Tragically widowed at a young age, Anna was thrust into the intimidating, but satisfying role of sole owner of a Kansas wheat farm. Tragedy strikes again as a tornado rips through her town, almost leveling her barn and home, and injuring her beloved elderly foreman. As she watches her only hope for recovery drive away down the long dirt road, she collapses in her driveway in tears, afraid, utterly alone, and almost destitute. The heat of the sun's rays cool as a shadow passes over her body. Firm, but gentle hands, lift to comfort her, but will she allow him to?

To Find Him Waiting
Copyright © 2019 Karen Louise
ISBN: 978-1-4874-2170-0
Cover art by Martine Jardin

Published by eXtasy Books Inc or
Devine Destinies, an imprint of eXtasy Books Inc

Look for us online at:
www.eXtasybooks.com or www.devinedestinies.com

TO FIND HIM WAITING

BY

KAREN LOUISE

DEDICATION

Dedicated to two angels in heaven, my parents. My mother's creativity and my father's work ethic and intelligence instilled values that have lasted a lifetime.

CHAPTER ONE

Even though it was Fall and the weather should be cooling, a merciless heat beat down upon Anna. The old swing looked welcoming as she climbed the steps to her porch. Easing her tired body down on the shaded, vinyl cushions, she groaned as her muscles and bones protested her every movement. Today had been more than grueling.

The scent of her own body drifted around her, and she cringed in revolt. Her once bright canary yellow T-shirt clung to her skin and was a sickening, muddy brown. She couldn't even imagine what her face looked like and really didn't want to find out.

The parched earth had billowed out about them in a spray of choking dust as they'd disturbed the soil, drifting to cling to their sweaty bodies. Looking at her hands, she grimaced at the dirt particles sticking to her skin like a million tiny freckles.

Her broken nails and calloused skin were true testimony to the work she did daily. Dirt lay caked under those once pretty nails, and she wondered when she had stopped caring about their appearance.

A light-hearted shout and laughter had her glancing into the distance, where her hired hands, Alec, Liam, and Greg, rounded up the last of her six head of cattle and herded them inside the barn.

The four of them and Pop, her beloved foreman, had spent the day harvesting the east field, and all were ready to call it quits for the day. With a grateful sigh, she realized this

1

farm would be nothing without them. They were such good young guys. She'd told them she would bring the cattle in, but they'd insisted they would before they left. Understanding had flickered through their youthful eyes when they saw her disheveled state and slumped shoulders. They knew she was exhausted, and exhausted she was.

She rubbed a grime covered hand across her forehead and felt the sandy grit. It was not a comfortable feeling for a woman who had always preferred to be clean.

Was it only two short years ago that life had been so different? She smiled ruefully as she pictured the naive young woman she'd once been. The happy person who often surprised the workers with lunch and cool drinks. The cheerful wife who gladly kept the house running and managed the books for the business. Most important of all, she would have been clean, at least most of the time. Not anymore. Now she pretty much did it all, and that included working hard at a business few women wished to take on alone.

Just two years ago, she still had Charles. Laying her head back against the cushions, she closed her eyes in weariness. As usual, thinking of him brought back the day her life drastically changed with vivid, heartbreaking clarity. A day that still gave her nightmares and woke her drenched in tears.

She'd been sitting at the dining room table recording the latest expenditures, feeling a sense of contentment as she paid the last of the monthly bills and still had money left over. Hearing the pounding hoof beats of a horse and the frantic shouting of her name, she'd rushed to the back door of their old farm house, knowing something had to be terribly wrong.

As Pop flew towards her, a sense of deep foreboding overtook her. Pop, an older, wiser, and usually calm man, never shouted. Breathless, he'd told her Charles had collapsed in the north field, the farthest field from the house.

She felt her own life collapse around her at his words.

Pop, with his infinite knowledge, said it appeared to be a heart attack, and they'd tried to revive him. It didn't work. By the time they'd brought Charles up to the house on their tractor the ambulance had arrived, but the medics hadn't even bothered pulling out their equipment after they checked him. She'd held the cooling fingers of her beloved as they told her there was no hope. Pop had been right. Charles had suffered a massive coronary and died quickly, barely even knowing it happened.

Shattered was too benign a word to describe how she'd felt. Charles was her everything, her whole world. She'd started dating him in ninth grade, fascinated that a senior was paying attention to her. She married the man she loved right after graduating and worked by his side on this farm from the tender age of eighteen up until the time of his death.

Happily becoming Mrs. Anna Scott, she'd moved from a small apartment she shared with her mom into this rambling old farmhouse while his dad was still alive. His mom had passed away just a year and a half before their marriage, and both father and son had welcomed her into their home and into their lives, grateful to have a woman in the house again. They told her often how they needed the touches only a woman's hands could bring, although at the inexperienced age of eighteen, those comments were confusing.

The two bachelors had enough to do keeping up with the farm, and they barely knew anything about running a home. That was very evident to Anna that first day when she walked in the back door and saw the stove caked in unrecognizable goop. Taking control of this home was a large and intimidating task for a young bride barely out of school, but she'd been determined to succeed. She had her own place away from the strained relationship with her mother and a handsome young man as her husband, and she loved it.

Both father and son had adored her, laughing good-naturedly when she'd burned their first few meals, even though she knew they'd been craving a good home-cooked meal. With a lot of internet research, cookbooks, and time, she'd become one heck of a good cook and eventually learned all the ways of caring for an ancient farm house.

Management of the business had come easily to her. Considering she lived in farm country, it was no surprise when she'd excelled in farm management courses in high school. Once she conquered her shyness and began pointing out small ways for them to cut costs and increase productivity, they decided she would be great at taking care of the books and quickly turned that over to her.

She'd often wondered if they hadn't relinquished that duty just a bit too quickly, but she didn't care. For the first time in her life she was a respected contributor and for the second time in her life, loved by a kind, responsible man.

Sadly, they'd buried his dad ten years ago in the family plot when he passed from a heart attack. His dad had been his best friend, co-worker, and had taught him all he knew. Charles had been inconsolable for weeks.

Anna remembered the tumultuous time all too well. Charles' grief had turned to anger, and with no one else around to vent on, that anger had been directed at her. It was the first time she and Charles had ever argued, and she recalled vividly the night she'd cried into her pillow when he'd slammed out of the house and gone to a local bar.

The next morning, hung over and contrite, he'd come to her with a huge bouquet of her favorite flowers, daisies, and had broken down as he apologized. Knowing the pain of his loss only too well, she'd held him against her and easily forgave him.

Remarkably, they'd never argued again after that. They'd

loved each other since they were kids, best friends, and that bond had only grown stronger after that one brief fight.

Unfortunately, life interfered as it always did, and she became a young woman who grieved for her one true love at only thirty-three years of age. He'd been everything to her, and the quickly passing fifteen years of their marriage had not been enough time to share with him the love she felt.

Her maudlin thoughts overpowered her, and she swiped a dirty hand against her cheeks to brush away a few tears that managed to escape. A storybook of time flashed through her head as she pictured the faces of those she'd lost in her life. Sadly, death had become too familiar. The ache of each loss lingered in the recesses of her heart, while the memories of each were stored away to recall at a moment's notice. The faces might fade over time, but their memory would never.

The very first loss her young heart had to face was Bella, her other half, the most important person in her young world. As twins, they'd always been together, holding hands wherever they went and sharing every adventure. They'd even shared the pneumonia she had rallied from, but her fragile sister had succumbed at the tender age of four.

Then there had been Miranda. Her kindergarten best friend had passed from a tornado, of all things. Like a scene from a movie, the monster storm had lifted a portion of their house and carried her away, crushing the young girl beneath the weight of the bathtub in which she had sought shelter.

As she remembered the terror of that night, she shuddered, the goosebumps briefly cooling her skin. Her father had held her against his strong, warm body and shared her tears as they learned of the losses their whole town had experienced.

Her dad, the first love of her life, had died when she was only eleven. Like her beloved Charles, her father had been

5

another man who'd kissed her goodbye in the morning and had never come home. Shot by a robber in his store, he'd struggled for four hours before passing from the wounds.

She choked back a sob as she remembered. She and her mother had clung to each other in the hospital and watched as he took his final breath. He'd been such a handsome man, with the same auburn hair she carried. The sob turned to a heartbroken chuckle as the memories of his goofy sense of humor surfaced through the pain. She spent a few minutes recalling some of his jokes that would keep her laughing for hours before she fast-forwarded through time to her husband. Losing Charles had been the final straw. To protect herself, she had no choice but to start building a wall around her heart.

Too many lives lost, too much pain. As she took a gasping, deep breath against the painful knot in her chest, his face rose in her mind's eye, and she gave up the battle to hold in the tears. Tall, blonde, and strongly built from farm labor, he had been all that was good, and she had adored him. With a gentle shake of her head, she thought of all the wasted years she and Charles had tried to conceive. They had shared their profound grief each month when nature let them know she wasn't pregnant, and slowly, over time, they gave up. The farm became their life. Adoption was not even considered. They simply stopped trying or hoping, maybe even caring.

The sound of the barn door closing brought her back to the present, and her first thought was of Pop. She knew when she lost him, it would hurt terribly, and she wasn't looking forward to that day. She'd had enough of heartbreak.

She had, at one time, vowed to stop her perpetually kind heart from loving, but it didn't work. There were still too many she cared about, both two and four legged.

Squinting against the harsh, unrelenting sunlight, she looked out on the land that was hers. The farm at one time had been her and Charles' baby. Working together, they'd made this farm what it was now, purchasing more land and upgrading it somewhat into the modern generation. In the beginning, it'd been great. Life had been hard and exciting, but with the slowing economy, the price of wheat had dropped, and taxes had risen. A small farm by most standards in Kansas, its income had never been substantial, but they'd always managed to get by.

When the budget tightened, they'd prayed for no catastrophes until they could build their little enterprise even more, but their hopes and prayers were not heard. As with her dad, Charles woke that fateful morning full of smiles, going off to work with a kiss to her cheek, and never came home. From a partner, she'd been thrust into the role of boss, the sole owner of three hundred and fifty acres of prime land. It wasn't easy being a woman in this male dominated industry. She had to grow up fast and become a hard, independent, and determined person if she was going to succeed and be responsible for everything, to oversee everything.

Because she lived alone, the old farmhouse required little cleaning, but there were plenty of repairs that needed to be done. Not the little nickel and dime stuff, but the kind that could bankrupt a person. The roof was over thirty years old, but at least it didn't leak, yet. Sadly, the windows were the original old wooden frames that constantly needed painting and caulking. They leaked the cold air of winter so horribly that when the temperatures began to dip, they had to be covered with plastic, the only way to get through the cold months.

She looked to the fields of wheat. The business had to go on or fold, and she refused to allow her husband's dream to go under. She owed it to him. She and Pop worked feverishly to keep it going. They hired the boys each spring and fall to help with the planting and harvesting and hired a local combine company to harvest the wheat. The rest of the year it was just the two of them taking care of the livestock, land, her vegetable plot, and a myriad of other chores that were part and parcel of a farmer's life.

She'd often wished she could hire another full-time worker, but it wasn't in the budget. Leroy Judd–who preferred people call him Pop–wasn't a young man anymore, and she was sure he would like to retire. She believed he stayed around just for her, and sometimes the guilt of that bore into her. She had no idea how she would survive if anything happened to him, but she also knew he was tired, and she was being selfish.

She had to make a decision about him soon.

CHAPTER TWO

When the fatigue of her worn-out body combined with the effects of the peacefulness of the late afternoon, she dozed off. Her head, heavy with weariness, rested against the old swing, but she jerked awake at the sound of Jake's deep bark. The sound came from the side of her house, and she wondered what had him so excited. It wasn't an angry bark, but one of a dog having fun. Who or what was he playing with? She hoped it wasn't some wild animal again.

Rising despite protesting muscles, she walked stiffly to the top of the porch steps to see what was going on just as her perpetually happy dog came into view. Excitedly jumping up and down on his two back legs, he growled happily as a stranger wrestled his favorite ball from his mouth and tossed it across the yard.

Her Jake, all eighty pounds of him, took off at a run with his tail wagging and a huge doggie grin on his handsome face. With his long, blue-black hair blowing behind him, he bolted after the flying ball. The man chuckled, and she turned her eyes to him as she walked down the steps to her lawn. Who was he?

His gaze darted to hers and he smiled, the simple gesture suffusing his face in warmth and kindness.

He was tall, over six feet by her guess, with raven black hair swept back from a sculptured and handsome, rugged face. His skin was a rosy tan, so different than her own creamy white. She guessed he had a Native American heritage in his lineage.

His shoulders and arms were muscular, his waist and hips narrow, and his thighs were thick and solid beneath his faded blue jeans. She could easily see he was either used to hard labor or took great pains to keep his body in shape. Either way, he was toned to perfection, and she took a quick moment to appreciate the beauty of the man.

If Jake hadn't felt so comfortable around him, she would have been concerned in the presence of this man's obvious strength. Anyone who could help defend her was far on the other side of her yard. Jake, however, was already back and shoving the frayed, time-worn, sloppily wet ball into the man's hands, wanting more playtime from his new playmate.

Jake knew who was enemy and who was friend, and he'd obviously determined this man was okay. She trusted Jake implicitly. With a dog's insight, he'd warned her off several times when she'd interviewed possible hired hands or when she was approached by a shady salesman. He was her right hand, her best friend, and as a woman who lived alone, a strong protector. She loved him with all her heart.

She stepped forward cautiously. "Can I help you?"

Throwing the ball, a bit further this time, he turned and walked towards her. His face was friendly, his manner perfectly serene, and she was at once captivated by the warm smile. It was odd, but for some reason she wanted to believe Jake was correct in his judgement of this man.

He extended a hand in introduction, and she looked at how clean he was. She held back with a shake of her head and a grimace as she showed him the filth that encased her hand.

"I don't think that would be wise."

He laughed and lowered his arm, withdrawing the offer. "My name is Dakota Powers, ma'am. I'm looking for work and have been visiting the local farmers, asking if they are hiring. One of them suggested I visit you, said you may be."

Fascinated, she kept her gaze glued to him as he spoke. Sensual and dreamy chocolate brown eyes with just a flicker of playful amusement sparkled at her in hopeful goodwill. Her gaze dropped from the infusing warmth of his eyes to his lips as they moved, and she shocked herself as she pictured the full lips touching hers. His words were friendly, spoken in a soft, smoky, deep voice, and she found the sound comforting and assuring. It was easy to relax surrounded by his good nature.

A loud, gurgling growl broke her observation, and he laughed, laying his hand across his stomach, apologizing. "I'm sorry. I think it's time for dinner."

She laughed along with him, but inside she worried. The man was obviously hungry, if his stomach was any indication, and poor if he was searching for a job. She felt a surge of compassion for him, knowing only too well how many were going hungry in the current economy.

Many a time, she'd struggled to feed her own family, but she always made sure Pop and her pets were fed before her own needs could be met. Pop would complain, but she would always shush him. She did what she had to do.

"I'm so sorry, Mr. Powers, but I'm not hiring right now," she said with a shake of her head.

As if to emphasize her words, her three hired hands and Pop exited the barn, joking and laughing. Without a wind to carry it away, their voices could easily be heard across the stretch of grounds to her and the stranger.

Pop noticed the stranger immediately and waved at Anna in their secret signal. She waved back to assure him all was well. She turned back to the stranger just in time to see the flicker of amusement disappear from his gaze, replaced by a look of defeat. If she hadn't been watching him closely, she would've missed the barely perceptible slump of his shoul-

11

ders. She did see it, though, and again felt compassion fill her at his plight.

She knew it must have taken great effort on his part, but he smiled, his look gracious and kind.

"Would you know of anyone who may be hiring?

"I honestly don't know, but you could stop at the Barkers' place. It's about five miles down the road. I know Jim Barker has been ill, and he might need a helping hand."

With a nod of his head, he thanked her for her time and started to turn away.

"Wait. Mr. Powers. Do you need something to eat?" She hadn't started tonight's dinner yet, but she could at least give him the leftovers from last night's meal.

"No, ma'am. I'll be all right, but I thank you for thinking of me."

He bent at the waist to wrestle the ball from Jake's waiting mouth, threw it one more time and laughed as Jake took off across the grassy field in pure joy.

He disappeared around the corner of her house, and curiosity compelled her forward. Slipping to the edge of the driveway, she peered at him, her gaze riveted on the mysterious stranger.

The care-worn jeans and dark red T-shirt both struggled to contain the strong masculine body. A shiver ran down her spine from the beauty of the man. It'd been a long, *long* time since she'd appreciated someone of the opposite sex and looking at this one sparked a memory of needs long forgotten. When did she forget about that tingling excitement from physical attraction? How long had it been since she had felt anything other than worry and exhaustion?

The engine of his surprisingly newer silver pickup purred to life just as a hopeful Jake flew to her side with the ball in his mouth. He stood with her as they watched the handsome, friendly stranger back up and drive down the road toward the Barkers'. Anna looked down at Jake and winced as he dropped the ball at her feet. Big, black, sorrowful eyes lifted to peer at her for a moment before he turned and walked away, his tail hanging down dejectedly.

"I'm sorry, buddy. I'd play with you, but I have to make dinner," she told her retreating friend, but he paid her no mind as he walked slowly towards the barn.

During this time of the year, playtime was hard to find, and she was sure Jake missed the one-on-one attention. He'd been Charles' dog and had accompanied him every day in his work on the farm. When Charles died, Jake had become Anna's dog by default and had switched his loyalty but like her, she knew in her heart that Jake still felt his loss deeply.

Flashes of memory tore through her mind of the hours they'd spent with Jake from when he was just a puppy to the time of Charles' death. Happier times, loving times. They would go for long walks, when they could find the time, and train Jake. Charles would spend a part of each evening tossing Jake's ball, and Jake would wag his tail in delight each time he brought the ball back to a hug and a loving word.

The day Charles died, Jake had lain by his side in the cart with his head resting on the chest of his best friend. That sight had torn at Anna the most, and she had collapsed by his side in their shared grief.

Her thoughts absorbed by Jake's retreating figure, she jumped in surprise when a piercing screech broke the silence of the day. Shielding her eyes against the glaring sunlight, she watched a beautiful, majestic eagle, wings spread wide in flight, circle the sky above before diving into her fields. When the noble bird emerged mere seconds later, he held a prize in his beak, and she shuddered at the gruesome sight.

"Blech." Anna turned to go inside, seeking the blissful relief of a shower.

CHAPTER THREE

Clean and feeling a bit more like herself, she quickly threw together a meal for Pop, Jake, and her little calico cat, Miranda.

Dishes done, she made her way back to her porch and her beloved swing. Claiming his own exhaustion, Pop said his goodnights and moved off to his own quarters above the barn, leaving her alone to enjoy the peace and quiet of the evening.

It was a bit cooler outside, and she eased her work weary body down on the cool vinyl and wiped away a bead of sweat running down her cheek. Late September was not easily giving up the reins of summer heat to the chillier weather of fall, and her precious hometown of Sweet Grove, Kansas was sweltering. She didn't have central air in this old house, only window units in the living room and her bedroom. The cost to run them was high so she used them infrequently. On the occasions when she did turn them on, it was for her Jake, who suffered in the heat. Otherwise, she relied on fans and open windows to cool the home. With her tight budget, she had to conserve every penny. Air conditioning was a luxury, not a need.

A gentle breeze kicked up, and she welcomed the air brushing across her skin, even if it was still warm. With one graceful leap, Miranda settled on her lap, and once Jake relieved himself, he came to lie down by her side on the porch floor, panting. He would enjoy the eventual return of fall and winter, too, she was sure. His long, black hair made life difficult for him on days like this.

The day was waning quickly, and as she rested against her swing, she watched through sleepy eyes as the setting sun cast an arc of amber light across the tips of the unharvested fields of wheat. They waved in the breeze, and she smiled softly at the beauty of the moving pattern. The wheat was the lifeline that kept them going. She both loved and hated it. She loved the checks that came with the sales and she loved to watch the results of their hard work grow and flourish from seed, but she often found herself hating the long hours of work and the worry when drought and disease claimed their efforts. She had learned quickly that a farmer's life was not an easy one.

Jake let out a huff and closed his eyes, losing his battle to stay awake. The crickets sounding off their mating calls, and birds chirping their goodnights were the only sounds that broke the silence of this peaceful twilight.

This was the time of day when she and Charles would sit in this very swing and reflect on their day. She looked down at the tears in the vinyl cushions and the rust eating holes in the metal and realized she should probably throw it away, but she couldn't bear to part with it. It held memories of Charles. She felt his loss here more than any other place, even in their bedroom.

The shared moments on this swing were the times to connect, to talk. Remembering how he would snuggle close and tell her how his day had gone clutched at her chest, bringing both a tender smile and brimming tears. Oh, how she missed him.

His voice had always been kind and gentle. She would listen to the soothing cadence until it lulled her into a relaxed state of mind. He always asked her how her day went and listened attentively, knowing full well she worked as hard as he. Charles had been a good husband, and even the passing of two years couldn't diminish the pain of losing him.

The mesmerizing dance of the wheat blurred and shadowed before her, and she glanced at the sky. In the distance, storm clouds moved swiftly in attempt to obliterate the glow of the lowering sun, and streaks of lightning lit from deep within the darkening clouds. She hoped it meant rain was moving towards them. Too many times she'd watch a storm pass them by to the north, forgetting they were there, and they needed the rain badly. It hadn't rained in over a month, and it was definitely not good for the fields or for her vegetable crop. Drought was a dire enemy.

An image flashed unbidden across her mind of the man who had stopped by earlier. He'd seemed so kind, and she hoped he'd found work somewhere and some food. It would've been nice to hire him, but until the money for the wheat sales came in, it would be tight. She couldn't afford another person added to the payroll. Besides, by the time the wheat sales were completed, she really wouldn't need any help until spring.

A nagging inner voice told her she probably should've checked him out, interviewed him for Pop's position, and let Pop retire. Again, though, she was being selfish. Pop knew every inch of this land and all the idiosyncrasies that came part and parcel with a farmer's life. Trying to substitute her irreplaceable friend wasn't something she even wanted to consider.

People stopping by looking for work wasn't unusual. Several had stopped by just this summer. Times were tough for all, and many were out of work. Yet, somehow this man was different. He hadn't tried to push himself on her, nor did he get belligerent as many had done in the past. Instead he'd been kind and respectful, almost humble. He'd actually impressed her with his gentle bearing.

She felt a blush of warmth cross her cheeks as she pictured his handsome face, making her giggle. Her stomach moved with the effort, and Miranda let out a disgruntled mew. A thirty-three-year-old woman with the burden of a farm to run couldn't think about men. She didn't even have time to socialize with neighbors anymore, but she could surely look at a good-looking man she would never see again.

With dawning realization, she burst out laughing. Miranda, angry at being disturbed again, jumped off her lap. The man must've been appalled when he'd looked at her. She'd seen her reflection in her bathroom mirror earlier, and she'd barely recognized her own face. Her long sweaty hair had clung to her neck, giving up the struggle to be contained under a beaten and filthy baseball cap. A dark layer of dirt had encased her face, except where her tears had made a smeared path down her cheeks from red-rimmed eyes.

She couldn't even imagine what he'd thought when he looked at her. Her laughter brought tears to her eyes as she pictured flirting with the man. He would've run as far and fast as his legs could carry him. She laughed harder, finding the whole thing hilarious. The laughter felt wonderful to her. She hadn't laughed in ages.

A rumble of thunder interrupted her musings, and she glanced towards the gathering storm. It looked big and was definitely moving. Hopeful, she went inside to close some windows, praying the dry ground would get a much-needed dousing.

Reaching to close a window in her living room, she jerked when an alarm went off on her phone, the sound loud and intruding in the stillness of the night.

Believing it was the usual alarms warning of an impending storm, she gave it no thought as she glanced down at the message. Tornado warning, her area. Not what she'd expected, and not good. Her first thought was of Pop and she hoped he had received the same message. Rushing to close the windows on both floors, she hurried back outside to the porch. The sky was darkening as the storm moved closer.

Worried, she texted Pop and sighed in relief when she got back a single *Yes*. Pop didn't like texting. He had resisted even carrying the phone, but she had insisted he do so after Charles' death. She believed in her heart the outcome of that horrible day might have been different if help had come sooner. She wasn't taking the same chance with Pop.

The town's air raid siren began its climbing wail just as the wind began to churn. The stiff breeze lifted and blew her freshly cleaned hair about her face. Her beloved Jake raised his head at the siren's blare and looked to the darkened sky. His nostrils twitched as he sniffed the air, and he let out a low growl of warning. Eerily, her swing began to rock back and forth on its own, and the trees swayed, revealing the backs of their leaves. To watch nature's reactions to a change in the weather was strangely mesmerizing.

Transfixed, she stood and watched the beauty around her. The evening had become a study of color, an artist's canvas. A definitive line of angry clouds rolled and tumbled in from the northwest with shades of turbulent purples, dark blues, and cool grays. Where the clouds had not yet touched the heavens, the color palette of a rainbow painted the sky with ribbons of soft pinks, brilliant oranges and yellows, and stark crimson reds. Against the shadowed gold of her fields and the varying greens of the trees, Mother Nature was on full colorful display. If it hadn't been such a frightening portent of things to come, it would also have been one of the most beautiful sights she'd ever seen.

Reality interfered, however, when a loud clap of thunder made her look toward the storm again. The tumultuous clouds rolling swiftly towards her catapulted her back to her childhood. She didn't want to go through this again, and growing worried, she gathered her pets and bolted inside.

She locked the door in a desperate, ridiculous attempt to hold off the power of a tornado and held on to her cat.

"Jake, come honey." Memories pounded through her head of the noise, the fear, and the devastation. Taking it seriously, she headed to the basement, the safest place.

Several years ago, Charles had fortified the walls of the downstairs bathroom, a small secure area tucked partially under the basement steps that his father had built years before as his own private room.

When his work was done, Charles had deemed that the four walls would withstand an assault by anything Mother Nature threw at them. There were no windows to the bathroom, only thick brick walls and a concrete floor. Its weakness lay only in the tiled ceiling over wooden beams.

Charles had done this work as a precaution. He'd never experienced a tornado, although he knew it was always a possibility when living in the Heartland. As she quickly herded the three of them down the steps and into the blissfully cool, dark room, she prayed he had known what he was doing.

Her phone blared out another alarm, and she jumped again at the sound, her nerves already on edge. Memories once more assaulted her, throwing her back in time to the night the star-filled sky had turned a turbulent greenish-black, and her life had changed. Her father had ushered them all down to the laundry room of their apartment building, assuring her mother and her that it would be a safe place.

At the tender age of six, she'd been terrified by the loud sounds and vicious winds. The storm had, fortunately, veered east before reaching them and had only done minor wind damage to her childhood home, but it had cut a swath

19

of destruction across her entire city and had stolen away her best friend. The curly blonde hair and smiling cherub face of Miranda had faded over time in her memories, but the closeness they'd shared would never leave. In some ways, she wondered if Miranda had replaced Bella in her young mind, but like Bella, Miranda had left her. Everyone left her.

She worried about Pop alone above the barn. She really didn't want to go through this again . . . the fear, the pain of loss . . . none of it.

The forecaster on her phone's news feed drew her attention, frightening her further. He was frantically waving his hands in the air as he spoke, and his voice rose as he demanded people take shelter quickly. She stared at the radar, engrossed, paling as she watched the storm inching closer and closer to her hometown. When the meteorologist finally stated that he was taking shelter also and bolted from the screen, her fear tripled.

Although no one could be seen at the tv station, the radar still showed on the screen, and she studied the storm's rotation. She was a mile or so outside of the city proper, and it looked like it was heading directly towards her small town. It also appeared to be traveling too close to her home for comfort. She hoped it would miss her and prayed it would turn and spare those that lived in Sweet Grove. Friends and neighbors she'd known her whole life lived in that small town, and even though she didn't get a chance to socialize with them much anymore, their lives were still important to her.

Muffled by the brick walls, but still audible, the siren again sounded its haunting moan. Shivers moved along her spine as Jake let out an eerie cross between a howl and a whimper. She quickly tried to call Pop, but his phone went directly to voice mail. Frustrated, she leaned back against the wall of the cool white bathtub. She laid one hand on Miranda who curled up on her chest and laid her other hand against Jake's head, holding two of the three she held most dear against her in protection. She hoped Pop was safe, her livestock were secure, and all three of her hired hands had gotten home in time to help protect their own families. A kind-hearted smile moved forward in her mind, and she prayed for him too. This was an unfortunate time to come looking for a job in Kansas.

CHAPTER FOUR

Only a few moments after she finished her prayers, the wind began. Anyone who had ever lived through a tornado knew the sounds to listen for, and she fearfully waited for the inevitable. Faint at first, the noise grew to a tremendous howl as it moved closer until it drowned out the pounding of her own heartbeat in her ears.

She jumped when a horrendous, splintering crack sounded just outside her home and recoiled when the walls quivered against a tremendous force slamming into the old wooden house. Terrified, she let loose a scream. Jake stood, his nails scratching against the tub floor as he tried to escape, and she grabbed his quivering body as an angry Miranda created a new set of scratches in her shoulder and arm.

Spellbound, she watched the tiled bathtub wall splinter before her. A few of the upper tiles lost their hold and clanked to the tub floor, shattering into ceramic fragments. With another whimper of fear, she curled Jake below her legs and hugged Miranda closer against her chest in protection.

The overhead light flickered and sputtered, and she once more sent out a prayer that they wouldn't lose power. Since the storm of her childhood, she wasn't all that fond of darkness. They had gone days without power during that storm.

She glanced at the ceiling above her. She had no idea what had happened up there and had no recourse but to wait to find out. The loud, roaring winds beat against the walls, and muffled tinkering sounds of shattering glass made her fears turn to full trembles. She wished for Charles or even her dad. Either one would hold her in loving arms and bring a sense of security in this storm. Again, she felt the pain of their loss. She was alone. She was always alone.

The noise of the storm heightened, becoming deafening, seemingly never ending. A dull whirring sound that hurt her ears made her curl into a fetal position with a quivering Jake intertwined in her legs and a suddenly docile Miranda tucked against her breasts.

With a final fluttering attempt to stay on, the feeble light above her died out, casting them in darkness so profound she couldn't see her cat mere inches from her face. Fear held her in its grip. Positive that death was coming to claim them all, she prayed once again. It was all she could do.

Jake trembled so forcefully, she didn't know where his trembling ended and hers started. If she thought the storm of her childhood was scary, it was nothing compared to being alone and facing the cacophony of noise and badgering vibrations outside these four small walls.

Yet almost as quickly as it'd begun, the turmoil quieted in an instant. The silence was almost as deafening as the previous noise of the storm. Her ears rang with the stillness, and her heart beat erratically, but she was alive. Jake and Miranda were alive. The question, however, was—was there anything left upstairs?

On uncooperative legs, she stepped out of the tub while still holding Miranda. Jake needed no encouragement and leapt out of the tub quickly, running to the door in his anxiety to leave. She followed the sound of his panting until she bumped into him.

She slid her hand down the wood until she found the knob and swung the door wide. The only light to guide them was the filtered gray glow from two small windows near the ceiling, and she squinted into the darkness. Taking a tentative step from the safety of the room Charles had built, a room that had saved them this night, she sent out a word of thanks to him for his foresight.

As if in a horror film, her old house creaked and moaned, threatening to crumble at their feet. Her toes screamed in protest when she kicked something hard on her way to the stairs and she let out a curse of frustration.

Miranda's claws once more dug painfully into her shoulder, and Jake walked by her side, leaning his warm body against her leg, as if he didn't want to lose the contact. All three of them were already shaken up by the night's events, and she didn't know what else awaited them.

With each step she climbed on the creaking wooden stairs, her trepidation grew. What would she find when she opened the basement door? Would she still have a house above? Was there significant damage? If so, how could she rebuild? Was Pop okay? What about the livestock? The fields?

The questions created anxiety as she swung the door wide to her kitchen and glanced around. She saw nothing except the dull, gloomy light at the windows, which wasn't very helpful. The room was nothing more than inky black shadows, and her eyes still struggled to adjust.

With a hand stretched in front of her, she inched her way across the floor until she found the drawer she sought and searched through the piles of junk for her flashlight. Relief poured through her when a harsh ray of light replaced the nothingness surrounding her.

The kitchen walls appeared secure, and she breathed just a bit easier, but as she looked toward the dining room door, she grew almost too afraid to see what was on the other side. Cautiously creeping forward, she swung the door open to her dining room, a very large space that served as both dining and living room.

Her beautiful white lace and costly curtains were now torn strips billowing in the wind. Varying sizes of shattered glass glittered across the floor, reflecting her flashlight, and two of her dining room chairs were on their sides. As far as she could tell in the single beam of light, that was all the damage on this floor.

Fearful, she glanced up the stairs to the darkness above, and prayers once again swirled through her mind that all would be well up there also, but she knew. Without even seeing the evidence with her own eyes, she knew the crash she'd heard and felt had to have been something very bad.

She set Miranda down with a cautious whisper to stay away from the broken glass and started up another set of stairs. She paused halfway when she felt it. A humid breeze lifted the sweaty tendrils clinging to her face and neck, a wind that shouldn't be there. She'd closed all the windows.

When she stepped onto the landing of the second floor of her precious home, she choked back a sob. The flashlight was no longer necessary. She could easily see that a tree had crashed through a large section of the roof and wall and was now almost resting on her bed.

A jagged and gaping hole revealed swirling angry clouds above. A light rain fell in her bedroom, turning her old wooden floor into a quagmire of wet leaves, broken branches and puddles. Her closet, which had held most of her better clothes, hung at an odd angle over her driveway below and was now a hollow shell. Her clothes were gone.

Memories of the devastation she'd experienced as a child assaulted her once more. Homes destroyed, lives lost. The pain they'd all felt. She shook her head at the devastation these storms caused.

Turning, she inspected the second bedroom, which was miraculously fine, and the bathroom had fared well from what she could see in the dim light. All in all, she should be grateful she still had a home, but as she returned to the doorway of her room and looked at the damage, worry wrapped her in despair. How would she repair it, and how could she possibly afford it? Would insurance cover this?

With a dog's innocence, Jake ventured into the room to inspect, lapping at the rainwater, and she called him back quickly. She didn't know how sturdy the floorboards were and didn't want him falling through to the floor below. She didn't even know if she could venture far enough to reach any of her everyday clothing in her bureau, which had slipped and fallen from its original position against the wall to lie wedged against the tree trunk. What was she going to wear?

Saddened by the loss and fearful for the outcome, she felt her tears begin in earnest. Standing still in the doorway to her room with the dark night sky incongruously visible above and rainwater falling in a mist around her, she felt the weight of the world on her shoulders. If she'd felt alone before, it was nothing compared to what she felt at that moment.

Her head rose in alarm as with a dawning clarity she thought of Pop, and she quickly raced down the steps and out the back door of her home. She ran in bare feet across the field with Jake on her heels, but when she raised the flashlight to guide her way, she instead skidded to a stop on water-soaked grass. While teetering on unbalanced feet, she saw the catastrophe before her.

Where once had stood a large grey weather-beaten but sturdy barn, a battered shell remained. In one corner, the broken support beams of the roof stood poking out into the night sky like cannons ready for battle. The walls below the beams were mostly gone, shredded as though a great white shark had taken a big bite in a frantic need to feast. She let out a cry of fear when she realized the area of damage had been Pop's apartment. Was he alive?

Turning in a semi-circle, she scanned the bright light around the mess. She could see that Pop had—with his infinite wisdom—let the livestock out to run and fend for themselves. Black and white dots of a few of her cows were huddled together near what was left of another of her trees. One whole side of the ancient maple had cracked and lay across her lawn.

The frantic clucking of her chickens could be clearly heard above the mooing cows. They were obviously upset that their warm, comfy rest was disturbed. She had no idea where the horses were and hoped they were not injured and came home on their own.

There was still no sign of Pop.

Breaking into a run once again, she didn't get far before she slipped and fell, landing with a splash on the hard, slick ground. She grunted as her hip and wrist screamed from the impact, and Jake ran to her side, kissing her cheek, worried.

"I think I'm okay, buddy." But it took a herculean effort to stand and test the painful areas of her body for movement.

They hurt, but they worked, and she limped towards the area where Pop's one-bedroom loft was supposed to be, although now it resembled a yawning hole against the night sky.

She screamed for him, frantic to find the man who was like a father to her. He just had to be okay. She couldn't go through this again. Not yet, not now, maybe never if she could wish it away.

Stepping carefully over boards that at one time had been part of her barn and were now scattered like a dropped box of toothpicks, she screamed Pop's name once again. Where was he?

The outlying tendrils of a brilliant flash of lightening lit the sky and briefly illuminated the mess around her. It was unbelievable. Seeing Pop's stark white refrigerator lying on its side, she moved in that direction. She had to be close.

"Pop! Where are you?" Fearing the worst, she called out over and over. She had to find him.

She was almost ready to give up and call for help when the wind carried a feeble cry to her ears. "Anna."

"Pop! Pop, I hear you. Keep calling to me!" She moved in the direction of the voice, but as he called again she got twisted around. The breeze was playing with her, carrying his cries away from her. Not being able to find him, she fought panic.

"Pop, keep talking to me!"

Jake let out a bark, and she swiveled in his direction, shining the light near some remnants of furniture. A dirty hand waved feebly from a pile of rubble, and cautious relief pounded through her.

Her aching hip protested her every movement, but adrenaline kept her hobbling over wreckage to his side. Kneeling at his side, she looked at the debris that covered him. Although her worry made her wish to rip it all away quickly, she moved carefully, fearful of what she would find.

When she finally had removed the boards, sheet rock, and debris from his upper body, she drew in a breath of shock. This sturdy but aging man looked nothing like the last time she'd seen him just a few short hours ago. Blood oozed from a large slash across his forehead, and dirt covered his face, hands, and clothes. The light rain only made it worse.

"Where are you hurt?"

"Everywhere," came the croaked reply with an attempt at a chuckle, followed by a moan.

"Do you think anything is broken? Can you sit up?"

He made to move and moaned again, raising his muddy, grass splattered hand to cover the bloody gash.

Anna pulled her cell from her pocket and hoped for a signal, releasing a pent-up breath she hadn't even known she was holding when she saw four bars. She called for help, but she knew it would be some time, if ever, before they got there. She had no idea how much damage they were handling in town and resigned herself to the fact she was the only one who could help him right now.

She asked him again if he could sit. "I think so," was the feeble reply.

Grasping his hand, she tried to help him up, but it was hard. He was a large man, a dead weight and slippery wet from rain and goo. She couldn't pull him, but maybe she could push him to a sitting position. Moving behind him, she grasped him under the arms and lifted. Unfortunately, her feet slid on the wet ground, and her face landed with a soft thud on his shoulder, her elbows taking the brunt of the impact with the earth. Not only was he injured, but he was covered in the mud and debris, his feet still buried below a heavy timber. The weight was too much for her.

"I'm sorry, Pop."

He let out a strangled grunt of response, and she scrambled to untangle herself. Giving it another shot, she dug her bare feet into the ground while the mud oozed between her toes and lifted the injured man from the damp chill of the earth.

It took great effort, but she managed to get him sitting, and she hugged both injured man and her wet dog tightly against her. Relief poured through her that she hadn't lost any of them to the storm, until she shined the flashlight on Pop's gash. Her stomach turned at the sight. She could see the bone of his skull, and the cut was at least four inches long, starting at the middle of his forehead and extending backward. The bleeding was profuse and worsened by the trickling rain. Lines of red ran down his face between brown clumps of dirt and blades of grass. He looked like something from a battlefield, and he needed help quickly.

"Pop, we have to get you to the house. I have to clean you up and get you to some help."

However, saying it and doing it were two entirely different things. His head protested each movement, and after freeing his lower legs from beneath the fallen timber, she saw that his right foot was twisted at a weird angle. She was certain it was broken.

Thunder and lightning began again, the wind whipping against all three of them. Jake was soaked, his hair plastered against his skin, and her own hair hung in stringy rivulets down the sides of her head. This was beyond dangerous to be in the middle of a field in a storm. Without letting Pop know, she cried frustrated tears that blended with the rain trickling down her face.

CHAPTER FIVE

Two brilliant blue lights flashed from behind her house and across her field. Her tear-blurred eyes confused it with another bolt of lightning until she realized the light stayed constant.

"Pop, I think help has arrived!"

She might have let out a groan, but even the discomfort in her hip couldn't stop her from bounding to her feet with a cheer at seeing those two welcome beams. They turned off, but she swung her one single light toward the driveway and waited, almost collapsing in relief when Sheriff Regan himself came around the corner of her home moments later.

"Martin, Martin, over here." She waved the flashlight as she screamed across the field, and he heard her. Already an intimidatingly large man and now covered in heavy rain gear, Martin Regan cast an imposing, shadowy figure in the ray of her flashlight, but she knew him well. He'd been Charles' classmate, a high school football player, and had been her and Charles' friend for all these many years. He'd even stood as a witness at their wedding at the courthouse, and she couldn't be happier to see such a friendly face.

He trotted towards them, and as he neared, she quickly explained about Pop's injuries.

"He needs to go to the hospital, Martin. I think his ankle is broken, and that cut on his head will need stitches."

"Let's get him inside and I'll take a look."

Without another word, he cautiously lifted Pop in his arms. Although Pop cried out when his ankle was jarred,

31

Anna grunted in exasperation that Martin could lift him so easily when she had struggled to move him at all.

She limped in pain but still did her best to race ahead of them and open the door to her kitchen. Her bare feet left a path of mud and grass and all of them created rivers of water on her hardwood floors, but at this point who cared? Her whole home was in shambles.

Spreading out an afghan, Martin placed the injured man on top, and she quickly curled it around Pop's shivering body.

Leaving them for a moment, Anna hobbled up the steps to her bathroom and groped for her first aid kit, towels, and clean face rags in the closet.

The reflection of Martin's brilliant flashlight lit her way back down the stairs, and as she approached, she could see the frown that marred the man's face while he spoke to Pop. She laid a towel over Jake's shivering body and knelt by Pop's side, gently placing the cloth on his head. He let out a hiss, and she grimaced.

"I'm sorry, Pop." She couldn't stand to see him this way. It wasn't natural to see this robust man laid low.

Martin's voice spoke at her side as he examined Pop's ankle. "Things are bad all over, Anna. The northeastern side of the city has taken a direct blow. Several businesses and homes were hit hard. Injuries and fatalities are unknown at this time, but our two medic units are out on calls, and the hospital has called in any staff available. We've asked for reinforcements, but who knows what the other towns are dealing with. With the power out, we don't know right now who else was in the storm's path."

She toweled her hair and some of the water from Jake's fur as she watched Martin unbutton his heavy yellow jacket and grab the mike hooked to his shoulder. His deep voice was concerned as he asked if either medic unit was available yet for transport. Although the answer was garbled and breaking up, Anna could recognize the level-headed voice of the dispatcher on the other end. She was the mother of one of her hired hands, Liam. The woman had been a dispatcher for more than twenty years and knew her job well.

They could barely make out what the woman was saying. Battery powered communication was weak at best, but they did hear that the medics and engines were currently out on calls. Worried, Anna looked to Martin for advice.

Pop must have also heard, because he let out a moan. His hand quivered as he held the towel against his forehead, and Anna took over the job of holding the fabric that was quickly turning a pale pink.

On a sigh, Martin stood and buttoned his jacket.

"Don't worry, Pop. I'm going to drive you to the hospital myself. Anna, do you have an extra pillow I could use?"

She hobbled back upstairs and grabbed a pillow from the spare room, then watched as Martin wrapped Pop's foot in the pillow before lifting him. She moved ahead of him opening doors as Martin carried Pop around the side of the house, ducked under the heavy tree leaning against her home, and skirted the rubble that covered her driveway. Seeing the effort it took for this large man to carry the injured Pop over the devastation in her driveway, Anna couldn't help but wonder how she would've managed on her own. In no way could she have lifted Pop inside her truck, and it could've been hours before a medic arrived. Thank heaven for Martin.

She opened the car door and backed away as Martin gently placed Pop in the back seat.

"Anna." Pop's voice was a mere whisper, which sent a shiver of fear down her spine. "You stay here. Find the livestock. Call the boys to help you in the morning. I'll be all right, don't worry."

"I'll take care of it, Pop. You're the one who shouldn't worry. I'll get to the hospital as soon as I can."

"Just take care of the farm, my girl. A few cuts and broken bones won't stop this old man."

She tried to smile at his attempt at humor, but her fear for his health made the attempt a feeble grimace.

The rain had slowed to a trickle as she watched Martin back his car up the driveway and turn down the lane towards town. Pop could no longer see her, and the tears she had struggled to hold back fell in freedom. He was her everything, her friend, her advisor, and the one person she had relied heavily on since Charles' death. She had no idea what she would do without him and refused to allow herself to think about it.

Slowly the retreating red taillights disappeared to nothing, once again casting the night into quiet darkness.

How long she stood there she didn't know, but a bright moon eventually made its appearance across the shadowed land and bathed her in a white-blue glow. Worry held her in its grip when she pictured Pop's head wound. It was bad.

The leaves rustled in a bush as an animal moved out from hiding, and she realized she had to get moving. On a sigh, she turned to walk back to her home. Well, at least what was left of it. She gasped when she finally got a good look at the damage on this side.

The old maple that used to shade her driveway and the side of her old house was now destroyed. She had loved the way that tree helped to keep her bedroom cool during the heat of summer. The gnarled, torn roots rose at least ten feet from a dark gaping hole in the earth. The trunk stretched out above her lawn and driveway, leaning at a precarious angle towards her home. The branches on the right side disappeared into her bedroom as if they were dozens of tiny hands grasping for something to help hold the burdensome weight of the trunk.

Anna feared that one good gust of wind would send the precariously positioned tree crashing farther into her house, destroying it completely.

The wet and shredded bright colors of a few of her dresses wafted like ghostly figures in the creaking, broken branches high above her. Swiftly moving clouds danced across the moon, casting a shivering pattern of light over the damaged white house sitting as a backdrop to the quivering fabric. The image was so eerie, she almost expected an unearthly moan or a deadly scream to pierce the night.

A creepy-crawly shudder tingled through her body and raised the little hairs on her skin. The disquieting feeling of being utterly alone in the dark with no one around for miles made her move swiftly, gathering what few clothes she could find along the driveway and bolting towards the back of her home.

Rounding the corner, she came to an abrupt halt when she approached the porch and found a wet Jake sitting as if frozen, watching her. Reflecting the darkness of the night, his eyes appeared as deep hollow black holes in his face, making her even more frightened.

"Jake?" At her question, he jumped to his feet and wagged his tail, and she laughed at herself, feeling foolish for allowing her imagination to overtake her good sense. Shaking off her ghoulish thoughts, she dropped the few clothes she'd gathered on the porch and prepared for the task ahead.

"Looks like we have a lot of work to do, buddy."

Hearing the distant sound of her cows, she and Jake moved towards the scattered livestock. The power of her flashlight was ebbing, but at least the brown and white cows were a bright enough shadow against the night for her to see them. Herding them two by two to what was left of her barn, she ushered them inside and to a secure area.

She searched for the chickens. They'd scattered and were raising a ruckus. Fighting to capture the frantic little birds was quite a task, and by the time she gave up, some were still missing.

Just as the last little beam of light from her flashlight died out, exhaustion claimed every inch of her. She hoped the other missing livestock had found a place to bunker down for the night, especially her horses, but at this point it was too hard to muster any concern.

She limped heavily towards her home with Jake by her side. Tired, wet, sore, miserable, and alone, she wondered if she collapsed in a heap on the ground, how long it would be before anyone found her. It was a bit disconcerting to realize it could be days or even weeks before her body would be found.

Laying a hand on Jake's head and gently stroking her loving friend as he hugged her side, she inhaled on a shaky breath. As much as she would have liked to just give up, she had to fight the urge. She had too many lives dependent on her. Once again, she had to be strong. She wondered what it would feel like to be weak for once. What would it be like to let someone else be in control for just a little while? She shook her head at her foolishness. There was no one else, and there would never be.

"I guess we have to find a dry and hopefully safe place for us to sleep, huh baby?" Jake let out a low yelp of agreement. The night had been hard on all of them.

Miranda was pacing the kitchen floor when she and Jake entered, and she let her displeasure with the evening's events be known loudly as she circled Anna's legs.

Too tired to worry about food despite a gnawing hunger, she swung the dining room door open.

"Come on, guys. Let's go to bed. I sure hope it's safe."

Bone weary and with feet that felt like lead weights, she led her little pack up to the spare bedroom. Grabbing towels, she dried Jake as best she could. Peeling the wet clothes from her body, she washed quickly with what little water pressure she still had from the well and crawled beneath the warm blankets. With a damp Jake at her feet and a grateful Miranda at her head, she passed out on a fervent wish that her home would hold up for the night.

CHAPTER SIX

Anna had never liked the spare bedroom, the one Charles' dad had used for many years. It faced the east, and the sunrise was blinding in its intensity much too early for her peace of mind. For what little time she'd been able to sleep, she'd slept like a rock, but she needed more, and the sun was not a welcoming alarm clock.

Moaning, she rolled over to block the harsh light. Sleepy-headed confusion had her wondering why she was naked and in the wrong room until last night's events hit her like a rock. She peeked from beneath the covers at the closed bedroom door.

With vivid and painful clarity, she remembered what was on the other side. She had a tree in her room and clothes scattered across her lawn and high up in a tree. If that wasn't enough to cripple her, she was missing a good portion of her barn. Whether she wanted to or not, she had to get up, see everything in the light of day, and hopefully find the rest of her livestock. There was no one else to do it.

Thinking it and doing it, however, were vastly different accomplishments. Her strained muscles and bruised bones protested her every action. She felt like hell, but she had no choice. Glancing down to her side, she moaned as she saw the purplish evidence of her pain. Her thigh was a roadmap of bruises. No wonder she hurt. This was not a good way to start the day.

She rummaged in the spare room closet until she found some old boxed up clothes that had belonged to Charles' father and donned them, thankful she'd been too lazy to give them away. The clothes were a little baggy, but they would have to do. Sadly, she couldn't get to her undies and would just have to make do.

Opening the bedroom door, she carefully made her way out of the small room, fearful that any vibrations she caused would send the house crashing down around them.

Despite all her fervent wishes that the morning would prove the night had been nothing more than a nightmare, the scent of fresh air that greeted her told her the prayers had gone unanswered. No different from last night, a large tree lay across her roof, with broken and twisted limbs branching out around her bedroom. Sunlight poured through the ragged hole in the missing ceiling and wall, and Anna wanted nothing more than to let loose a stream of cusswords.

Cautiously entering the bathroom, she saw what she'd been unable to see by the beam of her single flashlight last night. A large crack ran down the center of the wall, stopping mere inches from the floor. She worried further about the stability of her home and whether she should even be inside the house.

She made her way down the steps and brushed aside the broken glass on her dining room floor, cringing at the broken windows and torn curtains. She swung open the door to the kitchen and looked around.

At least this room had been spared, although the window above her sink was a spider web of cracks. Sunlight poured through the window with a crystal-like effect, creating little shimmering rainbows, and she ran a cautious finger along the surface in wonder as she asked herself once again how she would recover from this. Was it even possible?

With a shake of her head, she knew she had to get moving. Things had to be done. Past experiences had taught her that life went on despite all it threw in your face.

Anna made her way to the coffee maker only to remember she still had no power. How would she function without coffee? The day was just getting worse.

Miranda made her way to the litter box, and Jake let his impatience show with a yelp. She turned and stared at the back door, afraid to see what the night's darkness hadn't revealed. She wished she could run and hide from it all, but sighing with resignation, she grabbed the handle and swung the door wide, releasing her exuberant dog.

The brilliance of the sun against the storm-washed blue sky was blinding, and she grabbed her sunglasses, but not before appreciating the boldness of her emerald green grass reawakened from the rain. The air was clear and refreshing. The storm had broken the oppressive heat, and it should be beautiful to behold.

Yet sadly, the beauty of the day lost its significance when she looked around her property. All about her was chaos. Darkness had masked the destruction the vivid daylight made extremely obvious. From the northwest horizon to the field nearest her barn, a large swath of her precious wheat was gone, a stark indication of the storm's winding path. Broken branches, leaves, and another split tree cluttered the land with debris near the side of her barn. A massive clean-up.

Crushed by the enormity of the wheat's loss, she headed for what was left of the old barn while on the edge of tears once again. She didn't know where to begin or how she would do it all, but she did know her first two courses of action were to find the rest of the animals and call her insurance company to see if anything was covered. Other than that, she had no idea what to do. She'd never been in this situation before, but she was intelligent enough to realize this was going to be an uphill fight.

Approaching the barn, she was overwhelmed with the level of destruction. Wood, furniture, appliances, food, clothing, and metal were scattered everywhere she looked. The shed that held some of her farm equipment was gone, its contents nowhere to be seen. The doors to her barn were intact, but worthless when most of the wall to their right had disappeared in the wind.

She felt small and insignificant as she stood in the middle of the huge mess and turned in a circle, taking it all in. This was all too unbelievable to be true.

Taking tentative steps among the wreckage, she saw that some of the missing chickens had found their own way home amidst the rubble and were gathered together under Pop's couch. On quick count, six of them were still missing. Another financial loss.

A loud neighing broke the quiet of the morning, and she looked up to see her mare, Maggie, trotting across the fields towards her, but where were the rest?

She questioned her faithful companion by her side. "Jake, it's just you and me, buddy. Can you help me find everyone?" She spoke to him as if he were human and chuckled at herself, but when his alert ears twisted and turned and he took off at a run, she watched his retreating body in amazement. It was almost as if he understood.

She hugged Maggie, and after checking her for injuries, led her to the gaping hole in the wall of her barn. Why bother opening the door?

Stepping inside the debris-cluttered barn, she looked for anything she could find of use. Fortunately, the chicken feed had gone untouched, and after sweeping a clean section of floor, she quieted their clucking noise by casting the food on the cleaned surface. Little heads bobbed up and down as they feasted, their immediate need met.

Finding very little alfalfa, she spread that out for the

cows. It would only hold them so long. Cows ate a lot.

She searched until she found a hammer and nails and made her way through the broken lumber outside, finding some useful pieces of the old barn wall. They would have to do.

Looking up occasionally at the swaying and creaking wood above her, she prayed those existing walls held as she hammered the broken wood to the skeletal remains of the former walls. She built a haphazard barrier, something that would hold everyone inside as long as nothing happened to make them crowd it. At present, that section of the barn wasn't much more than a lean-to. The repairs would have to be done quickly if she was to keep her livestock safe. Again, she sent a prayer to the sky above that she had coverage for this catastrophe.

The sun was high in the sky by the time she'd built the tiny makeshift fence where the two barn walls once met. She stretched, her back screaming at her to rest. Her hip and thigh beat a steady throbbing rhythm of pain with her every movement, and her stinging eyes fought to release a torrent of tears. She laid a hand on her stomach to soothe the growling. The gnawing from last night was now a full-fledged painful ache in her stomach. She needed food, and after getting a good whiff of herself, she needed a shower. Only one of those things would be available to her, though. Well pumps didn't work without power and what pressure was still in the tank would be used up quickly.

A familiar bark sent her out of the barn to find Jake being followed by two of her horses. A bit of the despair she had been feeling lifted at the sight of her Jake bringing them home, and she burst out laughing, relieving some of the pressure that'd been building inside her battered body.

Giving the dog a quick hug, she took the horses into the temporary structure and placed them with Maggie. They were crowded together, but it would have to do. She hoped they would not fight.

She was still missing two horses, one of them Pop's beloved mare. She worried about them, knowing she would have to start a search soon. Her horses were well-loved pets, but she had to be practical about the cost of replacing them. At that thought, her smile disappeared quickly as despair hit her once more. She was hurt, hungry, and alone with a huge, seemingly insurmountable mess, facing catastrophic costs to rebuild. Anna had had enough hard lessons to know life was not easy, but nothing had prepared her for handling the enormity of this calamity. With tears brimming and her shoulders slumped in defeat, she dragged her tired body back across the still-damp lawn to her home. It was time to call the insurance company and to call the hospital to find out about Pop. She hoped her phone still had a charge.

CHAPTER SEVEN

By mid-afternoon the insurance agent showed up, and she walked anxiously by his side for almost two hours as he inspected the damage. With each note he wrote on his iPad and each mutter of concern he voiced, she waited, watched, and hoped.

The inspection done, she sat nervously at her kitchen table as he dealt both the good and bad news. They had coverage, but Charles had chosen a high deductible of five thousand dollars to keep the insurance payments low. Shocked was too mild a word to explain how she felt, and depression pressed down on her as she heard him utter those words. Where would she get five thousand dollars?

The sun was lowering in the sky when she stood watching the nice-looking agent drive away from her home, taking all of her ardent wishes for an easy outcome with him.

Once again crippling despair and anxiety hit her like a brick, and she crumbled to the damp ground of her driveway. It was all too much. She was only one person. How could she handle this? Oh, how she wished Pop were here.

The agent had told her he was going to get the repairs started, but she knew the first five grand would have to come from her. She had no idea how she would get it. She'd lost a good quarter of her wheat to the storm, and the sale of the rest would just barely get them through the winter and supply them with next year's seed and salaries.

Her husband's sweet face rose in her mind's eye, and her heart clenched in pain. She couldn't blame him. As he'd always been during their marriage, she knew he'd been financially practical. She was sure he never imagined this happening, or if he had, she was sure he felt he could handle the repairs, but he wasn't here anymore. Nobody was here. She was in charge of finding a way out of this mess. Too many lives depended on her, and that was just a bit too frightening.

A gentle snort sounded from behind her back, and she swiveled in the dirt, raising a tear-streaked face to see Pop's mare lazily shuffling towards her. The old gray horse's breath tickled her neck as she nudged her ear in greeting and knocked her sunglasses to the dirt. The loving touch was her undoing, and Anna burst into great wracking sobs as she pressed her face against the beloved, long equine nose. Pop would've been devastated if anything had happened to this horse. Picturing Pop lying alone in a hospital bed only compounded her grief, and her sobbing increased.

As she held the sweet face of the mare, serious doubts about her ability to rise above this catastrophe brought her near to plunging into hopelessness. The realization made her draw her knees up and curl into a protective ball, sobbing and hiding from the pain around her. The sun beat down upon her, and she felt the back of her neck begin to burn, but still the bouts of weeping wouldn't stop. They consumed her.

A dark shadow, lengthened by the lowering sun, covered her body as strong arms lifted her. She curled against the strength, needing the simple touch of another person.

Strong arms carried her exhausted body easily around to the back porch and set her down carefully on her swing. Coming to rest beside her, he lowered her head onto his shoulder and held her close as she continued to cry. The force of her sobbing shook her body, and the arms hugged a bit more firmly as soft words of comfort whispered against her hair.

Slowly her inner turmoil eased against the warm strength until her the sobs became a gentle weeping. Arms circled her, holding her against soft fabric, and she melted into the feeling. For the briefest of moments, she wasn't so alone anymore. Hands moved in comforting, lazy patterns along her shoulder, creating a calming effect, relieving some of the pain deep inside.

She longed to give in the security and almost did, but with a jolting, spine tingling awareness that strange arms were indeed holding her, Anna pulled back and stared in horror at the man who held her.

"Oh, no! I'm so sorry. That was so wrong of me. Forgive me, please." she cried out in frantic embarrassment.

The sensual kindness she'd seen once before on his handsome face stared back at her, and he gave her a woeful smile.

"It's okay, really. I understand," he said softly in reassurance. "I ran into the sheriff in town, and he told me how bad it was here. He also said that your foreman was in the hospital. I came by to see if I could help."

She scrambled from his side as quickly as her bruised and worn out body would allow and backed away. A tree was lying in her bedroom, her barn was devastated, by her guess a quarter of her wheat was gone, trash covered her land, she had to come up with five thousand dollars, but he wanted a job?

A seething anger replaced the hopelessness. Her irrational mind wanted only to scream at him that he was a special kind of stupid, but she knew she wouldn't. She wasn't the kind of person to be nasty to another. She drew on every ounce of pride she could find, despite an unfortunate case of deep hiccups squeezing her chest and interrupting her speech.

"I thank you for the offer . . . but as I said before, I cannot afford to hire you." With a sweep of her hand she brought his attention to the devastation of her farm. "As you can see . . . I now face an even bigger problem. I don't even know how I will afford the repairs I need."

She sighed and hiccupped again, turning her attention back to his concerned face. "Your kindness is appreciated though. I wish you luck."

Swiping her hands across her eyes to blot the tears, she walked down the steps and collected Pop's horse.

Dakota sat on the old swing, observing her as she turned and walked across the yard, his mind contemplating how he could help. When he'd first met her, she was covered in dirt from long hours of working the soil. Today she was covered in a filth he couldn't begin to describe and smelled of rank sweat and hard work.

She was obviously not afraid of physical labor. She must be a very strong, independent woman to deal with such a heavy burden alone, but she wouldn't have to do it alone if she'd only allow the help.

Her hair was tucked up under a baseball cap that had seen better days, but several tendrils had escaped their confine, and the auburn tresses curled down her long, graceful back. She was on the lean side, as if she barely ate, but her arm muscles were toned. Her waist was narrow, and from his vantage point, he saw a well-rounded derriere which swung awkwardly side to side as she made her way to the barn.

She was tall, her legs long, but he noted her awkward gait with concern. She was limping. Had she been hurt in the tornado, or had she had that limp her whole life? He hadn't noticed it when he first met her, but then again, he really didn't remember seeing her walking at all then.

Her jeans hung baggy on slender legs as if she had just lost a good amount of weight, which would explain the leanness of her frame. From what he'd been able to see below the rim of her hat, her eyes were an aquamarine blue, although today they were bloodshot, red-rimmed, and swollen. They were perhaps the saddest eyes he'd seen since he left South Dakota.

He knew how low she had to feel. He'd also been in similar situations, and he knew well the gut-wrenching despair and hopelessness she must feel.

His eyes narrowed on her retreating frame, and he came to a difficult decision. Standing, he followed her toward the wreckage of her barn with Jake on his heels. "She needs help, little guy. Now she just has to accept it."

Jake wagged his tail ferociously as if thankful, and Dakota chuckled, rubbing the top of the intuitive dog's head.

The enormity of what he saw made him walk slowly as he took in the devastation around him. The field on his left was mostly destroyed, and he knew the pain she had to feel at the loss, especially financially. A corner of her barn was wrecked, and its contents lay scattered across the land.

In less than a day since a storm that had altered her life, she'd built two makeshift fences where the north and east walls met, obviously to hold her livestock in. He shook his head at the work, knowing she had to have put in some gruesome hours to get that done alone.

Taking a few tentative steps, he came up behind her and spoke quietly, not wanting to scare her, yet her back stiffened in surprised anyway when he spoke.

"Ma'am, I am not looking for money at the moment, just a bed and a meal. I don't ask for much. I'd be more than happy to help you out until your foreman is out of the hospital."

"Why? Why would you help someone you don't know, and for free?" She shook her head, not giving him time to reply. "No, Mr. Powers, I couldn't let you do that."

She set a bucket down on a hastily swept area of the floor and turned around. Lifting her right arm, she swept her hat off her head. Once released, the thick mass of hair fell in riotous, sweaty disarray around her shoulders, and with splayed fingers, she combed through the tangled mess.

Time seemed to slow as he followed the movement of her body gently swaying with her actions. Lightly rounded hips and a narrow waist gave way to small, high breasts that quivered against an aged denim shirt, the peaks obvious under the thinning material. She wore no bra.

Her face, still covered in a layer of dirt and tear-stained smudges, tilted back as she combed, revealing a long graceful neck. The magnificent hair, though, was what captured him the most. Deep mahogany, burnished from the waning sunlight, glowed warm and rich around a small, round angelic face. It was a beautiful sight, even in this disheveled state.

She sneezed, the sound startling him, and he quickly looked back to her eyes, which were now more visible without the battered hat. He was right. Her eyes were the aquamarine blue of a mid-winter South Dakota sky just before sunset, clear and pure. They brought back yearnings for his home with painful clarity.

Her eyes narrowed in thought as she studied him, and he waited. She was clearly waging a war within her mind, if the emotions flickering within the blue depths of her eyes were any indication.

On a deep exhale, she asked, "Have you ever done this type of work before?"

He smiled inwardly. She was at least considering hiring him.

Explaining that he'd grown up on a farm, he described his duties in great detail. "I'm sure you'll approve of my work if you only give me a chance," he finished, selling himself and hoping it was working.

Again, he waited as her mind played over all the possibilities. Jake, growing impatient with the two humans, nudged Dakota's hand. He glanced down and scratched the head of her friend before looking back to Anna to see her studying the exchange.

"Ma'am, I sense that you are a kindred spirit in how you feel about working the land. Nothing beats planting row upon row of seed and watching the fruits of your labor grow tall and strong, giving nourishment to many and a much-needed income to you. Nothing beats a job well done. I can help you, if you'd only let me."

He watched as a beautiful smile lit her dirty face.

"Besides, you are going to need extra hands, considering the damage you have to clean up."

A frown quickly replaced the beauty of her smile, and with a defeated slump of her shoulders, she shook her head.

Raising a hand, she pointed to the pile of debris outside the fragmented walls. "It won't work, Mr. Powers. My foreman's rooms are lying over there in those various piles of rubble. My own bedroom has a tree in it. There is only one other bed in the house. I would have nowhere for you to sleep."

"All I need is a sleeping bag or a couch. I am a simple man, wanting only to work the earth. I can sleep outside here with the livestock, if need be. You need the help. I'm offering the help. Give me until the end of the week, and if you're not satisfied, then you can let me go."

"I don't know." She looked to the dog by his side and then back up to him, a sigh giving vent to her obvious exhaustion. "I do need the help, so okay, let's see how this goes."

With this decision made, she found herself working side by side with a stranger. They sorted through Pop's scattered belongings, trying to salvage what they could. Dakota peppered her with questions about the farm, but never once asked her anything personal. Although she itched to know more about him and knew she probably should, she took her cue from him and withheld her own questions for the time being. There would be a time and place.

Without her asking him to do so, Dakota climbed like a monkey along the large trunk of the tree lying against her house and rescued her clothing. Standing at the base of the tree, she worried for his safety, especially as he slipped a few times. When he finally slid his way back down and dropped to the ground, she let loose a laugh of relief and thanked him.

Eventually the long day waned, and, exhausted, they headed inside her home. Cringing at the cost, she reluctantly called out for pizza to feed them. She still had no power and had no idea when it would be restored, but they had to eat. The food in the refrigerator had started to warm, and Dakota ran out to find ice, which was difficult, considering the whole town was still without power. She smiled and thanked him for his thoughtfulness when he walked in the back door with gallons of water. At least she could wash up.

Together they worked to pack as much food as they could in ice, but she knew some would spoil, and she'd have to toss it. Another loss she was ill-prepared for. It was all adding up.

Bedtime brought on a whole new set of worry. She refused to allow Dakota to sleep in the barn, stating the structure was not safe. She already worried that her animals had to be housed there. At least her house was a bit more secure.

Setting him up with blankets and pillows on her couch,

she lay in bed that night and listened to the sounds of him moving around downstairs. She started to question her sanity in allowing a stranger into her life, but he was such a kind and gentle soul, she found herself relaxing around him as they worked together and talked about farm life. A huge plus in his favor was that Jake trusted him, and she, in turn, trusted Jake.

True to his word, the next day he worked hard, and it appeared he knew exactly what he was doing. His knowledge of everything to do with the running of a farm impressed her, but with so much skill she had to wonder why he had been jobless. She really hadn't expected him to be as good as he was. As with others she had hired in the past, she figured she'd have to explain a lot, but he just set about each job as if he had worked there for years.

When Liam and Alec came back to work, the three of them got along great. She was saddened when the boys told her poor Greg had broken his leg during the tornado and was laid up at his home. He would be out of commission for a while.

Shielding her eyes against the mid-day sun, she watched as Dakota and the boys worked on clean-up. Their muscles bulged and their bodies glistened with sweat as they sifted through the debris to find more of Pop's belongings. Anna congratulated herself on letting Dakota stay. She wasn't sure how much they would've accomplished being another worker short. It'd already been bad enough losing Pop.

The rental combine arrived the following day. Between the three men and her, they spent the next two days harvesting the remaining wheat, preparing it for trucks that would haul it off for sale. No matter how difficult and precarious it was to work amid the devastation around her, she had to get the wheat harvested before it spoiled. Not to mention that she desperately had to have the money the remaining stock would bring her.

A few contractors showed up and covered her roof with huge blue tarps. Long supportive beams were placed on both the house and barn in an effort to keep the structures from falling down around them all. The actual work to repair both would take a few days until supplies were brought in, but at least there was some type of security in place.

The contractors told her how they had run out of tarps and had to go to neighboring towns to get more. Laughing, although they probably shouldn't be, they informed her that most of their town was covered in colorful shades of tarp. One of the contractors even told her that the town looked like a circus had moved in.

After two and a half days with no electricity, she was beyond ecstatic when the local electric company showed up to restore her power. As soon as it came back on, she went straight to her coffee pot and practically danced as the welcome aroma filled her kitchen.

The day after the last load of wheat left her farm, the insurance agent showed up again with his final paperwork for the repairs. As she sat at her kitchen table and signed a bunch of forms, her mind came to a decision. It was the only option she could possibility think of, as she had no other choices. She would have to go to the bank and apply for a loan. She had nothing to sell that would be worth five thousand dollars, and she had less than a thousand in savings that she really didn't want to touch. The bank was her last hope, although she had no idea how she would pay that bill either. Something would have to be given up, but what?

Outfitted in white sandals and a soft yellow sundress Dakota had rescued from her tree, she drew on every ounce of courage she had and prepared herself for a battle.

Swinging open the back door, she met Dakota walking up the steps.

"I'll be gone for a while. I'm going to the bank to apply for a loan to pay for the repairs."

"Is there no other way?"

She shook her head. The question again brought on her insecurities. Would the bank refuse her?

He backed up as she passed and walked around the side of the house to her truck. As she drove the ancient truck up the driveway, she looked in her rear-view mirror to see Dakota watching her, and she wondered what he was thinking.

CHAPTER EIGHT

It had been a hard fight, but after practically pledging her life to the banker and with a five-thousand-dollar loan hanging over her head, Anna made her way home. She was bone tired of the struggle. When had it become so hard? After her husband died, it'd been difficult, but never this bad. As each day, each month passed, she found herself questioning her choices.

Doubt about everything clouded her mind. Why did she bother to continue breaking her back every day? Why not sell the farm and get a nice cozy apartment somewhere? She could get a job in an accountant's office or something. Anything would be easier than the life she had been thrust into and reluctantly accepted.

As she turned the corner of her driveway and slowly drifted down the small incline to park, she looked at the vast land stretching out around her. At last summer was waning, and the air had turned a bit cooler. The leaves on her trees were just beginning to change color, the peak still a couple weeks away.

The old maple that had caused havoc on her house had been removed, although the tarps were still in place on her wall and roof. The cleanup of the debris was almost done.

For the briefest moment, the despair and the wreckage faded in significance as she gazed at the acres and acres of land around her. This was her property, her life, her responsibility.

Too many days her body hurt from the work load, but as

she sat on her porch most nights, she felt such a deep satis-faction in a job well done. She knew Charles would've been proud of her.

Exhaling deeply, her shoulders slumped. Could she give this up? The soil, the livestock, her home, Jake, Miranda and Pop were her life. It was really all she knew. She felt so torn.

The picture of Pop's sweet face came forward in her mind, and the landscape blurred when tears filled her eyes. She had been giving him a lot of thought lately. She'd been so busy she hadn't been able to see him yet, but she'd talked to him on the phone and planned a visit very soon. He told her he was doing fairly well, but the break in his foot was bad. After his release from the hospital on crutches and in a walking boot, he'd gone to live with a friend. He had no home to return to here, anyway.

Coming to a deeply painful conclusion, she'd decided to let him retire. He deserved it. This would be an abrupt end-ing to a fine career, but at least it would be an ending. The man had worked hard for over sixty-five years of his life. She would tell him in person when she visited.

Her focus was captured by the path of a colorful leaf as it left its summer residence and drifted lazily to the ground. Soon it would be joined by thousands of others that would become nothing more than ground up fertilizer for next year's growth. Life went on no matter what it threw at you, but for the past two years it had been throwing everything it could think of in her path. She was tired of it.

The pressure returned with a vengeance and created a pounding within her skull. Her shoulders ached from the strain of holding her head up stoically at the bank, and with a sigh, her forehead thumped down gently against the steer-ing wheel. The fields still needed to be burned and prepared for spring planting. They showed only the broken stubble of what would have been a nearly perfect, healthy crop. There was still canning to be done, but that had to wait until her home was repaired and cleaned. Hours of work lay before her.

Lifting her hand, she switched off the tired old engine on a sputter and thought back to Charles bringing her here as a young bride. She'd been so innocent, so happy with the thought of a home and family of her own. *My, how things have changed.*

Fatigue seeped through her body like a sickness, yet the fight to survive against all odds paled in significance when she thought of the loneliness. She was so very, very lonely. No one and nothing had prepared her for this. The queen had moved into place, checking the king. The last step before he was checkmated. She was tired.

With her heart a heavy weight within her chest, she eased herself from the truck and walked the short distance to her porch and sniffed. Something smelled heavenly, and it was coming from her kitchen.

With the slow shuffle of one who has been almost defeated, she quietly climbed the steps and opened her back door. Dakota stood in front of her stove with a large fork in hand.

Dark black jeans curved deliciously over rounded and muscled buttocks, and the deep red T-shirt she had first seen him in strained across broad, strong shoulders. His hair had grown a bit since he started working for her and lay against the back of his neck, the ends curling into adorable little semi-circles against his skin. His long, callused feet were bare on the cool tile floor.

Her gaze swept him from head to foot, and she found herself growing warm, imagining things she hadn't thought about in a long, long time. Picturing him doing things to her body she'd all but forgotten had her nervously dropping her keys on the counter and moving to the refrigerator for a drink.

Loneliness was making her desire what she knew she

couldn't and wouldn't have, but it would've been nice to feel the strength of another's arms wrapped around her in passion. It really would be nice to just have a hug. She missed hugs. She missed touch. She desperately missed a warm body next to her on the long, dark nights, a body that wasn't as hairy as her dog.

He laid the fork on the counter and turned to her. He smiled, his even, white teeth brilliant against his darkened skin, and she inwardly moaned. Handsome was the only word tumbling through her mind. He was a man so flawless, he made her skin tingle in excitement.

"I thought I would make you a late lunch. You hungry?"

At the double entendre her mind conjured, she shifted uncomfortably and shook herself. She forced the desire away, knowing only too well where it could lead her.

"Yes, I'm starving," she replied without looking him in the eye.

He placed two plates on her table, and the aroma made her stomach truly growl in hunger. He had actually fried chicken, and the golden-skinned, succulent meat had her quickly taking a chair opposite him. Still-bubbling macaroni and cheese beckoned her to dig in, and she picked up her fork, ready to devour it all.

The man could also cook. What other surprises were in store for her with this guy? He could do just about everything he'd tried so far, and he had impressed her enough that she was going to ask him to stay on now that she was letting Pop retire. Her brain was being practical, because she needed the help. Her heart, on the other hand, cautioned that she could be making the biggest mistake of her life.

"How did it go?"

She swallowed a fork full of macaroni and looked to his questioning eyes. "Well, let me put it this way. I'm praying no catastrophe ruins next year's crop, because I have a huge loan to pay off."

CHAPTER NINE

After devouring the perfect lunch Dakota had created, she was putting the dishes in the sink when a knock sounded at her front door, an odd sound. Her head sprang up in confusion, and Jake started a ruckus the moment he'd heard the sound.

Dakota had gone back to the barn, so she was sure it wasn't him. Anyone else in her life knew to come around back. On opening the old door with the loud screech of seldom used hinges, she cautiously greeted the strange man on her porch. Short and round, his head covered by a hat that struggled to stay on his large head, he smiled at her.

He spoke over the sound of Jake's continuing barks. "Mrs. Scott, I am Brandon Shoop from Fidelity Holdings. May I speak with you for a moment?"

She stepped out onto the porch and shut the heavy wooden door behind her, muting Jake's frantic noise. With her normal faith in Jake's intuition, she eyed the man before her with mistrust.

"How can I help you, Mr. Shoop?"

"May we sit?" Removing his hat, he backed up a couple steps as she motioned him to the two ancient rockers on her front porch. She could barely suppress a smile as she watched him gingerly sit down, as if afraid the chair wouldn't hold him. She found herself agreeing with his caution. The old chair might just collapse under the pressure.

"Mrs. Scott, let me start by saying I am very sorry for the troubles you've had lately as a result of the tornado that passed through. It saddens me to see how it has affected our whole town. We were fortunate no lives were lost, but there were many injured and too many homes and businesses impacted."

Behind his thick black-rimmed glasses his gaze met hers again, and she experienced a strange dislike. His eyes held a fierce intelligence, but a sly and devious shift of his gaze on everything around him as he spoke told her more than she wanted to know. Maybe it had to do with Jake's reaction, maybe it was a first impression, but she couldn't trust a person who wouldn't look her in the eyes for long. Something just felt wrong about this man.

Her eyes narrowed as she observed his appearance. He was dressed in a fine light-grey linen suit with a crisp white shirt that threatened to burst open against the thick bulge of his stomach, and a dark black tie lay rounded over his abdomen. Removing his glasses, he rubbed them against his shirt, revealing eyes showing the effects of overindulgence. His clothing, made of the finest quality, spoke of wealth and opulence, but the body it covered spoke more along the line of gluttony and greed.

"Mr. Shoop, may I ask how you came to know about my *troubles*?"

"I sit on the Board for your bank. I make it my business to know about our patrons." He shifted, and the chair groaned loudly, protesting the movement. "I know this is a personal subject, but I am aware of how your farm is struggling right now, and I think I have a solution. That being said, I hope we can speak as two intelligent human beings deciding on a course of action that is beneficial to us both."

Anna couldn't take her focus off him. Beads of sweat had broken out across his brow, despite the fact the day was not overly warm. The bright sun, beginning its descending path toward evening, cast the porch in a strong glow, but it wasn't hot enough to cause him to sweat. At least in her opinion.

His eyes continued to shift uneasily between looking at her and the bushes across the road, but his words were spoken in a firm, intelligent and authoritarian voice, a voice used to getting its way. He was hard to figure out.

"Go on."

"As I stated previously, I am part owner of Fidelity Holdings. I've been approached by a corporation that is looking to secure a large section of land in Sweet Grove to build condominiums and storefronts. They asked me to recommend a good parcel of land."

He placed his hat back on his head and tilted it to block the sunlight, which partially blocked her view of his eyes.

"I've spent considerable time studying properties in the area, and yours would be perfect for their investment. As you are a widow and have been placed in an unfortunate situation beyond your control, you must be feeling a tremendous pressure. I'm aware that your foreman is unable to work, and this must also be hard on you. We would like to offer to buy your land at a significantly beneficial price to you."

His words shocked her. Of any of the myriad of things she could've thought he would say, this was not among them. She'd only been to the bank that morning. How could he know so quickly about her financial situation? What exactly did he mean when he said he had studied her land? She'd never seen him before.

She didn't like him. Jake obviously did not like him, yet she had to admit that his offer was enticing. Hadn't she been thinking along the very same lines?

She couldn't deny she was under tremendous pressure and feeling like she was fighting a losing battle, but to give up Charles' dream felt like a betrayal to the man she had loved. To give up the only home she had known all these many years felt wrong. She just didn't know if she could do it.

She leaned forward in the chair, and he raised his head, meeting her intense scrutiny.

"Your offer is tempting. Please allow me time to think about it." She wouldn't let him know this was a war she'd been fighting for some time, one minute wanting to give up and the next vowing to hold on to the land she held dear. For some reason, letting this man think he'd touched on a nerve was scary to her.

She would think about it, though. She knew she couldn't go on as she was. Because she and Charles had no children, she knew there was no one to take over the farm when she died. It was also depressing to think that in ten or twenty years she wouldn't be able to do the work she was doing now, but that was the reality. Her mind became a battle ground as she warred with living an easy life or fighting to live the hard life she knew so well.

She heard a piece of wood snap as he fought to extricate himself from the clinging arms. She should be worried he'd be hurt, but she brought her hand to her mouth and mimicked a cough to hide a giggle that begged for release. Finally, the chair let him go, and she rose to stand face to face with the man. His height afforded her equality in stature, for which she was grateful. For some reason she felt that any show of vulnerability would be disastrous.

He smiled, a sugary false curve of his lips that didn't quite reach the sickly look of his eyes.

"I'm glad you are a sensible woman. It's too hard to run a farm alone. You will see in the end that what I offer would be extremely lucrative to you. I'll send out paperwork that you can read over. If you have any questions, please contact me. Here is my business card."

As he extended a hand with the card, she took it tentatively. His hand shook, as if he were either ill or excited with the prospect of getting his hands on her land. Once again, she felt uneasy as she looked to his name printed on the expensive little piece of stationary.

As he made his way to his car and eased his enormous stomach behind the steering wheel, she watched him with curiosity. He sure lived well. He obviously never had to count every penny he spent. She wondered what that was like.

Lost in thought, she contemplated his words until his car was a mere speck on the horizon and jumped in surprise when the door screeched once more behind her.

Jake squeezed between Dakota's legs as he exited, happy to be let out and explore. Sniffing the porch around the chair the man had just vacated, he let out a low growl, and she watched, mesmerized, as the hair on his back stood on end, a telltale sight to behold.

"Are you considering selling?" her possible new foreman asked.

"I'm not sure that is any of your business, Mr. Powers." She was a bundle of tightly controlled, confused, and turbulent emotions as she turned and walked from the porch and around the corner, away from the eyes she felt boring into her back.

Once out of sight, she stood hands on hips in the backyard and looked out over her land. She wrestled with anger and indecision and was uncomfortable with both feelings. She had occasionally thought of selling after Charles died but then had been too busy to give it further thought. Eventually her home became too important to her to sell, but the tornado brought all the uncertainties back with full force.

Suddenly her need to see Pop moved her into action. She grabbed her keys and purse, and she searched Dakota out once more, telling him where she was going. She needed advice and knew Pop was the best one to get it from, but as she walked into the small apartment Pop was sharing with a friend, shock made her stop and stare at the man she loved.

In pajamas and a robe, he sat in a large maroon recliner that dwarfed his thinning frame. His lower leg was covered by a heavy boot and lay propped on pillows. His once handsome face was a kaleidoscope of fading bruises and healing cuts below a row of staples that ran vertically along his shaved head. Small cuts and bruises lined his hands. She had no idea what his clothing covered, but she imagined he looked the same all over.

She could barely recognize him. His smile on seeing her, however, was still the same warm and happy beam of the man she knew so well.

She walked forward quickly and came down on her knees, gently hugging his mending body. At least she could do that, and she sent up a silent prayer of thanks that he was still alive, and she could hold him. Her need to unburden her woes on him paled in comparison to his frail health, and she felt ashamed of herself. This man was dealing with enough.

He asked her questions, and she answered them vaguely. She couldn't have him worrying more than he apparently already did. He congratulated her on a job well done in organizing the repair work and was saddened along with her that she'd lost a few chickens. She didn't tell him about the missing mare. He had spent years training and caring for those horses, and she knew it would upset him to learn one was gone.

The visit went on longer than she had first anticipated, and she felt guilty when she saw him lean his head back and lightly doze while they were mid-conversation. Kissing him softly on the forehead, she said goodbye to his friend and let herself out. In truth, though, she didn't really want to leave. If she could've stayed by his side, she would have in a heartbeat. Not only would she be hiding from the world, but she also wanted to be with her friend and care for him, although actually he seemed to be doing just fine without her.

When she left Pop, she went to visit Greg, taking him a few jars of the strawberry jam he loved so much. He always managed to be nearby when he knew it was time for her to prepare her preserves.

She shook her head at the difference between Pop and Greg and how they were doing. Greg was already up and walking with crutches, complaining that he wanted to get back to work. Pop's recovery would be much longer and slower. He'd made no mention of returning to work at all, and she'd made no mention of his retirement.

That discussion would come soon, though.

CHAPTER TEN

As was her custom, that evening she sat on her back-porch swing watching as the sun began its lazy descent. The colorful sky was much as it had been the night of the tornado, and she relived the whole night over again as she watched a slowly moving storm drift away from them to the east.

A shiver moved along her spine and brought her back to the evening around her. She didn't know if the shiver was due to her memories or the fact that the nights had grown cooler, but she rubbed her hands along her forearms to warm them. Miranda lay curled across her lap, and Jake sought either warmth or companionship this night and had jumped up on the swing and laid his body by her side. His chin rested next to the sleeping Miranda as he also dozed, and she smiled at their companionship.

Her hands gently combed through the hair of her beloved pets as she closed her eyes and relaxed, easing the strains of the day from her body.

It was in this tranquil state that Dakota came upon her.

She felt the change in the air and knew he was close. His nearness was always unsettling to her, at times making her appear the shrew and other times warming her a bit too much. Too many nights lately she had tossed and turned restlessly dreaming about a faceless man who held her tightly in strong, loving arms. They were dreams that hadn't started until this man entered her life. Why he was faceless in her dreams she didn't know, for the arms that held her with passionate strength were the same as those that worked by her side each day.

Without opening her eyes, she revealed her regret.

"I owe you an apology, Dakota. I shouldn't have snapped at you earlier. I'm just feeling a strangely overwhelming weight of pressure right now, but it's not your fault."

His pant leg brushed against hers, the contact barely perceptible, yet her traitorous body clenched in anticipation of more.

"I'm not sure if you have heard of him, Anna, but there is a wise saying by a brave warrior named Crazy Horse that may be fitting here. *A very great vision is needed, and the man who has it must follow it as the eagle seeks the deepest blue of the sky.* Seek a greater vision. Pray for the answers you seek. Ask for guidance."

She lifted tired, heavy lids to find him so very close, mere inches away as he leaned to pet Jake. The sky was an amber glow behind him, casting his face into cool shadow. Heavy black lashes circled deep and shuttered eyes as he petted Jake. There was no telling what he was thinking. He spoke little, revealed little. He hid his emotions well and remained a mystery to her.

He shifted, and mesmerized, she watched as his gaze came to rest on her lips. For the life of her she could not draw a breath. For just a moment she allowed herself the pleasure of imagining him holding her, touching her, kissing her. The picture formed in her mind of his dusky lips lowering to her own, and she warmed as she imagined nibbling on the full lower lip she had memorized in her mind.

The direction of her wayward thoughts upset her, and she sat forward suddenly, the movement knocking Miranda from her lap with a meow of protest. Jake lifted his head and stared at her in question, and a startled Dakota quickly backed up to avoid their heads colliding.

"Thank you for your insight. I need to give all of this a

great deal of thought."

The moment was odd and uncomfortable, and she wondered if he would say more, but with a slight shake of his head he backed away. "I will check on the livestock before I retire. Goodnight, Anna."

"Goodnight, Dakota."

His focus rested on her lips one more time, and to Anna, the burning sensuous look was testimony to what he wanted to do at that moment, but with another small shake of his head, he turned and walked down the steps.

She watched him as he crossed the lawn. Her faithful Jake also watched and with a stretch, jumped down from her side and left her, following him across the field. The traitor.

Drawing a deep, shaky breath to calm herself, she couldn't help but admire his long and powerfully built body moving with a peaceful ease across the grassy field. His tall frame created a long shadow across the broken remains of her wheat, and when he brought his arms up to play with a dancing Jake, she gasped. Their shadows had combined and almost looked like an eagle stretching its wings in flight.

Her attention flew back to the man, who began to run in comical circles around her dog, and she laughed when she watched Jake try to catch him. Dakota was an enigma to her. Appearing to be deeply in touch with his inner self, he accepted himself for the man he was. It almost seemed to her as if no stress touched him, only a deep inner calmness with life.

What she wouldn't give to be that way. To accept all that was thrown at her as her due and to work through each obstacle with peace and assurance that all would work out in the end. She tried to be that way but failed much too often.

Jake took off at a run toward a tree and appeared moments later with his beloved ball, shoving it into the outstretched hand of Dakota. With a lazy toss, Dakota sent the ball sailing across the lawn towards the barn, and Jake tore off after it.

Dakota followed. Was he really that calm and self-assured, or was he hiding something behind the cool exterior? She really knew nothing about the man. Had she really based her entire opinion of him on Jake's acceptance?

He could be running from the law for all she knew, but somehow, she doubted it. The man appeared honest and kind. How many would help a lonely widow for no pay?

Her eyes narrowed in thought.

Why was he here? Where was his home? Was he a con artist? She had so many questions. Questions that Charles and Pop would've told her she should've asked in the first place.

CHAPTER ELEVEN

For two weeks Anna endured a barrage of ear-shattering hammers and saws as the seemingly always shouting construction workers strived to fix her home. She might be getting a new roof and much needed repairs out of this, but the never-ending noise was too much. Holding off on fixing dinner for a while, she went in search of the peace and quiet she craved. She would go for a ride. It'd been days since she'd taken Maggie out.

Making her way through the rubble and endless trucks and equipment, she entered her barn, seeing almost immediately that Maggie was also restless and ready for a run. Neighing loudly in greeting, the horse stood anxiously waiting as Anna prepared her for riding. The work on the barn was only just beginning. The house was near completion, but the racket wasn't something she or any of her four-legged family members were used to. The noise and constant activity was stressing for them all. Even her chickens were barely laying eggs.

From the corner of his eye, he watched as the workers ogled her. She paid them no mind, as if oblivious to their observation. She slipped inside the barn, but he found that their staring eyes angered him. Giving a few of them some hard looks, he walked quickly to the doorway of the barn and watched her, acting no differently than the construction workers.

The ever-present tight jeans lifted and curved over her rounded backside as she tossed the saddle on the tall chestnut mare's back. Today the awful hat was gone, and her hair was gloriously unbound and cascading down her back. In the shadowed interior of the barn, it resembled a chocolaty red silk, and he felt a long abandoned and almost overwhelming desire to curl his hands into the thick layers and pull her close against him. His mind had been on her constantly lately, and he had valiantly tried to fight the intrusive thoughts, but seeing her this way, his traitorous mind pictured what his body already craved.

"Where are you going?"

At the sound of his voice, she hesitated and turned slowly. The thin weave of her blue-gray sweater stretched across her unbound breasts with the movement, and his eyes were drawn to the hardened peaks of her nipples. No wonder the men were ogling her.

Being around her day to day was becoming difficult, the allure of her almost too powerful to ignore. She was a strong, independent, and beautiful woman, and he admired her. Her smile made him happy, and her tears tore him apart. Her strength made him proud of her, and her weaknesses made him feel protective.

He should leave. He knew he should. He was becoming too involved, but he, in mind, body, and spirit, could not leave her alone, no matter how hard he tried to stay away. After all he'd been through, an entanglement wasn't what he was looking for, but the strength of his attraction to her couldn't be denied. Indecision had never been a comfortable feeling for him, and he knew he should pray to the Great Spirit for guidance.

"I'm going for a ride to get away from all this noise. I want to look at the fields and make note of what we need to do next. I'm way behind schedule. Winter will be here soon, and the fields haven't even been prepared," she said with a weary smile.

"Don't worry. We'll get it done. Do you mind if I tag along? I want to see how the fence is holding up after the repairs."

She hesitated for just a fraction of a second, enough that he wondered if she just wanted to be alone and he was intruding.

She grabbed a sleeveless jacket from a hook on the wall, then shrugged as she donned it. "Sure," was her simple reply.

After saddling the one lone stallion in her possession, they rode off across the fields side by side. Jake must have heard them, because he found them quickly and raced from where he kept his vigil over the workers to streak past them. He led the way in pure happy abandonment.

The noise of the constant sawing and hammering faded as they traversed the beautiful land and peace once more took over his heart as he rode by her side, but not for long.

"Dakota," she called against the cool wind trying its best to tangle her hair. "Tell me about yourself."

He sighed internally. He knew this would happen sooner or later. The woman was basically his employer, after all, even though he hadn't received a paycheck. She'd been highly respectful of his privacy so far, but she had a right to know about him, to a degree. He would tell her only what she needed to know.

He looked to the horizon as the sun began a slow descent behind the trees and shadows lengthened along the barren fields on which they rode. They only had about an hour before it was dark. The air was chilling quickly without the warming rays of the sun. It would be a cold night.

He'd delayed answering and knew it. With a slight turn of his head he glanced at her, but he saw no impatience. She rode companionably beside him, her eyes watchful of where her horse was stepping, waiting for him to respond.

"I'm not comfortable speaking of myself, but I am sorry I've kept you in the dark."

Shifting his gaze once more to the land before him, he told her as little as possible. "I am from South Dakota, where I lived on a cattle ranch. I was married for six years, but now I am a widower. My wife died after giving birth to our daughter. Our baby was stillborn."

His vision blurred before him, and he realized he was close to crying. He hadn't cried since the day he had buried his wife, and he really didn't want to reveal the depth of his feelings to Anna. They were his to share only when he was ready. He blinked to clear away the moisture and began again.

"She developed an infection after the birth that my family fought, but by the time we realized we were getting nowhere with her and got her to the hospital it was too late, or maybe she had just given up. I think she didn't care anymore once she lost the baby, and no amount of medicine could have helped her."

In respect for the woman he had loved so deeply, his voice grew softer as he spoke. Anna must have struggled to hear him, because she moved her mare closer to his stallion until the two horses rode neck and neck. She tilted her body nearer to his, and he tried to speak up, but relaying this story was hard for him.

"I tried to help her. I tried to reach her, but she gave up the fight for life, I think. It was the third that we lost. She told me she had failed me and then stopped talking to me at all. Children are everything in the Lakota tradition, and she felt her inability to bring a child to term was some sort of punishment. After she passed, I had to get away. I had to reach some peace with myself and the Creator after losing so much."

Shifting slightly in the saddle, he glanced to her and was unprepared for what he saw. She looked at him in horror. Her beautiful blue eyes filled in front of him, and he wondered at the strength of her reaction. He had noticed that she was childless. Was it by choice, or had she faced her own battle?

He opened his mouth to question her, but Jake let out a howl interrupting them, and as one they turned to him, following the direction of his pointed stare. That was when they saw it. Smoke. Smoke in a drought was not a good thing. Smoke at any time was bad, but especially with the land so dry.

Kicking their horses into a gallop, they took off towards the ominous dark cloud swirling against the wind.

Cresting a small rise in the earth, they found the north field ablaze. The dried chaff left behind by the combine served as a kindling for the flames. With the beginnings of panic, Anna watched the fire's quick progression in horror. Tiny flames like the smoldering embers in a fireplace coated the ground. Travelling quickly in the wind, the fire inched towards a grove of trees that separated the four fields.

The ground around those trees was covered in dried pine needles and thousands of dead leaves, more kindling for the creeping fire. If the fire reached that area, it could cause devastation, because that area was precious. Those trees surrounded the gazebo Charles had built just for her, her own private place to go for peace and quiet. She hadn't been there since before Charles' death, but she didn't want anything to happen to it and looked to Dakota for advice. He was already off his horse before she had a chance to open her mouth.

They'd already planned a burn but were terribly behind schedule because of the storm damage. No real barriers were there to stop the progression of the fire, and this blaze could quickly get out of hand if it caught the dried leaves in the grove.

She hoped the firebreaks they had created in the early spring were still functional, but she honestly had no idea of their condition. The combine had mostly likely ground them to oblivion.

Dakota jumped back up on his horse and began moving the massive animal in an integral pattern along the edges of the field, all the while keeping control of the creature who was wild-eyed as he watched the fire approaching. With firm commands he kept on, and she watched, confused until it dawned on her what he was doing. He was disturbing the earth, building up a layer of dirt against the fire and hopefully destroying or burying any vegetation that could ignite.

She didn't know if it would work or if they could cover so much territory quicker than the fire could spread, but lightning fast she joined him, helping him the best she could. Her mare was smaller, lighter, and she herself was lighter, but as he headed west she headed east. They worked together until they were both exhausted. Their horses were lathered and breathing heavily by the time they finally rested them.

Backing away from the flames, they sat atop their horses in the shelter of the trees and watched as the fire inched towards them and prayed their haphazard firebreaks would hold. Jake sat quietly by their side and waited also, seemingly mesmerized by the dancing flames.

The sun had long ago set. The soft amber glow of the fire was the only real light in the cold moonless night. Anna had always found fire soothing and enchanting, but an uncontrolled burn could be disastrous. She could do nothing except stare spellbound as she watched the remains of the chaff quickly being turned to ash and send fervent wishes skyward for a good outcome.

How had it happened? Fires didn't just start by themselves unless the spark from a malfunctioning machine created an inferno or there had been a lightning strike. No machines had been on this land in a few weeks, and there'd been no lightening since the devastating tornado. The ground was again dry and brittle. It was perfect for starting a fire.

Someone had either done this intentionally, or one of the workers had come out here to smoke and didn't extinguish the butt.

She knew the workers would be gone by now, but come the dawn she would ask, and come morning, they would investigate. Tonight, it would just be too difficult to see. The morning should bring the answers they sought, she hoped.

Easing her mare up alongside his stallion, the two friends nudged each other with their long prominent noses and Anna shivered as the night air overpowered the warmth of the fire. She wished she had dressed warmer, but there had been no way of knowing how this night would turn out.

She watched Dakota survey the fire. It appeared their work would be successful. The flames were sputtering out along the edges, now that they found nothing further to ignite.

"What do you think started it?"

He shook his head at the question as he eased his body from the tall stallion and ran his fingers through the hot soil. Grabbing a handful, he brought it to his nose and inhaled. After tossing it back to the ground, he stood and stretched.

She waited with patience along the edge of the field. As with most questions she asked him, he took his time before answering, thinking about his response. She was actually growing used to it.

"I don't know. I will come back in the morning to check."

"Why did you just smell the dirt?"

"To see if any type of accelerant was used, but I smell nothing odd, at least in this area."

He looked up at her and saw her shivering, his face showing concern.

"Come, let's get you back to your house."

She didn't argue his command.

CHAPTER TWELVE

The early morning sun heralded another beautiful, yet dry day. She stepped away from the bedroom window and dressed quickly, wanting to go inspect the north field with Dakota.

As she quietly descended the steps, her phone rang, loud in the silence of the new day. She grabbed it quickly, not wanting the ringtone to wake Dakota, but was surprised to see his blanket folded on the couch and his coffee cup washed and drying on the counter. He was already long gone.

The concerned voice of her mother came over the line as she peppered Anna with questions about how the repair work was going, but she knew her mother well. What she really wanted were answers about the man who was now acting as her foreman. It was no surprise therefore when the topic quickly turned, confirming her suspicions. Her mother, in the usual condescending tone that always agitated Anna, had been giving her a fit about hiring a man who'd given no references. For the hundredth time, Anna berated herself for ever revealing so much to her mother in the first place.

She tried to care about her mom, but it had been hard to love a person who was so judgmental and cold. The two hadn't been close in a long time, and she found herself just wanting her off the phone. She was anxious to join Dakota in the field to see if they could find what had started the fire. There was no sign of Jake, so she could only assume that he'd gone with Dakota.

Almost a full fifteen minutes later, she happily succeeded in hanging up, but not without a promise to call her soon. She fed Miranda and made a quick mug of coffee before she grabbed her coat and headed out the door.

The brisk morning air was immobilizing at first, and she shivered against the chill, her breath fogging the air in front of her. Winter was closing in, and they were still so ill-prepared.

Large white trucks topped with ladders were again parked in front of the barn as she made her way across the grass, the workers preparing to start their chilly day. She didn't envy them working outside in this weather. She knew the feeling only too well.

The job was more than halfway finished, and she welcomed the thought of having the peace and quiet of her home once more to herself. The rooms above the barn for her foreman were almost complete, and she was sure Dakota would welcome a soft bed instead of her ancient sofa to sleep on. Last night on the ride back from the field, she had broached the subject, and Dakota had accepted her offer of the foreman job.

She would have to dip into her precious savings, but she would give Pop a small pension and ask him to take it easy. His recovery had been slow due to not only the severity of the injuries, but also due to his age. She couldn't in good conscience expect him to come back.

Her mare nickered when she saw her, and Anna dug into her pocket for the bites of the apple she knew the horse favored. Running her hand along the long nose, she thought back to the day Charles had gifted her with Maggie. The long-legged chestnut was her wedding present, and the beautiful mare held a special place in her heart because she was still here, even if Charles was gone. With a gentle nudge against her hand, the horse was reminding her she still held her favorite treat and Anna chuckled.

"Impatient are you, my love?"

After feeding her a few bites, she prepared Maggie for a ride, but when she lifted the heavy saddle to lay it across the broad back, the mare sidestepped out of her reach.

"Whoa, girl, what's the matter this morning?"

With a grunt, she hefted the heavy saddle again onto the mare's back and watched in alarm as the horse reared slightly back and to the left, neighing loudly while tossing the saddle to the floor. Puzzled, Anna didn't know what to make of her horse's behavior. She'd never acted like that before.

Picking the saddle up from the ground, she began to once again lift it onto the horse's back when she noticed Maggie holding her right rear leg at an awkward angle. Worried now, she rounded the horse while calming her with gentle soothing words and pats until she reached the leg.

She examined from stifle to fetlock but found nothing out of the ordinary. No swelling or sores. Lifting the leg slightly, she looked to the hoof, and that was when she saw it. A nail poked out of the sole of the hoof on a weird angle, as if she had scuffed it into her hoof as she walked.

Carefully removing the nail, she cleaned the wound. It was minor, really, yet she knew that even a minor cut in the hoof could prove fatal if infection set in. She grabbed her cell and called the vet to make an appointment for him to check on her. It was another expense she was ill-prepared to pay, another meal she could possibly miss, but she also couldn't handle losing Maggie.

Inspecting the ground around the interior of the stall, she found three more nails. Weirdly, all three nails were poking up. Rage infused her at the worker's carelessness, and she went in search of the construction foreman. With hands speaking for her, she poked the air in rage as she shouted at the man for ten solid minutes. He spoke calmly at first, letting her know that there was no way one of his men had left nails in the horses' stalls or anywhere in the barn, but eventually his own anger surfaced. His voice rose, and they drew a crowd as he explained that they weren't even working on that side of the barn and they'd been careful of the livestock. Frustrated, Anna was having none of it. She was furious that her beloved mare was hurt.

The two were soon shouting each other down, neither listening to what the other said, and the onlookers watched and whispered at their sides. Her frustration at a boiling point, she let out an angry growl and stomped away from him after not getting the answers she sought. Her heart was pounding, and her face felt hot enough to warm the chilled air around her. She couldn't remember ever being so angry.

She saddled Pop's mare and set off for the field, racing across the land in high temper. She felt like she was dealing with one thing after another anymore, and her nerves were becoming frayed. Just to punch something would give her immense satisfaction. No one hurt her animals. No one.

The horse was winded and lathered by the time she finally slowed to a trot as she neared the scorched ground. Dakota was walking with meticulous precision along the blackened ashes, and Jake investigated along the edges. He had obviously been ordered not to accompany Dakota on his search. His entire being focused on his task, Dakota seemed oblivious to her arrival.

She carefully brought the horse closer, but her earlier assumption that he didn't know of her arrival was incorrect. She was about twenty feet from him when he told her to halt. Stopping the horse in her tracks, she asked him why.

"I'd appreciate it if you didn't disturb the land until I have finished inspecting it," was his only explanation. Still boiling from her encounter with the foreman, she felt her temper rise further at being ordered about like a child, but she stayed where she was, watching and waiting. There was nothing else for her to do.

"Dakota," she spoke in a whisper, as if her words would disturb the investigation. "What do you see?"

"Many footprints, but they could be anyone's. I only have this last area to examine, and I'll be done. Why are you on that horse? Where is Maggie?"

She was surprised he had even noticed what she was riding, and her surprise must have shown on her face when he finally looked to her for an answer.

"Each horse has their own sound, their own smell, their own trot," he explained. "I could tell you were not on Maggie."

He continued to amaze her each time he spoke. It was almost as if he was in tune with all around him. It could be eerily unnerving at times. Turning from her once again, he carefully scrutinized the ground, and while he did, she let her anger vent, telling him about what she'd found when she tried to saddle her mare.

He made no response as usual, but this time it aggravated her. As absorbed as he was in what he was doing, she wasn't sure he even listened. She sat waiting and fuming, but her eyes widened in anticipation as he bent and lifted something in his hand and held it. Finishing his inspection, he turned and walked towards her with a grim look and holding his hand palm up.

She could see blackened cigarette butts.

"I've found several of these now. Someone is a very heavy smoker or has been on your property many times. Do you know anyone who smokes?"

"Not really. Pop enjoyed a cigar from time to time, and I know some people in town who smoke, but I don't know of anyone that has been at the farm who does."

She took the butts from his hand and examined them. It was hard to read the brand name, as only a couple scorched letters remained on one, but she slipped them inside her jacket pocket. She would question the construction foreman one more time to see if any of his workers smoked. Why they would be out here in this remote field was beyond her, though. She'd never seen them go farther from the job site than her bathroom or kitchen.

Lifting her gaze from her palm, she locked eyes with Dakota's. "I'll ask the foreman about this."

He raised his left leg to the stirrup, and she watched in admiration the play of thigh muscles as he swung his strong body over the healthy young stallion and settled his large frame in the saddle. Together the three of them made their way back towards the house while she explained further about Maggie. As before, she watched for any reaction from him, but he remained calm and in control. Was that control hiding something?

A niggling doubt formed in her head. Strange things had started happening since he began working for her. She wondered if there was a connection, but what reason would he have for doing such things? She inwardly shook her head at the direction of her thoughts, reasoning that the two events were probably just coincidence. She would give it some time and keep an eye on him.

Absorbed by her own thoughts, she spoke little as they made their way back to the barn. He remained equally silent. It was now very late and dark, so the workers and trucks were all gone. Quiet once again lay across her land.

She was rubbing down the mare when she heard the creaking of a stall door and peaked over the top of the wall. Dakota had finished with his own horse and had gone to Maggie. He spoke to her softly, his voice as gentle as a spring rain that lulls you to sleep at night as he built Maggie's trust. Anna smiled and closed her eyes, allowing the soft cadence to move along her frazzled nerves and soothe her anger. It was almost as if he was speaking to her when he murmured that all was going to be okay.

"Anna, where are the nails you found?" Gone was the gentleness of his tone as he called out to her, and Anna jumped, her thoughts returning quickly to her frustration. She patted the horse's rump and left her stall, walking to Dakota.

"I handed them to the foreman when I confronted him about it. They matched the ones they've been using, but he swears no one has been anywhere near the stalls, and that they've left no nails on the ground to possibly injure any of the animals. He was quite adamant that they know what they're doing and have been very careful about that, but I can't see how you can watch every little nail you use. It had to have been them."

Dakota harrumphed at her words, but that told her nothing. She didn't know if he was disturbed that he hadn't seen the evidence himself or if he also doubted the foreman.

"She'll be okay. I will make a salve, and you can cancel the vet. I'll speak with the foreman myself." With those three short commanding sentences, he left her standing alone near the stall door. Staring at his retreating back, bewildered and still a bit put out, she followed him out of the door.

CHAPTER THIRTEEN

The two boys arrived mid-morning, and along with Dakota, they burned the fields. She made excuses and stayed home, as it really didn't require her help. She closed the door on their retreating backs and put in a call to Sheriff Regan.

"Anna, it's great to hear from you, pretty lady. How are you doing out there? Have you heard from Pop?"

Anna chuckled at the cheerful enthusiasm in his voice. The man seemed to always have a good attitude about everything. Even after the tornado, he'd assured everyone that all would be okay. Maybe it was his job, but she remembered he had been like that even in high school.

"The work is coming along nicely, but I'll be glad when it is done. It's noisy and messy. I did go see Pop, and I've talked to him several times on the phone. He's healing, but very slowly."

"I'm glad to hear he's healing, but we can't expect him to recover quickly at his age."

Anna hesitated for a moment, unsure how to delve into the reason for her call.

"Um, Martin, can you tell me anything about the man I hired, Dakota Powers?"

"Can't say that I can. He seems a nice enough fella, but I don't know much about him. Why do you ask? Are you having trouble? Do you need me to come out there?"

"No, no trouble. I was just curious about him. I really don't know him at all."

"Why the hell not? Didn't you interview him? I can run a

86

background check on him, if you want."

She ignored his probing questions about interviewing Dakota, embarrassed that she hadn't.

"No, I don't want to take up your time. I was just checking to see if you'd heard anything."

They spoke a few more minutes about how the town was recuperating before ending the conversation. She didn't want Martin to know about the strange occurrences just yet, at least not until she had a better idea of what was going on. Maybe they could be easily explained, and she didn't want to cause trouble for Dakota if he was innocent or put a strain on their relationship.

Jake trusted him, and she felt at ease around him for the most part, so maybe she was just letting her imagination run wild. She told herself that time would tell.

She had enough to do without adding worry about these minor problems, and chastising herself, she got to work. After throwing meat, vegetables, and spices to simmer in a large pot, she gathered cleaning supplies. It'd been a long time since she had a chance to clean, and with the construction work done on the house, the inside was absolutely filthy.

She hadn't slept in her own room yet. Her new mattress still sat in plastic. She hadn't even wanted to uncover it until the room had been cleaned. Building a whole new wall, part of a roof and repairing cracks in walls was a detailed job, the result of which was a huge mess. The bathroom had been retiled and the wall secured, and the result of that labor was thick grime on every surface. She was looking forward to showering in her own bathroom for a change. She'd been relying instead on the bathroom in the basement, which also had to have some repair work done.

The remnants of the construction filth were a thing of the past by the time she stopped scrubbing and held her hands against her aching lower back. It was done, the house was finally clean. The scent of her simmering pot of stew made an impact on her senses, and she walked to the kitchen to thicken the gravy in her stew and prepare the biscuits.

She hadn't made anything this good in weeks. With men moving through her home all day long, cooking had become impossible, and she and Dakota had survived on carry out and lunch meat. Not very healthy. Tonight would be different for them both. It was very cold outside, and a warm pot of stew with many of her own home-grown vegetables would be a refreshing delight, not to mention a nice surprise for Dakota.

With the stew simmering and the biscuits ready for baking, she raced upstairs to take a quick shower, washing away the day's labor. Finally, she could stand in the privacy of her own shower, and it felt beyond heavenly. With a small chuckle, she admitted that not having to climb two sets of stairs afterward was heavenly also. Things were slowly returning to normal, and she welcomed it with open arms. She wasn't a stickler for orderliness, but like most people she did like it when her life ran peacefully. Across her two years of aloneness, peace and quiet inside her home had become her life. It was all she really knew.

Tired, yet immensely satisfied with her day's accomplishments, she made her way downstairs. The setting sun cast an orange glow through the three front windows, and the intense rays highlighted the work she'd done. Every table surface gleamed with a high polish, all the windows so translucent they almost looked nonexistent, and the wooden floors were smooth and grime-free. The scent of furniture polish and cleaners warred with the fragrant smell of her dinner. It was an impressive day's work that pleased her.

A shiver moved along her body from the chill in the house. While she'd worked she hadn't noticed it, but coming from a fresh shower, she felt the cold deeply. Moving to the fireplace, she built a fire she hoped would be all they'd need tonight. She didn't want to turn on the old furnace just yet. She had to save a few more dollars.

After feeding Miranda and Jake their dinners, she popped the homemade biscuits into the oven just as the basement door opened. The slow squeaking of a hinge causing her to let loose a shriek of surprise, and she turned to see a freshly bathed Dakota step from the darkened doorway. She didn't even know he was in the house.

"You startled me," she burst out, feeling embarrassed at the obvious statement.

"I'm sorry. I heard you in the upstairs shower when I returned, so I knew the bathroom downstairs was free. The smoke smell was clinging to me. I had to wash it off."

Her gaze swept him quickly. He had dressed casually in charcoal grey fleece pants, which hung low on his hips, softly outlining the bulge of his manhood. She warmed as she pictured what he would look like naked.

She lifted her eyes reluctantly to see that a long-sleeved black T-shirt, the sleeves pushed up to his elbows, curved deliciously over a broad male chest and strong shoulders. She ached to lay her hand on the skin beneath and feel the firm texture of his body.

His long black hair, still wet from the shower, swept back from his forehead and revealed his ruggedly handsome face. The man was gorgeous, and she could barely take her eyes off him.

The smell of his manly soap reached her nostrils, and she breathed it in. Working around the fragment aroma of men each day, she loved the intoxicating scent of a clean man, and this clean man swamped her senses. A nervous excitement she hadn't felt in a very long time overtook her with the sensuality he exuded without even trying. Was it that she had been too long without a man, or was it this particular man that enticed her so?

Either way, she flushed in embarrassment at her thoughts and turned back to the stove before she revealed herself further. "Dinner will be ready in a few minutes."

Making nervous chit-chat, she set the plates and silverware on the table while he praised the work she had done, telling her the house looked great and the food smelled heavenly. Mundane talk passed between them as it had on so many days in the past, but for her this night was different.

Grabbing a beer from the refrigerator, he sat down at the table, and she watched surreptitiously as his thigh muscles bulged with the action. Why was his nearness affecting her so much tonight? Could he feel it, or was it just her?

A ridiculous urge to reach out and grab him, to beg him to take her on the kitchen table, surged through her. Never in her life had she felt such strong desire, and she questioned herself. When had she stopped thinking of herself as a woman with needs? When had she become a robot going about her day-to-day life? She had just blended in with the guys, dressing like them, working side by side with them, and more often than she cared to admit, coming home smelling like them.

It'd been over two years since she felt the welcome sensation of a man's eyes upon her with interest. It felt both exhilarating and intimidating each time she turned and found him staring. Tonight, it was her turn to stare. She couldn't get enough.

The timer went off, and thankful for the activity, she moved to take the biscuits out of the oven. Her hands trembled, and she chastised herself. This was ridiculous. The answer could only be that she'd been too long without a man. That was it.

Setting the bowl of stew on the table, she placed the biscuits on a plate and laid them next to the stew. She inhaled a deep breath and released it slowly, trying to build up the courage to sit across from him and forget this pulsing desire, but it wasn't going to be easy. She just knew she was going to embarrass herself.

She sat and poured herself a glass of wine, downing the contents in seconds and looked up to see his eyes narrow in curiosity.

"You okay?"

She nodded, unsure if she could utter a single intelligent word. She'd certainly been aware of him day to day, but never had the feeling been as strong as it was tonight. She'd simply forgotten about this side of life or had lowered it to a place of unimportance. There'd simply been no time to consider sex, but tonight while sitting across from this virile man, her entire being reacted to his nearness.

The hastily consumed glass of wine quickly went to her head, muddying her thoughts, and as she poured another glass she told herself to behave and slowly sip the second. It wouldn't do to be drunk and feeling the way she was.

He began to speak, his voice a low cadence, and between the wine and his calm voice she relaxed somewhat. He praised the meal and thanked her for preparing it, and he told her about the final touches on the barn and how the work should be finished by the end of the week. As usual, his inner peace worked its magic, and she soon found herself asking questions and laughing at his dry humor.

Anna looked down at the remnants of her dinner on her plate and up at the clock, realizing they had been talking for hours. It had been so refreshing to just sit and talk, to share with another person. She'd spent many a night sitting at this table all by herself or just forgoing dinner altogether when the thought of eating alone became a bit too pitiful. This had been enjoyable, but as she stood to gather the dishes, he stopped talking and the atmosphere changed swiftly.

CHAPTER FOURTEEN

She could feel the warmth of his gaze follow her as she moved around the kitchen. The close inspection made her nervous and clumsy, and she dropped the butter on the floor, horrified when it skidded away. On an inner groan of embarrassment, she quickly snatched it up and placed the tub back in the refrigerator. Why did he affect her so tonight? What was wrong with her?

As she filled the sink with water and suds he stood, and she closed her eyes in anticipation of his next movement. Even the scrape of the chair along the vinyl tiles felt like a sensual tease, and the hairs along her skin rose in tingles of awareness. On silent cat like footsteps, he came to her side and slipped the dish rag from her hands, grazing her fingertips with his own in a soft caress. The touch might have been barely there, but she felt a rush of excitement that left her unable to even speak.

She stood like a mannequin, awkwardly frozen in place as she watched the juxtaposition of his long, strong fingers tenderly wash the delicate plate that had just held her food and the fork that had slid past her lips. Her mind went wild imagining those fingers sliding along her body with the same sure strokes, teasing her body to fulfillment.

When his fingers slipped inside a water glass to wash it, she fantasized that his fingers were actually entering her own body. Her imagination was wild, her focus glued to his hands. She felt as if she was slipping over the edge into insanity as she dreamed of those hands bringing her to ecstasy. An enticing heat radiated from his body, and she yearned to lean closer, to wrap herself around him. Her body tilted towards him until a bark made her jump.

Jake stood at the back door, and she looked at him, surprised that she had forgotten he was even in the room. Moving quickly, she let him out for his final run before bed and looked back to find Dakota's gaze on her once again. He smiled inquisitively, and she moaned. He was just too handsome for his own good.

She might have been inwardly trembling with need, but she chastised herself for her foolishness and returned his smile, walking to his side to dry the dishes his hands had just held. She had to at least pretend she wasn't going crazy.

He began to talk, and she welcomed the distraction, but something was wrong. At dinner his deep voice had been soothing and informative, but not now. Now it was a sensual purr along her nerve endings, and heaven help her, she wanted to purr right back. Maybe she was going nuts. Maybe it was the rarely consumed alcohol. Whatever it was, a longing moved along her body until a burning fire danced in a place that hadn't felt any sensation in a long, long time.

With just the two of them eating, the dishes were quickly done, and she took a step back. Without even realizing it, he had reduced her to a quivering bundle of nerves before he even set aside the dishrag. Yet, when he turned to her, she could have smacked herself. Here was a man who was always in tune with all about him. Of course, he could sense something was wrong with her. Through narrowed eyes he studied her stance, the nervous licking of her lips and her shallow breathing. She was a fool if she thought she could hide it.

The moment was unbelievably awkward. He stood not eight inches away, their bodies close, yet too far away. She looked down at the towel she clutched in her hand and quickly set it on the counter. When she looked back up, she sucked in a breath at the intense look in his eyes. He was a man so perfect, her breath froze within her chest. A muscle twitched in his cheek, revealing his own angst.

He took a step forward, and she backed away, unsure if she should allow this even though her body craved it. He took another step, and again she backed away. It was if they danced a dance of passion, of give and take. He took another step, and when she stepped back this time, the kitchen counter pressed against her backside. She had nowhere to go. Only an inch or two separated them now.

Her body felt the allure of him, and like a moth to flame, she had no choice but to allow it. She was afraid of the burn, but helpless to stop herself, powerless to deny her own needs.

He grasped her gently by the arms and pulled her closer and her arms rose to encircle his neck as lips met lips. Breaths mingled as she leaned against his hard frame. His hands left her arms and slithered along her back to wrap her tightly in an embrace meant to melt. His hard, sinewy muscles met her tender, reawakening flesh, and the feel of his hot body created a rush of liquid heat between her thighs.

His kiss was searching and inquisitive, while hers was frantic and needy. It was unbelievable to her how much she needed this. Their tongues dueled. Their bodies melded. Their arms held on.

How long it could've lasted or where it would've ended she didn't know, but a loud bark outside the door interrupted them, and they separated awkwardly. He turned and went to the refrigerator for another beer, and she moved shakily to the door, trembling from head to foot.

Jake burst through the door in a rush, accompanied by a blast of frigid air. Shivering despite the inner heat, she made her excuses to Dakota and bolted from the kitchen, quickly running up the steps to her bedroom, where she stood trembling with a nervous excitement. What was she going to do? He was her employee. She couldn't act like this, but she could not recall ever feeling this sexually energized in her life.

Suddenly her clothing was choking the life from her. Her breasts strained against her top, and her jeans constricted her swollen femininity. She quickly stripped, letting the cool air of the bedroom caress her inflamed skin. She bounced up and down on the balls of her feet in nervous excitement, while she prayed for goosebumps to chill her discomfort, yet there was nothing. She almost felt as if her body could heat the room instead of the room cooling her.

She had just showered earlier, but a fiery need burned a path along her skin, coming to rest in a spot that had not felt a man's touch in too long a time. She ran to the bathroom, needing an icy relief. Turning on the shower, she jumped into the cool spray and shivered against the fight going on between the cold of the water and the heat of her skin.

Having him so close day by day and touching him earlier in the kitchen had her in a state long unused. He had smelled of earth and wind, life and masculinity, a scent that inflamed her body and made her skin crawl with renewed sensations.

She rested her fingertips against her lips as she thought of *the kiss*. She could not remember ever feeling such consuming passion before. Certainly, her husband had never awakened her with such intensity.

In an intimate act she had never felt the need for before, she lowered her fingers to touch herself. They met a thick, pooling moisture so different from the water that coursed down her body, as well as the tingling swollen evidence of her arousal. A shudder of excitement ripped through her.

One kiss did this to her?

After drying quickly, she slipped back into her room and shut the door. She threw back the covers and collapsed on her bed naked as the day she was born, the chill of the sheets doing nothing to cool her body. Nothing was dousing the fire within. She ran her hands along her heated flesh, grazing and circling the sensitive pebbled peaks of her breasts with her palms until she moaned. Moving her hand across her quivering stomach, she circled the swollen, throbbing nub centered between her legs and clenched, the feeling unbearably sweet.

That his effect on her was this strong was frightening. Her fingers paused. Should she go to him? What would he think of her if she did? How would it change things? Could she be brave enough to walk naked down those steps and make her needs known?

Her bedroom door opened with a soft whoosh, and she gasped as her focus flew to the doorway. Her inquisitive hands flew to her sides, clenching the sheets between anxious fingers. Embarrassment warmed her face from being caught touching herself but was quickly forgotten when she looked to him.

The branches outside the window bent and swayed against a brutal wind, and their moonlit shadows played across his body, revealing a naked, sinewy, confident, and beautiful male. If this was the effect he was going after, he was a master at his craft. The sensual picture was hypnotizing.

Immobilized, she memorized all she could see as her gaze traveled his body. From the swell of his biceps to the curve of strong shoulders and down across dark male nipples and a taut rippled stomach, he was perfection. When her eyes came to rest on his thick manhood proudly thrust before him, she no longer bothered to breathe. Her muscles tightened and quivered in anticipation of what that body could do.

He walked further into the room and closed the door slowly until a resounding click shut away the outside world. It was now just the two of them. He didn't seek permission to enter her room. He didn't ask if it was okay to be naked in front of her. He just knew. With the inner perception of all things around him, he knew that she needed him, that her body was calling for only him.

Her fingers glided restlessly across cool cotton sheets, eager to touch him, and she watched anxiously as he walked across the room and placed one knee on the foot of the bed. His gaze held hers for just a second before sweeping along the long length of her body with the look of a panther stalking its prey, ready to devour. Her body quivered under the powerful scrutiny.

She keenly felt her already aroused breasts expand, and her nipples became almost painful as they tightened under his sensual look, hopeful for his touch. She couldn't even explain what was happening to her down there–at the place between her legs that wanted him before her conscious mind even gave permission. Never had she felt such yearning. Her body was overpowering her mind, taking control, demanding release.

He rested on all fours between her open and welcoming legs and continued to study her with a predator's unwavering attention to detail, slowly, tantalizingly. His eyes looked to her wet core and traveled to the hardened peeks of her breasts, and she could swear she felt the touch of his gaze everywhere it rested.

The simple act of breathing became difficult for her when he moved, slowly, sensuously, inching over her body, immobilizing her between powerful arms. Muscular shoulders flexed, arms bulged with the approach, and his dark locks curled and framed his perfect face. Deep brown eyes, almost black in the dismal light, captured hers with a molten intensity, speaking volumes about his own pent up need for her.

His intent look dropped to her parted lips, and he bent to kiss her in an almost savage, hungry plea for her deepest, darkest wants to be unleashed. She warred with being terribly afraid and unbelievably excited about what would come next.

Backing up slightly, he pierced her gaze. "It's your decision, Anna. Do you want your hand to ease the fire burning inside, or do you want me?"

Embarrassment flooded her at his question, but she catapulted into full desire when her focus dropped to his moist full lips, thinking about the effect of his kisses. "You."

This was no marital bed duty or innocent first-time encounter. This was sex. Primal, raw, mind-blowing wants and needs between two willing partners, both fueled and quenched.

Her kisses matched his with demand. Her hands fumbled and grasped. She touched every part of the hardened body she could reach, wanting to feel what her vivid imagination had pictured beneath his clothes. She could feel the pulsing weight of his erection against her leg, teasing and tickling, igniting her starving body even further.

When his mouth left hers, she whimpered from the loss, trying to pull him to her once more, but he refused. He moved lower and his hands surrounded her tender breasts, enveloping them like a bra, and she lifted to the warmth. When he clasped a nipple between two hot lips, she bucked beneath him. Her tiny breasts swelled to fill his hands, aching beneath his touch and hungry for more.

Her body felt liquid and on fire all at once. His hands roamed her skin, tracing every curve, every indentation. His touch was light against the downy hairs, sending a tingle straight to her bones. She squirmed. Her skin rippled and quivered with his every stroke. He worked a magic across her body she hadn't known existed. He touched her both reverently and passionately at the same time, appreciating her and devouring her with equal intensity.

If possible, it seemed as if his lips grew hotter as he burned a trail down her abdomen, almost inflaming her to the point of climax, but when he reached the juncture of her thighs he paused. She closed her eyes, her breath becoming shallow as she waited. She didn't need to look to see what he was doing—she could once again feel his eyes devouring her.

Liquid heat rushed to her core, and she moaned, feeling herself opening and her juices flowing under his scrutiny. He blew a soft breath across the heated moisture, cooling it slightly, and she shivered. She waited for his touch. Waited for more, but none came to the place she needed him the most.

She thought she heard him chuckle as he denied her. The heated kisses began again across her inner thighs, and she gritted her teeth in frustration. He moved down her legs, away from the part of her that burned with desire for him.

When at last a warm, work-roughened hand slipped between her thighs, she cried out, and her hips rose to meet the welcome intrusion. His fingers tickled and teased their way through her moisture, eliciting soft words of pleasure she had never uttered in her life. Wanton and wicked, she abandoned all pretense of being a good girl. Her legs spread wider of their own accord in an invitation to feast. She was on fire, frantic with the need for release.

She bucked as the warm fingers slipped between her folds to enter her, moving slowly in and out. She was so close she could feel the warmth of impending orgasm along her skin.

Raising her knees, feet braced, she lifted to him. "Dakota," she whispered frantically. Grabbing his arm, she pulled at him. "Please . . . I need you."

He came forward and held himself above her. The tickle of his cock against her opening was the only part of him that touched her, and she lifted her hips until an inch of him spread her.

Still holding off, he bent to kiss her.

Frustrated and on the edge, she groaned loudly against his mouth and tugged at his hips.

He broke the kiss and looked down at her with a teasing grin. "Anna, honey, breathe. I'll take care of you."

"Please."

His smile changed to a sensual lift of the corners of his mouth as he brought his body down upon her own, and with one supreme thrust, glided into her waiting canal. She could not believe how good it felt. He was thick and hard, filling and stretching her. The heat of his body matched her own as they began their dance.

With head thrown back and eyes focused internally, she met him thrust for thrust. Her fingers grabbed, her nails digging into his shoulders. Her hands rose to fist dark locks of tousled hair and pull his mouth to hers. She was frantic. She was alone in her ecstasy, but intimately tied to another human being as she scrambled for the peak she sought.

She felt brazen, sexually awakened. "Dakota," she begged. "Faster, harder, please."

With a low chuckle that rumbled through his chest, he acquiesced to her wishes, driving and pumping, drawing her closer and closer to what she craved.

Quivering to her very toes, she rejoiced in the pleasure. She realized with a jolt that this was what she had dreamed of on so many lonely, frustrating nights. She could now put a face to her dreams.

The world centered around their joining, the pleasure

building and building. He swiveled, grinding against her mound, and she shattered, her cry vibrating around the room as wave after wave of long-lost pleasure pounded throughout her body. She distantly heard him echo her as his release followed closely, their mingled sounds of completion shattering the silence and creating a howl of curiosity from Jake who obviously lay waiting outside the bedroom door.

She chuckled for a fraction of second before her body commanded her attention. It didn't want this pleasure to end, and it grasped for more. More fun, more abandonment, more anything. The quivering of her muscles around his shaft waned and died, and she exhaled in frustration as he relaxed against her. Too quick, it had happened too fast, and her entire being wanted more.

Her time with her husband had been nice, their sex life good, but this was another realm altogether. She had found something she didn't even know existed, and she was reluctant to let it go.

"Anna, what's wrong?" His intuitive question tickled the sensitive area of her neck, and desire surged again.

She giggled like a young girl, the sound foreign to her. "I want more."

His chuckle this time was deeper, the low, primal male sound rising from within his chest at her words. The rumbles sent a vibration through the side of her breast, and her nipple responded by tightening in need.

"Then I must oblige," came the gravelly reply. Rising on his elbows, hands resting on each side of her hair, he looked to her with infinite tenderness. The darkness of his eyes rested on her swollen, parted lips that waited impatiently for his touch.

When he lowered his mouth to hers, the kiss was softer this time, slower. Their immediate appetites had been calmed for the moment. With infinite precision, he ran a path of tender kisses and soft touches along her silken flesh from head to foot but still not *there*. He enjoyed teasing her, it seemed.

Each inner elbow was loved, each inner thigh was lathed, each earlobe suckled, each nipple drawn to a hardened peak, but he didn't touch her there. She thought she would scream from the need.

Having had enough and with a touch of frustrated anger, she reached for him, the object of her attention only partially aroused. His sharp intake of breath shattered the silence of the room, and she felt the silken strength of him harden beneath her fingers.

Looking from his swelling member to his shadowed orbs, she uttered words she never in her life imagined saying. "Dakota, fuck me."

Even in the gray light of her room, she could see brief surprise light his face, but it was immediately replaced by a heat that made her second guess her words.

With a small grunt, he lifted her to sit on his lap. He rested on his haunches, entering her as she glided down.

"You do it this time."

Emboldened, she did exactly that.

Chapter Fifteen

Anna awoke the next morning to a pleasured lethargy that sent her curling beneath the warm covers and relaxing for a few more minutes. She didn't want to move. She hadn't felt this good in a long, long time. Her body was calm and sluggish after a night of incredible sex and sleep without dreams or worries.

Dakota was gone from her bed, and she found she was reluctantly grateful. A blush from her toes to her nose bloomed as she remembered their night together. With an embarrassed giggle, she grasped that she had taken a lover. Her. A woman who had only ever been with one man in her entire life had taken a lover, and what a lover he had been.

The lingering scent from a night of sexual release lay heavy in the room and on the bed. Mingled with the masculine, musky perfume of her lover, it rested like a soft blanket on her skin. She breathed it in and pictured the night he had given her.

He had been so attentive, so caring as he brought her to pleasure three times before he finally covered them with a blanket, and they'd simultaneously succumbed to their sated exhaustion.

She pictured him leaning over her as their desire mounted. Never having thought she was anything other than a plain country girl, she would never have imagined attracting such a gloriously handsome man. His face was model perfection, and his body was the kind she had only seen on TV or in movies. Strong, hard, and muscled, she had luxuriated in touching every inch of that textbook perfect body as they pleasured each other.

She warmed, squeezing her thighs together as she thought of his manhood. Charles had been smaller and thinner, but not Dakota. She never knew men came in such different sizes. She'd actually never thought about it much.

Dakota was thick and long, filling her with a heated friction that ignited a fire within her. Even now, remembering how he had moved with skill and determination within her body made her squirm beneath the covers wanting more.

As was the way of her mind, the memory faded as reality and panic seeped back in. She grew pensive. How would this affect their working relationship? What would this mean for the future? She didn't want an entanglement. She refused to love another. Losing Charles had devastated her, and she couldn't venture into that possibility again.

Her comfy feelings disappeared after she allowed her mind to turn to worry. She stretched and rose slowly, achingly aware of what had transpired during the night. She snorted on a chuckle as once more the powerful, mind-blowing passion she had experienced moved over her. It had been good, but also so very wrong.

After washing and dressing quickly, she made her way downstairs, still carrying the blush of their lovemaking mingled with a flush of anxiety. She found him sitting at the kitchen table drinking a cup of coffee, looking casual and relaxed, and she cringed in embarrassment.

She'd never considered the possibility of being with a man again. Life had been too hectic to even think about that side of life, but now the man who had made her moan into the night sat in front of her sipping his hot drink and gifting her with a soft, knowing smile of greeting.

She didn't return the smile, shuffling instead to the coffee pot and pouring her own cup before taking a seat opposite him. Focusing on a scratch in the worn tabletop, she couldn't bring herself to look him in the eye again. She just couldn't let him see her apprehension, but she had to find the words to explain.

"Dakota, what we did, how I acted." She paused, humiliation flooding her again. "I don't know what to say. I'm so embarrassed."

He watched as she nibbled on her lower lip. Flames of her embarrassment darkened her cheeks, but he wouldn't let her slip backwards. Last night, while they had washed the dishes, it was blatantly obvious she was a woman in need, that she desperately wanted to experience passion again, to touch, to feel the warmth of human contact. She was alone, and he knew she was feeling profound isolation in her struggle to survive. Anything with a heartbeat needed the warmth of touch, the comfort of love or friendship, and the strength gained from support and caring.

His eyes dropped from her look of discomfort to the coffee cup encircled by his fingers, contemplating his own life. He knew only too well what she was going through. He had needed the warmth of her touch, also. They were two floundering souls who craved a moment of tenderness and found it in each other's arms.

There was nothing wrong with that. He had given her what she needed and wanted while releasing some of the burden on her shoulders, and at the same time, his own.

The tips of her long tresses waved as she took a sip from her cup, drawing his attention to the curling ends that rested on her breasts. He had slipped his fingers through those baby-soft tendrils while kissing the perfect symmetry of the lips that now curved along the rim of her coffee cup. Yes, he had helped her remember she was a woman.

What he hadn't expected, though, was discovering a very passionate and remarkable lady, and that bothered him a bit. He found he was growing attached to her in a way he hadn't felt since he lost his wife, and he wasn't at all sure he was comfortable with the feeling.

She set the cup back on the table, and slender fingers capped by broken nails fiddled with the wedding ring that still circled her finger. This woman before him was strong, a fighter, but she was also human. He would guess she had forgotten that. She had forgotten to think about herself as she struggled to tend to this farm and care for all that lived upon it. She had placed herself in last place, the final one to get any accolades.

The awkward silence stretched on, and he contemplated the right words to say until finally he said what was truly in his heart.

"Anna, what we did was wonderful. I don't want you beating yourself up over it. You are a grown woman with wants and needs like any other woman, and I am a man sitting across from a beautiful woman with wants and needs of my own. There is nothing wrong with what we did."

He pushed the chair back from the table as he stood and went to the sink, rinsed his cup, and laid it on the sideboard. When he turned, he was momentarily taken aback by the look of incredulity on her precious face.

"You think I'm beautiful?"

He walked to her side and lifted her hand. Pulling lightly, he raised her from the chair. Wrapping two hands around her slender waist, he tugged her up against his body. Gently encircling her within his arms, he whispered against her ear as he held her. "You are very beautiful, inside and out." He leaned back and captured her gaze. "Has no one ever told you that? Everything about you is beautiful. From your beautiful mind protected by your rich auburn hair, to the deep blue of your eyes that look for the good in everyone, down to the breasts that cushion a loving heart, you are beauty."

Her lips trembled, and he realized she was struggling to hold back tears. He kissed the tip of her pert little nose.

"Even after the night we had, I desire you and could easily carry you right back up to that bed."

Her lips curved in a sensuous, teasing grin at his words, and he had no choice. He claimed them, crushing her womanly body close against his strength.

Lost as she was in his warmth, she did not welcome the sounds of the workers and voices coming from outside the house.

Dakota broke the kiss, yet held on to her. "I have to go. I'm sorry. We will talk more of this."

She started to withdraw from the circle of his arms, but he pulled her back and kissed her once more.

With a long-suffering sigh, he released her, kissed her forehead gently, and moved away to don his jacket.

Chilly air met her with the opening of the door, replacing his warmth as he left. She wanted him back here in her arms, telling her again that she was beautiful. That hug, those kisses, his praising words had felt so good.

She listened to the soft timber of his voice as he greeted the men. Moving to the window, she parted the curtains and watched as he crossed the lawn, matching the quick strides of the workers. Jake tore across the grass and met him, pushing his head under Dakota's hand for a scratch, and Dakota petted the head of her most precious friend.

She giggled when a thought, unbidden, popped into her head that she had seen that gorgeous man naked. He had intimately touched her with that very hand that petted Jake.

She had gripped in pure passion the buttocks that faced her as he moved across the lawn, and it had all been so wonderful.

Slipping a hand inside her pants, she cupped herself. She was ready for him from just a kiss, which was unbelievable to her. She had never experienced this type of consuming passion with her husband.

Confusion trickled in again to slap her in the face with his departure. What was going on here? What had she done? Why had she allowed her traitorous body to overrule her sensible mind? Had she committed a grievous error in sleeping with him?

Dropping the curtain, she washed her hands and grabbed her jacket and keys. She needed to go visit Pop. She needed some wise advice.

Chapter Sixteen

Pop smiled and greeted her warmly as if nothing was amiss, but looking at the changes he had undergone since her last visit caused her so much guilt. He pulled her into his arms, and she returned the embrace, hugging the frail frame gently. He had continued to lose weight during his recovery and was no longer the robust man that had worked hard on her farm. He now looked every inch a man in his eighties that she knew him to be, and seeing him this way broke her heart and scared her.

If she had let him retire long ago, he would not have been at her farm that night. This was all her fault. The rational part of her mind told her she was being foolish to accept this guilt, but her heart told her differently. The way he looked worried her.

He grabbed her hand and squeezed.

"It's so good to see you."

He drew her to the sofa and sat next to her, holding her hand. The healing, thick pink scar with the pockmarked dots from the staples ran backwards from his forehead, and a boot still held the fractured ankle. Both were vivid reminders of that horribly frightening night.

"Tell me how it goes at the farm. I've missed it."

She had no choice. She had to talk to someone and poured her heart out to him, telling all that had happened since last she visited. She explained that the repairs were almost done, and he shook his head sadly when she finally told him about the loan to pay for it all. She told him about the mysterious fire in the north field and the nail in Maggie's hoof. By the time she got to the strange man who offered to buy the farm, she was talking so quickly Pop could only interject questions here and there. He let her talk, let her ramble as she released her pent-up frustration, and when she was finished, he sighed.

"I wish I'd been there to help you, my girl. It sounds like you have been through hell, but tell me, how is the young man you hired to replace me? Is he helpful to you?"

With a tell-tale blush, she looked at the wizened eyes of her friend.

"Ah, I see," was all he said.

"I'm so confused, Pop. I don't know much of his past other than he moved from South Dakota, and he was once married. His wife died shortly after giving birth to a stillborn child. He said he left right after that. That's all I know."

"Have you asked him?"

Pop, unlike many other men, advocated talking above all else. He felt that all squabbles, all confusion, all troubles, could be settled by talking and listening, to actually learn where the other person was coming from. She'd heard those views often. A wise and caring man, he had often wished the rest of the world would accept the same outlook, and he at times would grow angry at the division created by not listening to each other. He had employed his philosophy often when the boys had gotten into squabbles at the farm, and it had always worked.

"We started to talk one night, but that was when we discovered the fire. We haven't really talked about anything since."

"Then I think you need to ask him. Give him a chance. If you don't like what you hear or if you actually find out he is an exceptional man, at least you will have your answers."

She shook her head, her voice catching on the lump that

had formed in her throat. "I'm scared, though. What if he wants more from me? That would be something I can't give him. I just can't love again."

"Nobody said you had to love him, honey. Nobody said you have to give more than you are ready to give, but don't you think you should at least know him?" On a chuckle, he added. "More than just physically."

She averted her gaze away from the wise eyes as humiliation swept through her.

Thankfully, he turned the conversation away from Dakota and asked more about the man from Fidelity Holdings. The two of them talked for another hour about her indecision on what to do with the farm.

A little before lunchtime, she kissed him on the cheek and left him, but not before promising to visit him more often. As usual, his intelligence and insight helped her to weigh the pros and cons of her life, except for Dakota. That conundrum would take some thinking.

As she waved goodbye and climbed into her truck, she felt much more relaxed and confident about Shoop, but sad that Pop no longer lived within walking distance. She missed his wise counsel and his love, for truly they loved each other. He'd become the dad she had lost so early in life, and she'd selfishly relied on him maybe just a bit too much. It probably wasn't fair that she had thrust him into that role, but she had, and he had never complained.

Pulling into her driveway, she met her mailman, and after grabbing the post, headed into the house. Dishes were in the sink, a testimony that a few of the guys had used her kitchen, and after making a sandwich for herself, she sat down and sorted through the mail.

A letter for Dakota. How strange. Who knew he was here? She stared at the return address and postmark. "Dakota Dairy Farm," she whispered as she read the name. The postmark was in South Dakota. How funny. Dakota had worked for a farm named Dakota Dairy in South Dakota. She laughed at the irony.

As she set the letter aside, her attention focused on the thick packet atop her mail. Fidelity Holdings. With a bit of trepidation, she ripped the seal and unfolded the papers. The bite of her sandwich stuck in her throat, and she choked as she read the figures. He was offering her a substantial amount of money to sell off her land. If she was careful and invested wisely, she would never have to work again. It was very tempting, but with the wise council of Pop, she'd come to realize she couldn't give up her home.

Standing, she walked to the sink to get a drink of water and looked out at the vast landscape that belonged to her. Her home was beautiful. There was something indescribable about the work she did. Nothing beat the satisfaction she gleaned from tilling the ground, planting the seed, and at the end of summer, harvesting a bumper crop of wheat that would feed many. She also couldn't imagine letting go of her livestock. They'd become like family to her. Each one had their own personality.

Her cows and chickens were not used for meat. They supplied her with milk and eggs. If she had a good year, her patch of land next to the barn supplied her with enough vegetables to see them through to the next growing season. Anything else they needed came from the local store. It was a good, honest, and healthy life she had set up here, even if it was a hard one. She couldn't imagine losing it, but that money was very tempting.

Dakota walked in as the sky was turning the dusky pink of evening. He looked tired and dirty, but he gave her a smile as he entered and sniffed the air appreciatively at the scent of simmering spaghetti sauce on the stove and garlic bread in the oven. She greeted him just as warmly, feeling much more confident than she had earlier when he'd left her dazed and alone here in this kitchen.

Noticing that a certain four-legged family member was not with him, she questioned him about Jake.

"He left us a long time ago and came back in this direction. I thought he was with you."

Alarm surged through her. Jake would never miss dinner, and he rarely, if ever, wandered off alone for long.

Pushing past Dakota, she went out back and hollered Jake's name, and bringing her fingers to her lips, let out an ear-piercing whistle to call her friend home. No response. Fear overtook her, and racing back inside, she turned off the burners and oven, grabbed a jacket and headed back towards the door.

Before she could lay a hand on the doorknob however, Dakota laid a hand on her arm, staying her. "Anna, relax, he's probably just exploring. He'll come home soon."

She pulled away from him. She knew her dog. She knew all his quirks and habits. She knew that Jake would come home when it was dinnertime. He had done so since a pup. Jake never, ever missed a meal.

She yanked the door open, and before she could shut the door in his face, she looked back at Dakota, scowling her frustration. "I know my dog. Something is wrong."

With a resounding click of the door latch, she ran towards the barn to saddle her mare. Once saddled, she grabbed a flashlight and took off to where Dakota and the boys had done the last burn, screaming Jake's name over and over. For three hours, she flashed her light into every copse of trees, across all the fields, and around the barn. There was no sign of Jake.

Bone tired, hungry, and with tears freezing her cheeks,

she headed back towards the house. If something happened to that dog she would be inconsolable. He was her best friend. She couldn't handle another loss.

Approaching the barn, she met Dakota who was also on horseback.

"I've looked everywhere," came from both of their mouths at once, and concern registered on Dakota's face. Something was wrong, terribly wrong.

When they finished rubbing down the horses, they walked side by side back to the house, an integral part of their lives missing. The mood was somber. Anna's heart beat heavy in her chest as she imagined the worst-case scenarios.

Later, she sat nibbling absent-mindedly on a piece of garlic bread, bundled under thick blankets on the back porch. Every few minutes she stood and whistled again for Jake. He would be cold. He would be hungry. He could be hurt. He would be afraid out there in the dark. These thoughts had tumbled through her brain over and over for hours now until she felt ill with her fear.

Dakota sat by her side and held her as she told him funny stories of Jake as he grew up and of all the goofy things he got into. She explained the horrible things he had eaten, some of which landed him at the vet's. Sometime in the middle of the night she fell asleep on his shoulder as exhaustion finally claimed her.

He lifted her and managed to get the door open. For such a skinny girl, she was a lead weight as he carried her inside and laid her on the couch. He covered her with the blankets that had kept her warm during their vigil and walked back outside to stare into the moonless night. Where was that dog? Why were such weird things happening around here? Was that the norm in this place?

With one final sweep of the land, he gave up and went back inside to collapse on a heavily cushioned chair by her side, resting his own tired bones for a few hours.

CHAPTER SEVENTEEN

In those few seconds of time between deep sleep and wakefulness, memories assaulted her. Her eyes flew open and she glanced around the large room as her nerve endings came alive with panic. There was no friendly tongue to greet her good morning.

Her Jake was missing, and she had to find him. She pondered for the briefest of moments as to why she was on the couch but cast that aside as she jumped up and ran upstairs to wash and dress.

Dakota was still asleep in the chair as she flew back down the stairs. Heedless whether she woke him or not, she slammed through the door to the kitchen. Quickly making a mug of coffee, she donned her coat and hat and went out back once more. Anxiety had her feet quickly moving to the stables. Even if it killed her, she would find her dog.

The sun was just beginning to crest the horizon. The early morning glow painted the sky with vivid pinks and cool blues. The same hues had painted the day's ending just twelve hours earlier when she had discovered Jake missing. Her mind imagined all types of scenarios, which made her quicken her pace to a full run for the barn.

She would keep searching. He might be lying somewhere hurt or in pain, and the daylight would help her find him. She was sure of it, wasn't she?

The boys were no longer working, so she could not enlist their help. She'd have to do this herself. She hoped Dakota would join the search when he awoke. Somehow, some way, she had to find her dog. After futilely searching the west and north fields and the area around her gazebo again, she was near to tears, frustrated and scared.

The sound of hoof beats had her quickly exiting the trees that sheltered her private sanctuary with hope for good news. Dakota sat waiting next to Maggie. He rested atop the stallion with all the regal bearing of a warrior, and she sucked in her breath at the beauty of the man. His hair was tousled from the ride, his lips full and closed, his nose long and proud, and his eyes, as he looked down at her, were the color of her favorite candy — deep, dark chocolate.

He wore no jacket, seemingly oblivious to the chilly morning, and she stared in fascination as his muscled arms and thick thighs bulged and flexed as he kept control of the enormous horse. He was a man in the strongest sense of the word, and if she were not distracted by the magnitude of her worry for Jake, she would have pulled him from the horse and dragged him inside her gazebo, begging him to take her. The truth, however, was she was almost sick with her worry, and Dakota took a back seat to her fear.

When he told her he had found no trace of Jake, she felt deflated, and her stomach rose to meet her throat as her worry consumed her.

Deciding to split up once more and keep in touch with their phones, they headed in different directions, but four hours later, they gave up the fight.

There was no sign of Jake. Not even his favorite ball could be found.

Her stomach was protesting the long hours with no food, and her head pounded with fury from grinding her teeth.

She brought her horse back to the barn and took care of her, but she performed the duty on autopilot. She had grown numb inside, and she remembered this feeling all too well from when she'd lost Charles, the inner sense of no control of her life. She couldn't lose Jake, too.

Once again, a niggling doubt about Dakota entered her mind. He was the last one with Jake. Grasping for a common thread among the many occurrences of late, she came up with two, and one of them bothered her immensely. All the weird things that had happened recently had been since he came to the farm. She questioned again whether he was behind all of this and what his motives were if he was. If she found out he was the culprit, she would be humiliated that she had given herself to him.

As she was closing the massive door to the barn she watched, hopeful, as the object of her thoughts rode hard across the frozen ground of the south field. What had he found?

"What is it?" she shouted at him before he even had a chance to stop.

"I found strange tire tracks where tracks shouldn't be. I don't know whose they could be or if that had anything to do with Jake being missing or not. They are just off the road near a tractor path. It could just be that someone lost control and slid. I don't know, but it's suspicious."

Her frustration grew. She was frightened, cold and hungry, and possibly so was her poor dog. Dakota became the vent for her irritation.

"Why didn't you pay more attention to Jake? He was in your care! If anything has happened to him, I'll never forgive you!"

Her fingers curled into fists, ready to punch something. She wanted to scream her anger until her throat was raw. She turned and walked away from him swiftly, before she did something she shouldn't. She was furious with him for not watching Jake more closely, furious with herself for lying with a man who might have harmed her dog, and furious that life had taken another frustrating and twisted turn.

"Anna, he will come home," were the last words he spoke.

She placed signs all along the road from a mile past her home and then back down towards town. She called Martin and asked him to let his deputies know to be on the lookout for her Jake. For three days they watched for him, and for three days she alternated between crying and snapping at Dakota. Poor Dakota found it wiser not to talk it seemed.

She was being a bitch, she knew, but she couldn't help herself. A low humming fear had taken root in her body, and nothing she did could stop it. She couldn't eat much of anything, and she couldn't sleep. The not knowing was driving her insane.

Dakota rode the cold, barren land each day searching, and she didn't know whether to think he was just as concerned as she was or putting on an act. Whenever he came near, she backed away. If he did try to talk, she turned away.

She found herself hugging Miranda so much the cat protested and took to spending time in any room where Anna wasn't. She was losing it and didn't like the feeling.

She had laundry to do, livestock to care for, and groceries to purchase, but she found she only wanted to sit on her back porch and scan the horizon to see a smiling black dog fly across the land towards her.

On the morning of the fourth day, a car pulled into her driveway, and she flew out of her house to see who it was, her heart full of hope that it was good news about Jake. When she saw the sleek black car she was crushed, disappointment tearing through her. The man from Fidelity Holdings.

She prepared herself to give this most unwanted intrusion a piece of her mind as she stomped towards him. Venting on him and releasing some of her anger would give her immense satisfaction, but she was stopped in her tracks by a familiar sound. Muffled, but clearly recognizable was an excited yip of recognition followed by the low, familiar bark of her Jake.

After easing his rotund body from the car, Shoop opened his back door, and Jake came bounding from the back seat, running towards her with the usual big smile on his face. A strangled cry, somewhere between joy and relief, poured from her as she dropped to her knees and encompassed her beloved friend in a stronghold, not wanting to ever release him.

"Mrs. Scott, I found this guy roaming through town and recognized him. I'm glad he was willing enough to get in my car, so I could bring him back to you."

Her dislike of the man was forgotten for the moment as she lifted her head and looked to him with happy tears brimming.

"I don't know how he got all the way to town. He's never done that before, but I'm very thankful that you brought him back to me. I've been so scared." She looked back to Jake just as a few tears overflowed. "Thank you."

She smiled at her beloved mutt and buried her face in his hair but drew back at the stench of cigarette smoke clinging to his fur. She wondered about its significance.

"Mrs. Scott, I know this is a bad time, but I was wondering if you'd had time to look at my proposal."

She stood, reluctantly breaking her hug with Jake, yet keeping her hand resting on his head. She knew she had to be truthful with Shoop, but at least now she could be kinder, considering the gift he had brought her.

"I'll be forever grateful that you brought my Jake back to me, sir, but I've given the matter a lot of thought, and I don't want to sell. Maybe one of my neighbors would be willing.

They have land much like mine, but I'm not ready to sell at this time. Your offer was very generous, but I can't lose my home."

The changes that quickly passed over his face as she spoke were almost comical, from the pleasant smile when he'd begun the conversation to the ruddy red anger by the time she finished her few sentences.

He gave her a sickly smile. "I understand, but I ask you to think again about my offer. It would be beneficial to sell for a woman who runs a farm all by herself. This is too much work for you, and you shouldn't be out here alone, now that Pop has retired."

The front door made its usual creak as it opened and seconds later Dakota's authoritative voice rang out across the driveway.

"She's not alone, sir. She has a new foreman."

If eyes could literally pop from a man's head, this surely would be the day she would see it. Shoop's astonished globes bulged grossly as he scrutinized Dakota from head to foot while the anger continued to suffuse his face.

"When did you hire someone else? Wait, I know you. You're the man Martin was talking about who was looking for work in town. I thought you left."

His gaze darted back and forth between her and Dakota, and if it was possible, his frustration and anger grew even stronger. "How can you hire a complete stranger? You know nothing about this man!"

"That's really none of your business, sir."

A purple vein began to bulge in his temple, and Anna feared he'd have a stroke right here on her property. He had given her the creeps since the day she met him, but she'd never really been fearful. Today she found herself almost shrinking from him. His anger was truly frightening, but she wouldn't give him that satisfaction.

That he knew too much about her life was scary, but she felt some relief that he hadn't known about Dakota's presence in her home. He must not be watching as closely as he had previously said.

Tall and immensely commanding, Dakota walked to her side, his look just as menacing. "I'd like to ask you to leave."

Shoop's eyebrows shot up in indignation as he barked in laughter. "You have no right to ask me to leave. You have no rights here at all. This land belongs to Mrs. Scott, and hopefully soon to me!"

He continued to bellow while Dakota took purposeful steps towards him, and Jake growled low by her side, baring his teeth. Feeling the danger, Anna stepped forward before a fight could begin.

"Please leave. I've given you my answer. I'm not selling."

The large man backed to his car with each step Dakota took towards him, but he continued to speak to her. "I advise you to think about what we discussed. I'll be back for your final answer, once you have given it some serious thought."

He opened the driver's side door and bent to enter, but gave her one parting, scary last word of warning. "Who knows what could happen to you out here alone, once this vagrant takes off again."

Dakota was almost at his side, and Shoop moved surprisingly fast for a man of his size as he squeezed his body behind the steering wheel and drove backwards out of the driveway in a puff of dry Kansas dirt.

Anna's heart was pounding. She turned to Dakota and jerked back in surprise.

His hands were clenching and unclenching by his side, his body trembling. His breath blew from his nostrils like a bull ready to charge, and menacingly dark orbs, narrowed in fury, watched as the car disappeared down the long road to town. He was poised to fight, looking as if he could kill, and it was scary to her.

She'd never seen him angry, and this was a side of him she hoped she never saw again. She laid a hand on his arm to comfort him as she willed her own heartbeat to slow.

"It's okay, Dakota." He turned to her, and she smiled. "It's okay. He's gone, and look! Jake's home."

CHAPTER EIGHTEEN

Dakota looked down at the dog and back to the road while taking deep breaths. He knew this all too familiar anger would do him no good. The same type of anger had consumed him when his wife had withdrawn from him, and he had been powerless to stop her quick decline. He had raged against the world and the injustice of a deity who would take her from him, going nearly out of his mind with the pain.

Once again, his feelings for a woman were bringing out his protective side, a fighting side he disliked. He'd been taught from as far back as he could remember to live in harmony with others. It was the Lakota way, but this man posed a threat to Anna. His last sentence came dangerously close to a real threat. He didn't trust Shoop at all.

Soft murmuring made him turn back to her, dropping his gaze to where she had gone down upon the earth. She held Jake tightly against her body and cried through her joy that she was finally holding him again. Amazingly, she'd quickly left her own anger at Shoop behind, dismissing it as unimportant now that she had her dog again.

Her voice grew muffled as she buried her face against Jake's side, and he had to strain to hear her.

"I can't believe he is home, but he's so filthy, and he smells of cigarettes. I wonder where he's been?"

Taking one final cleansing intake of air into anger-strangled lungs, Dakota let it go, releasing it into the cool afternoon air. He lowered himself to her side and gently rubbed Jake's head, receiving a wet kiss for his efforts. That the dog was happy to be home was obvious in the kisses he gave both of them, but where had he been? They would probably never know.

"Good to see you, buddy," He sniffed along Jake's fur. "You're right."

She bounced to her feet, and he had no choice but to relax in the face of her exuberance.

"I'm cleaning him up. Jake, come on, boy." The dog rose slowly as if exhausted from his travels and followed her into the house. Her hand still rested along his head as they walked side by side.

Dakota leaned against the kitchen doorframe, smiling as he watched her sit cross-legged in front of a warm fire and towel Jake dry. Not until his midnight black hair shined with brilliant blue undertones in the firelight did she set aside the towel. She picked up a time-worn brush and began to gently work through the knots of the dog's thick fur, murmuring to him in a soothing voice. The whole time she worked, she never allowed her hands to leave the strong body of her dog.

Her love she felt for that dog, actually all of the animals in her care, was palpable. She cared about everyone and everything around her, and he felt himself drawn to her, wanting to be a part of the love she felt and be something important in her world.

Shoop's menacing scowl rose in his mind's eye, and he frowned. The man meant trouble, and if he harmed Anna, Dakota knew he'd never be able to hold back his anger. He would kill Shoop and never think twice about it, no matter his family's teachings. "Anna?"

She looked up, her gaze following him as he walked across the room and eased into a chair by her side. "Can you tell me more about what happened before I came outside today? Have you ever seen Mr. Shoop smoke? What kind of explanation did the man give for having Jake? What did you do with the butts I gave you out in the field?"

Her effervescent giggle danced around the room as she caressed Jake. "So many questions."

She turned to answer him. With her head tilted in thought, her hair cascaded around her shoulders, and his breath caught. The wavering firelight cast her in a hallowed amber glow, the reflection highlighting her auburn tresses and turning them a dark cherry red.

The flickering light glowed behind the lenses of her expressive eyes, lighting them from within with a sparkle of peaceful joy. She looked ethereal and beautiful. The happiness that'd been missing from her for days radiated from her in waves, and he thanked all above for bringing the dog back to her, if only for being able to experience this happiness with her.

The cheerfulness remained as she answered him, as if nothing could lessen it now. "He's never smoked around me, so I don't know if he smokes. I've never smelled it on him, though."

She paused and using her head, pointed to the stairway.

"The butts are on my dresser. For some odd reason I saved them, although they do stink up my room." Almost as an afterthought, she murmured. "I should put them in a baggy or something."

She quickly looked back to him. "He told me he found Jake wandering around town and knew he was mine, but I don't know if I believe him. Jake would have never ventured that far."

Her eyes told the story of her thoughts. She would never be a good poker player. They narrowed with doubt as she looked to her front door.

"Something's not right. He said he knew he was mine, but

as far as I know he'd never seen him, so how did he recognize him?"

As if answering her own questions, her shoulders slumped, and she shook her head, deflated. "I guess it could be from the pictures I nailed to the telephone poles, so that tells us nothing."

Jake let out a whimper in his sleep, and she glanced back at her pet, rubbing a hand along his head in comfort.

With her face averted, her words surprised him. "Dakota, I owe you an apology. I took my anger out on you when Jake went missing and suspected you were the reason he was gone. I'm so sorry for mistrusting you."

She didn't need to say it. He knew the terror she was experiencing, although she had been pretty darn hard to live with. "I understood what you were going through. It's okay."

"No, it's not okay. I was awful, and I want you to know how sorry I am." Her gaze flew back to his, wide and questioning. "Can we match the tire tracks in the driveway with the ones by the field?"

"Interesting, but highly unlikely. Many cars have been in the driveway, and the ground is dry and may not show a track, but I'll go check anyway."

"Now? Will you be able to see it in the dark?"

"I can try, at least."

With that, he stood and left her, and she warred with herself whether to follow him or stay with Jake, but Jake won. She had missed him way too much. He let out a muffled bark, his paws moving as if he was running. She worried for him. His dreams were troubled.

A log shifted in the grate with a hiss of a newly burning piece of wood, the flames brightening the room. The light highlighted Miranda, whose paws thumped softly as she wandered down the steps and sauntered over to Jake, sniffing along his fur.

Anna watched, fascinated as the cat's mouth hung open and her eyes stared off as she contemplated his scent. The wonders of animals.

Walking around to Jake's face, Miranda began to bathe him, or perhaps she was drying what remaining moisture clung to his fur. Who knew? In his exhaustion, Jake never moved as both Anna and Miranda groomed him, and that worried her further. She wished she knew what he'd been through.

She sat with them for over an hour until her back protested the hard floor. Then she quietly stood and went to a front window to look for Dakota. She'd thought he'd be back by now, and as if her thoughts conjured him, his dark shadow walked up the edge of the driveway, kneeling beside the tire tracks with flashlight in hand.

With lightning speed, she let herself out of the house and joined him, standing quietly while he inspected the tracks against an image on his phone. He shook his head as he stood.

"From what I can tell, they are not the same, but it's hard to be sure. It's hard to get a good track in dry dirt," he said with a touch of exasperation.

She could've kicked something. She'd been hoping they'd found their culprit. "That doesn't necessarily mean it wasn't him, though. He even could've used another vehicle."

"Possibly, but we have to leave open the possibility of someone else. Anna, can you ask the sheriff to look into this for you?"

With a bit of alarm, she met his gaze, not sure how she could do what he asked. If she caused trouble for Mr. Shoop, he could convince the bank to call in her loan. She explained to Dakota what could happen if she angered him further.

CHAPTER NINETEEN

The November morning was brutal, and despite being bundled up, Anna shivered against the wind whipping across the open land. It was hard to believe Thanksgiving was just a week away. The year had gone by so fast.

Glittering frost coated everything in sight, and Anna knew that soon the snows would come. The thought made her smile, though. She loved the snow. She always enjoyed just standing and watching it. There was something so peaceful about listening to the world quiet as the snow blanketed the earth, and there was nothing more beautiful than watching the ethereal beauty of everything turning to a frozen, clean white.

She turned her head towards the barn and wondered where Dakota was and whether he was tending to the animals. After finding the livestock warm and fed when she checked, she walked back out into the frigid air to look for him. Jake was also gone, so she assumed they had to be together, but there was no sign of either one.

Wishing she had thought to grab her sunglasses, she covered her eyes against the painful glare of the rising sunlight as it sparkled on the ice crystals covering her land. She swiveled around looking for signs of life, and a movement caught her attention on a field further up from her barn. Her Jake ran in playful abandon across the ground, chasing who knew what, and off to the side Dakota stood looking out towards the horizon.

She followed his gaze. The morning was a beautiful sight

to behold. Dazzling white clouds, pushed by a brisk wind, danced across the mid-fall sky, changing the colors of the land into a speckled pattern of sun and shade. The air was crisp, and clean, and invigorating, yet Dakota stood with only a small jacket against the chill, impervious.

The ground crinkled and cracked as she approached, and as she got closer, Dakota knelt, the morning sun caressing him as if it recognized a kindred spirit.

She was almost upon him when she observed a circle pattern he'd drawn in the earth, and in the center knelt the man she had known intimately. The arms that had embraced her so lovingly were held out by his sides in a gesture of submission, and his face was cast upwards, his eyes closed as if in prayer.

Anna knew little of the Native American Indian other than what she'd been taught in school, but with each day by his side, she came to have a little more insight into their ways. Dakota impressed her. He always stood erect and proud, and he almost always remained calm and understanding, while she screamed or cried as she lost control.

She wished desperately to learn his peacefulness. What would it feel like to trust in the outcomes of life no matter what they were and to learn acceptance for those outcomes? She longed to know. Could he teach her?

He startled her from her thoughts as, with a tranquil and respectful voice, he began to speak. She could not understand what he was saying, the guttural words foreign to her. She stood motionless until he stopped talking. Jake let out a bark and she looked to him, but Dakota never moved a muscle. He remained in the same position of obeisance. She wondered if he would begin again, but he uttered no further words.

She longed to be by his side but was afraid she'd be intruding on something spiritual. Entering the circle as quietly as she could on frozen ground, she knelt down beside him, hoping to join him in his tranquility, wanting only to experience this magical moment.

Without vocally acknowledging her by his side, he dropped his arms and lowered his head. With his left hand, he reached for her, grasping her hand in a strong hold.

Chills quivered along her spine as a shattering cry from above had all three of them looking up. An eagle, wings spread in regal beauty, circled high above calling to its mate, and within moments, she joined him. Together they dipped and circled the brilliant morning sky in a wavering dance of beauty and flew off, becoming two small dots on the horizon.

Dakota remained kneeling, still looking at the sky for a few more moments before he stood and helped her to her feet. Drawing her close to him, he enclosed her within his arms.

"Was that a prayer, Dakota?"

"Yes."

"What did it mean?"

"In Lakota tradition, we pray to the Four Directions."

"Four directions?"

Her head rested against the chill of his jacket as she listened to him, engrossed in the words he spoke.

"We see the world as having four directions. Each direction has a special meaning and color."

He broke off the embrace and pulled her outside of the circle. He sat on the cold hard ground and brought her down to sit on his lap, their bodies warming each other.

"I'll try to explain. The east is yellow, or in Lakota, Wioheumpata. The east is the direction from which the sun comes up in the morning, bringing a new day. It brings us a new beginning and helps us to see things with a new understanding."

He tilted his head and rested his cheek on her hair before he spoke again, his breath a fog around her face.

"The south is the Southern Sky, or the Red Sky, and the Lakota name is Itokaga. This is when the sun is its most powerful, warming the earth and allowing growth. The west, or Wiyokpiyata, has the color of black, because this is where the sun sets, ending the day, signifying the end of life."

His laid his hand on her thigh, and she watched, enchanted, as his fingers traced a lazy pattern across the soft denim.

"And finally, the north, Waziyata. The north brings the cold winds of winter which cleanse the earth. It is said that if someone can stand in the face of these harsh winds, then that person has at last learned patience and understanding."

Her hand covered his, stilling his movements, and she curled her fingers within his grasp.

"However, when my people pray with the Sacred Pipe, we add two other directions, sky and earth. We pray to the *Great Spirit or in our language,* Wakan Tanka. The Great Spirit lives high in the sky like the eagles we just saw. The sky is the color of blue. Earth is green and is our Mother. All about you is a part of Mother Earth. Rocks, dirt, trees, four legged and two legged creatures, everything. Mother Earth is the direction from which we receive our nourishment."

"Why do you pray with a pipe?"

"Ah, I have much to teach you. The pipe is our link between the earth and sky. Nothing is more sacred to us. The smoke in the pipe is our words. When we exhale the smoke, it goes out and touches everything on Mother Earth, uniting us. The fire in the pipe is the Sun, which brings us life."

Moved by the force of his words, she curled deeper within his hold.

"Why do you draw a circle?"

"It is a prayer circle. The Lakota believe the journey of life and death is a circular process. When we stand in the center and pray, it represents us standing in the center of the earth."

"Dakota, it's all so beautiful."

She didn't know what had just happened but knew deep inside she had just learned and experienced something truly special. Tears filled her eyes.

The beauty surrounding her, the crisp air, the peacefulness of the man wrapped around her, and the calming way he spoke eased her mind and heart. She gave in to it.

The heat of the sun was beginning to melt the ice, resulting in a white misty fog wavering and drifting just above the ground in a ghostly dance. Jake came and sat by their side, and the three of them watched the sun climb high in the sky.

CHAPTER TWENTY

For Thanksgiving, she decided she would prepare an elaborate meal and invite Pop to join them. Things had settled down recently, and all had been quiet. In a jubilant mood, she planned to roast a small turkey and all the fixings. It wasn't the smartest move, but she pulled out the last of her savings to pay for it all. She would suffer for it later, but she was determined to have a nice holiday, and at least there would be leftovers.

As if she was feeding an army, she spent two days baking pies and prepping the foods she would place before the three of them on her seldom used dining room table.

She rummaged through old totes in the basement and found her good tablecloth and napkins. She hated going up to her dusty old attic with the creepy spiders, but she climbed up the stairs and pulled down her china and special silverware, feeling almost giddy that she'd have *family* around a table again, for it had been years since she'd done this.

Her mother had asked her to come stay with her in Florida and be with her for the holiday, but Anna had been adamant in her refusal. She wanted to be home. She ruefully acknowledged to herself that she preferred to be with Dakota.

Dakota, though, had grown pensive as the day approached and often quietly observed her Thanksgiving preparations without saying a word. Caught up as she was in the joy of the holiday, she gave no thought to his quiet introspection.

The morning of Thanksgiving, she happily picked up Pop and brought him back to his previous home and introduced him to Dakota. As the two sat in the living room getting to know each other, she moved back and forth between the kitchen and dining room preparing the table and their feast.

She didn't interrupt them or ask for help but left them alone to talk. Her ulterior motive was to pepper Pop with questions when she drove him home as to what he thought of Dakota.

She was surprised a little later when she carried the wine glasses to the dining room table and caught what they were discussing.

Pop, always a sensitive man to the lives of others, asked a question she'd never considered. "Young man, do you celebrate Thanksgiving?"

She stopped what she was doing and watched the change come over Dakota. His calm face shuttered against the question as if hiding a world of pain.

"I will honor Anna's wishes to celebrate, but no, we don't celebrate Thanksgiving."

Anna stood frozen in place as she looked to Pop with wide eyes. Had she really messed up?

"What does this holiday mean to you?"

Dakota leaned back on the couch and stared at the football game on the TV. As always, he contemplated his words before speaking.

"Thanksgiving is a day for the white man only. To the Native American, we mourn on this day."

"Why?"

"Are you prepared to hear this?"

"I asked, didn't I?"

Dakota shook his head and smiled at Pop's reply.

"There was indeed a first Thanksgiving where the Pilgrims and the Wampanoag came together in New England for what we call a Harvest Celebration. The Wampanoag brought great gifts to the meal like venison, fowl, and lobster and stayed for three days afterwards as all celebrated. It appeared all would be well with our new white brethren."

Dakota looked to Pop with a sadness in his eyes that Anna had never seen before, and she grew frightened of what would come next.

"They remained at peace for sixteen years afterwards, but in 1637, while the Peguot warriors were away, the colonials raided their camps and killed about 500 women, children, and older men. Those they did not kill, they sold off to slavery in Bermuda and the West Indies. By the time the colonials were done, over 300,000 Indians were murdered or sold. So, no, we don't have any reason to celebrate Thanksgiving. Their words of peace and harmony were false."

The glasses in her hand came down with a clunk on the table as his words sank in, and he turned his head in her direction. Their gazes connected, and his spoke to her on a deeper level, revealing the devastation the American Indian had endured once her ancestors stepped foot on this land.

Pain clutched her heart at how unthinking she was. She'd been so caught up in the idea of family around the table at last that she hadn't considered his viewpoint.

"Dakota, I'm so sorry." With a sweep of her hand, she pointed to the elaborately placed table. "I never meant to offend you."

He stood and walked towards her, and she nearly came undone at the patience he showed while her heart was torn with guilt. Her hand gripped a chair back, and he uncurled her fingers, lifting them to encompass within his own.

"I am here today for only you. I've been able to see what this day means to you just by the work you have done to make it a good day. I don't celebrate Thanksgiving, but I will celebrate the coming together of friends to enjoy a great meal."

By the time he finished talking, she was a wreck, and tears flowed freely down her cheeks.

"Please don't cry, Anna. It is time for us to enjoy the good food I am smelling and for us all to talk and get to know each other better."

As she loaded the rarely used dishwasher with the mounds of dishes the meal had produced, she thought about the changes she had undergone this day. Pop had also been quiet and contemplative when she'd taken him home. She never had to ask him what he thought about Dakota. As she bent to kiss him goodbye, his parting words nearly did her in.

"He's a good man, Anna."

She knew he was. Dakota had remained calm and respectful of her feelings during dinner even while the overwhelming guilt plagued her. She'd been pleasantly surprised when the two men easily fell into conversations about wheat, livestock, and the future of farm life. The meal had gone relatively well, despite the shadow that hung over the day.

As with everything about Dakota she'd learned so far, she was impressed with his quiet fortitude.

Jake scratched at the back door, and she moved to let him in. Her gaze caught a movement, and she winced when she saw Dakota once more kneeling in her fields in prayer. No sunlight caressed him in a golden glow today. Only the deep gray and purple clouds of mourning hung low in the sky. Her heart went out to him.

Closing the door, she walked to the dishwasher and turned it on while thinking about Dakota, the man. He was getting a bit too close to her heart. She refused to allow herself to love him, but he wasn't making it easy.

139

He was noble, kind, generous, and just a bit too beautiful. His intelligence, raw sexual appeal, and deep spiritual and physical awareness was intimidating to a small-town farm girl.

Yet, through it all she still desired him, but he had not touched her again after their one night together. She wanted him to touch her. Her body craved the passion he had ignited.

She wanted to enjoy him for however much time they had together. She knew at some point he would leave, just as everyone had in her life, and if she held off on loving him, she'd survive. With an impish giggle, she reiterated her thoughts. Yes, she could at least enjoy him for a while.

They often talked late into the night or sat side by side on her living room sofa watching TV, but he never laid a hand on her. She figured if she wanted something from him, she'd have to be the instigator, and tonight was going to be that night. She'd waited long enough. It was his own fault that he had awakened something deep within her.

She needed to be with him, but first she'd finally bring up the subject of his previous life. She wanted — no, needed — to know more. She wanted him to talk about it all. What drove him to be here in the first place? She wanted to know more of who he was inside. Most importantly, she wanted to know more about where he came from and about his family, if he had any.

Letters were coming in more frequently for him of late, and he always took them outside to read them. Where he put them afterwards, she never knew. She saw no traces of them, and she respected his privacy. Oftentimes she would find him off by himself on the phone and wondered who he was speaking to. The secrecy was driving her nuts.

She laid her towel down on the countertop and left the rest of the cleanup for tomorrow. She was tired of looking at it.

She dozed in front of the TV and struggled to wake when Dakota walked in with tea for them both. The burning questions in her mind returned when she took the cup from his hand, but when he sat down beside her, she quickly realized he also had been thinking of questions, and his first question threw her for a loop.

"Anna, why have you never had children?"

Alarmed, she looked to his questioning eyes before glancing away, looking at the TV. The sitcom on the screen lost all meaning. The words the actors spoke faded as she became involved in her own thoughts. His request was intrusive, and not one she really wanted to discuss.

She must have been still for a long time because, with a sigh, he set his cup on a table and put an arm around her shoulders, pulling her close. With a warm breath against her hair, he told her, "It's okay if you don't want to tell me."

The strange part was she found that she finally did want to talk about it, to tell someone of her pain. With a shaky breath, she began her tale. "Charles and I tried constantly for years to have a child. It never happened."

He spoke not a word, but he tipped his head down to rest his forehead against her hair. He just held her close, and this long absent warmth and caring in her life was her undoing, bringing her to choke back the tears as she tried to explain her inner struggle.

"We both wanted a child. Children, I should say. The doctors said there was nothing wrong with either of us, but they must have been wrong. It never happened. I spent many nights crying after the evidence proved each month that we weren't successful."

"I'm sorry. You would've been a good mother."

"I'd like to think so, but I will never know. It was so hard. There were so many days I was so full of grief I could barely breathe. I know there are women who are happy not to have a child, but I wasn't one of them. I felt like something was missing in my marriage, in my life. The hardest part was seeing a woman with a baby in her arms and knowing I would never have that."

She leaned against him and let loose her heartache for all the children she'd never be able to hold in her arms. As he had before, he held her with his quiet strength as she poured her heart out to him.

She awoke a couple hours later with her head resting comfortably on his shoulder. Wine, heavy foods, the difficult emotions through the long hard day and the struggle to tell him about one of her most painful secrets had combined to be too much. She had drifted off again after revealing all.

Dakota had his head tilted back in repose against the couch, the angle causing him to snore softly. His strong, muscled arm still wrapped her in a cocoon, and she relaxed against the wall of his chest, relishing her contentment.

The evening hadn't gone as she had planned. She knew no more than before about his life, but their conversation about her inability to conceive had put a damper on her need to question him.

With a sigh she let her head fall back onto his shoulder once more and slept.

CHAPTER TWENTY-ONE

She opened her eyes to the sound of a truck clattering down the road outside her window. She was alone and lying across her sofa with a soft quilt across her body to protect her from the chill left behind by the cooling embers in the fireplace.

Surprisingly, she could hear the tapping of a soft rain falling outside, and the weather matched her spirits. Her body ached from sleeping in an awkward position, and her eyes were scratchy and tired. The sleep had done nothing to squelch her exhaustion. She wondered when this tiredness had overtaken her or if it had been there all along. Had she just never given in to the weariness that had encompassed her life since Charles had died?

On a moan that made her sound older than her years, she stood and shuffled her way upstairs to the bathroom. At least her responsibilities today would be minor, and she could take it easy. Winter was her down time, whereas spring, summer, and fall were her absolutely busiest times.

In the spring, the fields would be sowed and planted. The vegetable garden would need to be turned and planted. In the summer, the fields would be watched and tended to and the garden would need weeding, bug control, and harvesting. Then came the fall, the most back-breaking time of all. The wheat would need to be harvested and made ready for sale, the garden would need harvesting of the final crops, and more canning would need to be done for the winter.

The winter, however, was a time to relax just a bit. There

was still planning for the spring seeding, livestock to be tended to, and repairs done, but all in all this was their quietest season.

Washing and dressing done, she made her way to the kitchen and fed Miranda. Welcoming fresh coffee sat in the pot, and she made a beeline for it. After only a tiny hot sip, however, she heard a commotion outside her door and set the cup down, going to the door. Jake and Dakota were running around frantically chasing her chickens. What in the world was going on now? Why were the chickens out?

Opening the door just a crack, she hollered to them, but the brisk wind whipping across the open fields accompanying what was not rain, but sleet, blew her words away. Confused, she grabbed a coat and her hat and took off outside. Her cows were far away in a field, huddled together, and she could hear the great clatter of agitated chickens running amuck around the yard. Her confusion grew, and she raced to Dakota.

Holding her hat on her head against the bitter wind threatening to carry it away, she raised her voice to be heard. "What's going on? Why is everyone outside in this weather?"

His reply was a tense angry shout. "When I came outside they were all out here, everywhere. The barn door was open, and all the stalls and coops were open. Someone let them out."

The side of Dakota she'd never wanted to see again stood before in rage. Gone was the control. Gone was the inner peace and quiet that normally dominated his life. As before with Shoop, she could literally feel the anger pulsing off him. In frustration, he gave up on chasing the frantic chickens and grabbed a horse, guiding her back to the barn, his fury apparent in the steeliness of his spine.

Plucking her ice coated rooster from the frigid ground,

she carried him to the barn and stared in shock. The evidence that someone had indeed been in her barn was apparent. Every pen, every stall was opened to the dismal daylight beyond the barn doors. Signs of running horses were evident on the barn floor. Something or someone had frightened them all from their homes. The locks were broken or cut.

She quickly called Martin and asked him to send someone out immediately, and once that was done, she went back out to help Dakota. For almost an hour they collected and guided her livestock back inside. The horses were wide-eyed and unsettled until dried and safely ensconced in their stalls. The chickens raised a ruckus until they were also dried and placed in their coops. The cows as usual were complacent and went easily back into the cowshed, but the gate locks had all been damaged. Together they made makeshift ties to hold the gates in place until they could replace the locks.

By the time Martin entered at eleven in the morning, most of her barn was quiet and happy, except for her and Dakota. Martin listened patiently while they explained what had happened and examined the cut locks, noting all on his little flip-top pad of paper. Two other officers had accompanied him, and Martin put them to work looking for other evidence and dusting for fingerprints. Sadly, none were forthcoming, and Martin was not very enthusiastic about the possibility of catching the culprit who'd played havoc with their day.

Much later, while standing in her living room enjoying the warming heat of a roaring fire and a cup of steaming coffee, she gazed out the front window and watched as Martin and Dakota spoke quietly for a few minutes beneath the awning of her front porch. Their voices were low murmurs, indiscernible to her, but she knew Dakota would tell her what they spoke about. She was just a bit too chilled to be inquisitive enough to join them.

After shaking hands, Martin ran to his car while sheltering his head against the icy rain and carefully backed away.

A shudder wracked her body that had nothing to do with the chill of the morning. Somebody was out to get her. Very little of her suspected Dakota anymore. He'd never let the livestock out and then traipse around in the bitter cold to catch them again. The idea was ludicrous.

If anything, she figured it was Shoop, but what was his point, and how she could prove he was doing it? Was he trying to aggravate her enough to sell? Or was he trying to scare her into leaving? If so, it was a pretty underhanded way of doing business.

She was sitting at her kitchen table nursing her second cup of coffee when Dakota entered. The morning spent outside still sent a shiver deep in her bones, and she knew he had to be nearly frozen.

After removing his damp jacket and dropping it on the back of a chair, he sat down next to her and placed an icy hand across hers, curling the cold fingers into her palm, proving to her that she was right.

"You are frozen."

He chuckled. "I'll be okay. Listen, Anna, Martin and I talked. We have an idea, but this is only if you are willing to go along with it."

Intrigued, she raised her gaze from their intertwined hands to look at him.

"What is it?"

"I want you to fire me."

At her confused reaction, he chuckled, and the corners of his gentle, brown eyes crinkled in the way she found so endearing. She opened her mouth to question him, but he held up a hand to forestall any questions.

"I'll explain. We are going to put it about that you fired me because you suspected me of causing the damage recently, except I'm not really going to go anywhere."

Caught between his words and the desire that had been plaguing her, she watched the talented lips she'd fantasized about move as he spoke, and she pictured those lips against her body. Remembering the pleasure, he'd given her and lost in her thoughts of her night with him, she barely heard his next words.

"Martin and I will be watching the farm. He will also enlist the help of some of his deputies. At all times you will be under surveillance. We'll be watching to see if anyone approaches the house or barn after Martin puts the story of my firing around town. We have to find out who is doing this."

Her eyes lifted from his lips and looked at him in confusion. "What?"

He studied her, as if puzzled by her question.

"Are you okay? You are somewhere else, but I need you to listen to me. It's important. Martin and I have worked out a plan to have the house watched. Well, either Martin and I or two of his deputies. We want to see if anyone will approach the house while we keep an eye out somewhere hidden on the property."

No wonder her mind preferred to dwell on their night together. What he was proposing was scary, and she refused to think about it. Standing, she turned from him and walked to the coffee pot. She wanted and needed all the turmoil to stop. She tried to remember when her home had been a place of peace, but it seemed like ages ago.

"You are frightening me." What if they weren't here when Shoop, or whoever was after her came back? For she was sure they would come back. Shoop's words the last time she saw him came back to haunt her. One day she would be here alone and vulnerable.

"Please, don't be frightened. You have Jake and two of us will always have you in our sight. If they know I am around, they will do only minor things to aggravate you. If they think you suspected me as the culprit all along and fired me, they may step up their attacks, and we need to find out who this is. I need you to agree to this. I need you to be brave, Anna."

"I'm not feeling very brave. I'm scared."

"Even the brave are scared."

She huffed, not wanting wisdom at this moment. "Do you think it will work?"

As usual, he didn't answer right away and collected his thoughts before he spoke. He stood, walking to where she leaned against the countertop and brushed against her as he poured another cup of coffee. He was so close. All she wanted to do was lean into him, hold him — anything.

"We don't know. Maybe it will, maybe it won't, but it's worth a shot. We have to at least try."

He turned until he was face to face with her, also leaning casually against the countertop. All thoughts of the recent havoc in her life fled from her mind as she looked to the man who'd come to mean more to her than he should. *Hold me*, her mind screamed. She needed his hug.

Her dad had had the most wonderful hugs when she was young. He was a burly man, and she'd always felt surrounded in warmth and strength when he held her. All her childhood fears would wash away in the security of his arms.

Her husband's arms had been gentle and loving. Not the same as her dad's, but a wonderful feeling nonetheless.

Her mom had stopped hugging, but she remembered a time long, long ago when she still did. It was before her dad and Bella had died. Before she had changed into the cold woman Anna now knew her to be.

She exhaled. The loneliness and exhaustion held her in an iron grip. She'd been fighting for survival for so long. She was good at this life, but that didn't mean she didn't want help or someone to hold. She'd almost forgotten what it felt like to be held until Dakota.

He shifted the body she knew intimately against the countertop and sipped his coffee, appearing lost in his own thoughts. Unusual for him, he remained oblivious to the turmoil that raged inside her, testimony that his mind was far away.

When he finally spoke, it startled her. "We are at least hoping it works. We're hoping that whoever is doing this feels brave once he thinks you are alone and unprotected."

She was quiet as he sipped his coffee, watching as his lips puckered to blow a cooling breath across the rippling liquid.

"Dakota."

He raised his head and looked at inquisitively. He was so near, but still too far away.

"Hold me, please?"

The next afternoon brought another knock on her front door and she grew angry, almost stamping her foot in aggravation. The man wouldn't take no for an answer.

Opening her door to the now familiar leer of Mr. Shoop, she didn't even bother walking outside, but spoke to him through the screen door instead.

"Mr. Shoop, I told you before, and I will state it again. I'm not selling. Go find another person to pester."

Allowing her frustration and anger to overtake her normal good manners, she slammed the door in his face and felt immense satisfaction as the windows rattled from the force.

Chapter Twenty-two

The third night after Dakota supposedly left Anna's employ was cloudy and bitterly cold. He shivered, despite his downy winter jacket and thick cotton long johns. The weathermen had called for snow the next day, and the temperatures hovered just below the freezing mark, making him and the sheriff wish for their warm homes. They whispered together about the possibility their efforts were futile, that maybe whoever was behind this, quite possibly Shoop, had taken the hint and moved on. On a low chuckle, Dakota let the sheriff know that their criminal was probably smarter than them and was someplace warm while they were freezing their behinds off.

A deputy had been watching the movements of Mr. Shoop in town and reported no strange behavior. The past two nights he'd been at home. Tonight, the deputy told them the man was sitting in a cheerfully warm restaurant, happily devouring a plate of barbecued ribs, food the hungry deputy wished he was also enjoying.

They'd almost been ready to call it a night when a figure wrapped in a ridiculous Draculean black cloak came from behind the house, hugging the perimeter closely as he moved. The person didn't appear to be peering in the windows or trying doors, and that befuddled the two men.

Dakota whispered his confusion to the sheriff. "What is he doing?"

"I don't know. Can you see who it is? Considering his height against the bushes, he definitely isn't Shoop."

Dakota strained to make out the tall figure in the darkness. "I don't know many people around here, so I'm not going to be much help."

The figure turned and threw something across the driveway, and Dakota let out a curse when he recognized a red plastic gas can. An instant later a match was lit and held against the man's hands to protect it from the cold breeze. Already coiled and ready, Dakota jumped into action on a cry of outrage. He and Martin took off towards the alarmed figure just as the match was dropped to the ground.

Inside her warm house, Anna lay comfortably enveloped in a heavy blanket but sleeping fitfully. She hadn't slept well since Dakota left, frightened of what might happen next.

She thought she heard a muffled growl from Jake, but sleepily questioned whether it was only the sounds of the TV. When her faithful friend let out a yelp in front of her face, she came awake with a jolt.

She sat up, displacing Miranda, and looked at the hair that had risen along Jake's spine. A creepy sensation moved along her own back. "Jake, what's the matter?"

She let out a tiny scream of alarm when Dakota burst through her kitchen door and urged her to leave at once. He ripped the blanket from her body and moved back out of the room with lightning speed, and she stared at the swinging door in sleepy headed confusion.

What was going on? Jake began to kick up a real fuss, barking and running in circles, and it was at that moment she noticed the strange smell permeating the interior of her home. Smoke. Adrenalin now surged through her, and she slipped on her shoes, grabbed Miranda, and hollered for Jake to follow as she bolted out of the house.

The fire in front of her steps wasn't that big. It was merely a small path of flame struggling to ignite against the icy crystals coating her grass, but any fire near the ancient wooden house was dangerous. Jumping over the flickering light and urging Jake to do the same, she ran away from her home into the frigid night air and turned to watch the fire's path.

In nothing more than a sweat shirt and pants, it wasn't long before she was shivering violently. Her neck muscles tightened until she felt the beginnings of a headache. Her fingers turned to instant icicles, and the cold air wrapped around her legs like an ice pack. She gave herself hell for not grabbing her coat and clutched the furiously biting and scratching body of her cat against her to share their warmth, but both were now too cold to do any good.

Dakota came around the far side of the house beating and stomping on the fire, using the blanket that had just recently offered her warmth and comfort. She felt the pain of that loss. It was one of her better blankets.

Figures wrestled at the far edge of her driveway, and she recognized Martin, but the other was no more than a wavering shadow dressed in a dark dress. A dress? Dakota beating furiously at the flames. Jake crept towards the struggling figures. Fire burned everywhere. She wanted to help but had no idea where to begin.

A burst of fire flashed, and she gasped as it took hold, slithering its way up the wood siding to her windows, the flames created a mesmerizing path of destruction.

Dakota continued batting down the fire, but he couldn't see the driveway side of her home, and Anna's heartbeat became a frantic rhythm of fear that she would lose her home after all. She bounced on the balls of her feet as she hollered out to him about the more damaging fire, and he moved swiftly to where she pointed.

The low wail of sirens sounded in the distance, and she turned. The flashing red and white lights of the town's fire engines, police cars, and one medic raced down the road, the ear-piercing sounds getting louder and louder as they approached. She gravitated toward their safety, naively unaware they'd even been on the way.

Men and women piled from the engines, police piled from cars, and medics opened their doors. It became a frenzy of activity. Soon hoses were thrown to the ground, and she watched in fascinated horror as they hosed down her precious home. The cold water trickled and became an icy sheen against the charred siding. Orderly confusion was everywhere. Strangely, she no longer shivered as she stood watching, disbelieving that this could be happening in front of her.

So engrossed was she, that she jerked away in surprise when a hand came to rest on her arm.

"Anna, I need you to come with me." Martin stood solemnly by her side and placed his hand below her elbow to lightly tug her with him.

"What is it, Martin?" She followed him in confusion until they reached one of his deputy's cars, and she saw a figure in the back seat, kicking against the windows and seats, screaming loudly to be released.

"Anna, it's Liam."

Her confusion grew as she looked to the Sheriff.

"What about Liam?"

"Liam is the one who started the fire."

"What? No way. That's impossible. Why?"

"I don't know yet. He refuses to talk. I thought you would like to come to the station with me and find out."

With his usual canniness, Dakota materialized behind her, and she swung around at his voice. "Go, Anna, I will take care of things here."

"But . . . I don't understand. Liam? It can't be."

She looked to Dakota in disbelief, shaking her head. Liam had worked for her for the past three years off and on. She'd laughed and talked with him, worked alongside him. She'd even fed him on occasion. She'd known him most of his life, watched him grow to the young man he was today. She knew his mother. None of this made sense to her.

"Go to the station. See what you can find out."

After handing Miranda to Dakota, Martin led her to the front seat of the car, moved a laptop to the side, and protected her head as she bent to sit on the warm leather seat. Oddly, the warm interior caused her to begin shivering again, and she held her hands against the heater's warm blast, trying to feel her fingers and calm the trembling of her body.

A sniff sounded behind her, and she swung her body around and looked at Liam. He had quieted when she got in the car and sat with his chin against his chest in dejection and surrender.

"Liam? Why?"

He refused to answer her. He wouldn't even look at her. Her heart cramped as his betrayal sank in. She still found this difficult to believe. Something wasn't right.

The long night had been too much. It was nearing dawn before she'd crawled into her bed, and it wasn't welcoming to be awakened early by the deep cadence of male voices outside and below her bedroom window now.

Liam hadn't revealed a thing despite the hours of questioning, and she knew no more now than when she had crawled into the deputy's car last night. His mother had shown up at the police station, and they'd held onto each other in their confusion and pain. Liam's mother had apologized over and over, but Anna knew in her heart she couldn't hold it against the woman for what her son had done.

Martin had dropped her off in the early morning hours, assuring her he'd let her know if he learned anything new and had driven away to seek his own bed. Both of them were exhausted. At least Liam was locked up in jail and would stay there for the time being.

The lingering scent of smoke had still clung to her home when she'd entered and tiptoed past a sleeping Dakota. She remembered stopping on the stairs and watching him, bundled deep under the blankets with Miranda curled against his chest, only the top of her head peeping from within the warmth. Jake, her precious dog, had laid his long body between Dakota's legs, snugly enjoying the heat that radiated from Dakota. He'd lifted his head at her entrance and thumped his tail against the warm blanket beneath him but had quickly gone right back to sleep.

She'd wrongly suspected that kind and gentle man of causing all her problems, and she felt immense guilt. It appeared she'd also wrongly suspected Mr. Shoop. The man might be slime, but apparently, he wasn't a conniving slime.

That Liam could do this to her was a heavy burden on her heart, and all she wanted was some answers. She couldn't understand how the workings of someone's mind would bring them to do such things. The other instances had been mild and annoying, but no major harm done. He had stepped it up this time and damaged her home. The worst damage had been to the newly repaired wall and that angered her. The fact that he could have even killed her, Jake, and Miranda if Dakota and the Sheriff hadn't been around truly frightened her.

She thought on that for a while as she remembered the night before. Jake had warned her of the smoke before Dakota even burst in. Chances were they would have lived, but by the time help would have arrived, she was certain her home would have been gone. She smiled as she pictured Jake. He would have once again been her little savior.

She heard the voices once more as she made her way

groggily down the steps, recognizing Dakota's voice, but not the other. She wasn't in the mood to see anyone this morning and didn't want to face any more questions or the probing and prodding into her life. She'd had enough.

She needed some peace and quiet for just a little while, and she knew where to go to find the solace she craved.

Waiting until Dakota walked around to the front of the house, she slipped outside and shut the door quietly behind her. The urge to get away was overpowering. Traipsing over the charred remains of her burnt wheat, the frigid ground crackling beneath her feet, she moved swiftly towards her goal. She had no idea what condition it was in anymore, but she needed her gazebo.

When she finally reached the copse of trees, she slipped inside the shelter of towering leafless silver maples and tall blue spruce evergreens, hidden from the world at her level and open to the cloudy gray sky above. Her gazebo stood not too far ahead, and she hurried her steps, anxious to see it again, anxious for the solitude.

The year before she lost Charles, just as fall was winding down and winter began taking its hold on the land, he'd noticed how tired she was. She'd finished harvesting her garden and had spent days canning and freezing her abundant crops. It'd been a good year for her, and the work had taken a long, exhausting time.

More than that, he'd seen how she struggled to cope with the barrage of men who trampled through her home daily and the mountains of dirt and dishes they left behind. They tried to help her clean up, but she found them more a nuisance than a help. The deciding factor was the day she pulled out a plate that they had washed and saw the dried remains of food adhering to the surface. She'd do the job from now on.

To Anna, the work was what she needed to do, had to do,

but Charles had known she needed a break, a sanctuary, a place to call her own to come and rest.

She'd been completely unaware he noticed any of it, yet he had. Each morning as he left the house, she'd assumed he was doing things in the barn with the livestock or any of the other myriad of tasks that faced them year after year, season after season.

In the spring, almost exactly three months before he passed, he'd lovingly and excitedly taken her hand one morning and asked her to go for a walk. At the end of that walk, he'd guided her into the grove of trees and presented her with his gift.

CHAPTER TWENTY-THREE

The crunch of her boots on the crisply, cold tundra brought her closer and closer to her goal as the memories assaulted her. Charles had told her what had originally started out as just a simple, open-aired gazebo had changed as he worked. Wanting her to be able to come here any time of the year that she felt the need, he'd enclosed the side openings with windows that could be opened to let in the breeze or shut tight to keep out the cold.

She smiled as she remembered the roof. He had done a wonderful job with that. A sturdy tempered glass allowed an open view to the sky above. Whether sunny or cloudy in the day or even twinkling stars or turbulent clouds at night, the sight was always enchanting.

The walls beneath the windows were insulated, and in the very center of the precious, small enclosure, he'd built a fireplace that vented through the roof. How he'd managed all of this practically right under her nose was beyond her, but he had, and his thoughtfulness had touched her deeply.

When she'd stood in the room with him so long ago, she'd been overwhelmed by the beauty of his creation. Now, like a rerun of a favorite movie, the memories flowed through her mind until her chest hurt from the pain. He'd stood off to the side with a loving smile on his face as she walked in a circle around the fireplace, watching the wildlife scamper in and out of the trees through the windows that ran evenly around the room, interrupted only by the single door.

With clarity, she remembered one lone pregnant doe, her body heavy with her babe, standing outside the gazebo watching Anna as she had watched the little mother. The doe had been just as curious as Anna and had stood motionless for a long time as she observed her and Charles behind the glass, her soft brown eyes studying them both. When the gentle creature turned and moved back into the thicker brush, Anna had teared up, just as she was at this moment.

She couldn't stop thanking Charles for his precious gift.

Sadly, she'd only found time to visit the gazebo three times more before she lost Charles. With his passing, the building became a reminder of the love they'd shared and the thoughtfulness he'd shown her every single day of their marriage. She hadn't been able to bring herself here again, until today.

Desperately trying to choke back the tearful memories, she pulled the key from her pocket and opened the door. From her position by the doorway, she expected to see Charles standing by the fireplace, the last place he'd stood when they'd been together in this room, but no ghostly shapes haunted the quiet interior. No sounds came from inside at all. It was as it was meant to be, a place for peace.

As she closed the door with a soft click, the outside world ceased to exist. Nothing moved, nothing creaked or groaned. Absolute silence.

She ran her hand along a table and was surprised that only a light sprinkling of dust covered the dark maple wood. She'd expected to see a thick coating on everything and cobwebs hanging from the ceiling. Strangely, it was as if it had only been a couple of months since she'd last been there, instead of a couple of years.

Her ankle length boots made a soft tapping on the cool marble tiles as she made her way to the fireplace. The firewood her considerate husband had placed in a neat pile in the log holder was still there, wood that had been touched by his very hands. It was old and turning gray, and she hoped it would still ignite. It took a couple tries for it to catch, but soon warmth began to seep into the room, removing the chill in the long-unused space.

In lonely solitude, she circled the room looking out of the windows. As it was bitter cold outside, little moved, yet she knew in the spring birds would be hopping from tree to tree, rabbits would be playing in the sparse grass that grew beneath the shadow of the trees, and deer would take shelter and have their young amidst the dark foliage. This was a place of beauty in her otherwise harsh world, and it belonged only to her.

The thought only reinforced her decision that she could never, ever sell this land. Well, at least until she was forced to in old age, but not now. Almost every inch of this land held a memory for her that she couldn't let go.

She walked to the cool white leather chaise lounge Charles had bought her. His intention was for her to be able to come here and read or rest to her hearts content, but in the few times she'd visited she had preferred to spend her quiet time looking out the windows at the trees and the changing sky above. The books he'd so thoughtfully placed on a shelf to the right of the chaise had never been touched.

The room lost its chill, the fireplace doing its job, and she removed her coat and laid it across the cool leather. She sat down upon the warm wool and stared up at the bare treetops outside. Soon the snow would start. She could smell it in the air. The ground would be covered in a blanket of silent white, but today it was a barren, grey land sitting and waiting for new life to begin in the spring.

With her eyes stinging and a yawn overtaking her, exhaustion finally claimed her. She closed her eyes against the weight of the world on her shoulders and drifted off into a peaceful sleep.

Returning from the front of the house, Dakota had caught the barest glimpse of the auburn hair and light blue coat slipping into the trees and knew instinctively where she was going. Once he'd spoken to the sheriff and his men and after the insurance agent had visited again and inspected the minor damage, he sheltered Jake inside the warm house and followed in her footsteps until he reached the gazebo.

The windows showed no movement inside, but when he quietly opened the unlocked door and the fire's warmth enveloped him, he knew he was right. She'd sought escape.

A small fire still burned in the fireplace, although the logs were quickly becoming ash. He crept forward and added another log. Across the tips of the small flames, he saw her and went to her side.

He dropped to a knee and watched the gentle rise and fall of her chest. She slept a peaceful sleep. Soft reddish-brown lashes lay in repose against her beautiful alabaster skin. Four or five tiny freckles graced the top of her nose in a haphazard pattern, the effect making her appear young and innocent, and he smiled. She looked like a painting come to life.

Rich, warm tendrils of her thick and gorgeous hair lay in disarray across the stark backdrop of the white lounge. The firelight highlighted the auburn tones, turning it an almost fiery red hue, while the white, snow-laden sky above circled her crown in the barest whisper of a halo.

His eyes were drawn to the dried remains of a single tear that lay just below her left eye. Brushing a finger across it lightly, he removed the salty flakes. He didn't want to ever see her cry again. He hated the tears of women, for they meant heartbreak, and he hated to see their pain. Anna deserved happiness. She'd battled through too much.

161

Sitting back on his heels, he pondered the beauty in front of him. As hard as he had tried, he couldn't stay away from her. After the night they'd made love, he had backed off, trying to maintain a friendly, working relationship, but the fear that someone was out to hurt her coupled with being by her side day and night had become tormenting. The nights were the worst. Too many times he'd lain on the sofa beneath her room and imagined her lying across her bed above him, sated and resplendent in the aftermath of their passion.

Memories of their night together would sweep over him, and his loins would tighten painfully. He'd eventually give up on sleep and would slip outside, walking until the tension subsided. He'd loved once, and losing her had broken him. He'd sworn he'd never open himself to love again, but something was changing inside him.

He had prayed to the Great Spirit for guidance and advice. When no change of heart came over him, he accepted that maybe this was the path the Great Spirit had chosen for him, to give love another chance and to know another's joy. It was not his to question the Creator's wishes.

Coming forward, he kissed her rosy lips. "Anna," he called softly, and she smiled a serene smile.

On a whisper, she heard her name being called. He was beckoning to her. He wanted her, too. She'd been calling to him, searching for him in her dreams, and he came. Slowly she opened her eyes and met his. The passion she read in the dark orbs mirrored her own wants. She needed him. She needed to feel his strength. She needed his warmth. She definitely needed his body.

Raising a hand, she laid it against his cheek, still cool from the frigid temperatures outside. She slipped her hand behind his neck and gently tugged, and he came forward to meet her waiting lips.

This was where she'd wanted him for too long. Rejoicing in the feel of his lips against hers finally, she pulled, wanting him closer, demanding him to unburden this fiery need that just the sight of him created. Slipping off his jacket, he came down upon her heated body, and she sighed in contentment.

His kiss was so tender that tears threatened. He was treating her as if she would break. The moment was intimately precious and romantic.

He broke the kiss and pulled back, capturing her with a look of soft, serene gentleness. Giving up the battle to hold them back, she felt tears fill her eyes, but he cupped her face and swiped away a tear with his thumb.

"Don't cry, Anna. No more tears."

His lips came down upon her throat with even gentler kisses as his hand unbuttoned the front of her top. The soft material teased along her skin until she felt the cool air caress her heated flesh.

Her nipples, hard and erect beneath the flimsy fabric screamed for his touch, but he denied them. He kissed and caressed the hollow between her aching breasts as his hand moved along her ribs. Once he finished with those tender kisses, he slid her blouse an inch at a time to the side until his hand curved over a breast and his lips took possession. She arched into him, needing what only he could give her.

His fingers teased with feather-light caresses over the side of her breast as his hand reached to bare her shoulder. She trembled, waiting for more, wanting more. Never had she imagined that the sides of her breasts would be so sensitive to touch.

She wanted the restriction of their clothing gone. She wanted to feel him up against her body. "Dakota, too many clothes, help me."

With a chuckle, he rose and pulled off each piece of his

clothing until he stood naked and proud before her. With just the cold white sky a backdrop to his raven black hair and the shadowed flickering light of the fire dancing across the hard planes of his skin, he looked every inch the brave Indian warrior she'd seen in history books.

Her gaze travelled the long expanse of his body. Not a hair interrupted the broad expanse of his powerful chest. His stomach, flat and ripped, spoke volumes about the labor he put his body through daily.

Long, lean, but muscled legs ended in a dusting of dark hair from which his thick, engorged male need sprang forth. Her gaze snapped back to his. Smoldering male passion burning in in his eyes told her of his desire and growing impatience.

He interrupted her inspection. "I'm waiting."

She smiled impishly. "For what?"

He narrowed his eyes in false aggravation. "You also have on too many clothes."

"So, I have."

On an excited giggle she tried to stand. Her legs turned wobbly beneath her, and he held her to him as they removed her clothing.

When the last piece met the floor, they stood facing each other, bared to the world outside her windows. The crackling of the fire was the only sound in the room as they came together. Forehead to forehead, the tips of her breasts lightly touching the warmth of his skin, and their breaths mingling, he whispered of his yearning for every part of her body until she was giddy with desire.

Hands, arms, and mouths began to touch, and reach, and kiss. Quivering with the force of the want that had haunted her for months, she clung to him as an intense flame of desire exploded low in her belly and spread to her femininity.

His hot shaft came up hard against her bared skin, and

her quivers became trembles. She needed him with a desperation that almost frightened her.

He walked her backwards towards the lounge, never breaking his kiss, until the backs of her knees met the cool surface. With warm, strong hands, he slid her coat out of the way and lowered her to rest against the cushions.

She held out a hand, reaching for him, but he held back. It was his turn to inspect.

CHAPTER TWENTY-FOUR

Having never lain with a white woman before her, used to only the tint of an Indian maiden's skin, he found the difference mesmerizing. The soft grey light from the sky above covered her, creating the effect of freshly fallen snow under a winter sky, cool, white, and pure.

However, her eyes contradicted the cool exterior. The blue of her orbs had darkened and appeared almost cobalt in intensity as those eyes spoke to him, urging him to relieve her pent-up passion. Her breasts, small and firm, were thrust upward, the tips hard and pointing toward the heavily laden sky above. A flat firm abdomen quivered ever so gently as she lifted an arm to reach for him.

She was resplendent in her passion. Fire-reflective deep auburn locks fanned out around her head in a glorious display of riotous abandonment, and her kiss-swollen lips questioned his hesitance, beckoning him forward for more.

"Don't tease me, Dakota."

He chuckled, but the chuckle was not in amusement. He wasn't done admiring the woman before him.

If a man could explode just by staring at the body of a naked woman, then the sight before him could surely accomplish that task.

One leg was bent at the knee, the foot and knee angled outward on the leather surface of her lounge, opening herself to his view. The other foot still rested on the floor, the toes curled with impatience.

His eyes traveled the long, lean length of her legs to the

place where her thighs met, to the place where most men found their peace.

The amber firelight displayed her glistening core, blossoming under his perusal. He dropped to one knee and beheld her, her eyes softening in a smile as she watched him watching her.

A trace of her musk reached his nostrils, and his erection jumped in response. He willed it to behave as he lowered his mouth to her moisture. He blew a breath across her core, and she exhaled on a moan, the soft sound loud in the quiet of the room.

Her legs spread wider, her hips rising to meet him as he bent to taste the drops of moisture. Desperate hands came to his head and held him, and he chuckled again. His woman was on fire.

He parted her lips with his tongue, finding the little button he sought. Swirling the tip of his tongue over the rock-hard nub, he felt the quivering of her thighs as she struggled to hold them in place. He tickled, and teased, and suckled until he was sure she was as ready for him as he was for her. He backed away and placed a gentle parting kiss at the juncture of thigh and femininity and moved above her until the tip of his cock rested against her opening.

"What do you want, Anna?"

"You, please, now," she whispered in a breathless plea. With warm, soft fingers, she surrounded the length of him, and he drew in a breath, his hand reaching to halt her movements. His own passion was near to bursting. He had to stop her before it was too late. He lowered himself and rested deeply imbedded within her warmth.

With a pleasured cry, she welcomed him, clenching him in an iron grip. He held his body still and waited, willing his body to cooperate. "Stay . . . still," he pleaded.

An impish giggle sounded below him, and he growled as

she teased him, tightening her muscles rhythmically along his long length. He looked to her and narrowed his gaze in a warning, but her happy blue eyes twinkled with deviltry.

"Anna . . . no . . ."

She giggled again, and as she clenched one more time, he lost control and pounded home his own need. He worried he would leave her behind, but his Anna met him thrust for thrust until with lightning speed the world exploded around them.

The finish was quick, earth shattering, and unbelievably good. It was what both had needed and denied themselves for too long.

He began to laugh, which did nothing to calm his pounding heart.

She looked at him askance. "That's not exactly what you should be doing right now," she said in a mocking tone.

"I can't help it. You're a brat sometimes. I asked you to stop moving, but you took great delight in besting me."

"You teased me, so I teased you." They laughed until exhausted from their sated desire and the long night, then quieted. Whispering softly to each other, they drifted off.

Awakening a short while later, they began again.

Large, fat flakes fell from the sky above them to cover the roof of their world as they murmured endearments and caressed each other's bodies. No tension existed in the room this day. The outside world could go to hell as far as they were concerned. This moment was meant for them.

Lazily she rolled him over and came down upon the power of his body. Her hair fell in a curtain around them as she leaned to kiss him, to taste the man who was capturing a piece of her heart whether she wanted him to or not.

His fingers drew a languid, pleasuring pattern from her

buttocks to her back as she explored the heat of his mouth. She broke the kiss and rested her mouth against the warm column of his neck, lovingly kissing the pulsing beat of life that throbbed below her lips.

This was what she'd needed, wanted, from this man. She'd craved his touch to ease the loneliness surrounding her heart and ease the passion he always ignited within her. A thickness grew against her abdomen, and she giggled.

"What do you laugh about now?"

She lifted her head from the hollow of his neck and connected with his questioning eyes. A flash of deviltry sparked within her again, and she smiled. Wiggling against him, she began a slow tease of lips and fingertips along his skin, moving lower and lower.

As she found her place between his two strong thighs, she looked up at him. He had lifted his head, resting it against a folded arm, and was watching her intently. His smoldering dark-eyed gaze never wavered from hers as she gripped the iron strength of him in her hand.

Keeping her focus on him, she watched his reaction as she drew the tip of her tongue forward and licked the tip of his shaft, almost giggling again at the hiss of his breath through clenched teeth. He would find she could give as good as she got.

She ran her hand down the length of him, marveling at how such soft skin could encompass such steely strength. Inching forward just a bit, she lifted the heavy shaft. Encircling it with her mouth, she sucked the tip, much as he had done to her own already throbbing nub of desire.

When she came down upon the heat of him and swallowed his length, his hips jerked upwards, and he groaned his pleasure. "Anna."

The word was uttered on a whoosh of air, a plea for release, and she smiled as she slipped him from her mouth.

"Yes?"

His answer was a suffocated groan, as if he couldn't speak. She swallowed him again and moved. Up and down she pleasured him, suckling the tip and lightly nibbling before plunging once again.

She brought a hand down and cupped the sensitive sac of his testicles and caressed them gently while she gripped his iron firmness between two tightened cheeks. She drew on him, milked him, loved him over and over until he grabbed her shoulders trying to pull her upwards.

"Anna, stop. Stop, please, before it's too late."

Her laugh vibrated along his shaft as she denied him, as she continued to pleasure him. She had finally bested the master of self-control. She had brought him down.

The rumble came from deep within his chest as his orgasm overtook him. His hand shot to her head, holding her as he pumped his fluid within the softness of her mouth, and she swallowed until he slowed.

His hand fell to his side as his labored breathing relaxed. Still holding him within her moisture, she slowly slid up the length until she kissed the sensitive tip and let the tender appendage lie against his stomach.

She laid a hand across his softening shaft and rested her chin on her hand as she looked up at him, feeling immense satisfaction.

He felt her gaze on him but could barely move a muscle to acknowledge her. His wife had never done that, having found it distasteful. A couple of young girls had in his youth, but none could compare with what he'd just experienced.

Her hair tickled his hips as she lifted her head and kissed the tip of him again, and he jerked at the touch to his ultrasensitive skin.

When her slender body rose to slide across his own and her face came into view above him, he still could not find the right words to say.

"Wow," was all that came to mind.

She giggled. "Dakota?"

"Yes."

"My turn."

She slithered until her core rested mere inches above his face, and he grabbed her hips, bringing her down on his waiting mouth.

His lady was drenched, obviously aroused by what she had done to him, and he drank her in as he suckled and licked his way through the moisture.

In control, she set the pace, withdrawing and circling to reach the pleasure she craved. It didn't take long. Her cry of completion bounced along the walls. As she lost control, her palms came down with a crash to the lounge on each side of his head.

As he began drifting toward sleep, he heard the calls of a pair of eagles and sent a prayer of thanks for their blessing.

CHAPTER TWENTY-FIVE

On the morning of the fifth day after their passionate day in the gazebo, Sheriff Martin came to visit. Dakota had been out tending to the livestock, and Anna had been doing laundry in the basement when she heard the click of hard-soled shoes on the wooden floor above her.

People typically came and went in her home. The door was always open to those who knew her best, but she hadn't been expecting anyone today. Setting down the sheet she'd been folding, she made her way upstairs to see who was in her house.

Opening the door, she found Martin sitting on an armchair patiently waiting for someone to arrive. He stood when he saw her, always the gentleman, and she smiled at him in greeting, but instantly sobered as she realized the reason behind this visit.

She came forward and hugged him yet spoke warily. "Martin, it's good to see you. Please, sit back down."

He took a seat on her sofa while she anxiously came to rest on a chair facing him.

"How have you been, Anna?"

The question took her by surprise for a moment.

"I've been okay."

"It sure has gotten cold, hasn't it?"

He was being evasive, and they both knew it. In the ways of friends who had no patience for indirect talk, she narrowed her eyes at him until he sighed.

"You know why I'm here. I came to give you an update

on Liam."

She'd been expecting to hear something soon but didn't really want to know why he'd wished her harm. It still hurt deeply. Never would she have imagined that he would've been the one behind the mischief and attack. Liam had always appeared as a kind and gentle soul, and he'd always worked so hard for her. It just didn't make sense.

Sorrow softened her eyes as she looked to her friend. "I still can't believe this."

He shook his head in shared disbelief. "Nobody really can, and of course, the whole town now knows and has been rocked by the scandal. His mother is taking this especially hard. As you know, I see her every day, and not a day goes by that she doesn't stop by my desk and apologize. There've been several times I've found her crying at work. It's sad."

Lowering her eyes, she looked to her hands clenched in her lap and released them to rest on her knees, tapping lightly in nervousness. "I already told her I didn't hold it against her. I hope she believes me. I care for Liam, too."

"We've all told her, but I don't think it's done any good."

Clearly agitated by what he still had to impart, he stood, back ramrod straight, and walked to her window to look at his police car in the driveway.

"I wanted to let you know that Liam still hasn't given a statement and he has lawyered up."

A movement caught her eye, and she turned to find Dakota at the doorway to her kitchen. His ability to walk with catlike, quiet stealth and to know when he was needed still unnerved her, although she was beginning to begrudgingly expect it.

"What does that mean?" he asked as he walked closer, taking a seat beside her.

Martin turned and met Dakota's questioning stare.

"It means he's told us nothing, plain and simple, but we

may be getting closer to knowing more without his help."

Anna moved forward to the edge of her seat. "Come on, Martin, tell us what you know. You're driving me nuts."

Martin chuckled but sobered immediately. "Liam has made bail. An anonymous benefactor posted bail for him yesterday, but we all know nothing is really anonymous, anymore. I've found out that Brandon Shoop hired someone to post his bail."

Bolting upright, Anna screeched, "I knew it!" Both men winced, but she didn't care. "I knew that man was behind all of it. I'm confused, though. How did Liam get involved?"

"We don't know yet, and just because he posted his bail doesn't mean he was behind any of this. He could claim he was just being kind. I'm still doing my investigation, but I wanted to warn you. If he was behind this and thinks no one knows of his involvement, he may try more desperate tactics. I want you to be aware. We will be watching your property, but we can't be here twenty-four-seven. Just be careful."

The warmth of Dakota's fingers slipping between her own gave her support.

Clearly not missing a beat, Martin lowered his gaze to where they were joined.

Well, the secret was out now.

The crackling chatter of the dispatcher calling to him over his radio broke the tension, and he reached to lower the volume.

"I have to be going, but again, please be careful. Lock up this house. I walked in easily. I know you're used to being lenient with the locks on your doors, but I ask that you be a bit more careful for a while, if not forever. Times are changing, Anna, and we have to change with them."

Liam's mother once more called to him over the mic, and Martin said in parting, "I'll be in touch when I learn more."

With that, he walked through the swinging door to her kitchen, and in moments she heard the click of her backdoor as he closed it.

Standing, she walked to the window and listened to the low mumble of his voice as he talked to dispatch. Within moments, he climbed into his waiting patrol car and backed away.

"What's so special about my property that someone would wish to harm me over it?" she whispered to the air, but Dakota heard her.

"It's prime property. The land is good, and it's mostly flat. Very little grading would need to be done, and on top of that, Shoop sees you as an easy target, because you are a childless widow."

Raising a fist, she banged it against the window frame in anger.

"I am not an easy target. This is my home, and he will not get it."

"That's the fire you need to fight him, Anna. Keep that spirit."

Although feeling a bit like a child in a fit of temper, she raised her voice anyway. "I don't want to fight. I don't like fighting. I want everyone to leave me alone, and I want Shoop to be gone. I want Liam to explain why he did what he did." Her voice lowered as she whispered her true wish. "I just want everything to go back to normal."

The heat of his body pressed against her back as his arms circled her waist. Needing the comfort, she leaned into him, if only for a little while.

"Ever since I met you, my life has gone crazy, and I can't take it anymore. I want my peace and quiet back."

His voice, soft and low, spoke behind her head.

"Since the day you met me?"

"Yes!"

His arms slid from her sides, and she worried at the loss of his warmth, second guessing her words.

She turned to him in time to see a look of profound sadness touch his face, before it disappeared behind his normal mask of calm assurance.

"No! Dakota, no. That's not what I meant. It's just that I used to have a life of order and peace. I worked hard, yes, but I came home to a quiet home, a clean home, with just Jake and Miranda. There's just been too many people around. Too many crazy things going on, and I can't cope."

He backed up a step. "You want the peace and quiet you always talk about back again. You want to go back to just you, Jake, and Miranda."

"Yes! Is that too much to ask?"

"Would you like me to move out? To move over the barn?"

"I don't know. Maybe." She stepped closer to him. "I don't know what I want anymore."

For just a moment, tenderness lit his eyes as he looked to her, but it was quickly gone, replaced once more with a shadow hiding his feelings.

"Thought should come before speech. Remember that."

He turned and walked away, swinging through the kitchen door softly. In seconds, the backdoor clicked shut, again, and her stomach clenched with her worry. What had she done?

He stayed away until he knew she'd gone to bed. With the cat-like silence she sometimes hated, he slipped into the house and gathered his few belongings, but before he carried them to the cold, lonely apartment above the barn, he quietly opened her door and watched her sleep.

He contemplated the complexity of the woman who slept

curled in a ball in the center of the queen-sized bed. Her angelic face was hidden beneath a mass of tousled hair, but he knew it well. He didn't need to see her to know how beautiful she was, although why she didn't believe it, he couldn't understand.

Not just her face was beautiful, though. The woman inside was all that was beautiful and human. She was definitely human, but she tried to be invincible. To him she was strong, yet weak, young, but old in experience, sensual, but seemingly unaware of it, intelligent, but capable of doing the dumb things humans did, and sometimes unable to accept her own flaws.

She was also protective of herself. She wanted him only when her needs overpowered her and pushed him away the rest of the time. She refused to let him inside her heart. Twice they had made love, and she still wore her wedding ring. He often found her twirling the ring on her finger, and it grated on his nerves, but he'd never mentioned it.

He closed the door and silently left the house and her behind, his heart heavy.

Later, as he lay down on the single mattress in the barren apartment that still had no food, curtains or any other adornment, he wondered why he kept trying to find love and failing.

Was it that he could freely give his love but the two women he'd given his heart to were incapable of returning that love?

No, his wife had loved him. He knew it. Yet that love had changed and slowly died as they lost each child.

He closed his eyes and shivered against the cool dampness of the room.

Maybe it was time to accept defeat with Anna and go home.

Chapter Twenty-six

The day before Christmas, Anna awoke feeling like death was coming to claim her. Her head pounded, her throat was raw, her stomach queasy, and her body ached so terribly she didn't want to move a muscle or bone. She was supposed to fly out that night to visit her mother for the holiday, finally quieting her persistence, but moving anywhere beyond her bed would take more effort than she could muster.

She hadn't told her mother about her involvement with Dakota. She wasn't sure she was ready to share him with anyone, although she wondered if she had anything left to share. He'd moved to the apartment over the barn after their words, and her house had once more become quiet. She found that it had strangely become a bit too quiet. She had grown used to him being in her life.

She really didn't see him all that much, except for the times she went to the barn to check on her livestock or to ride Maggie. He remained polite and considerate, but there were no more kisses or gentle touches to warm her lonely heart. There were no more shared dinners or nights watching TV by his side.

Occasionally, he knocked on her door and sheepishly asked if he could steal some food. With tremendous guilt, she had packed bags of canned foods and a few meats and had written him a check for some of his back pay. She couldn't be responsible for him starving to death.

It was plain to see by his masked expression that she'd hurt him, but she was so terribly afraid. In just a few months her life had been turned upside down, and nothing made sense anymore. Her biggest fear was he was falling in love with her. She'd seen it in his eyes when they had made love in the gazebo, and she didn't want that. She wanted only to enjoy what little time she had with him.

She knew he had another life and that he'd leave, someday. As with all the others who had left her, he would one day become nothing more than a memory. He would become someone she could think back on and cry or smile about when the loneliness invaded once again. No, she couldn't allow her heart to become involved this time.

With a groan, she also knew she had to move, or she'd have a problem. She stood, wincing when her feet met the cold, wooden floor, but she had no choice. Not even a cold or flu could stop Mother Nature.

However, standing caused an issue she hadn't foreseen, and she just made it to the bathroom before she was sick. After being violently ill, she cradled her head as she leaned over the sink and brushed her teeth. She felt wretched. What a way to celebrate a holiday.

Shaky and weak, she held the walls to cautiously make her way back to her bed, shivering as she crawled beneath the warm covers and hid her eyes from the blindingly painful sunlight coming through the windows.

The sound of Jake bounding up the steps made her grimace, and she ground her teeth against the clicking of his nails on the wooden floor. A cold, loving nose pushed against her face in concern, and she opened her eyes to her best friend, wishing she could greet him with a smile, but the movement would be too painful.

"Hi, buddy. I'm not gonna be much good for you today." Her gravelly, raw voice was unrecognizable to her, and obviously to Jake, also. He tilted his head and studied her, then prodded her one more time, smelling her face. Apparently

satisfied she was who she was supposed to be, he leaped onto the bed.

The jerking motion of the mattress made her cry out as a
knife slashed its way across the inside of her head. She
grabbed her skull, trying to stop her brain from bouncing
around. Just moments later, the man who normally moved
about silently also pounded up the steps. Why was everyone
walking so loudly this morning?

"Anna? Was that you? Are you all right?"

She didn't know how or why he was in the house, but his
presence was welcome—and necessary. His concern was obvious as he came to her side and knelt down.

Opening her eyes to no more than a mere sliver, she
looked at him—freshly shaven, eyes bright and questioning,
and smelling like heaven. She groaned at his healthy state.
She hated him at the moment.

"Go away," she croaked through her raw throat, closing
her eyes against the pain in her skull.

Cool hands came to rest on her wrists and lowered them
to her sides, and then one of them pressed against her forehead.

"You're sick," was the obvious statement.

"Ya think?" She was feeling sorry for herself and cantan-
kerous, but she realized she was also being a bit mean. She
reckoned she'd been mean enough to the man lately. "I'm
sorry," she groaned into her pillow.

"You've got a fever. I'm going to get you some medicine."

He stood and walked away, his footsteps loudly echoing
inside her bouncing brain with his exit. Where were his cat-
like footsteps when she needed them the most?

Jake laid his heavy body across her legs, his senses clearly
telling him something was wrong. His warmth was soothing
as it heated her frozen toes yet did nothing for the shivering
in the rest of her body.

By the early afternoon, Dakota had brought her tea with herbs, acetaminophen for her head, twice, heated up some chicken soup, and had bathed her hot forehead. If she hadn't felt so awful, she would've enjoyed his tender care, but it was impossible when she was sure death was right around the corner, waiting.

As the late afternoon sun turned a dusky moonless blue, the pain in her head had lessened enough for her to call her mother and cancel her trip.

"Do you need me to come there and help you?" was her mother's quick reply when she heard her daughter was ill, for Anna was rarely sick.

"No, Mom, don't be silly. I'll be okay. It's only the flu. I just need to sleep. I'll call you when I feel better, but Mom, please, do me a favor and cancel my flight for me. I'm sorry that you will lose the money. I'll find a way to repay you."

"Don't worry about it. These things happen. You take it easy."

When silence on the other end of the line penetrated Anna's foggy brain, she set the phone down and slept.

And slept.

She slept for three days, barely remembering the moments when Dakota forced tea and medicine down her throat. Through a fog, she seemed to remember another voice in the room, but she had no idea who it was and didn't care. Another tornado could've torn through her home, and she couldn't have lifted her head to see it.

She awoke on the fourth day feeling much more like herself and asked Dakota if she had been dreaming or had there been another person in her bedroom.

"I called the doctor and had him check on you."

"You did what?" Her voice rose with the question, and her hand flew up to hold her head against the pain. It wasn't hurting if she lay still, but the jerking, low shout had jarred her, and she was painfully reminded she still wasn't feeling her best.

Lowering her voice to a whisper, she confronted him. "Why did you call the doctor? I can't afford that. I'm barely making it as is."

"Stop worrying about it. Get some more rest and we will figure it out later."

Her last thought as she drifted off was *there is no money to figure it out later*.

On the fifth day, she felt human again. She needed to get up and get her energy back. Rising, she made her way to the bathroom, but again she barely made it there before she was sick. Unfortunately, there was nothing in her stomach to empty, and she wretched with the dry heaves off and on for over ten minutes.

When she finally opened the door of the bathroom, Dakota was standing there.

"I don't know what's going on. I feel better, but my stomach still isn't quite right."

He had placed a cup of tea and some toast by her bedside, and she grimaced when she saw it.

"Please, get that out of my sight," she begged.

Crawling back into bed, she pulled the covers over her head and hid.

Just before lunch time, he came back into the room. Through narrowed eyes, Anna watched him as he moved to her. With cup in his hand, he sat down on the side of the bed, the action rolling her limp body towards him.

"You're going to eat this soup. You can't get better or gain your strength unless you get some food in you. Besides, we have to get you moving and cleaned up. I made a one o'clock appointment with the doctor. I talked to him, and he wants to see you."

She couldn't figure out if she was mad at him for wasting more of her money or feeling sorry for herself, but she started crying.

"Anna, honey, please, don't cry. We'll get this all taken care of, but we have to get you well."

As if she were a child, he fed her the chicken noodle soup, which went down surprisingly well. Once she'd eaten every drop, he helped her to the bathroom to bathe. It was the first shower she'd had in days.

She could literally feel her pores opening under the invigorating hot spray, cleansing away days of fevered sweat. Standing almost motionless, she let it beat against her flu-ravaged body until her muscles relaxed, her breathing eased, and the water grew cold. By the time she was done, she felt energized for the first time in a week.

Able to dress herself in comfortable jeans and a sweatshirt, she smiled a bit at her accomplishments.

She was still weak though and moved gingerly down the steps, fearful of falling. Dakota must've heard her slow, thumping gait. He swung through the door from the kitchen, moving swiftly across the room and up the steps, as if fearful for her. Wrapping an arm around her waist, he guided her down the final steps. She felt cared for as she curled into the cushion of his arm, rested her head against his chest, and thanked him, her guilt once more assailing her from the way she had treated him lately.

She sat on her couch, happy to be out of her bedroom for a change. "I'm feeling better. I want to cancel the doctor appointment. It's a hundred dollars I can't afford right now."

He stood not three feet away, looking uneasy, as if warring with himself to force her to go or cancel, but he gave in to her wishes and called to cancel the appointment.

By evening, they sat together on her sofa eating and watching TV. He'd been considerate of her stomach and made scrambled eggs, toast, and tea, and by bedtime she felt so good that, despite all her misgivings, she took his hand

and led him up the steps.

The next morning however, as she rose from her bed, her hand flew to her mouth, and she once more took off for the bathroom.

A little while later she exited on shaky legs to find Dakota sitting on the side of the bed waiting for her.

"I'm scared. Something's wrong with me. Maybe I should have kept that appointment yesterday."

His gaze traveled the length of her, and she was afraid of what he saw. She knew she had lost weight she couldn't afford to lose. Did she look terribly ill? Was she even uglier now?

"Why are you looking at me like that?"

He opened his mouth but closed it, as if unsure whether he should ask what was on his mind.

CHAPTER TWENTY-SEVEN

He gave her another strange look, and she grew uncomfortable as she watched uncertainty pass over his face.

"I'm sorry to ask this. I know it's very private, but when was your last period?"

The question startled her, and she barked out a laugh at the absurdity, but with a dawning realization she groped her way to the bed and sat down next to him.

"No. It can't be. Charles and I tried for years to have a baby. I can't get pregnant. It's ridiculous."

She gasped, and frightened, she turned to him and gripped his arm in a firm hold. "With all that has been going on, I didn't notice. I should have had it weeks ago. Dakota, this can't be happening. What am I going to do?"

She waited for him to say something, anything. Where were his words of wisdom? Where was his deep insight that always soothed her? She shook her head, refusing to believe she could be pregnant. It wasn't possible. "It has to be something else. This has to be some type of sickness. I know I can't get pregnant," she insisted.

His lips came to rest in her hair, and a feather soft kiss pressed against her scalp. He still didn't say anything, and she grew even more anxious. Whether she was pregnant or sick with some disease, she wasn't prepared to handle it either way.

"Talk to me!"

"Anna, hush."

She tilted her head back, their eyes connecting in a shared

anxiety of the future.

"I think that first we need to take you to the doctor and get you checked out. If you are pregnant, we'll talk about it. If it is something else, it's best we find out what it is. I'm calling the doctor again."

He kissed her once more on the forehead and stood, walking from the room. Moments later, she heard him downstairs. His voice was a deep mumble through the floorboards as he talked to the doctor's office. Upstairs, she sat alone, frozen in her fear. This was supposed to be a simple flu that she would get over within a few days. Now, in the space of a few minutes, her world had shifted, again. Her heartbeat, an erratic thumping within her body, felt as if it would pump its way out of her chest.

Why did life keep throwing large boulders in her way that she had no idea how to move? What type of sickness did she have? She still refused to believe she could be pregnant. A baby?

She shook her vehemently side to side. No. She wasn't pregnant. She was too old to have a baby. The child would be seventeen when she was fifty, for heaven's sake. Not to mention that her life was too busy already. She barely even got a chance to rest now, except for a while in the evenings.

How could she take care of a baby? How could she afford to feed one? What about the diapers, and clothes, and crib? Her mind was in a full-blown panic by the time she heard Dakota's footsteps on the stairs.

"They're going to fit you in on their lunch hour in twenty minutes. We have to go now."

Her body shook as she stood, her knees wobbly beneath her. A wave of nausea hit her, and she stood absolutely still, breathing calmly, praying it would pass. It did, fortunately.

Nervous, she fumbled with the buttons of her blouse as she dressed. Once that task was completed, numb with fear, she followed him down the steps.

Her Christmas tree stood abandoned in the corner of the living room, the flickering lights silent, the few presents underneath still unwrapped. She had completely forgotten about Christmas. What a great holiday this had been.

With Jake and Miranda safely locked inside the house, she slowly followed him to his truck, feeling as if she was heading toward a guillotine. Overly dramatic, she was sure, but she was dreading what news this visit would bring.

She nibbled on a piece of bread during the trip to the doctor's office, desperately trying to quiet her stomach. It did little good. This ride had never seemed so long before. The minutes stretched out before her interminably as her anxiety built. What if she was ill? Would she die? What would happen to the farm then?

The wait to see the doctor was horrid, the minutes ticking by like a dying battery in a clock, the hands moving ever slower until finally, time stopped. So high strung was she that when she heard her name called, she jumped in nervous energy.

Swiveling in her chair, she turned to Dakota.

"Please come with me. I'm scared." She couldn't do this alone.

He came willingly, holding her hand for support and helping her to disrobe and put on her incongruously happy, flower-patterned gown. She grabbed his hand, and he helped her sit down on the exam table. Once she was seated, whether from nerves or whatever was wrong with her, her hand flew to her mouth in horror as she valiantly tried to stop the vomit that rose in her throat. Her efforts did no good as she sprayed the contents of her stomach across her body and the floor.

"Oh, dear Lord, I'm so embarrassed."

As always, Dakota was Dakota, and in the calm way he

approached almost anything, he helped her clean up the mess and asked the nurse for another gown. Several times, she caught him covering his nose from the smell, but he never said a word, and her humiliation grew.

"I'm so sorry."

He smiled but again never said a word. His patience in the face of her mini nervous breakdown was getting annoying.

On a quick knock, the doctor entered and made a face at the odor, asking what the heck had happened. Anna was sure that from head to foot she was the same color as a new red apple. Never had she faced such embarrassment.

"I'm so sorry. I'm afraid I was sick."

The doctor had the grace not to laugh, although Anna was sure she caught a glimpse of a smirk. He walked to a nearby countertop and grabbed a can of air freshener, spraying it around the room and eliminating the odor she had left behind.

"Okay then, let's talk. What's happened since I last saw you?"

Frightened, she struggled to raise her voice above a child-like whisper as she explained about her illness. Dakota interjected information here and there, and they both patiently watched as the doctor scribbled it all down in Anna's chart.

When he stood and set the chart aside, she knew the time had come for her exam, and her nervousness grew again.

"Okay, let's check you out."

He turned to Dakota, "Would you like to stay young man, or would you prefer to wait in the waiting room?"

There was no way she was allowing him to leave now. Even before Dakota could open his mouth with a response, she let her feelings known. "He's staying."

"I guess I'm staying," Dakota answered on a chuckle.

Dakota leafed through a magazine while the doctor examined her from nose to toes. When the time came for the doctor to ask her to scoot down and put her feet in the stirrups, she blushed furiously.

In her nervousness, she'd never even thought about this part of the exam. She'd never even thought of him doing this type of exam, but considering the issue at hand, it was only reasonable.

She cast a quick glance at Dakota. He had seen her naked. He'd made love to her, but this was a whole different ball game for him to see her with feet in stirrups, spread eagle. She was mortified, her face reflecting her embarrassment. She wasn't even sure it had gone back to normal, anyway. Maybe it would stay this color through this whole appointment.

She looked down at her spread knees and back to Dakota, but he was still reading the magazine. She had asked him to stay, and she was too embarrassed to ask him to leave now.

The doctor examined her, pressed low on her stomach in a few places and stood to slide his stool out behind him.

"You can sit up now." With an outstretched hand, he helped her up, then walked over to a chair and sat, opening her chart.

Dakota set the magazine down and came to her side, and she clutched his hand in a firm grip as she waited for the verdict.

"When I saw you at your home, you had every indication of having the flu, but I think there were two things going on. One of which I was unaware of."

He looked up from his writing, and his eyes softened as he gave her a smile.

"You give every indication of being, by my calculations, about six weeks pregnant, but it's very early in the pregnancy. We will run tests to be sure."

She could not return his smile. His confirmation of her

deepest fears shook her to her core, turning her stomach. She let loose with a gurgling burp, which to her ears sounded like a strange sound of nervous strangled air and whatever could have been left in her stomach.

Her hand again flew to her mouth. Dakota released her other hand and stepped backwards as she burped once more, but fortunately that was all she did. She flushed as she watched the men relax. Her mortification could not get much worse.

Dakota, drat him, chuckled at her side and wrapped an arm around her shoulder, guiding her head to rest against his shirt.

The kindness was her undoing. She couldn't help it. A choked moan sounded throughout her chest as she burst into tears, frightened.

"Anna, this isn't welcome news?"

The doctor had been with her though all the years of trying and not succeeding. She quieted and peeked at him from within the shelter of Dakota's arms. "I don't understand how this happened. How did I get pregnant?"

With the familiarity of someone who had known her since a young bride, the doctor's mouth twitched, and Dakota laughed, easing the fragile tension in the room.

Their reaction, however, only increased her humiliation, making her feel dumb. "Oh, for heaven's sake, I know *how* to get pregnant, but how can I *be* pregnant? I didn't think I could get pregnant!"

The last words were almost a shout, and Dakota squeezed her hand to hush.

The doctor smiled at her in a fatherly fashion. "We don't always know why these things happen. The fault could have been with Charles, or maybe, the fault was just with the timing. We will never know, but I can assure you that I believe you are well and truly pregnant."

He scribbled some notes and stood, handing her a few slips of paper. "These are the prenatal vitamins I want you to start, and here is the name of an excellent OB/GYN. Her office is also in this building."

Reading the name scrawled across the piece of paper, Anna relaxed somewhat. She didn't need him to give her this name. The doctor was already her gynecologist.

"I also want you to go get bloodwork done to be ready by the time you have your first OB appointment."

Dakota watched her closely as the doctor spoke, wondering if her eyes could get much wider. The large aquamarine orbs seemed to take up the entirety of her precious face. It was as if she could not believe the words the doctor was saying, as if she had entered some alternate reality. He imagined that for her it probably was. He'd been through this too many times, yet for her it was new and strange.

His work done, the doctor said his goodbyes and left the room, leaving them alone to face the reality of this new development in their lives.

Her hands shook as she tried to dress, and he laid his own over hers, stilling them.

"It'll be okay," he promised, but he grew concerned when she began to mumble incoherently about stupid doctors and finding money for this when she still had a loan to pay and life going a bit too crazy anymore.

Once she was dressed, he guided her out of the office, her face pale, her body quivering. She actually began to scare him.

After he placed her in the truck and went around the front and entered his own side, she grabbed the sleeve of his jacket in a stranglehold that surprised him with its strength. Fragile, sorrowful eyes revealed her innermost fears, and his gaze dropped to the hand clutching his arm, the knuckles white against the fabric. He waited, instinctively knowing that the words she'd utter wouldn't be good.

"I'm so sorry. Please believe me — I never meant for this to happen. I want you to know I hold you to nothing. I always thought I couldn't get pregnant. I give you permission to go. You can leave whenever you want. I'll be okay."

The words flowed from her in a jumbled, anxious rush, and he wanted to comfort her. He knew he should comfort her, but if she had slapped him across the face with all her might, he couldn't have felt more pain from what she said. With a calmness he didn't feel, he patted her hand, lifted it from his arm, and started the truck.

For a moment, she stared at her hand hovering mid-air, feeling as if she'd been discarded. What did the pat on the hand mean? Was he relieved? Would he take her at her word and leave? They both had thought she couldn't get pregnant. Was he angry with her, thinking she'd tricked him?

She had to let him know that wasn't true. If she had had any indication that she could've gotten pregnant, she would never have done what she did, or at least not without protection. Guilt enveloped her and laid like a brick on her mind.

"Dakota, I mean it. I don't want you to think I did this on purpose. I hold you to nothing."

He turned a corner, taking the curve just a bit too harshly, and she grabbed the door handle, gasping at the speed.

"Stop talking, Anna, please."

She stared at him, silenced, and watched the hard stare of his eyes as he concentrated on the road. She didn't quite know what to do or how to make the situation better, and that worried her.

They once more rode in silence, but this silence was deafening inside the cab of the truck as each warred with their own thoughts.

She was carrying a baby. Counting back the days, she realized she had to have gotten pregnant during their time in the gazebo, which made her doctor wrong about how far along she was, but what did he know, he wasn't a gynecologist.

One glorious day in her gazebo, and she was carrying a child — his child. She couldn't believe it. She laid a hand on her lower abdomen protectively. A baby. She had a life growing inside of her. For so many years she had tried and cried, but here she was, pregnant. She shook her head in amazement.

Glancing at Dakota as he maneuvered the road ahead, she saw that he was now frowning, the deep furrow between his brows marring the beauty of his face. A muscle twitched in his jaw as if he was grinding his teeth, and she couldn't help but wonder what this meant to him.

Was he now sorry he ever offered to help her months ago? Honestly, they really hadn't known each other that long, and now they were going to have a child? A car cut them off, and he slammed on the brakes, letting loose a rarely used cuss word. His anger was palpable, and it frightened her.

She looked to him in horror as she suddenly remembered the story he had told her about his wife losing her babies. She hadn't considered how scary this had to be for him. Yes, maybe it would be best if he left, just in case. She wouldn't want to put him through that again.

A woman bundled against the cold weather strolled quickly by the truck pushing a baby carriage, and Anna grimaced. What would she feel like if she lost a child, to experience the pain he had felt? Could she cope with that after wanting a baby for so long? She'd only just had this pregnancy confirmed, yet a protective feeling washed over. Even if she could never afford this baby, she was beginning to get just a small inkling of how his wife must have felt.

CHAPTER TWENTY-EIGHT

As Dakota opened the door to her kitchen, the two of them entered to a rambunctious Jake who bolted out the door after greeting them. He obviously had to go, and apparently, Anna felt the same. She swung quickly through the kitchen door and hurried up the stairs.

Sitting down at the kitchen table, he rested his head in his hands, feeling a bit stunned by the day's revelations. It would take all the strength he had, but he wouldn't leave her alone and pregnant with his child, whether she gave him permission to stay or not. Permission. Even now that word angered him.

He sighed with worry, knowing that if she lost the baby or if she also died, he would face that outcome as well. This wasn't the time to turn coward and run. He'd done that once after losing his wife, but this time, he would be the man the Great Spirit wished him to be and stay strong.

His family had been supportive after the death of his wife and child, but their clinging had annoyed him, and their calls for prayer had grated on his nerves. At that time, he did not want to pray. He'd wrongly felt that the Great Spirit had forgotten him or perhaps was punishing him for some past wrong doing. He'd spent many days and nights hollering at the heavens, bellowing horrible words at a deity he felt had abandoned him.

Now, after much thought and eventual return to prayer, he realized this was his life. This was his path. Life handed you some hard times, and it gave you some wonderful times. His time here with Anna had been good for the most part and had helped him to heal. She alone had been the catalyst that helped him to heal.

Her love of life and her sometimes crazy and misguided strength had closed the gaping hole in his heart and soothed his turbulent thoughts. Her body had cushioned him, lovingly pushing away the desolation that had become his life and giving him a reason to go on. He couldn't imagine leaving her alone, never lying with her again, or never knowing if she had delivered his child.

He couldn't help but wonder how his family would receive this news. The last they had seen him he had been mourning the loss of his wife and child and in anger, then left them. Now he had to tell them he had fathered another. They would wonder about his reasoning and worry about this child just as he would. He also wondered how they would receive the news that this child would be half-white. A few within their community had married white women and men, but no one in his immediate family had done so, yet. He would be the first. Would they accept her? The baby?

He heard the tap of her shoes on the stairs and rose from the chair, drying his eyes, not even aware that he'd been crying. Turning on a burner on the stove, he filled the teapot to prepare her favorite tea and shield himself from her eyes. He didn't want her to see the evidence of the pain she'd caused by her words or to know the fear within him. She had enough to deal with.

The door opened on a soft swoosh, and he listened as she moved quietly behind him, sliding a chair from the table and sitting. He quickly glanced at her and winced. Like a child afraid she would be chastised for some wrong doing, she sat quietly, hands folded on the tabletop, as if waiting for her punishment.

He couldn't recall a more awkward moment in his life.

The rise of the teapot's shrill whistle broke the loud silence of the room. Swiping his fingers across his eyes one more time to erase the evidence of his own pain, he turned off the burner. His actions were the stuff of reflex as he prepared the tea unthinkingly, dipping the bag, stirring in the sugar.

He walked to her side, set the steaming cup in front of her, and crossed to the refrigerator to grab her cream. Moving around to the opposite side, he sat, staring down at his own cup. Neither looked up. Speaking to the chipped, white teacup, he gave voice to his thoughts.

"Anna, you wounded me in the truck when you said you wouldn't hold me accountable for the child. That you gave me permission to leave was inconsiderate. I am the father of that baby. I had just as much a hand in the creation of that child as you and have just as much right to be in that child's life."

Hearing a choked sob, he cringed. He didn't want to bring her more pain or come across meanly, but he had to tell her how much she'd hurt him.

"I will admit that I am scared. You know my history, but what if this child grows strong and is born healthy? How could either one of us deny that it is wanted? I will be here for you through the whole pregnancy and afterwards."

When he finally looked up, he was crushed. She made not a sound, but tears threatened along the lids of sad and broken eyes that looked to him without the slightest flicker of hope.

"I don't want you to cry. It'll be okay. We will make it okay."

Her laugh was a bizarre bark of incredulity, mocking him. "How can you say it will be okay? Look at what we face. I'd given up on ever having a child, but now that the reality of this is in front of me, I wonder if I will be a good mother."

She looked to the teacup as if surprised it was in front of

her and picked up her teaspoon, staring at it. Sighing, she dipped the spoon into her tea.

"But most importantly, I'm scared because I–I mean we– cannot afford this child, and how can I have a child and care for it when I have so much work to do around here? I'm not saying I don't want this baby, but I can't see how it will work. We will have to hire help, and we can't afford that. There are too many obstacles, and I don't know what to do."

Her voice was tremulous, her anxiety clear. She grew quiet, and he watched as she put teaspoon after teaspoon of sugar in the tea he had already sweetened and stir it absentmindedly in small circles. He knew she didn't even know what she was doing and that he would have to stop her before she took a sip. That tea would be awful.

Dakota lowered his eyes and stared at his hands as they surrounded his own cup. The silence was loud as they each dealt with their own confused emotions, but he knew he had to calm her, assure her.

"I have seen you with Jake and Miranda. I have seen you with the animals in the barn. You watch over them with the eyes of a mother. You care for them with the love of a mother. I cannot think of a single person who would be a better mother than you."

A noisy, bubbly sniff was the answer to his words. She was crying so hard her nose was running, and he stood to reach for a napkin. She grabbed it quickly.

Sitting again, he struggled with what he knew he had to say. He had kept this from her. He had kept his past private. Heck, he had kept pretty much everything quiet, but in the face of her fears he knew he had to give her some relief.

"You don't have to worry about money."

"What?"

He looked up at her. "You do not have to worry about money. I have money."

She stared at him for a moment until a comical look of disbelief crossed her face and she burst out laughing. When he forced himself to remain impassive, she quieted. "What are you talking about? How can you have money? You have been working here for almost no salary, for heaven's sake."

Her eyes widened, and she pinned him with a look of disbelief. "You've borrowed food from me. I had to give you money to stock the apartment. Why, even the first day I met you, your stomach was growling from hunger."

"I borrowed food from you in order to check up on you. I was fine. I didn't need you to write me that check, and if you check your bank account, I've never cashed it. As for the first day we met, it was only hunger, which I took care of at the diner in town, after I left you."

She looked at him incredulously. "You were checking up on me?"

"I had to make sure you were okay. There's nothing wrong with that."

She shook her head and brought her forehead down to rest on the table, speaking to the cool tabletop.

"You can't have enough money to raise a child. Do you have any idea how much money it takes? There's a crib, diapers, clothes, bottles, doctors, babysitters, and I don't even know what else. You can't have that kind of money.'

Her hand hit the teaspoon that lay beside her cup, and she looked at the tea again as if she'd forgotten it was there. She lifted the cup to take a sip, and before he could stop her, she choked on it.

Standing, she walked to the sink and dumped it before she swiveled around and looked at him. "Oh, my God, my mother. What will she say?"

He'd had enough. She was going to drive herself crazy if she kept this up, and she would take him along with her. The chair kicked out behind him as he stood.

Going to her, he grasped her gently by the upper arms and forced his voice not to reveal his frustration.

"Who cares what anyone else thinks? What we think should be the only thing that matters. A child is the greatest gift we can give ourselves. There is a Lakota proverb, Anna, that you need to hear. *The ones that matter the most are the children.* This child will be valued and loved. This child will be cared for and nourished–together. You and me. We created this child, and we'll protect it."

She lowered her gaze to his stomach, as if still unsure and too afraid to reveal herself if she looked to him.

He placed his hand under her chin and felt the trembling. Lifting gently, he revealed what was in his heart. "Anna, I love you. I love that you are having our child. I am glad that we could do this."

The tears began again as he pledged his love, becoming a waterfall coursing down her cheeks. He continued to hold her gaze, trying to figure out the myriad of emotions that played across her features.

"You love me?"

"I wouldn't say the words lightly. I've loved once before. I know the feeling well, and if the Great Spirit has seen fit to grace me one more time with a chance to love, then I thank him."

Her lips trembled when she smiled through her tears. Reaching up, she wrapped her arms around his neck, brought him down to her salty lips, and kissed him.

As they broke the kiss and held on to each other, he waited, but she didn't say the words back. Her silence was like a second knife to his heart. She relied on his help, she'd had sex with him, but she continuously held him away from her heart. He called himself a fool again and wondered what he'd gotten himself into this time.

CHAPTER TWENTY-NINE

Early in the morning almost a week after her doctor's visit, a low growl awakened her. It had to have been hours before dawn. The sky outside was still a deep, dark blue with only the light of a half-moon filtering through her window.

Dakota had moved back from the barn when they'd discovered she was pregnant and now slept by her side, and she really didn't mind anymore. He was helpful each time she raced to the toilet. Her stomach raged a war every time she even thought of standing up.

She stirred groggily to see what was bothering Jake and found Dakota alert and already on his feet.

Jake's growl became a long, low howl that made her skin crawl. She wanted to see him and reached to her side, flipping on the light, blinding them all for an instant.

Looking at Jake, she saw the hair on his back had risen, and his ears stood up at attention, flipping back and forth in effort to capture the sounds he heard. She knew her Jake. If he was unnerved, it was something she needed to pay attention to.

With a wave of his hand, Dakota motioned for her to turn the light back off, and she obliged, casting the room into gray shadow once more. The pale moonlight softly lit his features as he stood by the window, searching the darkness outside with the eyes of a hawk.

"What is it?" she whispered.

"I don't see anything. I'll take Jake, and we'll check it out. Please, Anna, stay here where you both will be warm and safe."

Throwing on clothes, he rapidly made his way down the steps. She rose and went to the window to stand where he'd just stood moments earlier. In mere seconds, she watched as Dakota and Jake made their way out the back door, Dakota slipping his arms into a jacket as he followed Jake's lead. He took Dakota across the field and towards the grove of trees that sheltered her gazebo and she grew alarmed that someone could be lurking in those woods. Would someone destroy her gazebo?

She watched them both until the night covered them and still stood waiting for any signs of trouble. The night was deathly quiet without Jake and Dakota and so very dark. Darkness hadn't been her friend for a long, long time and she wished for their quick return.

An unusual creak sounded just outside her bedroom door, and on edge, she swung around to peer into the darkness. A strange pinprick sensation moved along her spine. This wasn't just her normal fears.

"Is someone there?"

Eyes squinting, she searched the shadowy doorway to find the source of her unease and blinked against a flash of metal that shouldn't be there. A shiver stole over her body as she realized it was a gun pointed directly at her.

He separated from the shadows and moved forward, and she cringed as the ghostly gray features of his face materialized in the filtered moonlight.

"Mrs. Scott, I find you alone at last."

"Shoop, how did you get in my home?" She hissed the question at him, angry that he had fooled them all.

"It's easy. Once that man of yours ran out the back door, I was able to slip in."

"Why are you here?"

"I have this little problem, Mrs. Scott. I don't like it when people thwart my plans."

She backed up a step, wanting desperately to get as far away from him as possible, but with a gun pointed at her she knew she wouldn't get far.

"I don't understand. Why my land? What's so special about this property?"

"It's simple, really. It's what I want, and I always get what I want. I stand to make a pretty penny from this sale, and I plan to go as far away from this God-forsaken town as I can get. Come with me, Mrs. Scott. I haven't much time before your lover returns."

She sucked in a breath at his words, wondering how he knew she and Dakota had been intimate.

A chuckle, cruel and grating, sounded from deep within his throat. "Surprised? You shouldn't be. I'm very good at what I do. I make it my business to know all. Maybe you shouldn't be so open about your lovemaking in front of windows, but I found it most exciting to watch. You are quite a hot-blooded woman."

Bile choked her as her stomach rose up to meet her throat. He'd watched her and Dakota in the gazebo. That was the only time he could've seen them. Such a special time between them was now forever marred by the thought that his probing eyes had been watching, that he had seen them naked and in the throes of passion.

His muffled laughter echoed around the room at her silence. "I'm thinking, maybe, I'll see if I can spark that kind of fire in you before I am done with you, hmm?"

He moved swiftly and grabbed her by the hair, pulling her close against him. His cold, wet lips smashed down upon hers. She raised a knee to injure him, but he was quick. Backing away, he growled an expletive and grabbed the sleeve of her nightgown, yanking her towards the stairs.

"Come with me, if only to protect the life that grows within you."

When she tugged away from him, he yanked her forward, losing his patience.

"Quickly now, we haven't much time."

In his haste to pull her, she slipped and tumbled into him. Cursing, he grabbed her up, hauling her the rest of the way down.

"Where are you taking me?"

Continuing to drag her forward, he muttered one scary word. "Away."

Her fear could not get much worse.

He didn't bother with the back door where he had entered but turned the key in the front door and tugged her across the porch and front lawn, the gun glinting as it wavered in the pale moonlight.

The night was bitterly cold. It wasn't long before she began to shiver violently in her old flannel nightgown and bare feet, the ice-covered snow crunching between her toes as he pulled her.

If not for the gun, she would've fought him, but she wasn't just Anna anymore. She was carrying another life inside her own, and she didn't want to bring on any unnecessary violence—if she could help it—until Dakota found her, until someone, hopefully, saved her.

Her stomach heaved, and she gulped against the wave of nausea until her mouth watered with the effort. Whether from the terror of being dragged away from home by this man or the baby, she knew she was going to be sick. She was not going to be given a choice.

As she opened her mouth to warn him, the contents of her stomach flew down the side of his coat and pants, and he let go of her long enough to curse.

"You bitch!" The name was uttered in a furious, angry hiss between clenched teeth. He couldn't shout, yet she was sure he wanted to. He was incredibly angry, but he knew Jake or Dakota would hear him if he hollered. He wasn't stupid, this one. He could, however, let his anger go in another way. With just a flicker of warning, his arm rose, and she moved just in time to avoid his beefy hand as he swung towards her face.

Having never been hit before in her life, she cowered as he stepped forward, fearful that he would try to strike again. "I'm sorry. I can't help it."

"Bullshit! This is why I don't involve myself in this messy side of things, but that bumbling idiot from town screwed everything up. He's the one who should be doing this!"

He lurched towards her once more and grabbed her by the throat, his face inches from hers.

"Don't piss me off."

Wrapping her hands around his fingers, she dug her nails in, fighting his brutal strength. Just as stars began to burst in her vision, he released her and laughed as she fell backwards. Coughing and gagging against the discomfort, she rubbed the area where his bruising fingers had just lain. He was going to kill her, and the child she had waited so long to hold would never be born. Tears threatened, but she wouldn't allow them to fall. She would show this man no weakness.

Again, he grabbed the sleeve of her gown and yanked, dragging her with him. Her toes were beginning to freeze, making her feet uncooperative, and the shivering had turned to great shudders throughout her body. Struggling to breathe with the pace he set, she wondered where he was taking her, but as they rounded a bend in the road, she saw his car.

Panic stricken, she knew if she got in that car she'd be lost. She had to stay out of that vehicle.

She slowed her breathing, counting the breaths in an effort to slow her racing heart, to think clearly how she could save herself, to slow time. Searching her brain for something to delay him, she grabbed hold of one image in her mind, and in what she hoped was a perfect imitation of what she had seen on TV, she rolled her eyes up into her head and collapsed in a less than graceful swoon to the ground. The snow was painfully cold and melted against her nightgown swiftly, but she had to try her best to slow him down.

As he was still holding on to her arm, the action of her supposed fainting jerked him sideways and knocked him off balance. His voice rose this time as he began cussing once again, and she prayed Jake would hear. She called to both Jake and Dakota over and over in her mind to save her, to save her baby.

"Get up, you bitch. I've had enough of your crap. If you had only sold to me in the first place, none of this would have to happen."

At her lack of response, he grew angrier and dragged her across the snow. Rocks and sticks painfully poked her in the side, but she didn't help him. She made herself a lead weight, slowing his progress. Her mind silently screamed for Dakota to find her or to find some way to defend herself. She had to get out of this mess somehow.

Once he reached the car, she peered at him through narrowed eyes and fought the urge to giggle. He looked to her and the car door comically as if trying to decide how to get her inside. He mumbled barely intelligible words, and she hid her face and smiled. She'd do all she could do to stop this maniac.

Bending over his enormous stomach with a grunt, he struggled to wrap an arm around her middle. He clawed at anything he could find and yanked her roughly up against his body. Her swoon was no longer effective when she gagged at his odor. He'd been sweating profusely despite the cold, and the smell of that sweat mixed with her vomit and the stench of stale cigarette smoke that clung to his clothes and breath, did weird things to her stomach.

She began to wretch. Unfortunately, there was nothing left to purge.

"Don't you do that again! Get in the car."

Opening the back door, he shoved her in, and her ankle connected painfully with the metal door frame. At her cry of outrage, he slammed the door, barely allowing her time to pull in her feet. Anger was quickly replacing her fear. She had to fight.

It was warmer inside the car than the frigid temperatures outside, and her cold, wet body wanted only to stay where it was until warm again, but her desire to live pushed her. She wasn't going to give in easily to this lunatic, and she kicked at the door with leaden feet.

He pointed the gun at her face. "Stop it!"

She quieted, but she watched with observant eyes as he struggled to squeeze his massive girth behind the steering wheel. Before he could put the key in the ignition, she saw her chance, quite possibly the only chance she would get. He hadn't thought to lock her door, and throwing the door open, she took off. Maybe he wasn't as smart as she thought.

Her feet felt like concrete slabs, and she ended up running awkwardly on her heels, slipping several times, but she ran. Adrenaline pumped through her as she ran for her life, despite the pain, the cold and the fear that a bullet would pierce her body at any moment.

Chapter Thirty

He searched the woods around the gazebo, growing frustrated that he couldn't find the source of Jake's unease. There were fresh footprints in the snow, but no sign of anyone having broken in.

Confused that the dog had led him in this direction when there was nothing much here, Dakota rounded the back end of the building, shining his light in the windows and across the wooded area one last time.

Coming around to the doorway, he saw Jake. The dog stood motionless, his ears alert and his nose held high in the air, twitching. With a low menacing growl, he took off out of the woods, all four legs carrying him as fast as he could go.

Jake was a mere shadow, bolting across the snow-covered field by the time Dakota broke from the trees. He was heading straight for the house

Anna! He took off after the dog. Jake knew something.

There was no sign of Jake by the time he got to the house, and Dakota questioned the dog's instincts again, but on pushing through the kitchen door to the living room, he saw what he'd feared. The front door stood wide open, the large room frigid cold evidence of what had transpired. Miranda stood at the door peering out and mewing pitifully.

Wasting no time, he raced through the open doorway to the porch, and that was when he heard it. A sharp, high pitched scream of pain. Terror gripped him that she was hurt. The scream came again, but lower in register this time, and he realized it didn't sound like Anna, but he didn't know what it was. That scared him further. He headed in the direction of the scream, running as fast as his legs and lungs would allow.

He ducked instinctively when a shot rang out, the deathly sound echoing over the barren fields. A cry of pain rent the night, yet what followed that cry was unmistakable. A terrified scream unlike anything he'd ever heard, the sound chilling him to his bones. *Anna.*

He moved forward quietly, with the snow cushioning his steps. He crouched down and inched along the side of the road. Scattered leafless bushes left him little to hide behind, and the crescent moon creating a pale glow on the snow didn't help, but the tense situation in front of him gave him some coverage. No one was thinking about him at this moment.

Shoop stood mere feet away, waving a pistol, the smell of the recent firing still lingering in the air. Anna was crouched beside Jake, who whimpered in pain.

Anger pulsed off the man as he urged Anna into action. "Next it is you, bitch, if you don't get in this car. That man of yours will be here soon, and I need a doctor because of that mutt. Move it!"

Anna rose from her place by Jake's side and faced him, and Dakota watched the amazing transformation. Whether it was brave stupidity or resignation, she stood as tall and proud as she could and awkwardly shuffled towards Shoop.

"Go ahead. Kill me. It's what you wanted. If I'm gone, there's no one to inherit the farm. It reverts to the state, and then you can buy it, right? But guess what, you idiot. You're too late. I already drew up a will, and if anything happens to me, the farm is left to Dakota, so you'd still get nothing, and if you think Dakota wouldn't hunt you down and kill you for harming me and our child, then you really are dumber than I thought."

Disbelieving, he scoffed at her. "You have no will, your stupid bitch. I checked already."

"Ah, but when did you last check? When I started having problems and knew my life may be in danger, I saw my lawyer. The will was just registered last week at the courthouse. You've lost, Shoop, so go ahead, do what you want with me, but you'll still not get my land."

The man stepped back as Anna advanced. The gun shook in his hands at her words, and Dakota watched the terrifying scene before him.

"You're lying. If that was the truth, you would've told me already."

"Well, I suppose you'll find out the truth one way or the other, won't you?"

Hidden behind a small evergreen, Dakota paused. When had she done that? Or was she bluffing? Why would she do that anyway?

This was no time to think on it, and after eyeing up the situation, he moved again. He wasn't sure if Anna could see him as he inched towards the round man from behind, but he prayed if she did notice him, she wouldn't give him away. He also hoped as he tackled him, the gun wouldn't go off and hurt her. Too many things could go wrong with this whole scenario.

Shoop bellowed angrily.

Behind him, Dakota used the distraction to lunge forward, buckling the man at the knees. Unfortunately, the rotund figure crumpled backwards and came down hard on Dakota's back, driving the air from his lungs, Dakota felt the beginnings of a faint as his body was crushed. He shook himself, forcing the faint away. He couldn't fail her. He would not fail another woman.

Anna gasped and ran forward, wrestling the gun from Shoop's hands and turning it on the man who had hurt her

Jake. "I'll kill you for what you did to my dog. Move! Get off Dakota, now!"

The gun was aimed at the man's head, and after letting loose a disgusting cussword, he rolled over and allowed Dakota to scramble out from underneath. He staggered to his feet and stared at Anna.

The gun wavered in her hand as she trembled, and Dakota stood motionless, fearful of what she would do.

"Anna?"

She didn't hear him, or maybe she simply ignored him as she stumbled forward and placed the pistol against the back of Shoop's head. A click of the hammer drawn back, horribly loud in the tense moment, seemed to jolt her awake. She looked at the gun and then to Dakota, visibly trembling.

Before the gun could go off accidentally, Dakota rushed forward and snatched it from her hands.

Immediately she turned and ran back to Jake, dropping down with a thud by his side.

Dakota pulled his cell from his pocket and dialed the police. Still holding the gun on the angry, bellowing man lying face down in the snow, he backed up until he could see Jake. The dog was alive, but obviously grievously hurt. Dark red blood oozing from a hole in his side glittered ominously in the moonlight. Anna clung to him, inconsolable as she grabbed what little clothing she had left and held it over the dog's wound.

Dakota's stared in disbelief when he realized what she was wearing. A soaked, torn, and filthy winter nightgown lay plastered against her skin, and her feet were bare to temperatures below freezing.

Switching the gun from hand to hand, he quickly removed his jacket and urged her to put it on. Slipping from his soft moccasins, he made her put them on despite her protests. They might be damp and overly large, but they were still some protection from the frozen ground.

Shining his flashlight on her face, he saw that her lips were blue and trembling. Her lashes, frozen from her tears, stood in stark black spikes against a face that had gone deathly pale. He was scared for her health and that of their child and looked down the road for signs of help, but the long road was dark and barren.

He waited and wished for them as he held the gun on Shoop, and it was maybe ten minutes before he heard the welcome sounds of sirens above the angry protests of Shoop and the cries of Anna. He wiggled his toes, trying to thaw them to the point of feeling and wondered how she had managed to be without shoes so long in this cold. Unbearable pins and needles of pain began to take over his feet, but he would have given up anything to try to warm her.

Lights flickered along the road, and the sirens grew louder until they reached them, and then a semblance of silence followed once more as each siren turned off.

Martin was the first out of a car and ran up to them, taking in the situation before him.

"You, Gleason, handcuff that man," he shouted to the deputy approaching.

Two medics came forward and looked around, not sure at first who was injured, and he watched with concern as Anna begged them to help Jake. They were people from town and knew her well, friends for years. They spoke to her kindly, ready to argue the laws forbidding her request, but both men were powerless when Anna turned her tear-stained face on them and pleaded for help for her Jake. They sighed collectively as one of the men lifted the dog carefully and carried him to the waiting ambulance.

Dakota pulled the other medic aside as he watched Anna's clumsy, frozen progress towards the ambulance and urged him to check her out, that she'd been exposed to the cold for over an hour. He cautioned the medic that she was pregnant.

Once Anna sat bundled inside the warm ambulance, he went to Martin.

"What exactly happened here, Dakota?"

Dakota kept his toes moving, trying his best to ignore the throbbing as he and the sheriff walked towards Shoop. It had taken three sets of handcuffs interlocked to secure the large man, and his arms were more by his side than behind his back because of his girth. He was still bellowing obscenities while being led by the deputy, his plans foiled by their collective efforts.

Dakota told the sheriff all that happened, as best he knew. Anna would still need to be questioned about what took place before he arrived, but they could pretty much figure out the events of this night.

A siren once again broke the silence, and Dakota relaxed somewhat as he watched the ambulance race down the road towards town, content that they both would receive care. Martin offered him a ride in his car with his siren on to follow, but Dakota knew Anna. She wouldn't go first to the hospital. She would make a beeline for the vet and wake him. She wouldn't care about money this time, and she wouldn't care about herself, despite being pregnant. Her first thought would be for Jake.

"I'll take my truck. I know where she is going. Thanks, Martin. I hope this is all over now."

With that he sprinted awkwardly away from the scene to his truck and stopped when he realized his stupidity. Frustrated that he was being slowed down even further, he ran back inside the house to grab his keys and find some shoes. On a rush of thought, he ran upstairs to his luggage and reached inside to grab a little something he hoped would help.

As he ran back down the steps, Miranda walked up to him, crying, and he bent to pet her.

"All will be okay, little one. I hope. We'll be back soon."

After soothing her cries, he locked the front door and ran to his truck, sliding along the driveway in his haste to get to Anna's side. He knew where the vet's office was. She had pointed it out to him when they had gone to visit her doctor.

He broke all speed limits in his haste to get to her side, and not much later he pulled into a space in front of the building and shut off the motor. A single, muted light shined from within, as if it were nothing more than a night light. Nothing moved. No sign of an ambulance or Anna, and he questioned whether he was right to come here. He knocked on the door, and when no one answered, he wondered if he should've gone to the hospital instead. Maybe Jake had passed, and the ambulance had taken Anna directly there.

Turning to leave, he paused when the door opened and a soft, golden light from inside created a path in the snow. In the shadowed light of a nearby street lamp, she looked the image of an orphaned waif in her dirtied, torn nightgown and swollen, red-rimmed eyes. The tragic image broke his heart.

"Jake?"

"He's in surgery. It's very serious. He lost a lot of blood."

He lifted her into his arms and carried her back to the waiting room, found a chair that would handle their weight, and settled her on his lap. Her skin was still very cold to the touch, despite a blanket the veterinarian had given her, and it worried him. He wanted to demand she go to the hospital, but he knew his words would fall on deaf ears. Instead, he wrapped her tightly within the blanket and held her, allowing his heat to seep into her chilled body.

Time ticked by slowly. Anna alternated between softly

crying against his shoulder and dozing as they waited, and Dakota prayed. The bond between this woman and her dog was strong, the love apparent to anyone who saw the two of them together. He didn't even want to think what would happen if she lost him.

The first rays of dawn crept through the window before the door to the back office opened. Anna awoke when she heard her name being called softly. Spatters of blood covered the man's clothing, and the weathered face looked exhausted.

"I removed the bullet. Unfortunately, I also had to remove about eight inches of intestine. His road to recovery will be long and intense, but unless infection sets in, he should be okay."

"Can I see him?"

"You can, but he is still sedated. I will keep him that way for a while to help him recover. He has been a good dog for me, Anna. You should be proud of him."

"I'm always proud of him."

She walked to stand in front of the doctor. "How long of a recovery do you think he'll need?"

"He'll be here at least a week or two, and then he can go home, but he will need to be kept very quiet for quite a while as he heals."

They followed the vet to the surgery. The normally cold, sterile room was filled with bloodied instruments, gauze, and towels. Her Jake lay sleeping on a surgical table. His beautiful long black hair had been shaved away across his entire stomach, and white bandages were wrapped from back to front holding an even larger bandage across the side of his abdomen.

Dakota knew that seeing her Jake like this would tear a hole through her heart. His own heart broke as he watched her walk forward and lower her head to rest on Jake's, her teardrops wetting the soft black fur.

"Thank you for defending me, baby. Thank you for being brave. Thank you for being in my life. I'll get you through this, I promise."

Dakota stood quietly near the door, and the vet walked from the room, giving her some privacy.

Her voice was a tremulous whisper in the cold lifeless room as she spoke to him. "Dakota, I know no prayers. Do you have one we can say over him?"

She turned to him, and his heart contracted under the weight of her pain. Watery blue eyes looked to him for wisdom and comfort. Although of a different hue, he had seen eyes that earth-shatteringly sad once before. He hated to see her cry. He hated a woman's broken tears.

"I know of no specific prayer, but perhaps this will help."

He walked forward and laid a beautiful turquoise stone by Jake's side, but Anna was too upset to even ask him the meaning. Clasping her hand, he laid his other hand on Jake. Anna mimicked him, laying her right hand against Jake's head. He breathed deeply and looked to the heavens above.

"Wakan Tanka, hear our prayers. We ask for your help. If you can but bring your healing hands to our beloved family member, we will be forever grateful and in your debt. If you choose to bring him home, we ask that you take him gently and to grace us with your strength as we heal."

Anna crumbled down and cried.

CHAPTER THIRTY-ONE

Every morning for the next week Anna awoke and ran to the bathroom. With each trip to the bathroom the same words tumbled over and over in her mind. If this was what pregnancy was, she was sorry she'd ever wished for it. It was exhausting.

It wasn't just the mornings, either. Many afternoons she found herself speeding towards the nearest toilet or sometimes even a sink if the need struck her too hard.

Each morning she got sick, she struggled to get control over her turbulent stomach so she could go see her Jake, who, despite all he'd been through, was showing wonderful improvement. That she couldn't see Jake this morning saddened her, but today she would see her OB/GYN for her first appointment, and she was beyond nervous and excited. There were no more lingering doubts in her mind she was pregnant. It could be the only thing causing such horrible nausea and tender breasts.

As she swung through the door to enter her kitchen, Dakota opened the back door, letting in a rush of bitterly cold air, and she shivered. "Brrrrr."

He laughed. "Everyone is fed and happy. Are you almost ready to go?"

"I'm hungry, but we might as well just go. There's no sense trying to eat. It'll only come back up, and I'm sure not doing that again in a doctor's office."

She did grab a bottle of water and take cautious sips as they made their way to the truck.

As they drove together, they discussed Jake's progress and when he would come home. Neither one mentioned the reason for this trip, because they both shared a reason for being worried. His wife's struggle lay like a shadow over her pregnancy.

For the first time in her life, Anna walked into her doctor's office as a pregnant woman. Other women and a couple of men sat in chairs around the room. Some of the women had bellies showing their advanced pregnancies, some were just beginning to show, and still others had tummies that were flat like hers had been for too many years.

Remembering all those times she'd sat in this room and held back tears of frustration when jealousy had consumed her, she felt a sense of unreality. This was just not what she had imagined she'd be experiencing the next time she saw this doctor.

Dakota sat next to her in calm self-assuredness, leafing through a magazine. She could've smacked him. Inside, she was a bundle of nerves, although she didn't allow it to show on the outside. Her stomach roiled, and she begged it to calm. She was sure this office had seen worse, but she didn't want to be the one who gagged and vomited on its floor. Not again.

Dakota showed her a picture of a dog that looked almost like Jake from the magazine, which again launched him into a conversation about the care he would need when he came home. She knew he was trying to keep her busy and her mind off the impending visit, and surprisingly, she found herself being swept up into the conversation.

Dakota had built Jake a slightly raised bed that he'd placed near the fireplace in the living room, as Jake would not be allowed to go up and down steps for a while. Anna had rounded up old blankets and sewn a soft cushion for her buddy to rest on. Special soft foods the doctor had ordered were purchased and waiting. All was in place. They just needed their little patient.

Her name was called, and Anna jerked, almost forgetting where she was. She stood and held her hand out to Dakota, again needing him by her side for this strange, new experience.

Dr. Maria Alexander greeted her as she took a seat, and Anna introduced Dakota. Short, sweet, and cute, this woman had been her doctor for a long time, and Anna trusted her implicitly. She'd consoled her during each visit when she had wept over her inability to get pregnant, and after all the expensive testing, she'd been the one who told her there was nothing wrong with either of them. Nobody knew why it didn't happen.

"I received a report from your general practitioner and the lab results he had drawn. I hope congratulations are in order?"

Anna smiled at her. "It is now. At first it was a scare and a surprise, but now . . ." She rested her hand on her abdomen.

"I'm happy for you. I know very well the struggle you've been through. Now, your lab results are good, and they confirm your pregnancy. Let's get you back into an exam room and check you out, shall we?"

The doctor motioned for Anna to follow her, but Anna stood and grabbed Dakota's hand, tugging him with her. She wasn't doing any of this alone.

Smiling, the doctor told them to go to exam room four and instructed Anna to disrobe and put on a gown. Shutting the door softly behind them, she left them alone in the room.

Anna looked at Dakota and smiled shakily.

Her nervousness was endearing, and he returned her smile. This was all so new and exciting to her, a happy time. He shared her joy, but it was also scary to him. She handed him her clothes, and he set them on a chair and turned just in time to tie the pale green gown behind her back. Moving off to a corner, he lifted the blinds and looked out the window as Anna wiggled up onto the exam table.

He had been through this so many times. Each time brought the typical anxiety that had warred with happiness, but for him and his wife, each time had ended in pain. She had miscarried early in the first two pregnancies. The third went full term, and they were both ecstatic, only to face devastation. His grandmother had warned them of trouble, that the infection his wife was battling had caused a problem with the baby, and he'd rushed her to the hospital.

The machines they hooked her up to had told a sorrowful story and his poor wife had been faced with the choice of a caesarian section or going through the labor. Either way, she would be delivering a baby that had passed.

His heart clutched around the remembered pain of that day. He hadn't known it at the time, but it had been the beginning of the end for them. Lifting his eyes to the cloudy winter sky, he prayed once more to the Great Spirit to guide him and give him strength, for he truly needed it at this moment.

The door opened behind him, and he let the blind fall, turning as the doctor entered.

With a physician's efficiency, she put on gloves and cheerfully chatted with Anna while a nurse set up all the necessary stuff that was needed for the exam. Anna blushed at the questions the doctor asked, and Dakota found himself smiling at her. Those same blushes had graced his wife's face with the first pregnancy.

Life was repeating itself as he stood by passively watching while her body was poked, prodded, and pushed. The same actions he'd seen in the past. They might be familiar actions, but that didn't ease the anxiety he felt. He knew he'd worry over her until the baby was safely delivered, if it was safely delivered.

The doctor asked Anna questions about how she felt, and Anna bemoaned her misery with the endless nausea and vomiting and that she'd lost five pounds as a result. On a sad chuckle, she told the doctor that her pants had begun slipping down her hips, and she missed eating.

"It won't be long, Anna, before you won't even be able to squeeze into those pants."

Gadgets were placed on waiting tables and all sorts of things strange to a man were passed around as the doctor sat between Anna's legs and Anna lay quietly staring at the ceiling. Dakota was uncomfortable with it all.

"Okay, we're all done here. Get dressed and meet me in my office."

Once more Dakota helped her with her clothes and followed her, worry wrapping around him like a cold blanket.

Anna's hand quivered as she reached for him, once he sat down beside her, and he held her hand in support, watching her nervousness closely. Meeting him had changed her world as she knew it. He wasn't sure how he felt about that. If he hadn't been there, who knew what would have happened to her after the tornado and with all of Mr. Shoop's shenanigans. Coming to learn exactly how strong she was, he figured she would've persevered, although at what cost? If he hadn't been there, though, he wouldn't have planted a baby in her womb, and this child was becoming very important to him and apparently, to her.

He wanted this baby with her. He needed this baby with her, and he needed this woman beside him, but she remained a conundrum to him. She still hadn't uttered the three words he wished to hear, and even now as they sat in a room waiting to hear about their child, she wore the damn wedding ring from her husband.

He hated the feeling of insecurity her resistance built deep within him. She could tell him to go at any moment, and where would that leave him?

The doctor came through the door in a rush and sat down behind the desk.

"Anna, all seems well. I would put you at about ten to eleven weeks along. You have a long way to go yet. I want you to set up an appointment to see me once a month until you're closer to delivery. I also want to set you up for a sonogram."

Anna shook her head slightly, as if confused at the doctor's words. "No, that's wrong. I know exactly when I got pregnant. It was right after Thanksgiving. In fact, it was November twenty-forth. I should be about eight weeks."

The doctor glanced up from her paperwork at Anna's words, but didn't contradict her. Instead, she typed a few more words on her laptop.

"When did your morning sickness start, Anna?"

"I got the flu at Christmas, and the vomiting never stopped after I felt better from the flu."

"Hmmm, that's a bit early for morning sickness, but with you being sick at the same time, it might account for it. I'm going to increase your B6 vitamins. Many times, that helps women with morning sickness. Also, I suggest you keep a supply of ginger ale and crackers in the house. Sip the ginger ale and eat a cracker or two when you first wake. That can also be very helpful with the morning sickness. Hopefully all of that should end by sometime in the late third month, although it has been known to go a lot longer for some."

Informative and efficient, the woman rattled off more instructions before standing.

"I can see you're nervous, but don't worry. We'll get you through this." She smiled, giving Anna some encouragement.

When she had left the room and Anna stood, he heard one single word. "Whew."

Jake came home three days later, but keeping him calm and quiet became a chore neither one relished. He wanted his life to be as he'd always known it and begged to go out and explore. He was unhappy with the cone around his neck and struggled with the bulk of it. The work of keeping him inside and making sure he left the cone alone for the most part fell almost exclusively to Anna, as Dakota was preparing for spring planting and out of the house more than he was in.

Anna found that the only time she could get Jake to truly rest was when she slept by his side, and she found herself sleeping often. Slowly, her baby grew, and slowly, her four-legged baby healed.

CHAPTER THIRTY-TWO

Anna awoke to a gently falling late winter snow. She lay perfectly still as the doctor had advised and she'd practiced each morning. If she stayed still for a while, the nausea lessened.

When she stretched into the warmth of the covers, she realized this morning was a little different. For some reason, she felt glorious. She'd slept deeply, and no queasiness greeted her as she awoke.

Tentatively sitting up, she still felt no turmoil in her stomach, and she smiled but told herself not to be too rash. She stood and walked to the bathroom, the first morning she'd been able to do so without rushing madly for the toilet.

She showered quickly and brushed her teeth. Today was a checkup at her doctor's and then her sonogram. She was beyond excited to see her baby. Already at only fourteen weeks pregnant, her stomach was quite rounded and hard, with the tiniest butterfly winged movements. The first time she felt it, she thought it was a tickle and scratched it, but it didn't go away, and when she realized she was feeling her baby she screamed in joy, which almost gave Dakota a heart attack.

Wrapped in just a towel, she opened the bathroom door to find Dakota walking into the room, bearing her customary ginger ale and crackers.

"Dakota!" Her brilliant smile was not the norm he had

grown accustomed to the past few months. He was taken aback at first, but finding her radiant glow infectious, he smiled at her in return.

"I want bacon! I want eggs! I want toast and orange juice. And I want coffee so bad, even if it has to be decaffeinated!"

With a giddy laugh, she ran up to him and threw her arms around his neck. "I feel wonderful!"

Despite holding her ginger ale and toast, he encircled her within his arms, holding her as tightly as he could. This was what he'd been waiting and hoping for. She had suffered horribly for weeks, barely being able to eat except in the late evenings. He'd wished and prayed it would end, and, hopefully, it now had.

"I'm not sure we have any bacon, but I'll go look, just for you."

He kissed her forehead and backed away as she began to do a little dance around the room in happiness. He chuckled at her enthusiasm, laughing outright when Jake barked and wagged his tag, loving the joy in the room.

Cathartic relief poured from deep inside, as if a burden had been lifted from his shoulders. He had feared for her with the weight loss while she carried his baby. His wife had never suffered this badly with the sickness.

Her parting shot as he left the room to check on the bacon had him laughing.

"If we don't have bacon, we are stopping at the diner on our way to my appointment. I'm ravenous."

True to her word, she made him stop at the diner, and truer to her word, she ate and ate. He didn't know where she put it all. She drank copious amounts of fluid as if she'd been dehydrated, and he smiled in happiness for her. Even the waitress got a kick out of the amount of food she ate. Her eyes were bright, her cheeks flushed, and the smile that graced her face was beautiful. She was happy, gorgeous, and simply radiant, and he had fun just being with her.

Big, fat snowflakes coated everything in sight by the time they got to her doctor's office, and they were surprised to see that they were the only ones who showed for their appointment. The warm, inviting waiting room was completely empty.

"I feel bad, Dakota. I made them wait for me when they probably wanted to close."

"They aren't shoving us out the door, so that's a good sign."

The empty waiting room was a gift that eased her nervousness. They brought her straight back to the exam room, which was a delight, no interminable wait today. After being weighed, the doctor came quickly into the room.

"Good morning, Anna. We will get you examined and on your way before this snow gets too deep."

Fighting the feeling of guilt, Anna climbed up on the exam table. Snow had never bothered her in the past. She owned a four-wheel drive truck, and Charles had taught her how to drive in rough weather. She never gave it a thought that others might not feel as comfortable behind the wheel as she in this kind of weather.

As the doctor examined her, Anna lay thinking of the little life growing inside of her, so it was a surprise that she heard the doctor's questioning voice.

"Anna, are you positive you know when you got pregnant?"

Wondering why she asked, she assured her that she knew the exact date.

"What time is your sonogram?"

"Eleven-thirty, why? Is something wrong?"

"Not really, but I'd like to see the results of the sonogram.

You are just a bit larger than I would've thought at this stage of your pregnancy. I just want to see the results. You are absolutely positive of the date? There wasn't an earlier time that you were with Dakota?"

She had been, but the timeframe was wrong. At her assurance, the doctor's brows drew together in concern. Dakota had stayed in the waiting room this time, and she wished she had asked him to come in. Her doctor's frown scared her. Was this what had happened to his wife? Was her baby in danger? Did she suffer the morning sickness all this time just to lose the baby?

"I'm going to call them and make sure they're still open. I'd like you to go over right away if you can."

The doctor opened the door to leave, but Anna stopped her. "Wait! Is this something I should be worried about?"

"Let's just wait and see what the sonogram shows. You may just be carrying a larger baby. Given the size of the man waiting for you in the waiting room, it's a strong possibility."

The doctor shook her head, chuckling at her own joke, and Anna grasped onto her words with hope, but still worried. By the time she got to Dakota, she was in her typical basket case state, and Dakota stood, worry spreading across his face when she rushed to him.

"Anna, what's wrong?" But before she could answer, the receptionist called out to them, telling them that the radiology office had been trying to get a hold of her to cancel, but on her doctor's insistence, stated they'd stay open until she got there, if she hurried.

Explaining it all to Dakota on a rush out the door, Anna pulled on his arm in her haste to get to the truck.

The roads were indeed filling up with snow, and the drive was slow, but Anna didn't care. . She laid her hand across her belly and kept it there.

227

She refused to believe anything was wrong with her baby. Even at this moment, she felt the flickering of life within her womb. All had to be okay.

As soon as they got to the center, they were both ushered straight back. They lifted her shirt and lowered her pants. Spreading a cold gel on her stomach, she watched in fascination as they ran some type of wand over her stomach, pushing down uncomfortably. She had to pee badly, and this was making it very hard not to lose control of her bladder.

"Anna?" She looked to the face of the sonographer. "Do you have any history of twins in your family?"

Tears filled her eyes and quickly spilled down along the sides of her face. Frustrated, she swiped at them. She was so tearful anymore. Seeing her distress, Dakota came to her side quickly.

"What is it, Anna?"

"I was a twin. My sister, Bella, died very young." On a choke, she muttered, "I was Anna, she was Bella. When my mother wanted us both, she'd just call out Annabella."

"I'm sorry."

She jerked and looked at the woman doing the sonogram. "Wait. Why did you ask me that?"

The young woman turned the screen towards Anna.

"You see the little heartbeat right there?"

Again, Anna teared up and nodded as she saw the proof that her baby was alive.

"Well, do you also see the little heartbeat right there?"

Anna made not a sound as the realization of what she was saying sunk in. She'd been worried about being good enough to raise a child and to have enough money to raise one. Now they were having two?

"I have two babies?"

"Yes."

Swinging her head to face Dakota, she could have

laughed if she hadn't been so shocked herself. The normal rosy hue of his handsome face had paled, and his usual sexy heavy-lidded eyes were wide with wonder and something akin to fear. Nothing much shook up Dakota, but this surely had.

"Dakota, are you okay?"

He tore his focus away from the screen and looked to her, his dark chocolate orbs appearing just a bit moist. He cupped her face in his hands and leaned in for a gentle kiss.

"Thank you," he whispered against her mouth.

The ride home was dangerous, the pace slow, but Dakota handled it with aplomb. He would do everything in his power to protect his family.

His family! He had a whole, big family.

It might not have been the most romantic of occasions, but after making a split-second decision he pulled the truck to the side of the road.

"What's wrong? Why are you stopping?"

"Anna, will you marry me?"

Her reaction was not what he wanted. She quickly looked away from him and grew pensive as she stared out of the window. In the cool gray interior of the truck, with thick, fat snowflakes lying heavy on the world around them, she finally looked back to him. Their gazes briefly touched before she quickly turned away again.

"Dakota, it's too soon. I can't answer that, yet. Please, forgive me."

Crushed again, he said not a word. Defeated, he slipped the truck into gear and began the difficult drive home.

CHAPTER THIRTY-THREE

Anna sat on her swing and watched Dakota and the boys sow the seed that would be her lifeline for the next year. Dakota had been adamant that she wouldn't be allowed to help. She was to rest, take care of the home, the business side of things, and herself. He wouldn't allow her to tire herself out working the fields or even to scrub a bathtub. She found herself rather grateful for the edict, as her energy was quick to leave her nowadays.

The early spring breeze was still just a bit crisp, and he had wrapped her shoulders in a soft, light blanket before leaving to work her farm. The air was refreshing after being cooped up in the house for the long, cold winter, and she breathed in the scent of spring. The sun was high in the sky, warming the ground, preparing it to nourish her crops.

A memory pushed its way into her mind of the day Dakota had held her and told her about the four directions. She glanced up at the sun briefly before the brightness had her looking away. The Southern Sky warmed the earth and allowed growth. She'd never thought much about his words after that day, but now as she watched the men work, she realized how true it was.

The North had brought a bitter winter with bruising winds and heavy snows, keeping them sheltered indoors.

She rested her hand on her stomach, lovingly caressing the lives she carried. The East had given them brand new beginnings, the best direction of all to her.

The West, well, the West had been quiet for the time being. She needed no more death in her life. She refused to look to the West.

Dakota's voice carried over the wind, and she glanced at him. His intelligence astounded her at times. With each word of wisdom or heartfelt prayer he uttered, she came to realize how noble and intelligent the American Indian really was, at least this one.

Never before had she encountered someone with such a tie to all around him, and it made her wonder what his family was like. Would they have the same great strength and wisdom as Dakota?

She rubbed along the bulge of her belly and wondered. Would her children inherit the same wondrous traits, and would he stay around long enough to teach them?

A kick against her ribs made her grimace. She was so large it was unbelievable to think she still had a little less than five months to go. She would be the size of a house at this rate. At times, it felt like a war was going inside her stomach, and she couldn't imagine what it would feel like as she got closer to delivery.

Otherwise she felt wonderful, except for the constant need to tinkle. For the first time in her life she had bigger breasts, and she got quite a kick out of it. She had to buy bras. She'd always been so small she'd never bothered. Now the weight didn't feel comfortable unless she supported them. She often found Dakota staring at their fullness, and she'd laugh. Men were men when it came to boobs.

She scanned the field until she focused on Jake, who stood watching as the men worked. Like her, he was slower these days. His recovery continued, but the vet said he was making remarkable improvement. He didn't run yet, but he did love to go out walking, and that was one exercise she could allow him to do. Nothing could keep that dog down.

Her eyes teared as he sat down and rested on his belly.

Her poor little guy. Remembering the night she'd thought she would lose him, her heart clutched painfully, and a tear spilled over and rolled down her cheek. If that was love, then these babies were in trouble, for she would worry over them constantly.

Her hand felt a slight movement as some part of a baby pushed and squirmed, and she couldn't help it—she giggled. Her babies. She still had a hard time believing it.

Miranda jumped up onto the swing and tried to find her lap, mewing pitifully when she found the task impossible. Anna patted her chest in invitation, and her loving little cat climbed up to rest her body on her plump breasts, snuggled her chin against Anna's neck, and began to purr.

A sense of happiness and security surrounded her, and she sighed in relaxation. Life was quiet at the moment.

Liam had been released on probation and had come straight to her to apologize. Shoop had found an easy target with him. Because Liam's single mother couldn't afford to send him to college, when Shoop offered him a large sum of money to cause minor trouble, he thought it a good way to get away from this small town that was smothering him.

He had explained that he wanted to get an education and make something of himself. Shoop had done his homework well by picking the easiest target.

He'd told her when Shoop had stepped up the pressure and told him he wanted the house burned to the ground, he had refused. He'd told Shoop he cared for the lady of the house and wouldn't want to see her harmed. Shoop had grown angry and told him he would tell everyone of his involvement if he didn't cooperate.

Liam wasn't stupid. He knew somehow what he'd done would get out anyway, and he got the final revenge. He'd made sure to bungle the job, setting the fire poorly, but he'd made a show of doing the job and hoped he'd still get the money for school. Unfortunately for him, that didn't happen once Shoop was sent away to prison.

Liam had sat in her kitchen with his mother by his side and cried when he related the story, and Anna had easily forgiven him. It was not in her nature to hold a grudge. Well, except for Shoop. She would hate him forever, and she was sure no one would blame her.

The piercing shriek of her ever-present eagle made the three men and Jake look to the sky where the large majestic bird hovered almost motionless above them. His only movement was the gentle swaying of his body in the breeze.

His shadow against the radiant sunshine was massive along her field, and she gasped when she realized the shadow covered Dakota. Shuddering, she wondered if it had some type of meaning in Dakota's world. Its constant presence in their lives had to mean something, and she promised herself to ask Dakota about it.

One of the guys must've said something funny. Laughter broke out among them, their voices carrying over the wind, and Anna smiled. She cared about Dakota and stupidly wished their lives would stay like this forever, but she knew there'd be an ending someday. Dakota had a home and a family he was hiding from. She had a home here. The two couldn't mix. At present they were playing house with no entanglements or promises, knowing it would end.

Tears sprang easily to her eyes at the thought of him leaving her. He'd said he wouldn't, but she wasn't a fool. After she had turned down his offer of marriage, his words of forever and love were never uttered again.

The deepest loss for her was his touch. They'd not made love again. He rarely even touched her, unless he was helping her from a chair or up the stairs, and she missed the warmth of his body. For some odd reason at this time in her life she craved it, but each time they went to bed he said his goodnight and turned away from her, leaving her frustrated at the rejection. It was torture to be so close to him and not being able to touch. She'd tried it once and almost cried when he had flipped back the covers and left the room.

He looked to her rarely, but on the few occasions when he did, his eyes told his story. They were shadowed and self-protective each time they briefly connected. She knew she'd hurt him. He was still attentive to her needs, but he just wasn't the same.

She hadn't mean to hurt him, but she still adamantly refused to love. The thought of loving and possibly losing that love terrified her. She couldn't feel that pain again.

Besides, there were too many things to consider in loving Dakota. Would his family accept her? Would he want her to give up her home and move with him? She just couldn't give up this land and all it meant to her. Too many questions and not enough answers.

She lifted her hand and stared at her ring. How could she love another when she still couldn't let go of the one she'd lost? Her brain hurt just trying to figure out what to do, and her peacefulness left her in a rush.

CHAPTER THIRTY-FOUR

With only six weeks to go in her pregnancy, she leaned over her massive belly and attempted to do the dishes. Dakota approached her, took the dishrag from her hand and drew her to a chair. He pulled a chair close and sat, finally looking into her eyes for more than just a few seconds.

"I'm sorry, Anna, but I need to go home. There are things I need to tend to. I received an urgent call today that problems have arisen."

She sighed inwardly as her heart clutched painfully within her chest. He broached the subject she'd known would be coming sooner or later, but she'd hoped he would wait until after the birth. She felt strangely hollow inside, although she knew she shouldn't. She'd been expecting it for months.

She looked away from him. She was too afraid to look at the man she'd become dependent on. It was hard not to be dependent when you looked as she did. She was huge. Her gait was unsteady as she lugged around this weight, and her ability to do even some of the simple things had vanished. She'd come to rely on him to help her with so much.

She whispered the question she had dreaded. "When will you leave?"

"Will you come with me and meet my family?"

Their questions came out simultaneously, and she swung her gaze back to his. He wanted her to go with him. This had been something else she had feared, the possibility of losing her home. Although overjoyed at his wish to remain by her side, she struggled with the answer.

"I don't know if I can. It wouldn't be a good impression to be a blimp the first time I meet your mother. Besides, these two are heavy to carry, and my time is close. That would mean leaving my doctor and finding someone to care for the farm."

"We will only go for a week at most, I promise, but I have no choice. I have to go home, and I don't want to leave you alone right now in this house with no one to watch out for you. You don't have to worry about my family. They are asking me to bring you to meet them."

"You told them about me?"

He slid off the chair and knelt on one knee in front of her as the dark, sensual eyes she had come to care for so deeply looked at her incredulously. "Of course, I did, Anna. They know everything. Please, come with me."

Despite her misgivings, she found herself a week and a half later sitting in the front seat of a comfortable rental car wondering how she got there. She had acquiesced to Dakota's pleas, which was against her better judgement for so many reasons, most especially leaving her home behind.

The bottom line was she was more fearful of losing Dakota's presence at this scary time in her life than she was over being so far from home or facing the total strangers at the end of this journey. She didn't want to admit to herself that she needed him, but she did. She'd been on her own for so long, but it wasn't easy to be independent when you were the size of a small truck. It was unnerving to find herself suddenly reliant on someone else.

Her doctor had cautioned her about the travel. She was already two centimeters dilated, and she urged her to be careful, which only heightened her anxiety. She warred with herself whether to go or stay and had almost denied him, but Dakota had been so sweet in his pleading.

Sweat coated her body as the oppressive summer heat beat down on the black rental car, and she struggled to get comfortable. The air conditioner blasted cooling air across her body, yet it did little to help. She was miserable, tired, and feeling cranky.

The back seat of the car was taken up entirely by Jake, who alternated between dozing and staring out the windows, enjoying the scenery. Though the drive was only a little over six hours, they stopped often to let Jake run and do his business and for Anna, unbelievably heavy with pregnancy, to move around or visit the restrooms along the way.

He still used a cane, but Pop had recovered from his injuries for the most part and had been enlisted to oversee things at the house. He would not be required to do physical labor, only oversee. The boys had been hired full time to run the day to day operations of the farm, and she felt comfortable that they knew what they were doing.

Anna cried like a baby as she said goodbye to Miranda and Maggie, but Dakota assured her it would only be for a week. Ten days at the most. She would see them soon.

She fidgeted with a loose strand of cotton on one of her newer maternity tops as they drew closer and closer. She was fearful of meeting his mother and worried if she would be accepted as easily as Dakota seemed to feel.

She saw his home well before they reached it. The signs along the road they travelled advertising Dakota Dairy Farms were hard to miss. The flat land stretched out forever, and everywhere she looked, according to Dakota, belonged to him.

Dakota had once told her he was a simple man, not requiring much, but what she saw in front of her eyes was not so simple. She should be mad at him for keeping this from her, but his reasons for hiding from his pain were understandable. She wondered how he felt coming back to the place that held such tragic memories.

As they drove down the two-lane country road, her eyes took in everything around her. The farm was massive. The outbuildings themselves stretched for hundreds of yards. To the left was a large sprawling ranch-style white brick home, landscaped with small evergreen bushes all along the front. What drew her attention the most was the smoke that billowed from what seemed like hundreds of colorful tepees and small houses far to the left of the main house. She questioned him about them.

"We are a community. Each tepee and individual home houses someone who works at this farm and their family if they have one. The Lakota believe in generosity and teamwork. If someone of our community has been a bit more fortunate than others, we don't regard it as a competition. We view it as an achievement for all, and we share. These people are all my brothers and sisters."

She watched him as he spoke, then profoundly moved by his words, turned back to study the land before her. If only the whole world could be this way. If only those who achieved would help those less fortunate and work as a community, sharing all. Maybe then there wouldn't be such poverty, greed, and crime. It was powerful to think about.

They came to a gate with a high arched metal sign stating Dakota Dairy, and she thought back to the day she had giggled at Dakota working at Dakota Dairy in South Dakota. What an idiot she'd been to think it all had to do with the farm being in South Dakota. It was Dakota's farm that just happened to be in South Dakota.

By the time he pulled up in front of the beautiful house and helped her from the car, she was quite nervous, and her stomach roiled with anxiety. She leaned her tired body against the car and held on to him.

"What if your family doesn't accept me?"

"All will be well, I promise. You'll find out soon enough."

Frustrated by his constant calm demeanor, she looked up to see an older woman standing at the front door. She was tall like Dakota, but where Dakota was muscular, this lady was willowy and very beautiful. Her coal black hair, streaked with a few slivers of gray, was the only sign she was older. Her face was smooth. No lines or wrinkles interrupted the sun-kissed hue of her perfect skin. Time had been a friend to the lovely woman in front of her.

Dakota turned, and she watched the transformation of his expression. Gone was worry. Gone was the stress of the long drive with a dog and a heavily pregnant woman. Gone was the grown man. It was like he was a kid again as the two exchanged tender smiles. It took seconds for Dakota to leave her and rush to the woman's side. He wrapped the woman in his arms as if they hadn't seen each other in years as respect and love radiated between the two hugging forms. She had to be Dakota's mother.

A pang of jealousy tore through her at the obvious affection these two shared. Anna's own mother was somewhat caring, but she couldn't remember ever feeling the emotion she witnessed before her. Her mother had changed somewhat when they'd lost Bella, but when her father had passed, well, her mother had pretty much withdrawn, hiding behind her fear of loving. Anna, being young, had imitated her, at least until Charles had come along and she had allowed herself to feel love again—and look where that got her.

They spoke to each other in hushed tones as Anna waited, and she wondered if this was the love she could have with Dakota if she only let it. It was easy to see he adored his mother, and she thought back on the times when he had treated her with the same adoration and she had rebuffed

239

him.

Dakota kissed his mother's forehead and brought her down the steps to Anna. Nervous and worried about her acceptance, it took all her willpower to look the woman in the eye, but Dakota had been right. She'd worried for naught. The kind woman looked to her and down to her massive belly and smiled a benevolent smile, putting her at ease.

"Mother, I'd like you to meet, Anna. Anna, this is my mother, Mina Powers."

With the same inner peace she had come to know so well in Dakota, his mother extended her hand and took Anna's own in a gentle grasp.

"Anna, welcome. Please come in and rest. I know you must be exhausted."

Clearly reminding those outside of the car that someone was still waiting inside, a loud bark broke the conversation, and Dakota laughed. "We forgot one important member of the family."

Once Jake was released, he was as before his wound, running in circles, releasing pent up energy and lifting a leg here and there. She laughed along with them at his antics until a wave of exhaustion hit her. She needed to rest.

"Jake, come honey," Anna commanded in a weary voice, and the obedient dog complied, but it was apparent to all that he wanted to explore.

Dakota laid a warm hand against the small of her back, guiding her up the two steps to the enchanting house. They passed through the doorway to a large foyer with hallways branching off to each side, and she looked around at the grandeur of his home. She had never lived in anything so stunningly beautiful. Heck, she had never even been anywhere this beautiful.

The foyer was decorated in stunning, brilliant whites and cool blues, and a sense of serenity lay upon the house like a security blanket, comforting and inviting.

The calming effect was quickly shattered when a shriek that broke the sound barrier sounded from down one of the hallways. In mere seconds a gorgeous young woman flew past Anna and straight into Dakota's arms, wrapping him in a tight embrace and kissing him on the cheek.

Realizing her mouth hung open in surprise, Anna quickly closed it, but still stared at the shapely young girl clinging to Dakota. Her hair was long and thick, reaching her buttocks, but the color was unlike anything Anna had ever seen in person. It vibrated with a vivid mixture of golden blonde and bright streaks of vibrant pinks and oranges in the modern fashion of the young.

Flawless sandstone skin graced her face, and unbelievably long black lashes framed eyes the likes of which Anna had never seen before. They were the same golden brown as the soil she maintained every day on her farm, and they drew her in to the point that she couldn't stop staring at them. Her smile was heart-stopping, and all of this beauty sat atop a body Anna would kill for. She was torn. Should she smile at her obvious joy or be jealous that this woman was in Dakota's arms? Who was she?

Laughing at something the young woman said, Dakota kissed the tip of her nose and stepped back. He turned to Anna and held out his hand, beckoning her.

"Anna, this rambunctious young lady is my baby sister, Winona, who is home on holiday from college. Winona, this is my Anna."

Anna's eyes rounded a fraction at his use of "my Anna," but she checked herself quickly when she found the two women watching her intently.

Winona walked to Anna and enveloped her in a hug, and Anna stiffened. Not used to demonstrative displays of affection, Anna felt uncomfortable, but the young woman was so kind she tried not to let her discomfort show.

"Welcome, Anna," she said, gracing Anna with her stunning smile. Her youthful happiness was infectious, and Anna was drawn in, smiling in return.

Only able to remain quiet for so long, Jake chose that moment to remind her that he was in the room and nudged the back of her knee. She let out a gasp as she felt her legs fold, her enormous belly upsetting her center of balance. Amid the clatter of excited cries of alarm, six arms quickly caught her before she could fall to the floor.

"Thank you," she uttered, flushing in embarrassment. She felt like a beached whale around these slender people.

With a kindness known only to those that truly cared about animals, Winona squatted in front of Jake and graced him with a gentle smile. "That wasn't very nice of you, young man."

Her poor Jake had the grace to look ashamed of himself, and everyone laughed.

"Would someone introduce us?"

"This is Jake. Jake, this is Winona," Dakota said, while keeping his hand on Anna's arm in support.

Jake sniffed the hand Winona extended and wagged his tail with a ferocious force, clearly comfortable with another new friend, and Anna smiled, relieved. She had worried how he would handle this trip. Neither one of them had ever been this far from home before.

His mother's smile was benevolent as she watched her daughter interact with Jake. "Anna, Winona has a way with animals. Rarely does one not like her, and if they don't, she goes out of her way to win their trust."

Winona placed a hand under Jake's chin. "Would you like to come get a drink and a bite to eat, little sunka?'

Obviously worshipping the beautiful young woman, Jake followed Winona obediently down a hall towards the sounds of clinking pots and dishes. His tail swung so far to and fro, he almost slapped his own ribs. He'd truly found a friend if she was going to feed her perpetually hungry dog.

She turned to Dakota, her eyes questioning. "Sunka?"

"Lakota for dog."

"Ah," she uttered. This only confirmed her feelings of being so out of place in this world, and her discomfort grew.

Dakota's mother smiled in understanding and invited her to come sit and rest. Anna gratefully followed, needing to get off her feet. Although she could not see them, she could feel her ankles swelling and knew she had to sit and prop them up. The long drive had been a bit too hard on her.

They entered a coolly shadowed, charming pale blue room, and she paused to take it all in. A sofa took up a greater part of the room in a full half-circle and a large round table stood in the center, topped with a colorful mosaic pattern of an eagle. On the walls everywhere she looked were pictures, hundreds of pictures. Some were obviously newer, some old. Some were absolutely ancient, captured with the large flash photography of the early days of photographs.

Some people stood, some sat in chairs, some even sat atop a horse. Some smiled, some looked downright forbidding. A few were in contemporary clothes of jeans and T-shirts or a suit or dress, while others stood regal in traditional Indian garments. Interspersed throughout were huge, majestic oil paintings of men adorned with beads, feathers, and brightly colored clothing as if they were men of rank.

She turned around in a full circle, her head swimming from the many strange faces staring down at her. To say she felt dazed was an understatement. This was a huge family. All she had was her mother, and the realization of the differences between their two worlds was wildly intimidating. When at last her gaze rested on the final group of pictures, she jerked in surprise.

An ancient woman stared at her in calmness, almost as if her face were a picture itself. She sat in a chair that appeared older than the woman herself, calmly rocking back and forth.

Even with her steady gaze on Anna, her gnarled fingers worked with the needle and threads in her hands. Stark white hair framed a time-worn and weathered face, but her eyes looked to Anna with clear wisdom and strength.

On a table by the woman's side sat several photographs of a young woman and man dressed in traditional Indian clothing. Time had stolen this woman's beauty, but the facial structure and eyes were the same.

Anna smiled a cautious smile in her direction and lifted her face to Dakota for guidance.

"Anna, you will meet a lot of people in your visit here, but none are more precious to me than my grandmother."

He walked forward and knelt on one knee in front of the ancient woman, stilling her active fingers in a curtain of his hands. "Unci, I'd like to introduce you to Anna."

"Come here," the old woman commanded in a voice strong for such a seemingly fragile person.

Anna was tired from the drive, and the babies were heavy and kicking up a fuss inside her. All she desired at that moment was to sit or lie down, but she glanced at Dakota to find him watching her in hopeful anticipation.

She internally sighed in frustration. She couldn't embarrass him, nor did she want their first impression of her to be one of a whiny brat. She willed herself to walk forward and stand before the woman who was eyeing her with steely intimidation.

Her back ached, her feet hurt, and she wanted a nap. She fought the exhaustion claiming her as she looked down at the piercing gaze. The woman released the garment she'd been working on and raised her hands, laying them on Anna's stomach.

Paper-thin lids closed over wizened eyes as her long, thin, twisted fingers circled her stomach, poking and pushing until Anna felt like she would erupt in anger if the woman didn't stop.

Everyone from the cashier at the local grocery store to the kind old man at the gas station had wanted to touch her enormous stomach, but this was more than touching. This was an intrusion.

She stole another glance at Dakota, who stood by his mother's side. Both respectfully observed his grandmother's movements as if it was normal, and for some reason it angered her.

The old woman's voice softened as she turned to her grandson. "Dakota, she has given you two fine sons."

Dakota smiled, but looked to his grandmother with curiosity. "No, Unci, we've had a test, an ultrasound. One is a girl and one a boy."

"They are wrong. You have two strong sons. They will be born here," she commanded.

Anna gasped, but didn't say a word. This old woman was crazy to think she knew more than modern medicine. They'd seen the ultrasound, for heaven's sake, and knew what they were having.

His grandmother's last sentence finally sunk in, and Anna swung her head around and pierced Dakota with a questioning, frantic look. This was ludicrous. She wasn't going to have her babies here! She was going to be in a hospital with doctors and nurses and all the things necessary for a healthy birth.

With a small shake of his head he looked to her, his eyes twinkling in a conspiratorial wink, and she felt herself relax, almost smiling.

245

He bent down and kissed the older woman on her cheek and backed up. "It's nice to see you again, Unci, but I'd like to let Anna rest, if you don't mind."

Anna felt the weight of their stares on her body as Dakota led her from the room, and she shuddered. When she at last heard their quiet mumbling fade behind her, she let out the breath she hadn't realized she'd been holding.

CHAPTER THIRTY-FIVE

A gentle knock on her door brought Anna groggily from a peaceful sleep, wondering who could be interrupting her chance to get some rest. She and Dakota had been here a whole week already, and she was growing increasingly tired and more and more uncomfortable. Pressure on her lower body these past couple days caused her to move more slowly, to pause often. Her children were heavy.

Everyone had been wonderful to her, but she was so very weary. She wanted to go home.

She'd met more people than she had met in her lifetime and knew she would never remember the names. Some names were foreign to her, and some were as everyday as her neighbors in her own home town.

Only one among them all had been distant and cold, and Anna had asked Dakota about her.

"She is the mother of my late wife. She may resent you being with me, but she won't interfere. Her heart is heavy from losing her only daughter and her grandchildren. She still deals with the grief, and she prays for guidance."

His explanation had brought her to tears as she tried to imagine the woman's pain.

The door opened quietly, and Anna blinked as she struggled to bring the face at the doorway into focus. She was still so tired.

Winona's brilliant smile peeked from behind the wood and greeted her warmly, followed closely by a low bark. Barreling through the door in his usual exuberant style, Jake took a leap and jumped on the bed. Through a groaning laugh at his antics, Anna sheltered her stomach as he showered her with wet kisses and bounced around the bed.

"Anna, lunch will be ready soon. Are you hungry?"

When Anna had assured her she was indeed hungry, Winona smiled again. "When you are done, Unci would like to talk with you."

With that the door clicked shut leaving Anna alone with Jake. "Holy cow, Jake, what does the old woman want now?"

Even after a week the lady still scared her, and she often found her watchful eyes following her as she shuffled from room to room. She truly wondered if the woman wasn't just a bit crazy and everyone was coddling her, but she never voiced her question to Dakota. It was clear he worshipped his grandmother.

She rose from the bed carefully. Everything she did nowadays was done with care. Her belly stretched out so far in front of her she could not find her feet and most times never even saw the floor below her.

Her stomach growled with hunger, but she knew before she even went to the table she wouldn't eat much. Meals had become smaller as a result of the babies taking up so much room, and she pictured her stomach the size of a walnut squished up against her ribs. She was growing more and more uncomfortable and wished for the birth and home.

Today was no different as she sat at the table with the smiling group of skinny people. This lunch wasn't going down easily. Whether it was from her shrunken stomach or the impending conversation with the person she was told to call Unci, the food had lost all taste and didn't sit well.

Once done with her attempt to eat something, she reluctantly made her way to the living area and walked before the ancient, intimidating woman. She was sure her knees were visibly knocking, although she couldn't see them anymore to verify her suspicions. She often wondered if she'd ever see her knees again.

The clicking of the ever-present needles working a fine intricate pattern of lace ceased as Anna approached and the old woman motioned her forward.

"Come here, child."

Anna started to sit by her side, but the woman stopped her and once more placed her hands against Anna's stomach. Bending her head forward, she rested her ear against the growing babies, and Anna waited, once again feeling the inspection intrusive.

"Something has been bothering me since we first spoke. I needed to touch you again. I'm sorry. I was wrong. You do have a daughter and son."

At Anna's self-satisfied smile, the old woman clucked her tongue and spoke again. "But, what no one has seen is that you have two sons and a daughter."

Anna felt her self-righteous smile quickly disappear at her words. She swallowed against the bile that rose to her throat and wavered as she groped for an arm to the chair the old woman rested upon. Unci had to be crazy. She just had to be. Triplets?

"No, Unci. I mean no disrespect, but you're wrong. The sonogram showed two babies."

"They are the ones who are wrong. Your little girl was hiding from me, but she is there, and she is healthy and strong." Knotty fingers reached for the hand Anna had glued to the armrest and pulled her to a chair at her side. "Sit, your time grows near. You need to rest."

"I'm not due for another few weeks yet. I'll be home by then." Anna rubbed her hands along the large protrusion of her stomach and looked to the old woman. "What makes you think I carry three children?"

"I can feel them. I can hear their hearts beating strongly."

This conversation was scaring her, and with the beginnings of rising panic, she searched grandmother's eyes for signs of insanity but found nothing more than the milky gaze of aging, yet unwavering vision. Her heart began to pound a bit harder within her chest as a panic attack took root.

"No, I won't accept that. I can't have three children at once. It's impossible. I worried how I could handle one with all the work I have to do at the farm. Then they told me two. I'm sorry, but you must be wrong. I cannot care for three. At the rate I am going, someone else will come along and tell me there are four in there!"

"Calm yourself, child, it's not good for you or the babies, but I'm not wrong. You will see, and you'll do what you must. What will happen will be part of your path, and you will rely on Dakota and your family here to help you."

Setting her lace-work to the side, the steely-eyed gaze assessed Anna. "My grandson tells me you don't wish to marry him."

Uncomfortable with the probing question, Anna broke contact with the prying eyes and looked around the room. She took a few deep breaths as she tried to calm her heart.

The face of a stern man in a full headdress stared down at her with regal importance, and Anna felt chastised for her outburst in this home of peaceful tranquility, or was it just her own insecurities in this house full of tradition? She still felt so out of place.

His eyes bore into her own as if sending her a message, and she felt her back stiffen with a resolve to explain.

"It's not that I don't wish to marry him. I'm just confused. I was married once to a wonderful man, and losing him broke my heart. I'm not sure I'm ready to give myself up to the pain of loving and losing again. I've buried too many already."

Almost as if the stern man on the wall changed before her, his visage didn't look as menacing, and a creepy crawly shudder moved along her spine. She quickly dropped her focus to her clutched hands before she spoke again. "Truthfully, I'm not even sure about my place with Dakota. We're so different. Our cultures are so different. I have a home and responsibilities, and so does he. It's too much to overcome, I think."

She lifted her eyes to the sharp vision of the elderly lady and searched for a clue to what she felt. "Besides, I'm not sure if he loves me still. I've made things difficult for him, I'm sorry to say. I think he acts only out of a sense of duty to his children now, and I can't bind myself to a marriage like that. The loneliness would be unbearable."

A small, aged bark of a laugh escaped the old woman, and she reached for Anna's arm.

"I see him when he looks at you. His eyes are filled with his love, but you refuse to see it."

A foot pushed against her stomach as a baby stretched, and Anna groaned as she straightened to accommodate the action. Grandmother's hand rested on her abdomen and felt the movement, and she smiled.

"If what you say is true, child, maybe he's afraid to voice his love again. Words do not come easily to the foolish men. Open your eyes to what the world is trying to tell you. Look inside your heart, and I believe you will find him waiting there."

Shame filled her at his grandmother's words. He'd voiced his love, and she had rebuffed him. If that had happened to her, could she bring herself to say the words again?

"Anna, you and Dakota are living together. In my culture you are already married."

Hands as fragile as time curled upon her own, the bones

gnarled and bent. Skin as thin as the silk she worked revealed blue and bulbous veins, yet the strength in those fingers was powerful.

"The answers to your questions will come easily once you accept his love."

Anna once more lifted her gaze from the firm, almost pleading grip on her hand and looked at the old woman's face. Her eyes filled with tears as she realized that maybe she'd wronged this lady. She wasn't so formidable or scary. She was extremely wise. Her eyes saw all. Her ears heard all. Her mind understood all. Her tired body might be failing, but a strong woman of infinite wisdom rested behind the fragile exterior.

"Unci, you scare me when you speak about having three children at once. I'm very sorry, but I pray you are wrong. One was scary to me. Two put me in a panic. I can't be strong enough for three, but I will think about your words regarding Dakota."

Anna scooted forward awkwardly and after several tries, hefted her body to a standing position, prepared to leave, but again the bony fingers grabbed her hand.

"When do you and Dakota plan to leave?"

"Very soon, maybe tomorrow or the day after. I don't know. I have to get back to my farm and relieve the person who is caring for it. Besides, I have an appointment with the doctor next week. I already missed one."

"You cannot travel tomorrow child."

"Why?"

"The babies will be here by tomorrow night." She still held her fingers in an iron grip, and Anna wondered why.

"Anna, give my Dakota a chance. He'll be good to you."

Anna gently pulled her fingers from the gnarled grasp and turned to go, her heart pounding at her words. Confused, Anna tried to count. If she was right, the babies weren't due for at least three weeks, and she had read that first babies never came on time, but was that the same when you carried more than one? She couldn't have the babies, yet. It was too soon. She had to get home and fast.

She moved down the hallway with one hand curled beneath her large, protruding stomach to support the weight and the other resting against her aching back as she sought the solace their large chamber offered. She had to think, but she had too much to think about. Fear wrapped around her at the thought of three children. His grandmother had to be wrong.

Dakota's handsome face and kind smile rose in her mind's eye. What was she going to do about him? She had to make a decision, but in reality, she saw only heartbreak in her future. They had two very different lives.

That night she and Dakota packed to leave early the next morning. He wanted to stay a couple more days, but Anna was adamant, crying over her fears and pleading with him to take her home. She argued that they'd already stayed longer than he'd originally promised.

She wanted to see her doctor to find out if what Unci said was true. She wanted to lie in her own bed and have her babies in her own hospital, with a doctor who knew her and nurses and other staff to see to her care.

Gripping his arm tightly, she told him that having her babies in a strange environment, an environment steeped in traditions so unlike her own was frightening. His grandmother's words had frightened her. She needed to face this time in her life in what was familiar, comfortable.

Her tears and fears were his undoing, and caving to her wishes, Dakota told his family while they gathered at the dinner table that they'd be leaving at first light. A small smile played around the old woman's lips at his words.

"You will not have the chance, Dakota," she said quietly.

Respectful eyes around the table turned to her when she spoke. Her wisdom was accepted, but not to Anna. She avoided the old lady's gaze as she fiddled with her food.

Unbeknownst to Anna, the gaze from the wise old eyes of his grandmother met Dakota's and twinkled. He smiled as he accepted her wisdom.

CHAPTER THIRTY-SIX

A s she had the past few mornings, Anna rose the next morning slowly. The night had been hard. She had tossed restlessly, unable to give in to the exhaustion that plagued her body. The babies were pressing on her back, and it ached ferociously. She couldn't find a comfortable position at all, and the result made her tired and cranky.

At the breakfast table, she hid a yawn behind her hand and pushed her food away, stating she was not hungry. When Dakota tried to get her to take a few bites, telling her it would be a long ride, she'd snapped at him and immediately regretted her foolish behavior.

"I'm sorry, Dakota, everyone. I didn't sleep well. The babies are making my back hurt."

Dakota's mother and grandmother exchanged knowing glances and rose from the table in unison, walking to her side.

"Come, child," the older woman commanded.

Anna knew of his grandmother's suspicions and vehemently rejected them. Looking to Dakota in fear, he nodded and smiled encouragement. She wanted to kick him.

"I'll pack the car, Anna."

Not sure if he was lying or not, she rose on shaky legs and followed the two women, surprised when they entered her room and told her to disrobe.

This was too much.

She grew angry with their command and shook her head in defiance. "I will not."

She didn't want these relative strangers to see her naked. It was unnatural and intrusive. She wanted to go home.

"Anna, please, let Unci look at you. She has birthed many babies." Mina coaxed, placating her. "She needs to see if you can travel or not."

Voiceless for once, Anna reluctantly removed her pants and underwear and lay down across the bed. Embarrassment turned her face a blood red. This was wrong. Everything was so strange, so foreign. She didn't want to be there. She wanted her old, comfortable bed and her Miranda by her side. Thinking of the cat she missed so much brought tears to eyes. All she wanted was home.

The old lady walked to her side and laid hands on her stomach once more. Feeling for what, Anna didn't know, but she pushed against her suddenly quiet children. Spreading Anna's legs, she looked at her most private place and when the old woman placed fingers inside her body, Anna let fall her frustrated tears. She was scared.

"You are ready, Anna. Your labor has begun. You will birth three babies soon, maybe even before this day is done."

Her heartbeat thudded erratically inside her chest. She cast a frantic gaze at Dakota's mother, but the woman had moved away and out the door.

"It's too soon. I can't have them, yet. I want to go home. I want Dakota."

"Not now, Anna. Let's take off the rest of your clothes. Mina is gathering a gown for you to wear. Then you must stand and walk. That will ease the passage."

Anna struggled to rise, and a hand as old as time grabbed her in a firm grip to help her from the bed. She knew that labor could take forever, and her house was only six hours away. They could make it in time, couldn't they? She wanted Dakota. She wanted to beg him to take her to her own doctor.

"I want Dakota," she begged.

The door opened, and Mina stepped back inside. Anna heard the whispered murmurs of a crowd outside her door before Mina shut the door firmly in their faces. She'd obviously become a curiosity.

A rush of warm liquid oozed between her legs, and she cried out in frustration. She'd read about this in one of her books. Her water had broken. She was truly in labor and far from her home.

Frightened and shaking, she let Mina help her shed the rest of her clothing and ease her swollen body into a softly flowing gown.

"Come, we will walk."

Opening the door to the curious gazes, they exited. With a look of concern on his face, Dakota came forward to grasp Anna, but Mina turned him away.

"Be gone, all of you. This will be a long day." Turning to Dakota, she laid her palm against his cheek with love and understanding, "Come back later, son."

With the respect due the lady of the house they all dispersed, except Dakota. He stood just out of her reach watching Anna closely, understanding written on his handsome features.

They exchanged unspoken words as their eyes met and again, she voiced her desperate plea. "I want you. Please, Dakota."

He came to her side and wrapped his arm around her, and she clung to him fiercely, the only person she truly knew well in this sea of strangers.

If not for his firm grip around her, she would've fallen to the floor when the first contraction hit. She let out a cry when the pain felt like it would rip her in two, and the old lady clucked her tongue in her annoying way. "We've only just begun. Let's walk."

They walked and walked. Other than a few times he left to eat or do something else required of him, he stayed by her side as they moved through each corridor. Mina related stories of her ancestors and the lives and struggles they'd all endured. Anna tried to listen, but knew she'd heard little between the contractions that wracked her bloated body.

Fear—fear unlike anything she'd ever endured, even when tornadoes threatened her life—took hold of her body and mind. Nothing was going as it should. Strangers were in control of her very life, of her body. She held on to Dakota like a lifeline dangling from a floundering boat.

Minutes passed to hours, the time moving so very slowly. With each passage of the hour, her pains increased, coming closer and closer together. Her groans of discomfort echoed down each hallway, letting everyone know of her agony. She didn't care.

She felt as if the babies were pressing low, ready to enter this world. She'd had enough, and with a hand gripping the back of a chair as another pain passed, she grew beyond weary, her legs shaking beneath her.

Her voice was a prayer for relief when she begged them. "I can't go on. I must rest, please. Please, let me lie down."

Mina walked her to the living space and nodded to his grandmother, and the old woman rose from her chair.

"Let's see how we progress."

This time they ushered Dakota away, and Anna protested loudly as the door closed behind him. The two matriarchs wouldn't allow him in the room no matter how much she begged.

She looked about her in confused wonder. Everything in the room was changed. A strange smell permeated the air from something burning in a small bowl on a table near her bed. The bed itself was covered in protective cloths, and the room had been made warm. Everything had been made ready.

She paid it little attention when she was finally able to ease her rotund body down on the bed. She was so tired. She just wanted some sleep, but sleep was not hers at this moment, for a pain shot through her again, and she cried out.

The old woman once more spread her legs and again inserted two old fingers inside her body, but Anna no longer cared what the woman did or who looked at her body. She just wanted relief.

"It's time."

Mina stood from where she'd been resting beside Anna. Releasing the firm hold Anna had on her hand, she went to the door and opened it slightly, murmuring something to the anxious Dakota outside.

"Anna, the first baby's head is low. You'll soon feel the need to push."

Somewhere in the recesses of her mind, Anna heard a drum begin a steady beat and wondered at its significance, but before she could question it, another horrific pain doubled her over, and again, she cried out. They were coming so closely together now she could barely take a breath before another gripped her in a tight hold.

Nothing was as it should be. She should be in a hospital with medicine to ease this pain, yet here she was in a strange home, in a strange state, feeling every cramp and every movement of her babies, every pressure to push. That was when it hit her. She needed to push.

Rearing up and with a gravelly dry-throated growl, she pushed. The need was great to expel the life within her. For two and a half hours she pushed until sweat poured from her body in the overly warm room, and she felt she could push no more.

"Aku la, Anna. It is now. I see the head, push."

With a cry of pain and exhaustion, she pushed, feeling as

if a knife was tearing through her body as the babe entered the world in a rush. Experienced hands moved quickly, and soon a boisterous cry of a new life reverberated around the large bedroom.

Wrapping the tiny bundle tightly, they laid the child across her breasts, and Anna saw the raven-black, full head of hair and bright blue eyes of her son. She laid a finger against the soft cheek in wonder. He looked so much like Dakota already.

Swiftly they moved him away as they prepared for the arrival of the second baby, and Anna slipped into a brief sleep.

How long she slept, she didn't know, but it felt like mere minutes before she was crying out again. Another contraction tore through her body, and the need to push followed quickly thereafter. She struggled against the pain. She was not strong enough for this.

Day had turned to the deepest dark of night as she bore her children into this world. A whole twenty-four hours was almost gone as she panted through her pain.

This child came more quickly, slipping easily into her new world. Once more they placed the tiny bundle into her arms. She was bald except for the finest whisper of downy black hair and large eyes that looked straight at her mother with boldness and curiosity. Anna barely got a chance to lay her hand against this child before she fell asleep. She was exhausted.

A light touch shook her shoulder. "Anna, wake. Your baby wants to be born."

Anna waved the hands away. She wanted the voices to hush. She had already birthed two babies. That was enough, but the pains began again and swept away any chance of rest. Once more she cried out. She just wanted to sleep, but there would be no sleep. Perhaps never more.

Pushing with the last ounce of strength left in her body,

she felt the last of her three babies slip from her body. It was done.

She never saw the third child, for the blissful relief of oblivion overtook her.

CHAPTER THIRTY-SEVEN

A kiss as soft as a feather rested on her lips, and she recognized the scent of the man who touched her. She smiled, instantly catapulted back to the gazebo when he had awakened her this way and made sweet love to her for hours.

"Please wake up, Anna."

She moved a leg, the discomfort she felt between her legs bringing her eyes open fully, and remembered the result of that day.

Dakota was gazing down at her with a tender look of concern resting on his handsome face.

"The babies?"

"They're good. They are small but fine and healthy, and they want their mother."

Their mother. She was a mother. The enormity of those words hit her like a brick. She was both elated and scared to death.

A gentle, understanding female voice came from behind Dakota. Anna knew it to be his mother. "Anna, sweetheart, you've been asleep for two days. You need to wake up and meet your family."

That Dakota had been worrying was obvious to Anna as she studied the face looking down on her with such concern. His hair was tangled and oily, his eyes swollen and red. He looked as if he'd not slept at all.

"Two days, Anna. You had us worried," he admitted.

Anna tried to move and winced again at the discomfort.

Her body had paid a big price and was letting her know each time she moved a muscle.

"I guess I was pretty tired." The obviousness of her statement made her giggle, bringing smiles to the two occupants of the room.

"Dakota?"

His look was so tender and loving when he looked to her in question that she almost burst into tears.

"I've been asleep for two days?"

"Yes, you have."

"That means I really, really need to visit the restroom."

He choked on laughter and stood, lifting her heavy, swollen body and carrying her to their adjoining bathroom.

"Dakota, I think I can walk."

He set her down near the commode and left, shutting the door behind him, and she giggled, but let out a squeak of alarm when the door opened, and Mina entered.

"You will need me."

At least ten minutes later, pale-faced and trembling, Anna walked from the bathroom holding on to Mina's arm. Dakota was instantly by her side and sweeping her up into his arms again. This time she didn't mind that he carried her, and she held on until he laid her down gently on their bed.

Mina came forward with a tiny squeaking bundle and laid her in the crook of Anna's left arm. In moments she was back with another and laid her in the opposite arm. When she came forward with the third, Anna looked at her in alarm.

"I've run out of arms!"

Laughter, cathartic and welcome, lifted the spirits in the room. She glanced at Dakota, who laughed the loudest. With a jolt she realized he must have spent the past two days in fear she would die, just like his wife, and this laughter was a cleansing relief for him. She had scared him. Her heart warmed to him, and she gave him a gentle smile.

He took his son from his mother, and Anna finally glimpsed her tiny son. He was so much smaller than his brother and sister, appearing almost fragile. She looked to them in awe. She truly had given birth to three human beings.

"We have to name our children, Anna."

One by one Anna looked at the tiny faces of her children. It seemed just a moment ago that she was an independent, childless woman running a home and business. She remembered being tired most evenings after a hard day of work, but she also remembered the pride in her accomplishments.

Gazing lovingly at the three little faces of the babies her body had nourished and given birth to, she realized what real accomplishment was. She had done this. Well, she and Dakota had, but she'd carried them in her worn out, swollen, and very tender body.

Memorizing each little face in turn, she thought of names. How could she recognize their Indian heritage, but also give them names that would work well in the outside world?

Looking to the father of her children, she smiled tentatively. "What do you suggest?"

"I've given it a lot of thought while you slept. I think our little girl should be Mika, and I like Elan and Dyami for the boys."

She knew by now that every name had a meaning. She had been told Dakota meant friend, and she knew Mina meant eldest daughter. They had even checked out her own name and told her that Anna was a Hebrew name and meant favored by God. She had never known.

"What are their meanings?"

"Mika means clever raccoon. Elan means friendly, and Dyami is eagle."

"Why is my daughter a raccoon? I don't like that." Embarrassment flooded her face at her outburst.

"I'm so sorry, I didn't mean—"

Mina stepped forward and lovingly laid a hand across her granddaughter's head. "It's of no matter. Look to your daughter, Anna, and you'll see."

Anna looked down at the tiny girl lying in the crook of her arm and did indeed see why they'd chosen that name. Thick black lashes circled eyes that were dark brown, wide and large. Those bold eyes stared at her intently, listening to her voice, mesmerizing her face. She remembered seeing her little girl right after birth and at the bold way she'd looked at her then. Intelligent and observant eyes filled the small face.

With a smile, she turned to Dakota. "My little raccoon. These are good names."

Little Dyami let out a cry, and Anna felt it straight through to her breasts, realizing finally that they were part of what ached so horribly on her body.

With a gentle touch, Dakota's mother placed her hands against his back and pushed gently.

"Dakota, leave us. Anna needs to feed her babies."

"If I have been asleep for two days, who has fed them?"

Dakota kissed the top of her head and left them.

"One of our tribe has been helping to care for them. We didn't know if or when you would wake. We tried to wake you, but you wouldn't. Dakota stayed by your side the whole time, worrying that he would lose you, too." His mother's words confirmed her suspicions, and as Mina taught her how to feed three hungry babies, she contemplated Dakota's place in her heart.

For the first time in over four days, Anna cautiously ventured from her room. Brilliant sunlight bathed the hallway through a tall window, and she narrowed her eyes against the pain. The curtains in her room had been nearly closed for days, leaving only enough light to see by, and the intenseness of the reflective light against the white marble floor was harsh.

As if she were seeing the world anew, she moved down the long hallway. So much had changed in the space of a week. South Dakota was now the official birthplace of her children. Not exactly what she had planned.

She didn't know where her children were. They'd been carried from the room by three capable women while she had showered. She heard no sounds of crying and could only assume they were asleep somewhere.

The familiar tapping of nails on the floor brought a huge smile to Anna's face. Jake. She had missed him, and apparently, he'd missed her too. His tail beat a steady rhythm against her leg as he circled her and smelled along her clothing.

She wasn't quite up to bending to the floor to pet him, so with a gentle voice she asked him to follow her to the living space. The dog, against all household orders, jumped up onto the large sofa and curled into Anna as she took a seat and received many days of pent up love. Jake would always be her first child.

Doggie kisses satisfied for the moment, Anna noticed his grandmother in her favorite spot, and with a sheepish grin, looked at her apologetically. She'd told this woman she was wrong, she couldn't be carrying three children, she wouldn't deliver here. The shame warmed her face for telling this wise woman that she knew more than her.

"I'm sorry I didn't believe you, Unci."

"No need to apologize, child. Modern medicine does not know all. I have birthed a hundred and sixty-nine babies. Well, a hundred and seventy-two now. I know all the signs. I have seen it all."

She stood, and old, tired bones and worn body moved slowly towards her. "How do you feel?"

"Like I pushed three watermelons from my body."

The wise lady chuckled and sat down beside her, grasping her hand in a bony, but firm grip.

Surrounded by the ghosts of Dakota's ancestors, Anna held the cool fingers of the ancient woman who had become dear to her. Her profound knowledge and her deep insight into human nature made her a force to be reckoned with, but her gentle yet steady care of her while she was in labor and afterwards, when her body had felt as if it had been beaten, connected her to the highest matriarch of this family.

"Will you leave us now, Anna?"

Anna nodded and hugged Jake to her side. "As soon as the children and I can travel. I have a home and fields to tend to, animals to care for, and a vegetable garden long forgotten. I can't imagine what it all looks like."

"I'd like you to stay. I would like my great-grandchildren to know their heritage, but you must follow your own path."

"Thank you for understanding."

"Anna, listen to what I tell you. Hear my words. Just because your life is stormy now, doesn't mean it always will be. Eventually, the sun will return."

Anna looked to her in confusion, unsure what she meant or why she said what she said. The old woman stood and with shoulders bent with time, slowly walked away. As she watched her disappear into a room, she wondered if she would ever understand the meanings behind the woman's many sayings. Yet she was intelligent enough to know one thing, and the weight of it bore down upon her shoulders. She would let her down when she left, but there really was no choice.

She peered down at Jake, receiving a wet kiss across her chin for her effort. Holding on to the familiar beside her, she thought of this place, Dakota's home.

If she were here, she'd have many hands to help her, and if she were here, she'd have much less responsibility. Yet, if she stayed, she would lose her own home. The property she had fought so hard to keep from Mr. Shoop would be gone. She was so confused, she didn't know what to think. Those three babies sleeping somewhere in this house meant everything to her, but her home and all the land meant a lot to her, too. It was part of their heritage. She couldn't just let it go.

Sighing, she realized if she was truthful with herself, Dakota meant everything to her, also. She had a family here if she chose it. She had three children who would now rely on her for everything from nourishment to education to guidance, and on and on. It was daunting to think about when she imagined doing it alone.

If she asked Dakota to come back with her, what would be his choice? He was the head of this household. He was the owner of all the land around him. He had many who relied on him for their lives, and she would be selfish to demand he make such a difficult choice.

How he'd stayed away so long before was beyond her, and that spoke deeply of his promise to her. Knowing the responsibilities of her small farm, she could only imagine the weight Dakota carried on his shoulders with this large enterprise.

Footsteps sounded behind her, and she turned to see the mother of Dakota's first wife approach with Mika in her arms.

"Your daughter needs to be fed."

Laying the small bundle in her arms, the woman moved off quickly.

As Anna watched the quiet woman glide away, her heart broke for the pain she had to be enduring. She never knew what to say to her and couldn't imagine what it felt like for her to see her three babies. The grieving lady should've been holding her own grandchild in her arms.

A disgruntled squeak made her turn back to her little girl. Her little girl. A girl who would grow to become a woman and maybe have a child of her own one day, if she so chose. Already, she couldn't imagine the pain if she lost her.

Jake stood and sniffed along the baby's body as she bared a breast for her daughter's greedy mouth.

"Jake, this is your sister."

CHAPTER THIRTY-EIGHT

She sat on her bed struggling to feed the children, a bit frustrated as the boys fussed and sucked greedily at her breasts. Their small hands gripped her tender flesh, the fingernails biting into her skin in frantic need for the hunger pains to stop, and she found herself anxious for them to be done.

Her frustration was forgotten, though, when Dakota walked into the room, and she gazed upon his beauty. His body moved with a fluid ease, and when he approached and sat down carefully on the side of their bed, she took a moment to appreciate the entirety of the man.

The tender smile that graced his face when he watched his children suckle touched her deeply, yet it caused a pain to sear her heart at the thought of taking them away from him.

"You have given me such wonderful gifts, Anna. What can I give you in return? How could I possibly repay you for these sacred lives?"

Her eyes filled, and her heart clenched as she thought of taking them away from him.

"You don't owe me anything. We gave each other these gifts. I lived all those years of my life thinking I couldn't have children, thinking I'd never know the joy of holding my own baby in my arms. I remember the pain of wondering what was wrong with me, and look—you gave me three children at once. Your gift to me is much, much better, and I thank you."

He lowered his head, and she wondered why he was intently studying his folded hands in his lap. "I'd like to talk to you about something."

She knew before he opened his mouth what he wanted to talk about. It didn't take a Ph.D. to know he would ask her to live here.

"I don't know, Dakota."

She must have surprised him as his eyebrows rose in question when he looked to her. "You don't know what?"

"I don't know if I can live here."

He laughed, a deep chuckle that jiggled the bed, and the finally quiet babies' arms jerked up in unison at the sound.

"Shhh. If you wake them, you'll tend to them. Help me, please. My arms are killing me."

She placed a tiny baby in each arm and watched as he rose gently with infinite patience and care to carry them to the waiting cradles. He stopped to gaze down at their daughter before returning, and she drank her fill of his long, muscular length and his dark locks falling around his face as he bent over. When he turned to walk back to her, she felt a surge of conflicting emotions tumble through her mind and body as her need for him waged a war with her need to leave.

He lay down by her side, cupping a tired breast in his hand, and she warmed at his touch, yet when he gazed at her with a look of insecurity, everything ceased to matter. She couldn't recall a time he'd ever looked at her with anything other than a calm assurance of the man inside. That she'd done this to him was a heavy burden to bear.

"How did you know what I'd ask?"

"It wasn't hard to figure out. You are essentially chief here. These are your people. You need to be here to run your business and take care of them."

She slinked further down into the bed until she lay facing him and captured his sorrowful gaze. "Why did you leave,

Dakota?"

A work-roughened finger grazed her nipple and circled out to touch the rest of a breast as he considered his words, and she waited.

"I couldn't look around me without seeing her standing in every doorway, every corner of a room. I saw her in the fields. I saw her in our bed. I believed I even saw her in a cloud one day. The pain of failing her wouldn't let me be. I had no choice but to leave for my own sanity. I had to find my way."

"Do you see her now?"

"I see only the woman who would be my wife if she would just accept me."

When she had no response to his words, she watched as hope was replaced by the familiar shadow passing over his eyes. He stood, going to the door.

With his hand on the doorknob, he uttered words that stung. "I've watched you for many months now, Anna. You wear your fear like a shield. You hide behind that ring on your finger." He shook his head sadly. "I can't make you love me, Anna, and I can't change your past, but I can help you write a new future if you would only allow it."

The click of the door as it shut behind him left her feeling strangely abandoned and thinking about what he said.

Sitting cross-legged in the middle of the living space floor with cushioning blankets below her, she watched as her precious little children kicked and waved at their new world. They were so tiny, so beautiful. She still couldn't believe she was a mother, let alone to three babies at once. If she allowed herself to think on it too hard, it frightened the hell out of her.

Her daughter still watched her with unwavering eyes,

and she wondered what she saw when she observed her so intently. Did she see a woman worthy of being her mother? Did she see a woman fighting a war inside whether she should marry or continue to be independent? Could she give in to love and bear the pain of possible loss? It had nearly devastated her before. Could she go through it again? Could she lose her home?

Her mind flew back to her and Dakota's last heart-wrenching discussion about her leaving. Just thinking of it, she could almost feel the warmth of his hand and how his thumb had grazed her tired nipple in wonderment and tender care. That touch had ignited a longing she still felt deep inside. The man could just look at her a certain way and melt her resistance.

Dyami burped, bringing her back to her children in front of her. Milk slipped from the sides of his mouth, and she rushed to clean him up.

Should she try to live here among all these people? Could she? Solitude had been her way of life once. Was it possible to acclimate to always being surrounded by this huge, devoted family? Could she learn their ways?

Most importantly, could she give away Charles' legacy? She was no closer to finding the answers she sought, and the uncertainty hung heavy on her shoulders, dragging her down with the weight. She was causing both herself and Dakota pain with her indecision. In the end, she could cause her children pain. She was a woman torn.

A knock sounded on the front door, and she raised her eyes to watch as a young girl of maybe fifteen dashed down a hallway to open it. A voice asked for her, and Anna's heart clutched within her chest at the need for the familiar in her life. Her mother had come.

She laid a sleeping Dyami down next to Mika and carefully stood without disturbing them. Rushing forward, she flew into her mother's arms, clinging to the body of the woman who had given her life. Her mother would never understand how much she needed her at this moment. Even if their relationship had been strained, she was still her mom, and Anna was surprised at how much it meant to her that she was there.

Her mother returned the hug just as fiercely, surprising Anna somewhat.

"Anna! I am so glad to finally get here. I've been traveling forever." She stepped back and looked at her daughter. "You are looking pretty good for a woman who just gave birth to three kids!"

Anna rolled her eyes at the lie but laughed. She knew her mother was being kind, for a change. Anna knew what she looked like. She had a long way to go to get back to the trim figure she once had, if such a miracle ever happened. Her stomach still looked as if she was five months pregnant, and she hated it.

"It took me longer than I'd hoped to arrive, but Dakota asked me to stop by your home and bring you a couple of things."

A man, obviously a hired driver by the uniform he wore, walked up beside her mother and placed a small carrier on the marble floor.

Anna stared at the case and looked back to her mother in surprise, the almost ever-present tears filling her eyes.

Carefully coming down on all fours, she opened the door and grasped the small protesting body that emerged. Her Miranda was here. With her. She might have been kicking up a fuss, but Anna didn't care. She still hugged the tiny frame against her.

As he always did, Dakota materialized from nowhere and placed a hand under her arm, helping her to rise. Overcome with emotion, she crushed Miranda against her breasts, then threw herself into Dakota's arms, and kissed him, surprising him and the crowd that was forming.

"Anna." She reluctantly pulled away from Dakota and turned when her mother called to her. "There's more, sweetheart."

She stepped to the side to give Anna a clear view of the front driveway. Hooked to the back of the large truck that had brought her mother and Miranda to her side was a horse trailer, and Anna's breath froze in her chest in disbelief.

Still clutching Miranda to her chest, she shakily walked out into the brilliant and warm South Dakota sunshine. Could it be?

The driver was lowering the gate to the trailer, and within moments he was backing her beloved Maggie from the confines of the trailer. Her Maggie. Her Miranda, and her Jake, all in one place. With her, with her three children. With Dakota. With her mom.

She couldn't handle the surge of emotions that rose within her, and grabbing her mother, she broke down and sobbed against her shoulder. Dakota had given her a gift after all.

Never one for too much sentimentality, her mother pulled away quickly and turned to Dakota.

"Well, young man, where are my grandchildren?"

The crowd had grown and gathered along the front steps and inside the foyer to watch the new arrivals. Standing in the midst of those who had congregated in the foyer rested her children in the arms of Mina, Chumani, the mother of Dakota's first wife, and another woman whose name Anna couldn't recall. With tears of happiness still wetting her cheeks, she took her mother forward to meet them.

CHAPTER THIRTY-NINE

The mood was jubilant among everyone. These were happy days.

With the arrival of her mother and Anna finally feeling a bit better, Dakota had called for a celebration. For a week they'd done just that. Anna had been drawn into the euphoric festivities, finding the joy of their tradition embracing and heartwarming.

There was dancing, which Anna wasn't up to taking part in, and worshipful prayers of thanks. There was more food and drink than Anna had ever seen in her life, and she found herself eyeing it wistfully as she remembered the days she had gone without.

Everyone seemed to be smiling, and everyone shared a warmth and love the likes of which Anna had never felt before. She found it oddly embracing to a loner such as she.

Her quiet mother stayed by her side for most of those days, not only to be an aide to Anna, but also because her mother was intimidated by the large crowd of people always moving and working in and around the sprawling home. Like Anna, her mom lived alone. She was surrounded by her circle of friends in the condominium complex in Florida, but her own condo was just that, her own. She was used to solitude. She was used to peace and quiet.

The day before her mother was to make the long trek back home, she sat beside Anna on the immense sofa in the living space and held her granddaughter in her arms.

"Now that we finally have a few minutes alone, would

you like to tell me why I didn't know any of this was going on?"

Regretful and guilty, Anna felt remorse over not including her mother in the past year of her life. She'd told her only what she wanted her to know. Now that she was a mother herself, she realized she'd probably stolen some joy from her mother's life.

"I've been selfish, Mother, and I'm sorry. I'm not sure I can explain what was going on with me."

She sighed and turned towards her mom. "At first, I was unsure of Dakota and what was happening between us. Then I truly just wanted him all to myself as I learned about him. I was having some fun for the first time in years and didn't want anyone to ruin that."

Her mother grimaced, and Anna momentarily felt like a heel, but both knew what she said was true.

"When I discovered I was pregnant, I was scared. I didn't know how to care for a child or if I even wanted to have a child after so many years of trying. I guess I'd gotten used to the fact I couldn't get pregnant—or at least I thought I couldn't get pregnant."

She hesitated before she spoke again, knowing exactly how painful her next words would be.

"Then I was told I was having twins, and I worried how you'd feel at that news. Not a day goes by that I don't think about Bella, and I guess you do too."

As she'd wished for so many times in her life but had learned to live without, she again yearned to feel the warmth of her mother's body. Laying her head down on the slender shoulder, she thought back over the turmoil and changes of the past year.

"When I first felt a baby move, I grew fearful that I'd lose them like Dakota's wife, and I guess I sheltered myself and them. I never even told anyone in town I was pregnant until it became obvious that I was. I know I probably haven't explained myself very well, but I truly am sorry I didn't tell you."

"Oh, Anna, what have we done to ourselves? Where did we go wrong?"

Her voice broke on the questions, and Anna lifted her head to look into the tearful eyes.

"Sweetheart, I will not sit here and lecture you. You've been through enough the past few years, but I'll tell you my heart broke to get a call from a stranger telling me my only child had given him three children in one day, and I never even knew she had gotten involved with someone or had gotten pregnant. I really didn't believe him when he called. I thought it was a joke. You and I had talked so many times, and you never gave a clue as to your life."

"I'm so sorry, Mom."

Her mother shook her head.

"No, Anna, don't be sorry. This fault lies entirely with me. We're not as close as a mother and daughter should be. When I lost Bella and then your father, my heart grew cold against love, and I'm afraid I took that out on you. You were left with a shell of a mother and pretty much had to raise yourself. I believe that's why you married so young. You were running away from me. I'm the one who should be sorry and ask you for forgiveness."

She stared at her mother's quivering chin as she confessed her regrets, and when her mother twisted on the sofa, Anna raised her head to see the sadness in the blue eyes so like her own. Something was going on here that Anna couldn't understand. Had the birth of her children helped to mend the rift between her and her mother? Was this another gift Dakota had given her?

Mina burped, and her mother patted the tiny back and sighed. "I don't want her growing up afraid of love, Anna.

Can we fix this?"

The question startled her. She'd wished for her mother's love so often and had always been pushed to the side, not important to the woman. She had at times hated her for it until she eventually grew indifferent.

Her mother was right. It was why she'd married so young. She'd wanted her own home, and she'd wanted separation from the loneliness and heartache her mother caused. She'd found that with Charles. Maybe in hindsight, she'd married Charles for the wrong reasons, but it had still been a good marriage, and she didn't regret it.

Staring into the face of the woman she had spent too many of her young years craving love from, she wondered. Could her mother and she repair the division between them? Could she open herself up to the possibility of more rejection from her?

The lonely child within pushed forward and she put her arms around the person who'd given her a lifetime of pain, holding on tightly to her daughter and her mom.

Seeing her mother off the next day was harder on Anna than she expected, especially now that they were trying to repair the rift between them. For almost the entire day of her departure, Anna's eyes were wet more often than they were dry. She felt closer to her mother now than she had since she was a small child, and it was hard to accept her leaving. She wanted more time with her.

Therefore, it was not welcoming when Dakota joined her that night in their bed and once again pushed for her stay.

"I know you don't want to talk about this, but I have to bring it up. I'd like you to stay and let the children grow up here to know their family and our traditions. I ask a lot of you, I know, but we can sell your land and put the money away for the children. You know you have a home here."

Anna rose from the bed and paced around the large chamber, frustrated that this discussion had to happen today of all days when her heart was already heavy.

She had warred with herself over her plan to leave for days, and she felt deep in her bones that she'd come to the right decision. She'd just put off talking to him about it until her mother was gone and she found the right time. Dakota was going to force her to tell him anyway.

"I've done nothing but think about my decision. The weight of it is crushing me."

Turning around mid-stride, she found him sitting on the edge of their bed, his body on full alert as he watched her with the eyes of a hawk. They shared an anxiety. They shared hope, but unfortunately, they hoped for two different things.

"I can't. You know I can't. My place, like yours, is at my home. I can't let Pop continue to run my farm, and I can't sell. That land is my responsibility. It was left to me. It was my husband's dream. Like it is here for you, my home is also our children's' heritage. I need to go as soon as I am ready to travel."

Dakota's body was rigid anger when he rose from the bed, and she wondered whether to go to him or back away. Should she try to comfort him, or should she flee? Desperate to let him know her own struggles, she walked up to him and laid a hand on his chest, feeling the pulsing of his angry heartbeat just below her palm.

"I'm sorry. Like you, I struggled with this decision, but I don't know what else to do."

The look he gave her was controlled emotion, but she knew he was angry and hurt—either out of respect or from fear of what he might say, he said nothing. He turned and left the room. She knew this about him by now. He always left when he struggled with his anger.

Her mind battled its own turmoil, torn in the face of Dakota's anger at her refusal. When she left, she knew she'd lose Dakota's heart, and that thought scared her. Would he fight her for the children? Would he try to take them from her in a court battle? How would it all end? Could she travel back and forth? Most importantly, could she give in to Dakota's wishes and accept him fully into her life, accept his love? Always she held him just a step away from her heart, afraid. What would it feel like to let him in?

Dyami woke and began to fret, and she walked to the tiny cradle. Scooping him up, she shushed him before he woke the others and took him to her bed, baring her leaking breast for his hungry mouth.

As she held the smallest of her children and watched the tiny mouth suckle, his teeny fingers curling and grasping the fullness of her breast, she teared up. How could she lose her children? But what kind of monster would rip them away from him? Would he even just let her leave?

She thought she had made her final decision, but in reality, she'd been lying to Dakota and herself for she really was no closer now than she'd been a few months ago. She was trying to choose the right path but didn't know which direction to take. She chuckled through her tears as the picture of Dakota's grandmother came unbidden to her mind. She was starting to sound like her now.

CHAPTER FORTY

H er ears tuned in to the familiar sound that rose above the clip clop of Maggie's hooves against the hard earth. The rhythmic whacking cast her thoughts four hundred miles away to a small farm in Kansas where she and Pop had created the same sound every fall.

The landscape before her, so very different from her homeland, faded as she retreated into her mind's eye. An old, white shingle house with leaking windows, a well that struggled to meet their needs, and flat, fertile lands with precious, loved livestock shimmered in her memory. Her eyes moistened. The vivid pictures in her mind made her even more homesick, if that was possible.

What was she to do about her home?

She brought Maggie to a stop, searching for the direction of the sound and moved on, drawn towards the chopping and hard male grunts of physical labor.

A squirrel raced across her path with another following closely on its trail, and her eyes cast about her. A buck, in all its powerful beauty stood on a craggy group of rocks searching the vast, flat land. Did he seek a mate to end his loneliness?

This land was beautiful and quiet, but so very desolate, which only increased her profound loneliness.

She wouldn't have to be lonely if she'd only accept Dakota's love and live here, but again it meant selling the farm she'd nearly died for. Indecision was creating havoc with her nerves, at times freezing her in her tracks.

She'd entertained the idea of renting her house, but who knew what kind of devastation that would bring. Not to mention the discomfort she'd feel if strangers lived in the only home she had known in a long, long time. The thought of selling it brought the same feelings, strangers living in her house where she'd lived with Charles and met the man who now caused her such indecision.

Looking skyward, she sent a silent prayer to Charles to help her come to a decision and smiled at the beauty of the South Dakota sky. A deep aquamarine blue heaven lay as a backdrop to wispy trails of brilliant white clouds, blinding in their beauty as they reflected the radiant sunlight. Kansas skies were similar, but not quite as deep a blue as the dazzling display above her.

If she were honest with herself, she could get used to this. Her life here was much easier with so many hands to help her. She was treated with respect and caring and could come and go as she pleased. At home, she'd be doing a myriad of tasks until exhaustion claimed her.

For the first time in many years, she felt rested. Her duties lay only with the feeding and caring of her children. She could tell by the burgeoning of her breasts, they would be waking soon. She couldn't stay out here much longer, but the thought of going back into that house and possibly facing Dakota kept her out in the cool air riding on her beloved horse.

Their last encounter had been tense and painful, which only made her want to go home even more. To be around him every day was torment.

She knew she could never make him understand how much her property meant to her, that she couldn't just give it up. He should understand, though. His home meant just as much to him. Again, she questioned herself on how she could fix this or if she even wanted to anymore. She never

knew she could be so homesick. Home was security. A place
to go where the outside world couldn't find her.

The pounding rhythm of the ax grew louder as they am-
bled along the long dirt trail. She couldn't imagine who was
out here in the middle of nowhere chopping wood. Whoever
it was, was giving it all they had. Her curiosity was piqued.

Rounding a bend in the old dirt path, she reigned in her
horse near a grove of trees before she could become visible
to the man viciously pounding on the wood right in front of
her.

Form-fitting jeans stretched and groaned across solid
thighs and rounded buttocks with his labors, while his upper torso was bared to the sun above. With each arcing rise
of the ax, she watched the play of strong, firm muscles quivering and bulging with determined precision.

While she sat bundled within a thick jacket, he seemed
immune to the chilled weather. The broad expanse of his
back glistened with moisture, highlighting the sinewy
strength of him. Rivulets of sweat trickled along
the indentation of his spine before coming to rest at the
waistband of his jeans, and coal black hair hung in sweat-
drenched waves along his shoulders.

She had never seen Dakota like this. Oh, she had seen him
working plenty of times, but this was very different, as if an
obsession burned within him.

She sat quietly in rapt attention, watching the power play
of muscles as he swung the ax. The sight of his strength and
masculinity had her stomach clenching in need. She had
missed him, missed his mind-blowing ability to satisfy her.
Missed the strength of his arms as he held her, his kisses, his
nibbles on her body, and the teasing erotic whispers against
her skin. She couldn't deny their attraction to each other,
and she questioned her sanity at giving this up.

He muttered to himself as he worked, and with each hard

hammer against another piece of wood, the words he spoke came out harsh, guttural, and angry. He was not speaking English, and it frustrated her. She couldn't understand the words, but she could tell the tone and was sure they were directed at her.

What he was doing was obvious. Instead of expressing his anger to her at the frustration of their relationship, he was taking it out on the wood.

There was at least a four-foot-high pile of uncut wood to his right and an almost six-foot tower of splintered and shattered wood to his left. He'd been busy.

Her heart clutched painfully within her chest. Her indecision was destroying lives, but what choice did she have?

She'd hidden her indecision behind the walls of a white shingled house while Dakota walked away, releasing his own problems on a pile of wood They were a mess.

Maggie, seeing the familiar man before her, let out a neigh, and Dakota swung around at the sound. His body was stiff and ready for attack.

He stared at her, hard. No warmth crinkled the corners of his eyes this time. No brilliant smile infused his handsome face, melting her on the spot. His legs were spread in defense, the arm at his side holding the well-used ax in a raised grip. His smooth, muscled chest rose and fell with his labored breathing.

For the first time in their relationship, his anger was directed at her, and it was frightening. Turning Maggie swiftly, she raced back along the trail to the house.

CHAPTER FORTY-ONE

The children were fed and asleep. Her breasts were calm for the moment, and her body was feeling much better. The effects of all three were relaxing. She was feeling stronger and would soon be ready to make the trek home.

Although it was October, she was told they were experiencing a rare day. It had warmed into the sixties. She rested lazily on an open veranda behind the white stone structure of his home, leaning back against a cushion on one of several lounge chairs. Turbulent dark blue storm clouds could be seen in the distance, but for the moment it was heavenly letting the sun warm her. The weather would change again very soon. They couldn't expect it to stay this way.

Dakota's land stretched out as far as the eye could see, and she let her eyes absorb it all. To the right was the cattle housing, a massive gray and white building with two tall, dark grey silos to the left and a long low building to the right where the sounds of muted mooing could distinctly be heard. At least a couple hundred head of cattle were spread out across the field closest to the barn, grazing in the grass.

She gazed even farther to the right where three tall gray structures stood stark against the bright sky. Anna assumed they held the milk that was produced here each day. Two of the structures had a huge eighteen-wheeled refrigerated truck sitting out front, proudly displaying the Dakota Dairy Farm emblem.

She wondered about it all. Far too often she'd heard of how the government treated its indigenous people. She'd heard horror stories of unbelievable poverty and how many turned to drugs and alcohol as a way to cope. How did Dakota come to be here?

"Did you inherit this land, Dakota?"

The well-rounded buttocks of her lover became more prominent as he bent to rest his arms on the railing, peering out at all he owned. She appreciated the view. She could always appreciate looking at this man.

He'd come back to their bed the night she'd discovered him chopping the wood, but not until the wee hours of the morning, and he'd been gone before she awoke. With each rebuke she gave him, he pulled further and further away, and she admitted to herself she was suffering the pain of losing him, but it was what she had to do.

"This ranch was a gift. When I was nine years old, I came here to work. Times were tough for us and each had to work to help support the family. My father had just died, and I was thrust into the position of the man of the house, even though I was very young and still grieved for my father. My employer, Mr. Cooper was a strong, intelligent, white man who took me under his wings and taught me all he knew."

Standing tall and stretching, he moved closer to her and took a seat on the softly cushioned Adirondack chair beside her.

"The story is a bit similar to yours. He'd never married and had no children to pass his great legacy to. I was a young man in need of guidance and an income. He was an older man in need of a good worker. He became my mentor and eventually, a friend. We became very close."

Anna watched him intently as he spoke. As was typical for him, he maintained a calm outer appearance. Only a few times since she met him had she seen his anger. Many times, in their bed she'd seen tenderness. At all other times he remained in control. He related this tale as if telling an age-old story, showing very little emotion, which didn't surprise her much. He showed very little emotion around her anymore.

"After I'd been here for almost seventeen years, he became ill with cancer. He wasn't that old, and the cancer came as a surprise, as I guess it does for everyone. It was upsetting to think I would once more bury a man who had been a father to me. I figured that after he passed, I'd have to move back home to the reservation and try to find work, but I was in for a surprise. I'd actually started packing in preparation to leave after his funeral when his attorney came to me and told me that he'd bequeathed all of this land to me."

A movement caught her attention, and she turned to see Jake tearing across the grass in pursuit of a rabbit. Smiling, she watched as the rabbit disappeared into a hole in the ground and a panting Jake lay down across the hole, guarding his prize.

Dakota continued speaking, and she turned back to him to see him also watching Jake's antics.

"I knew I couldn't live here alone when so many of my tribe struggled just to make it through each day. That's when it hit me to bring them here, put them to work, give them a home and let them live in the traditions we cherish."

Bringing his fingers to his lips, he let out an ear-piercing whistle, and Jake rose to his feet to begin an exhausted walk home.

"So, you have been the owner of this land for ten years?"

"Yes, and it's been a wonderful place for all of us. Well, for a while it was wonderful."

Jake climbed the three steps of the veranda and found his water bowl, draining it before he came to Dakota's side and collapsed with a harrumph. Her dog loved it here. He'd made new friends, both two-legged and four-legged, and he had all new places to explore. He often ran wild and free for hours at a time, but as he did at home, he always returned at mealtime. The dog's stomach would always be his curfew.

"Tell me more about her."

"I don't think that's necessary."

"Yes, it is. I want to know about the woman who captured your heart."

He chuckled in a self-deprecating manner and lowered his hand to scratch Jake's head. He was quiet and still for so long she wondered if he would answer, but with an intake of breath, he told their story.

"Her name was Wachiwi. She was the daughter of my father's cousin."

Again, he chuckled. "Let me say she was a cousin far removed. When I met her, I just knew I would marry her. She was pretty and very kind. She found beauty in everything and had a voice like an angel when she sang. She walked in a quiet dignity and grace that many admired. When I lost her, I felt confused and angry and wondered what I had done to deserve such pain."

Speaking of the man who'd been his mentor, he'd spoken in a flat, monotone voice, but it changed when he spoke of his wife. She watched as he closed his eyes against the memories and with a lowered and sad voice, continued.

"She was tiny, no more than five-feet-three inches. She barely reached my chest. I remember that she always smiled. At least in the beginning. With each baby she lost, her smiles came further and further apart until she no longer smiled at all. Eventually all she did was cry. I couldn't reach her. I couldn't stop her withdrawal."

Reaching out, she laid a hand on his arm. The need to touch him as he revealed his pain overwhelmed her. He pulled away from her touch, and she was surprised how much it hurt. Why did he stay by her side if being around her was so hard for him? Was it to torture her? Or was he torturing himself?

"You pull away from me, but I was only trying to let you know I understand what you went through. I went through the same thing."

"There's a difference between us, though. I have chosen to move on from the pain, but you cling to it and use it as a shield to hide from the possibility of more pain."

On her gasp, he lifted heavy lids and looked to her.

"You know I am right."

"I'm not hiding. I'm just trying to protect my land."

She watched his face contort in a mask of disbelief.

"You have to make a decision. You can't just play with me. One minute you want me and the next you push me away."

One of his people walked out of the house, and he paused until they were far away from their conversation. Standing, he turned to her. "Go or stay. Take the ring off or leave it on. The choice is yours, but I need you to make a decision. You either take the plunge to love again or you want your home and the memory of Charles."

The warning beeps of a truck backing up made both look towards a milk carrier leaving, the truck full and ready to move on to the factory.

He watched the process for a moment before he emitted a long release of breath. "I have to go."

As he walked down the steps and headed across the long, grassy field, she crumbled inside. He was right. She was putting off making a decision, and it wasn't fair to any of them. Her body was healing. Her children were growing. She knew Pop needed her, that her farm needed her. She had to decide what she wanted. His words had been harsh and difficult to hear, but she acknowledged the truth behind them.

Why was she still here? What, exactly, did she want?

The familiar ache began in her breasts, and she rose to seek out her children, but before she went inside a feeling of being watched had her looking to the darkening sky. An eagle sat perched on the tip of a towering tree as if guarding all around him. She could barely see him against the grays and deep blues of the growing storm, but the widening of his wings against the rising wind captured her attention.

Wherever she went, there was an eagle.

CHAPTER FORTY-TWO

Her three little bundles, now nearing eight weeks of age, were growing stronger and gaining weight, although Dyami was still the tiniest of the three. They ate almost constantly, draining her. Their hunger was so demanding one of the local wives who was also nursing helped her every day.

Everyone was helpful, never really letting her lift a finger. She was special to them because of Dakota. It was obvious they loved and respected him. After experiencing his pain with the loss of his last wife and each of his children, they worshipped her for gifting him with three children at one time. She'd been told that to them, she had returned to him the spirits of the three children he had lost. It was an eerie thing to think about.

She spent her free time walking or riding, doing her best to repair the damage from carrying three children for over eight months. The weight was slipping away, her skin toning and firming, but very, very slowly. She still felt like a blimp.

She shook her head slightly. If she was truthful, she exercised to relieve the boredom and loneliness. The children slept for hours each day, leaving her with nothing to do. When she tried to assist in the kitchens or with cleaning, she was ushered from the room. Dakota spent more time away from her than by her side. If she searched him out, he would turn and walk away.

The loneliness was like a knife to her heart. The inactivity was causing panic. She was used to being active and working hard. Leisure time didn't sit well with her.

Mostly, though, she spent this time worrying over her indecision. She knew her fields had been harvested by now, but she wondered about her garden. Had it been also harvested? Had the food been canned or frozen? She was embarrassed to admit she was so wrapped up in her own worries, she'd forgotten to ask Pop.

She had to leave. There was a myriad of reasons she was still here, but foremost was her fear of being alone with her children, but they were old enough now. She was well enough to travel. She had no more excuses other than her fears.

She couldn't continue to leave all the work to Pop. He did call occasionally and send important mail for her to handle, but the brunt of the running of the home and farm had fallen on his elderly shoulders. It wasn't fair. What was supposed to be a week had turned into over two months. It was way past time for her to leave, and her mind asked her a question she couldn't answer. Why hadn't she?

Today she had bundled up against the winter air and searched out Maggie. While she prepared to saddle her mare, a strong young boy came up and took the saddle from her, doing the work she was used to doing. She alternated between being angry that she wasn't allowed to do anything on her own, to feeling oddly pampered. She would grow lazy in this life.

The sounds of hoof beats made her pause, and she turned Maggie to see who was approaching. She watched as the man who made up her dreams each night trotted towards her and came to a stop a mere foot away.

"You grow more beautiful with each day. Come with me. I need you."

"Is something wrong?"

He brought his horse up until he was just a few inches

away and leaned forward. Wrapping his hands in her long hair, he tugged her forward until their chilled lips met. He didn't let go until those same lips were warm and swollen.

"I need you."

Confused by his change of heart, she released the bridle to his waiting hands and held on as he trotted them back to the stables. He handed the care of both horses over to the same young boy who had helped her, and she quickly blushed as the young man watched him lift her from the saddle and kiss her again.

Briefly, she thought of resisting. It would do no good to lie with him again when she was planning to leave, but she reluctantly gave in. Her need matched his.

A sense of urgency radiated from him as he linked his fingers in hers and practically pulled her towards the side door of his home.

Laughing at his frantic desire to have her, she was finding it hard to breathe as he quickly tugged her forward and shushed her laughter as they got close. He obviously wanted no one to know they were inside.

With a soft push against the outside door, he looked around before pulling her through to the quiet interior. All were about their daily duties. They silently rushed down a hallway until they came to their room, and ushering her inside, he closed the door with a soft click.

Wasting no time, he quickly stripped himself of his coat, his breathing loud in the quiet chamber. Wanting him had never been an issue for her, and the fact that he needed her so strongly only further enhanced her own desire. Closing the distance between them until she was close enough to see his chest rise and fall with each passionate breath he took, she watched as he disrobed. When he slipped off his shirt, she sucked in a breath in appreciation at the toned, bulging muscles of his chest.

As she liked to do, she laid a palm over his heart, feeling the anxious rhythm inside his firm chest. His fiercely controlled desire pounded off him in waves that rippled deep inside her own body. Lowering her eyes, she saw the evidence of his desire stretching the fabric of his pants and giggled.

"Anna, I've missed you."

"I can see that."

He slipped her coat off her shoulders, tossing it to the side and guided his fingers under the edge of her top. His fingers teased as he glided his hands along her ribs to lift the garment over her head, but she stayed his movement, hesitant.

"I'm embarrassed for you to see me."

The gentle smile returned, so long absent from his handsome face. Oh, how she had missed it.

"No, Anna, don't be ashamed. Your body shows only the evidence of the gifts you gave me. Your body shows the hard work you had to go through to bring forth our children."

Shyness had her blushing as she lifted her arms and let him undress her. As her top came to rest on the other discarded clothing, he touched the soft, bulging skin of her stomach and ran his hand along the jagged, puckered stretch marks her large pregnancy had produced.

He knelt, lowering her pants slightly until they rested just above her mound and laid his lips against the scars, kissing each in turn. Her embarrassment turned to tears at the gentle kindness he showed her. He was beauty in all its forms, yet he was kissing her ravaged body as if she was the beautiful one.

She grasped his head in her hands, tugging upwards, and he rose to capture her mouth, pressing his heated arousal against the stomach he had just kissed.

With arms still encircling his head and neck, she held on,

295

for surely her legs would collapse with the surge of need coursing through her body. It had been too long since he had touched her, too long since she could touch him. She didn't know why he wanted to now or what had changed within him, but she was not going to turn him away. Denying him was only denying her own needs, and that would be foolish.

She had hurt him, and he had held her at a distance for a long time. The feel of him against her once more was heaven-sent. No matter what they went through, their physical attraction always remained, simmering and smoldering behind sometimes cool and sometimes angry exteriors, but always there.

He knelt before her once more and slipped her shoes from her feet, his fingertips gliding over the soles of her feet in a sensual caress. His face was mere inches away from her core, and the thought of him touching her there almost made her bounce on her feet in excitement. She could not wait.

He stood, his fingers tickling inside the waistband of her pants. The rough skin of his palms slid over her buttocks as he inched the material over her hips. She wiggled in impatience until the garment fell to her feet, and with one swift kick, she sent it flying across the room to lie in lonely abandon against the wall.

Except for her bra, the final barrier against his observant eyes, she stood naked before him, unsure of herself yet tremendously aroused.

A small smile played along her lips as he hastily removed the rest of his clothing, kicking his own shoes against the wall. So much for being quiet. The proof of his own desire thrust forward, thick, rigid, and seeking, and she reached to touch it, but he stopped her.

"No."

He raised his hand to undo the clasp of her bra but frowned when she blushed furiously and tried again to stop his hands.

"All will be okay, Anna. I promise."

With a flick of his long fingers, he undid the hooks, and heavily laden breasts were bared to his eyes. He cupped them, lifting the weight in his hands. Running his fingers along the pebbled tips, he stared, mesmerized, as a trickle of her children's life-giving milk wet the tip of his thumb.

Embarrassment flooded her despite his assurances. Her body was no longer the trim, perky breasted body of youth. She was now a softly rounded woman, a mother, but the ravages of childhood obviously meant nothing to this man, her lover.

Bending, he scooped her up into his arms with barely a grunt and carried her to their bed, laying her down on the soft mattress where she had only eight weeks ago given birth to his children.

She loved him. She wouldn't tell him that. She could not give in to living here. She'd made her decision. She was going home, but she truly loved this man who was sending shivers of desire along her body as he nibbled on her neck. He could've easily turned away from the strange body she now bore, but he didn't. That sent a powerful message straight to her heart.

She opened her mouth to speak, and he swept in, taking possession, demanding her response until their tongues dueled in passion and their breathing became labored.

He broke off the kiss as quickly as he'd started and began his carefully planned attack. He tasted the body he had come to know so well. Her skin was delicately scented by her own personal musk. It made him rock hard, but he steeled himself against the need to pound home his desire. This day was for her. He was determined to push her beyond pleasure, to a point of no return. To the point that she would remember this day forever once she left him, because he knew she was going.

He cupped the soft roundness of her breasts and gently tweaked her sensitive nipples as he nuzzled the hollow in between until she moaned. Replacing his fingers with his mouth, he suckled, tasting the sweet milk that nourished his children. His teeth grazed the tender, aroused flesh until she writhed and bucked beneath him.

She reached for him, and he stayed her hand, pushing it back to the mattress. He wouldn't allow her to touch, not today.

The scent of aroused femininity drifted around the room, spurring him on in his quest to make his bedroom a place to remember. He slid lower, kissing the rounded evidence of his children's birth and still lower. Her stomach quivered beneath his lips, telling him how highly strung and anxious she was for this pleasure.

Again she reached for him, her hands coming to rest in his hair, and again he clasped her by the wrists, lowering her hands to her sides, and moved lower to her core.

He rained gentle kisses on her outer lips before slipping his tongue between the folds and parting them, searching for the little bud inside. When he finally circled this most sensitive part of her, her shoulders came up off the bed in mindless passion until he laid a hand on her stomach, letting her know what he wanted as he pushed her down onto the comfortable mattress.

"Anna, be still. Let me make love to you." He knew she heard the words he dared not speak, one last time. This time together became poignant, for it meant a closing.

She moaned, the sound guttural and strangled as he pleasured her with his tongue. He slipped one finger inside her slick passage and then two, mimicking the strokes his engorged cock longed to do.

Trembling took hold of her body as her orgasm neared, and when she exploded around him, she gripped him tightly between quivering thighs, holding on to the pleasure.

He refused to stop. He continued lapping at her core until she came again and again, until she begged him to let her rest, but again, he wasn't done. He rose above her, holding her gaze, and when she again reached for him, he pinned her arms above her head before plunging into her slick heat. He drew her out once more, achingly loving the woman who meant everything to him. Not until her walls began to convulse once more did he hammer home his own need, bellowing as the almost painful orgasm overtook him and not caring who heard.

Anna felt as if she had taken a powerful sedative. Her body couldn't move. Deliciously satiated, she felt him slip to her side, pulling her languid body against his own. Lazily, her fingers caressed his arm in exhaustion. Her eyes grew heavy as sleep beckoned, and just before she drifted off, he whispered words she could not respond to.

"Don't leave, Anna."

She felt as if someone had just ripped her heart from her chest. There was no way she could ever tell him what he meant to her, but she knew she couldn't stay. With no way to respond to him without hurting him further, she began a soft snore of pretend sleep.

CHAPTER FORTY-THREE

On the morning after she had told Dakota she was going home, she walked out of her bedroom to an unnatural silence.

No one greeted her with a smile. No sounds of movement could be heard. No one was anywhere at all.

Walking into the kitchen, she found Chumani alone at the counter preparing vegetables. The long family table, usually filled with family breaking their fast and sharing their plans for the day, sat empty and cleared of all food.

She greeted Chumani and was shaken when the woman turned her back to her and walked away. Obviously, Dakota had told everyone, and she'd become a pariah. She was no longer welcome among these people.

She searched until she found a piece of still warm bread, and after spreading a thick layer of jam on the surface, crammed it into her mouth and left the room quickly. She had to have something in her stomach before she started this long day.

On instinct, she moved toward the living space to speak to his grandmother, but even she had deserted her post. Already questioning her decision, she could've used a few words of wisdom.

Feeling dejected by their quick abandonment, she made her way to the nursery and found all three of her children alone, awake, and quietly babbling to each other in a playpen. They were dressed and cared for, but it was rather unnerving to see them without supervision. This family was very loving and careful of children, so she knew someone had to be close, but where? Looking in the adjoining rooms, she still found no trace of anyone. That was when she gave up. She had no time for games. She packed up her children's belongings and moved her luggage and the babies small carry bags to the front door.

Dakota had accepted her leaving with his usual calm demeanor but had refused to drive her. He'd offered little help at all except ordering a town car, and she glanced at her watch. The car was due to arrive at nine, leaving her a little under a half an hour.

Thinking it was probably best to be well out of the house, she moved the bags once more and set them on the front porch.

The outside of the house was just like the inside. No one moved out there, either. No cars lined the driveway, no workers could be seen in the fields to the side. Not even a stray car traveled the road beyond Dakota's land. It was if she was entirely alone in the universe, and it was creepy.

Dakota was also nowhere to be seen. Knowing full well by now that he sensed her every movement, she knew he was staying away on purpose. She'd hurt him terribly, but what was she to do? Her home was her responsibility, just as his home was his to oversee. She had to get back before the full winter weather set in. She had to see if she had enough food to see her through the winter.

She made her way back to her room and crated Miranda, who preferred to hold her legs out to the side and fight, refusing to cooperate. She obviously didn't want to make the long move again.

Near to tears from the battle and stinging from the scratches, she carried the crate to the front door and set it by the door. It was too cold to place her outside. Loud, echoing plaintiff cries came from within the crate as her little cat voiced her displeasure at the confinement. It would indeed be a long ride.

Now she just had to find Jake and gather the babies, which was also not going to be an easy task. She'd have to carry all three of them by herself.

Rubbing her hand along the stinging scratches, she sighed. She'd best get used to carting her children around. She was going to be utterly alone with three little people, two pets, and a barn full of animals dependent on her for everything, and that was scary as hell.

When she'd told her mother about her decision to go home, she'd called her an unmitigated fool. That had hurt. Why she was refusing to accept Dakota's love and why she was questioning everything about their future together, she didn't know. She only knew she was afraid, and the thought of home gave her peace from her thoughts.

Maybe she needed to talk to someone. An image of Pop came to her mind, and she decided she couldn't wait to see him. He was her version of Unci, wise and sure. He was familiar. He was her family, and she missed him terribly.

The front door knocker shattered the silence of the house and had her jumping. The loud interference momentarily hushed her cat's protests, and Anna rushed to open the door. The driver was early, but she was grateful to see the first friendly face of the day.

It took over a half an hour, but the car was finally packed with all their belongings. She carried the babies out and stood there, realizing she had no idea how to secure them in the car. She'd never had the need to learn.

Fortunately, the driver of the car was a father and saw at once the dilemma she was facing. He held Elan and Dyami while he talked her through securing Mina, then held Dyami until she belted Elan. Finally, she unburdened him and secured Dyami into his seat. How was she ever going to do this alone?

Telling the driver she had one more thing to do, she raced out the back door and whistled for Jake. The tepees stood lifeless, no smoke curling against the sky from their tips. The cows could be heard, but their mooing was muted, as if they were far away or in their stalls in the long, low building. None stood in the fields. No people moved about, either. The land was cold, lifeless, empty and, again, very creepy.

Frantic, she whistled once more for her dog, but it was as if everyone had packed up and moved on, taking her dog with them. She knew that Jake wouldn't just abandon her. He must have been tricked into not being around. That blow hurt the worst, like a temperamental punishment of sorts from Dakota.

The driver walked to the back patio. In a frustrated voice, he informed her the babies were crying, and they had to leave, or he was dropping everyone back on the front porch. His fatherly manner had disappeared with the first cry of her children.

This wasn't going at all well.

With heartbreaking sadness, she thought of Maggie. She couldn't take her with them. She'd have to send for her later. Her only consolation was she knew her precious horse would receive excellent care. Otherwise, she would be afraid to leave her behind.

Miserable and more than a touch frustrated herself, she walked out of the front of the house and crawled into the back seat.

The driver moved off around the driveway, but not before closing the window between them. The crying was clearly getting on his nerves. Now even the driver was separating himself from her.

Dyami was only fussing, not yet setting up a screaming fit, so she checked Mina and Elan's diapers, fed them, and settled them back in their seats. By this point, Dyami was red in the face from screaming and Anna was crying profusely.

An hour and a half after she left Dakota, she at long last had three sleeping children, but Anna was still bawling like the babies she'd just cared for.

The separation window came down about halfway, and the driver looked to her with kind, fatherly eyes. Funny that the man was only kind when the children were quiet.

"You okay, miss?"

She looked at him and looked away. The window closed again, and Anna resumed her crying as she questioned her sanity.

Pop greeted her warmly, fussing over her three little additions to the household. Anna wrapped her arms around the man who had been a father to her for so many years and held on to him while pouring out her story of the last several weeks of her life through more bouts of tears.

The tears slowed, though, as the familiar arms held her, and when she at last looked up at him and really saw the man holding her, she felt nothing but shame. That was all she had been feeling this whole day.

He looked old, thin and exhausted, and she had caused it. It seemed as if everyone she encountered was feeling the effects of having her in their lives. She wasn't sure she could feel any more depressed.

If he had words of advice, he didn't impart them this time. With a couple shakes of his head, he looked at her sadly, as if disappointed in her. He told her he would stay in the apartment over the barn until the weekend, but after that he was leaving. Her humiliation at seeing what she'd done to him made her beg him to go home now. She would be fine, she hoped.

Reluctantly he left her, but not without telling her to call if she needed him. At six o'clock on a Tuesday evening a little over a year since she'd met Dakota Powers, she was alone again in her home with three additional lives dependent on her and her beloved dog four hundred miles away. Thoughts of Jake made her cry again, and that made her cry even harder because she was sick and tired of crying. When had she turned into such a crybaby?

She hiccupped and took a deep breath. This had to stop. She glanced around her kitchen and was pleased to see it clean and orderly, but she almost let out a wail when she realized how stupid she'd been. In her rash decision to leave, she hadn't planned. There were no cribs. There were only a few diapers. There was nothing she needed to care for her babies but a few items of clothing made by Dakota's family, the infant carriers, and her breasts.

She was in trouble.

Lugging her three heavy bundles upstairs to her bedroom, she removed the clothing they had travelled in and changed their diapers. Propping pillows all around her bed she laid each child around her as she sat in the middle and contemplated her life. When Charles had died, she had rallied herself and become the boss, running a three-hundred-and-fifty-acre farm almost entirely by herself. She was tired of being weak. She could do this. She was a strong woman. Hadn't she proved that already? It was time to stop feeling sorry for herself and to stop the tears.

Feeling empowered, she relaxed until Elan scrunched up his face and passed gas, scaring himself. His shocked cry woke up Mina and Dyami. As usual her calm and quiet Dyami only made a minor fuss, but Mina was one very unhappy young lady. She hushed each one in turn and changed them. She had twelve diapers to make it through the night. In the morning she'd call the pharmacy and have some delivered along with a few other supplies.

By six the next morning, however, twelve hours after the children had entered their new home, she was exhausted. Twelve diapers had definitely not been enough. Whether it was from traveling or something in her milk, each one of her precious children had developed a case of diarrhea with terrible gas, turning each little infant into a screaming mass of discomfort for most of the night. Reluctantly, she had resorted to using her towels.

She wasn't sure if she'd even closed her eyes all night, and they burned with the need for sleep.

This was not fun.

Just after eight, she dressed each baby the best she could and put them all in their carriers. Lugging them all to the kitchen, she made a frantic call to the pharmacy. The kind and understanding woman had promised she'd get their driver to bring her the diapers and something for the babies' gas as soon as possible.

With that accomplished, she called the local department store and purchased a crib. They could share the space for the time being as the cost of one almost bankrupted her.

Searching through her freezer and cupboards, she praised Pop for stocking her shelves.

She could do this.

She struggled, yet everything was going fairly well until the third Wednesday after her return home. Anna awoke before the sun had even risen in the sky to the sound of her crying babies and groaned. Blinding pain hammered behind her eyes, and her nose was so clogged she had to resort to mouth breathing. Her throat and lungs were on fire. Worst of all, she was freezing. This wasn't good. She couldn't be sick. What if she passed this on to her children?

On shaky legs that threatened to collapse beneath her, she went to the crib. Mika's fine, brown, peach-fuzzy head was covered in sweat, and her face was blood red. Anna panicked, touching her hand to the tiny forehead. She was too hot. Elan and Dyami were cool to the touch, although Dyami's nose was running. She breathed a cautious sigh of relief.

Her breasts were aching with the need to feed, and with a fever-muddled mind, she labored to lift each baby in turn and move them to her bed. She was unbelievably weak as she held each tiny bundle in her arms, fearful she would drop them.

Mika screamed her displeasure with life while she fed the boys, and as soon as the first one broke from her nipple and drifted back to sleep, she quickly grabbed Mika and placed her in the open spot. This was just too exhausting as sick as she was. She had to get the formula the pediatrician advised. She couldn't continue to do this.

Her normally sweet daughter was fussy against her breast, struggling to suckle with a clogged nose and fever. Anna found the fight to get her fed was beyond her capabilities. She knew her own fever was climbing, and she felt dizzy. She feared dropping a child or doing something to harm them in her fevered state.

Grabbing her phone, she called the only person she could think of, crying as she begged Pop for help. With Pop-like efficiency, he had a hired, private ambulance at her door within an hour, and she and the babies were whisked away to the hospital in town. There was no other choice on the two that were not sick. They had to come with her. There was simply no one to care for them. She praised herself for having put her children on her health insurance right away, but insurance only paid so much. This was going to cost a fortune, which only scared her further.

All four of them were placed in the same room to prevent spreading the germs, resulting in Anna getting little rest. She tried to sleep when they slept, and when they were awake, she fought to get them to accept a bottle. She was on heavy medications, so her milk was pumped and tossed, now worthless to her small children.

Three days after entering the hospital, Anna and Mika felt better under the care of the hospital, but Dyami and Elan were sick.

People came and went from her room. Some came to speak to her about how she'd pay the balance of her bill, some to give her advice on the children, and some with medicines upon medicines. Even more came to take their temperatures and blood pressure. Voices spoke constantly over the intercom in the hallway. Noise was a constant, and she craved silence and sleep, but none was forthcoming.

She'd been sick last Christmas, and here she was sick again this Christmas. Another horrible holiday. They were there for six days. By the time they were released, she was feeling better from a medical standpoint, yet exhausted from the need for rest.

CHAPTER FORTY-FOUR

The wind was wicked and harsh as it battered his body, but he welcomed the frigid discomfort. He felt it a fitting punishment for once again being a failure to a woman. He'd tried so hard to reach his first wife and let her know he loved her deeply and would always be there for her.

He had begged her to listen to him, telling her it didn't matter if they couldn't have children. He'd told her that only her love was important to him, but in her sorrow, she had turned away from him. She had shut him out of her pain and withered away before his eyes as he pleaded with her to hold on. He had buried her and his little daughter side by side and run away, unable to control his grief.

With Anna, he thought he'd done everything the right way. He'd tried to do all he could to keep her by his side and to let her know he loved her. He would have protected her, provided for her, cared for her, and stood proudly by her side as her partner in life, but once again a woman refused him.

He could've tried to demand she stay, but he knew with his independent Anna it would be counter-productive. She had to make this choice on her own. Although her final decision had devastated him, it hadn't surprised him. He'd pretty much known all long what path she would take, but he'd prayed for her to choose another course. Again, his prayers were not heard.

In his desperation, he stupidly entertained the idea of threatening to take the children, but that would only have caused hate. Hate was not what he wanted from Anna. They could have something very special if she would only lower that shield and allow him inside her heart.

What was wrong with him? Was he not meant to have love? Was this all his fault? Did he go about loving all wrong? His parents had always had a deep love and respect for one another. Everyone around him had strong bonds and deep commitments. Why couldn't he?

It was bad enough to lose Anna, but the worst was losing the children, his flesh and blood. In just a few short weeks they had become a part of him. Elan, strong, with a cry that let all know who and what he wanted. Mika, a brave and intuitive young lady who studied the faces of all who cared for her, and Dyami, small and fragile, yet patient and kind. His children, his babies. Powerful words, but they were gone. Anna was gone.

Once again love had been ripped away from him, and he was tired of it.

He wrestled between his desire to be by her side and the responsibilities that lay heavy on his shoulders. Should he give up everything and go to her? Who would stand in his place to run this huge business? No one else here had his experience. If he went to her, would he ever forgive himself if he abandoned his family? On the other hand, how could he live without Anna and his children?

He didn't want to travel back and forth weekly between the two houses. He wanted them to be on the same property, to spend every possible moment with them or at least know they would be there to welcome him at the end of his day. His life here demanded long hours. If he lived with her in Kansas, that life would be the same. He could not split himself in two.

In desperation and with a heart that couldn't possibly break any further, he raised his eyes to the crisply clear midnight-blue sky. Stars pockmarked the darkness with a million, brilliant celestial lights winking incongruously above him. As a child, his grandfather had weaved stories on how with each death here on this earth a star was formed in the sky.

With an educated mind, he knew it was fanciful, but inside his heart he hoped somewhere out there were those who had already left this earth. He wanted to believe his grandfather, his father, Mr. Cooper, his wife, and his unborn children all watched over him and that maybe they could guide him now when he felt so lost.

Tears welled in his eyes, quickly freezing against his lashes as he prayed for their help. He prayed for a light to show his path. He prayed for the woman who'd become his life. He needed her. His mind desperately searched for an answer while his chest clenched with a pain he was powerless to withstand.

A hand gently touched his as it gripped the porch railing, and he turned, lowering his gaze to search the wizened old eyes of his grandmother. She was bundled against the cold with just her eyes peeking between the layers of a scarf, but if she braved a night like this then she obviously knew he needed guidance. A movement caught his attention, and he looked up to see his mother watching the two of them behind the thick patio door glass, a look of love and concern in her eyes. His family once again felt his pain and knew he needed help. He needed some words of wisdom to help him understand.

He looked back to the little slip of a woman by his side. "I am suffering, Unci. I stand here again under the eyes of the Creator and wonder about my path. I am torn between my duty to my family and the woman I love and the children I miss."

The fragile hand gripped his, whether to offer him comfort or seek stability against the winds that threatened to knock her over, he didn't know. In respect, he tucked the tiny woman into the crook of his arm, using his body to shield her from the harsh, cold wind.

"We do not create our path, my child. Our path is set before us by the Creator."

He once more looked back to the night sky as his eyes filled with sorrow. Her words didn't help. They only confused him further. On a strangled voice, he spoke to the sky again. "Then how do I know what to do? Every time I think I've been set on the right course, I end up losing. Is this what my life is supposed to be? *O ma key yo.*"

His grandmother clucked her tongue. "You do not need help, Dakota. You need to open your eyes. Do you not see that the eagles have gone?"

He searched his memory. He hadn't really noticed. With such pain surrounding his heart, he had ceased to see anything. Everything had just become part of the scenery before him. He did his job each day, barely remembering what he'd done, and curled into his empty bed at night to mourn his losses, remembering all that had taken place on his bed. He had obviously become blinded to the messages they carried from the Creator.

"They have gone to watch over her, Dakota. She struggles with the same pain as you. She is torn between duty and love, and she desperately fears that love, but unlike you she is alone in her fight. She is struggling to survive with no one to help her. She is in trouble, and she doesn't know it."

He shook his head, knowing Anna had chosen to leave, chosen her own path.

"When Anna was here, she cried too much. She was in too much pain from missing her home. Yet if I go to her, I will have to leave my own home."

"It is good to cry, child. Tears cleanse the eyes and help us to see clearly. Let her cry until her eyes open to the right path. Her path is with you, but she is too afraid to see it."

He kissed the parchment-like skin of his grandmother's forehead as he held her close.

A blast of wind whipped against her, and she buried her face in his coat, her words muffled against his chest.

"Dakota, why can't you have both homes? Why does she or you need to choose?"

He looked down at the salt and pepper hair that protected his grandmother's amazing intelligence and thought about her words. He began to laugh as relief eased his pain, but it was all quickly replaced with a feeling of utter stupidity. Why had they been so caught up in choosing one home or the other when the answer was so simple?

"You are wise, Grandmother. You make me feel the fool."

She backed up until she could look up at him. "Not so wise, my child. I have just witnessed too much in my long life. You're not a fool. You are wise in your own way. You just thought of your wishes while she thought of hers. You forgot to meet in the middle, like so many do in our world."

He held her delicate body against his, wondering how much longer he would be able to do so. The physical life didn't go on forever. Again, he would lose a woman who meant so much to his life as she took her place in the stars.

The wind grew ferocious and another blast of arctic air robbed her of her breath. She gasped as the old lungs struggled against nature's wrath.

"The creator has laid your path. It is clear to all but the two of you. You have both been too blind to see but follow the eagles. Go to her. Bring her home. Love her."

A shiver wracked the aged body, and she tugged on him gently. "I'm cold, Dakota. You must be cold, also. Come, we go inside."

He walked her to her chair and again kissed her withered

cheek before moving away with an excitement for life he hadn't felt in a long time. He just had to convince one very stubborn woman, and that was his biggest hurdle of all. While his brain worked out how to make the plan work, he threw some clothes in a suitcase. Packed, he looked to his bed, the bed that had seen the joy of new life and way too much pain in recent weeks. He was determined to change that.

He went to his mother to explain all, but just before he walked out the door the phone rang.

CHAPTER FORTY-FIVE

The cab driver dropped their one little suitcase and several bags of things the hospital had sent home on the front porch and shivered as he stood waiting. As she searched frantically in her pocketbook for enough to pay the man, her children waited together in their carriers in the back of the cab.

She seethed internally that the driver didn't bother to help her with the carriers or help her get inside. He simply collected his money, deposited the children in the driveway, and left them standing alone. Dakota could teach this man a few things about being a gentleman.

As bitter winter winds whipped snow from the ground in a spiraling tornado-like effect and blasted icy pellets on all four of them, she lugged each child to the front porch and fumbled for her key. She had no idea where her key was for this entrance or if she even had one on her ring. With two heavy babies on one arm and one in the other, she gave up and fought the breath-catching winds whipping around her home to make a dash for the back door.

The screech of her ever-present eagle made her cast her gaze upwards for a moment as she ran, and she squinted against the brilliance of the clear winter sky. Since the first day Dakota had come into her life, the bird had become her constant companion. He even brought his mate to visit on occasion. Today she saw neither one, until she rounded the corner and approached her back porch.

An impressive figure, he sat alone on the railing watching

them. His gaze flickered down to the burdening weight in her arms and back to gaze into her eyes. His rich brown feathers lifted and ruffled, his strong body unflinching against the wind. The piercing black pupils centered within the pale-yellow eyes looked to her with wisdom and sorrow as their mutual observation connected.

He spread his wings in a wide arc, and she gasped, almost recoiling as he brought one wing forth towards her. She watched, absolutely spellbound, as the tip of the long wing touched the edge of her shoulder for just a fraction of a second. He lowered the wing, then with a tip of his head to her, spread the huge span of his wings and on a bounce, took off in flight. The interaction shook her, the meaning unclear, but she was left no time to think on it.

The children struggled as the frigid cold robbed them of breath and they began to kick up a fuss. She rushed to get them inside. Opening the back door, she took them in and deposited them with a small thump on the kitchen table.

Her thoughts turned quickly back to the strange encounter with the majestic bird. He had been alone, just like her. Where was his mate? Had it been injured? He had looked at her with such sadness before spreading his powerful wings and taking off in flight. What was his message? Was he showing sympathy? Could a bird show sympathy? She had no idea.

The house was freezing cold, and she shivered just as Mina let out a scream of impatience at being bundled up in the carrier for so long. Her scream sent the others jumping in alarm, and within seconds bright red faces and waving arms were letting her know they were unhappy.

She'd had enough. She couldn't do this. She had tried and even succeeded in some ways, but she needed help. No one could possibly run a farm, take care of a home, and raise three babies alone. It was impossible. The scary part was, this was winter, her quiet time. How could she do this once spring came and her farm work began?

After quieting each child, turning the furnace up high, and starting a warming blaze in the fireplace to get rid of the bone chilling cold in the unused home, she sat down on her living room sofa with her children at her sides and picked up her phone. She was going to have to call her mother.

She stared at the rectangular lifeline in her hand and knew a simple call would bring her, but she questioned her sanity on making such a move. How would that really help? Her mother couldn't stay here forever, and she knew it could be months, maybe even years before she would have to stop depending on her help.

The more important question was, did she want her here? Could she handle her condescension when she told her she'd made a mistake? She didn't want to admit her mother had been right when she said her stupid stubbornness was going to get herself and her babies killed.

It was hard to acknowledge to herself that she couldn't run this farm and raise these babies alone. She was proving everyone right, and it rankled her. She had been stubborn in her claims that she could do this alone, but she'd been proven the fool. Being strongly independent had its faults.

She needed the help, yet she hesitated. Setting the phone down on her leg, she continued to stare at it in confusion. She was left with three choices. Call her mom, continue to try to do this herself, or call him.

Maybe her mother wasn't the right one to call. She knew she'd come, but things were still so fragile between them. Did she want to try to mend their relationship while being dependent on her? It didn't sound like something she wanted to find out.

She looked to her three sleeping children. She'd told herself that her actions were the best for her children, but she was wrong and realized she hadn't really been thinking about them, only about herself. She'd seen what she'd done to Dakota but had cast it aside and allowed her fears to control her. Shame filled her once again. She'd hurt him over and over. Why was she so afraid to give him her love? Had she become her mother? Holding people at a distance?

Dakota was right when he told her she wore her fear like a shield. She was afraid to love and lose, but Dakota had lost his father, his wife, and three children and still had the strength to love again.

As usual lately, her mind was a mass of confusion as she struggled to reach a decision. She stared once again at the phone in her hand, wondering. Could she do it? Should she?

Those long and lonely hours in the hospital had left her with a lot of time to think about him. She truly missed him. It took her a long time to convince her stubborn mind that she needed him. She loved him with all her heart, and it'd be foolish to let him go, but she was still afraid.

The bottom line was, she missed talking with him. She missed the feeling of being cherished by him. She missed his strong arms when things got tough. She missed his calmness and bravery, and most of all she missed being loved by him. He had truly shown her about love.

As much as she loved this old house, it was nothing more than four walls. It did not hug her or love her back. This land was just land. It did not talk to her when she was lonely or smile at her with tenderness. She told herself she was hanging on to this land because it was her children's heritage, but the three sleeping babies in front of her didn't even know this place existed. They didn't give a fig about this house.

While a part of her would regret the loss of her home, the larger part of her yearned for him.

She loved him. It was as simple as that. She'd truly been

the fool. Now the question was, was she brave enough to make the call and beg him for forgiveness? Her eyes filled with the pain her life had become. Almost everything in it had been a result of her own stupid actions.

Unci's aged face popped into her mind as if she were here with her in this room, her calm intelligence gazing at her with the wisdom of a lifetime experienced to its fullest. "*You must follow your path, Anna, but do not let yesterday control today.*"

Her deep breath for courage was shaky as she lifted her phone and pressed the button to light the screen. Her heartbeat thudded in time with her fingers pressing the numbers, but before she could press the last two, she heard her back-door open.

Alarm lit along her skin before she realized she had to know whoever was coming in. Rising, she watched as her kitchen door swung open, and there he stood. His face was thinner than she remembered, and his eyes were circled in darkness, looking unsure of his welcome. Her heart broke at what she had done to him, another result of her foolish actions. With a sob, she ran to him and threw herself against his body, grabbing hold of her life. With a step back, he took the force of her embrace, wrapping her firmly in cold arms as his coat touched her warm skin.

"You came."

He squeezed a little tighter, as if to ensure she was real. "You needed me."

She looked up at him, searching his eyes. "How do you always know everything?"

He shook his head slightly and laughed in a self-deprecating way. "No, Anna. I don't. If I did, I would've known how to stop you from leaving me."

She lifted the phone in her hand, and he looked down at it.

"I was just calling you."

He smiled, the corners of his eyes crinkling in the endearing way she'd come to love.

"How did you know I needed you?"

"Pop called me and told me that all of you had been in the hospital and were coming home today. He also gave me a bit of a lecture. He's a wise old man."

Slipping off his coat and laying it across a chair, he wrapped her in his arms again.

She held on for dear life. She would never let him go again.

Wanting to stay this way forever, she let out a groan as three things happened simultaneously. A scratching sound and loud bark at the kitchen door, two of the three babies began crying, and she blurted out how sorry she was, which she wasn't even sure Dakota heard. A mini-pandemonium reigned.

He backed out of her arms and opened the kitchen door allowing a jubilant Jake to come rushing into the room, almost toppling Anna over. He whimpered and cried, and she hugged him to her, but the wailing of her children got louder, now joined by the third. She couldn't ignore them.

The hospital had sent her home with formula, and she rushed to prepare a bottle. Two would feast at her breasts, but one would need to feed from the hated bottle. She took turns getting them used to the hard, plastic nipples which they still fought against.

As she quickly heated the bottle, the crying ceased, and she wondered why. Going to the living room with the bottle in hand, she paused in the doorway, her heart contracting at the vision in front of her. Dakota sat on the floor in front of the fireplace crossed-legged. All three of their children were lying in his lap looking at him and giggling as he made silly noises. Jake lay by his side, his chin resting on Dyami. She melted at the sight.

This was what she had refused to accept in her life. She felt the pain around her heart ease as she gave in to his love. She had indeed been an unmitigated fool.

CHAPTER FORTY-SIX

Dakota moved the one lone crib to the spare bedroom as he claimed the need for privacy, and excitement warmed her at the thought of being with him again.

Once the babies were settled down, he kissed each one in turn before gathering her in his embrace and leading her to her room. With the soft glow of a full moon drifting across her floor, he stood before her as a man in love, undressing her with infinite patience, just as he'd done so many times in the past. When she stood before him with nothing on but the blush of need, he swiftly removed his own clothing, throwing them in a pile on a chair.

She giggled at his impatience, amused as she saw a slight frown cross his handsome face.

"Don't laugh at me, woman."

She flat out laughed until he pulled her to him and hushed her with an earthshattering kiss, pouring out his feelings with the swirl of his tongue against her own.

To be pressed up against his firm body once again felt so right. His heat warmed her. His love empowered her. His gentle touch moved her. Again, she asked herself why she'd fought so hard against this. Why had she not seen that he had indeed taken residence inside her heart, and no matter what she did or how hard she fought, he'd be there forever, waiting for her. He was her other half. He was perfect for her.

His hands gliding along her body elicited tiny goose-bumps while he lovingly possessed her with his kiss. Her body trembled as it remembered what his talented hands could do to her, and she leaned into the need.

She had never imagined this type of passion could exist until the first time he'd brushed against her quite by accident in her kitchen. A spark had passed through them at the touch, igniting them both, forever changing their path forward.

Their path! Alarmed at the thought, she opened her eyes and looked to him. He had indeed been her path in life, and she never saw it. Love surged within in her, warming her, filling her with a joy unlike anything she had ever experienced in her life.

She touched him, sliding her hands along the rock-hard planes of his stomach until they curled along the velvety strength of his need. He hissed a breath against her mouth. His body did its own trembling as she firmed her grip and slid up and down along his length.

He broke the kiss, and they rested forehead to forehead as she lovingly pleasured his shaft. He lowered his hands from her shoulders to cup her breasts. When his roughened thumbs teased along her nipples, she moaned into the quiet room and released him. She needed him–now.

She pushed him backwards until he toppled to the bed, and she came down on him, staring intently at eyes that looked to her with pure, forgiving love. She reached once more for his length and slipped it into her need before lying down to press her aching breasts against his chest.

Her body gripped him, holding on, never wanting to let go, and she paused as her emotions overtook her. He was beauty in all its forms. She didn't know what she'd done to deserve his patient love, and once again, shame filled her for what she'd put him through. She had to tell him what she felt. She had to unburden herself before she could go any further.

"Dakota." His gaze questioned why she'd stopped and looked at the tears that formed in her eyes. "I'm sorry. I was a fool. Please forgive me." A teardrop spilled over and landed on his neck, and she reached to brush it away.

"No more tears, Anna."

He rolled her over slowly until he rested between her thighs, never breaking the contact of their joining. Lips as soft as her babies' skin gently kissed the corners of each moistened eye before he found her lips once more.

He didn't speak again. He let his body tell her of his love. With each movement, he made her feel like a desired woman, not just a tired mom. With each thrust, he caressed her, lovingly reawakening her to the pleasure only he could give.

When sometime later her cry of completion could be heard throughout the house, he chuckled and laid a hand across her mouth, shushing her.

She would need to learn to be a bit quieter.

Somewhere in the middle of the night, an agitated whimper rose from the adjacent bedroom, letting them know that one of their babies was awake. He covered her exhausted body with a blanket and walked from the room.

Just before she drifted back to sleep, she heard the soft rumble of his voice as he spoke to his child, and she smiled.

Anna woke in the morning feeling wonderfully refreshed, but with burgeoning and painful breasts.

Dakota breathed deeply in sleep beside her, and she watched him for just a couple minutes. He had, with quiet assurance and infinite talent, given her hours of pleasure during the night. She'd only slept maybe four hours, yet the rest had been deep and replenishing. She leaned into him and kissed his temple before rising.

She felt gloriously wonderful this morning except for the weight pressing down on her chest. Checking on the babies, she found them still sleeping peacefully in the crib.

Moving quickly, she tiptoed down to the kitchen and reached for the pump to relieve the fullness.

It was in that humiliating position that he found her, and she blushed furiously before turning away from his inquisitive eyes. The hospital had shown her how to do this and how to save the milk for her babies. It was only the third time she had done it on her own, and to have him coming upon her while she fumbled with uncertainty was beyond embarrassing.

She cringed as she looked up at him and saw him intently studying what she was doing. Her heavily laden breasts were bare before him, and one was stuck to a pump that squeezed against her. Her blush was hot against her cheeks.

He moved, taking a seat in front of her and replaced her hands with his own. With deep interest, he took over the job of pumping the life-sustaining milk from her breasts. His ease with life, his acceptance of all things natural, overawed her at times. Where she was shy and afraid and struggled to cope, he was calm and patient, seemingly taking each day as it came. Never in her life would she have imagined sitting at a table in her kitchen while a man pumped milk from her body, but with him her shyness evaporated.

With his eyes cast down as he concentrated on the job he was doing, his long dark lashes looked to be resting on his cheeks. His coal black sleep-tousled hair was in disarray around his head, and the pure male scent of him filled her nostrils. His legs, thick and muscular beneath his soft pants, curved around the chair seat as he leaned forward, his slender fingers cupping her breast as he watched the milk drip into the bottle.

He was a man in every sense of the word. He was strong, virile, loving, and beautiful, and he was hers. A lump formed and lodged in her throat as she held back the tears.

She could've lost him forever.

"Anna, this is the last time I will ask this."

She held her breath as he set the pump and bottle on the table and took her hands in his. Deep brown, questioning eyes swept up from their intertwined hands to meet hers in a locked embrace.

"Will you marry me?"

Never in her life had she cried as much as she had in the past year. Well, except for maybe when Charles died. Even when they had lost Bella, she didn't remember crying. She'd shut herself away from the world, not understanding death at that young age. She sat here overcome with emotion. With eyes again shimmering with tears, her answer came out on a release of pent up breath.

"Yes."

He sighed, and she knew what the next question would be.

"Where do you want to live?"

"I don't know. How can I fight Shoop so hard to keep this land to only walk away from it, but how can I not be with you? Why are there no simple answers?"

"There may be a simple answer."

She looked to him in question.

"Hear me out and think about what I say. What if I ask one of my Lakota family members to come oversee your lands? What if we live at my home, but come here as often as you want? What if we still own both lands and manage them both? We don't have to give up anything. We can share the responsibility and keep both properties for our children."

She sat at her kitchen table on a cold winter morning with her mouth hanging open and her breasts hanging out, while a half-naked, sleepy-eyed beauty of a man proposed to her and then stated the obvious. She stared at him, feeling utterly stupid and shook her head in wonder. The absurdity of what they'd put themselves through hit her like a brick.

She began to laugh and cry at the same time, her nose running and mixing with the teardrops until she was a sloppy mess. A deep and cathartic release poured through her. When she looked to see Dakota watching her closely, as if she was slipping over the precipice into madness, she only laughed harder. Her stomach hurt by the time she calmed enough to speak. She grabbed a tissue and dried her face, quite certain of what she looked like at that moment.

"Oh, Dakota, if you'd only said those words six months ago, maybe things would've gone a lot differently."

He smiled the heart-stopping, crinkles in the corners of his eyes, brilliant flash of white teeth that always wrapped itself around her heart smile that she loved.

With his mind on all they needed to discuss he hadn't noticed, but as the sun's rays moved along the tabletop, a little gold band, sitting all alone on the far side of the table, glinted in reflection. They both saw the twinkle of light at the same time, and he turned to her in question. She smiled.

CHAPTER FORTY-SEVEN

All about her was activity. Her wedding to their chief was tomorrow and the whole land was swarming with people preparing or waiting for a joyous festival. Dakota had planned the vows to be exchanged during the spring pow-wow and so much had been done to make this a grand occasion. What he didn't know was he had planned their wedding on her birthday. She figured she'd tell him at some point.

Once he knew she would be his, he wanted the wedding to be perfect and put it off for four months. Those four months had flown by as each person was assigned duties to ensure the day was perfect for them all.

Her children were flourishing under loving care. Everyone wanted to spend time with them. Sometimes she had to beg to be left alone with her own babies. With so many women involved in their lives, she laughingly voiced her concerns that they'd never know she was their mother, but she didn't mind. She was being pampered and spoiled.

As the children were nearing six months of age, she was slowly weaning them from her breasts, leaving even more time for them to be grabbed up by everyone from Dakota's mother to his sister and on down the line to be spoiled as well.

Each afternoon over the past few months, her soon-to-be husband would saddle both of their horses and take her for long rides over the terrain of South Dakota, teaching her the names of the trees, the outcroppings, and the intricate ways of the Lakota. Several times, she peppered him with questions about the dairy side of the business, and he promised to take her to see it one day.

Today, as with any other day, he came for her shortly after lunch, and they climbed upon their saddled horses and rode out. Unlike the other days, though, he suddenly veered her towards the two long, low, white buildings.

Her excitement grew to be able to finally see the internal workings of his vast business. On opening the doors to the building that ran on forever, she gasped at the smells. She knew the scents on a smaller scale, but with so large a number of cattle in one place, the smell was almost too much. She held a hand to her nose as her stomach protested.

"Whew," she exclaimed, and he laughed.

"You get used to it."

The entire production line was fascinating to a small-town farm girl.

The impressive machinery for milking lined the center of the long floor, and Anna thought longingly of having at least one of these machines to relieve the pressure on her own hands from milking her cows each day.

Shades of brown and white and a few black and white cows stood hooked to the machines, their faces lowered to eat the expensive, nourishing feed before them. She knew without asking the others had been released outside to graze and enjoy the warm sunshine.

As with the running of his home, people came and went, each having a different responsibility. Some fed the cows the massive amounts of food a lactating cow ate each day. Some stood with long brooms pushing the food the cows had scattered back towards their waiting mouths, while others moved among the cows checking them for signs of illness or checking the teats for mastitis.

The cows were treated with love, for they were the reason

this family prospered. A woman in a white coat walked among them checking the feed, and Anna questioned Dakota as to who she was.

"She is a nutritionist who comes once a week, making sure our feed is good."

Anna walked around in wonder, amazed at the efficiency she saw. Her own farm paled in comparison to the huge production before her.

He walked her outside to the back of the building where hundreds of non-lactating cows were enjoying themselves. In a special fenced off area were four cows that grazed all by themselves with young children petting them and chatting with them like they were a best friend.

"Why are those cows separated from the rest?"

"They are infertile and should probably be sold off as beef, but the children have made them pets, and we've been reluctant to break their hearts by selling them."

Again, the man's kindness touched a special place in her heart. He would rather feed additional mouths than to show the children the harshness and cruelty of the world.

Slipping her hand in his, she gently gripped him, and he squeezed back.

"Come, I have something else I want to show you."

He took her to their version of a vegetable garden, which put her own tiny plot to shame. Rows upon rows of healthy and abundant crops could be seen for at least fifty yards, if not more. She couldn't even see the end.

He explained without really needing to that the late winter vegetables were planted in the first twenty rows and were almost ready for harvest. Men and women alike moved along the land, turning the soil and planting the spring crops. They planted all they'd need to keep the couple hundred people who lived here nourished for the upcoming year.

Anna had kept her crew fed on her farm with the extra help of a local grocery store. Here they were almost entirely self-sufficient. They had an abundance of milk and other dairy products. This land before her would supply the nutritious vegetables. When the cows were too old to produce milk, they were sold off for slaughter, which had her shuddering at the thought, but the meats were returned to grace their tables.

Anna realized that nowhere did she see the wheat for their breads, and she wondered where it came from. When she asked Dakota, he told her it was shipped in from a local grain manufacturer. Without him seeing, she smiled a knowing smile. She knew where they could get that at a much cheaper cost. She could finally contribute.

She awoke the next day full of excitement. The morning of her wedding had arrived, although she still hadn't seen her wedding dress. It had been a secret. A surprise, they'd told her, and she worried about it. No bride wanted to be kept from knowing about her gown. It was too special.

Aware that the women would be here soon to dress her, she slipped into the bathroom to shower.

She exited her bathroom a short while later with a small stick in her hand, hiding it quickly in the pocket of her robe when her door opened and a half-dozen women poured through. She'd have another surprise for Dakota this day. Either she was a bit more fertile than she realized, or he was a bit too potent.

The cheerful women surrounded her, and she quickly removed the robe, hiding it from the prying eyes. Very little went unnoticed in this family.

Sitting naked as the day she was born and now quite used to it, she relaxed as they combed the snarls from her freshly washed locks and sat in wonder watching their reflections in the mirror as they dried her hair and worked an intricate pattern of beads throughout the shiny locks.

When the door opened again, two women entered bearing her gown across outstretched arms, with grandmother following closely behind. Anna almost wept at the beauty of their creation. She knew many hours had gone into this dress. She'd peeked at them through doorways and seen them hard at work for the past few weeks. She had been beside herself to know what the gown looked like.

The white silk dress slipped easily over her head, coming to rest upon her body and ending just below her knees. A necklace of turquoise jewels was placed around her throat, the largest gem coming to rest between her breasts. A belt of the same blue design was secured around her waist, a round shiny stone also hanging low, resting on her mound.

Lace tassels adorned the sleeves and the same pattern hung from the bottom of the gown, giving the dress a floor length look.

She asked about the significance of the turquoise, for she knew everything had a meaning in this world still so foreign to her. A tiny slip of a woman spoke softly as she touched the stone between her breasts, telling the story of its heritage.

"In Indian folklore, it is said that the Creator loved the color of turquoise so much that once He had finished creating Mother Earth, He tossed all the remaining turquoise to the Heavens, creating the beautiful blue skies above. It is the color of water, sky, and flowers. Because of our Creator's love for the color, turquoise is now cherished above all else. It is both spiritual and life-giving and brings both good health and long-life."

It never ceased to astound Anna the stories handed down through generations in this gentle and welcoming group of people. Everything under the stars was significant to them and had a place. She corrected herself, for even the stars and beyond held meaning to them.

She stood and walked to a long mirror. The reflection before her brought tears to her eyes. She looked beautiful. Soft white boots adorned with the same jewels reached up to just below her knees. The exquisite purity of her gown shimmered in the sunlight pouring in through the windows as if it was crafted from opal.

On the outside she appeared chaste and innocent, but her body beneath the gown was bared to the smooth, cool silk and its gentle texture aroused the senses. She would be in a constant state of readiness until she lay with her new husband.

She touched the lace hanging from her arm and stared at the intricate pattern, realizing at once who had created this masterpiece. Searching the crowd of women, she looked for Unci and found her sitting on the edge of her mattress quietly observing all.

Anna walked to her and knelt, holding out a piece of the delicate lace. "You made this." It was not a question. It was a statement of fact.

A transformation took place in front of Anna's eyes as she watched the normally stern and in-control woman tear up in front of her. "I asked the eagles to bring you to him."

Anna kissed the wrinkled cheek and rested her face against hers for just a moment.

"I love you, Unci."

In a soft whisper, the old woman responded. "You have a surprise for my grandson today?"

Anna chuckled and kissed her again.

Chapter Forty-Eight

The sun. The life-sustaining star high in the sky brightened the landscape and created a rainbow on display among the mass of people waiting for her as she exited the house. Fabrics in every color adorned the men and women alike, almost blinding her with their brilliance. The honored traditions warred with the necessary modern, as many were in buckskin and moccasins adorned with feathers and beads, while still others wore suits and dresses.

Chairs and tables sat under a large canopy to her right with a long table bending under the weight of the food the family had prepared for this special day. Everyone was smiling and laughing, the atmosphere jubilant. Their chief would be happy.

Her mother materialized at her side, and Anna smiled to see her on the arm of Pop. Everyone she loved was here today.

"You look beautiful, daughter," she said while grasping her hands.

"Thank you, so do you. You fit right in, in this sea of color." Her mother laughed and hugged her.

She reached up and kissed Pop. "You look very debonair today," she said, then smiled when he blushed.

Anna looked about her, nervous, but so very excited. This was what everyone had been working towards for months, and the outcome of their labors was breathtakingly beautiful. She prayed all would go as planned, because this family deserved it.

Her eyes combed the crowd for him, and with a gasp and a tremor of anticipation, she saw her future husband parting the crowd as he came towards her. She didn't just see him, though. She felt him throughout her body.

He was garbed in a white tunic with blue beads that matched the jewels on her dress intertwined throughout the fabric. Black breeches hugged and outlined his lower body and black buckskin boots caressed his feet, coming up to a stop at his knees. His hair had grown longer than when she first met him and was braided down his back, ending at the shoulder blades. As if that wasn't enough to inflame her, his piercing gaze was dark and passionate, speaking to her about what he felt inside.

With a quick glance to the sky, she sent a silent prayer of thanks to the Creator and to God, maybe one and the same, for gifting her with this man. She didn't know what the future would bring, but she knew with her whole heart that however many days they had together, they would be full of love. She was ready to take the chance.

He stopped before her, and all else faded away when he looked to her. Their gazes connected in a secret handshake that just the two of them shared. Today, they would become one.

His eyes twinkled in happiness as he spoke. "You are lovely, Anna. Come, it's time."

He took her hand and led her to the center of a large ring of people. She felt the joyful eyes of everyone as she looked to the man who would be hers. This wedding day was so very different from her first, an impetuous trip to the local courthouse. This was beauty, tradition, and celebration.

Everyone broke into laughter as a few in the crowd were jostled when a jubilant Jake ran forward and sat at their feet, a pale blue scarf tied around his neck. He was dressed for the occasion and didn't want to be left out of the festivities.

Smiling, she watched a heavily pregnant lady friend of his come forward also but moving much slower than her Jake. She sat next to Jake, a bright orange bandana tied around her neck, and Jake turned to lick her cheek. Even her dog had found love among these very kind and accepting people.

A hush of respect came over the wedding crowd when an older man with a face scarred and aged with time joined them. He was dressed in bright yellow buckskin breeches and tunic, covered in deep red and blue beads. A band around his head was designed in the same colors.

He spoke to them of the sanctity of their vows and the importance of love above all else. He spoke of duty and the sacred calling of procreation. As he wound down, he spoke of living in goodness and purity in the eyes of the Creator. When he raised both hands to the sky above, she listened in wonder as the world quieted around them. Not even a bird call or rush of wind could be heard to break the silence.

His voice was a prayer as he raised his eyes to the vividly blue sky and spoke of love and rebirth. He spoke of cherishing the life-giving land and all that roamed upon it. He told the tale of a man's humbleness in the face of the Creator's glory.

She wanted to giggle but held herself in check when he spoke of blessing her and Dakota with many children to carry on the Creator's glory. They were doing very well on their own in that regard.

In deference to her and modernism, when he was done, a woman stepped forward and led them in wedding vows that were traditional to Anna. They'd been married twice.

A cheer rose up among the crowd of people when Dakota took her in his arms in the modern way and kissed her, sealing their vows, and the party began.

Hours later, he still held her hand in a firm grip as if he couldn't bear to lose her touch again. He'd barely let her go long enough to eat. She probably should have found it annoying, but today she found it more charming and sweet than possessive. She enjoyed it.

A guest said something funny, and he turned to her to share the joke, but the smile changed rapidly. The expression in his eyes heated as their eyes connected. He made his excuses to the joking man and pulled her through the jubilant, singing and dancing crowd, their forward movement impeded by congratulations and best wishes. By the time they broke from the hundreds of people barring their way, he was tugging from his impatience, some people behind them were laughing, and she was giggling.

Her laughter turned to a struggle for breath as she tried to keep up with him, and she urged him to slow, but the obvious bulge tenting his breeches told her of his intent. She had come to learn that when her husband wanted her, he wanted her then and there.

They'd walked a half a mile at least by the time they came to a copse of trees and he pulled her through. Trying desperately to catch her breath, she bent over at the waist, sucking in much needed air. She understood need, but this was crazy.

Yet as she finally stood, the breath she had struggled to control left her lungs in a rush once more. Trees of all kinds with the soft, light green new growth of spring towered to the sky. Others were low and thick, forming a protective barrier around a place of beauty.

She'd seen this area often on her rides, but thinking it nothing more than a forest, had not ventured close. She was sorry she hadn't. Like her gazebo at home, splendor had been hidden within the sheltering woodland. A small lake sat to the left, fed by a creek that trickled through a break in the trees. A part of the lake looked dark and cool under the forest canopy. The rest gave a warm and enticing invitation as it glittered in the spring sunshine.

Her eyes lowered to the ground in awe of the magnificence she saw. All around the lake and across the small enclosure were thousands and thousands of blue bells. Their tiny buds created a purple/blue blanket under the overhead sun.

With questioning eyes, she looked to him. "What is this place?"

"This is nature's miracle." He chuckled and looked about him as he spoke, as if absorbing it all anew.

"I found this place not long after I moved here as a child, and I came here often when I wanted to pray or to be alone when missing my family became overwhelming for me. It was a hard life in the beginning when I was separated from all I knew. The bluebells reminded me of home and made me feel closer to all I loved. It's always been kind of sacred to me."

He looked to her again and with a small, wicked smile, crooked his finger, motioning her forward. "Anna, *he you woe.*"

She tilted her head and stared at him questioningly and he smiled.

"Come here, Anna."

She stood just inside the shelter of the trees and stared at the man who was now her husband standing in the center of the enclosure. The gentle breeze rippled the tunic across his broad chest, the thin fabric outlining the power of the man. His look was intense and purposeful, and a flush of heat crossed her body that had nothing to do with the warmth of the day.

Letting her voice carry on the wind, she questioned him. "Dakota, here? What if someone sees us?"

"Then they'll see a husband and wife doing what husbands and wives do."

"That's not really an answer."

The gleam in his predatory eyes told her plainly that he wanted to devour her, and he motioned her forward again.

"Come here, Anna, or I'll come for you."

Anna had never in her life made love outside with the sunshine above and wildflowers at her feet. She looked at the wildflowers, and not wanting to harm them, slipped off her boots. As she carefully walked to her husband, the soft petals cushioned her skin like a bed of cotton balls, and an impish excitement coursed through her veins. She felt wild and free.

Untying the belt around her waist, she let it drop, and he pulled her to him, crushing the silken gown against his hardened body. With a kiss meant to melt all resistance, he curled his hands into her hair and held on, his mouth demanding. She met the force of his kiss with her own. Equals in every way, she took as much as she gave.

When his hands left the heated warmth of her hair and slowly lifted the silken dress to glide across her body, she grew lightheaded as erotic shivers tickled along her skin. This dress had placed her in a heightened state as soon as she'd donned it. Every sway of her body, every warm breeze that found its way under the gown awakened every nerve ending in her body. She'd spent most of this day ready for him.

Quickly, he stripped himself of his clothing, leaving them both free to feel the heat of the sun's rays caressing their naked skin. A soft, cooling breeze blew across them both, but did little to douse the fire their nearness always created.

Her husband stood proud, erect, and strong mere inches before her. She knew him well and could easily see the effort it took for him to hold his passion in check, but they were suddenly in no hurry.

A long finger came forward and curled to brush lovingly across her cheek, lowering slowly along her skin until it tickled the tip of a breast. The light touch created a firestorm of heat and moisture to rush to her mound, and she quivered. One single touch of his hand did this.

She raised her own hand and with the tips of her fingers, grazed his nipple, much as he had hers. The muscled flesh of his stomach rippled and flexed as she created her own firestorm within him. He was hers. Forever. She would never stop touching him. She'd craved touch for so long and now couldn't get enough of it.

His hands cupped the weight of her breasts. Though not quite as heavy as when she was nursing, they were still more than she'd had when they'd first lain together. His thumbs tickled the tips, and her eyes closed as her body arched into his touch, seeking pleasure.

She became greedy, caressing his taut chest and abdomen, running her hands down his hips and watching as his erection danced in response. She memorized every curve, every dimple, and every pore, seeing all anew in the bright light of day.

His hands dropped from her breasts as she moved behind him, running a finger down the length of his spine, remembering the day the sweat had trickled along the indentation. Her hands stroked and cupped the strong curve of his buttocks, and she watched as they tightened in reaction. She leaned forward and rubbed the hard pebbles of her nipples against his skin, and he'd had enough. He turned swiftly and knelt before her.

His fingers traced the silvery outlines of her scars, and she inwardly cringed. Time and Unci's ointments had made them less visible, but they were still there. They still embarrassed her, yet her husband caressed them lovingly, the soft movements making them feel erotic on her heated skin.

A kiss as soft as down touched her near her left hip as a finger slipped between her folds. It glided and tickled until she was moaning and quivering from the building pressure.

He wasted no more time. Gently, he eased her down to rest on the little flowers, their scent so intoxicating. Their gentle petals were like little kisses on her skin. She felt so decadent and ready lying bare and open in the middle of a clearing in the daylight.

"What do you want, Anna?"

"You, Dakota, always you."

Coming down over her, he slipped inside her waiting body. His long, muscled and powerful legs enclosed hers, bringing her thighs tight against his shaft buried deeply within her. He moved, the friction tight and new, creating a burning warmth.

Everywhere around her was warmth, on her skin, in her core, and in her heart. It sent her quickly catapulting over the edge, crying out her pleasure.

His body shook from his restraint, but he didn't let go. Moving within in her, he kept tantalizing and teasing until she once more felt the tremors of release wrack her body. Only then did he shudder against her, meeting his own completion.

He came down on his elbows, his hands fisted with emotion in her hair and stared into her eyes.

"I love you, Anna."

"I love you, Dakota. I fought it for so long, but I do. My eyes were blinded by my fear and I'm sorry for all you have gone through. I never meant to hurt you."

His lips met hers in love, the kiss tender and forgiving. She'd opened her heart and found him waiting there. Unci had been right.

Breaking the kiss, she smiled at him impishly. "I have something to tell you."

CHAPTER FORTY-NINE

She made her way slowly down the hallway, the bulk of her stomach impeding her way. At least this time around her girth was much smaller. This she could handle with ease. Unci wanted to see her for one last check up as she was due soon, and she looked forward to knowing when she would see her new baby.

Another little girl. Two boys and two girls. What a wonderful little family. She was unbelievably happy. Her Lakota family had accepted her easily, and she knew it was because she made Dakota so content. The sadness that had encased him for so long was gone, replaced by a jubilant, productive, and happy man. The whole farm stepped lively these days.

She found Miranda lying outside of Unci's bedroom door and chuckled. The two had formed quite a friendship. Knocking lightly on the door, she waited for a response, but there was none. Knocking again, she called out to her softly. Mina rounded the corner, her footsteps silent on the hard floor.

"Unci is not answering her door. Is she in the living space?"

With a mildly concerned look, Mina opened the door to the grand old woman's room and entered, Anna following closely behind. Miranda bolted between her legs and jumped up onto the bed, where a silent body lay.

Mina knelt by the side of the bed with a muffled cry, and Anna's heart clenched. She knew without asking what was happening and turned to flee the room.

As quickly as her body would allow, she moved towards Unci's rocker in the living room and held on to the ancient wooden arm. Heart pounding despair ripped through her. She refused to accept this. She had wanted no more deaths, especially when she was finally content with her life. No. She wasn't ready to face another loss. Unci had to birth her daughter. Unci had to be here to help her raise her family in the Lakota tradition. The lady had become closer to her than any female in her lifetime. She'd become the grandmother she'd never had.

Again, she'd let someone into her heart only to have it torn apart by them leaving her. She couldn't handle this.

Escape beckoned to her, and she bolted through the front door. The air had changed, turning frigid, and it hit her in the face, robbing her of breath. The sunshine was blinding in its brilliance, and it was wrong. It shouldn't be sunny. There should be clouds and rain. The whole world should be sad with the loss of such a great lady.

The way became fuzzy as she moved quickly towards the road and away from the house. Warm tears quickly turned cold against her cheeks. Swiping the moisture away in anger, she slowed as a twinge ripped through her side. The baby was not happy with her, apparently. Slowing her movements, she walked cautiously, exiting the huge front gate and turning down the road toward nowhere. She'd barely left the huge farm since she came to live here and had no idea where she was headed, but she had to leave.

There'd be pain in that house. There would be the mournful wails of the tribe members when they all learned that Unci was gone. There'd be tears and heartache, and there would be the loss. So much loss. No one would be able to replace her.

As he had in her driveway so many months ago, he found her alone.

With her arms wrapped around her rounded belly and her head hanging down, she knew she looked the picture of despair. Whether from the force of crying or from shivering against the bitter cold wind that whipped her hair around her head, she was shaking.

He dropped to the ground by her side to pull her against him and wrap her within his huge coat.

Stilling against the warmth, she raised her tear stained face to his and wept anew at the pain she saw reflected in his eyes. She had known his grandmother for a brief moment in time, but this man beside her had known the wise lady for all his life. She opened her mouth to apologize, but he spoke before she could get the chance.

"Anna, I should give you hell for being out here like this. You risked your life as well as the baby's being exposed to this cold."

He kissed the top of her head and rested his cheek against the cold tresses. "But I won't. I know your grief only too well. Come, let's get you home."

He urged her to stand and kept her within the shelter of his coat as they made their way back down the long road, willing the warmth of his body to replace her shivering.

"I'm sorry for your loss. I didn't know her for very long, but she became very important to me. I loved her as if she were my own grandmother."

"I'm happy you got a chance to love her before she left us."

She lowered her gaze and ran her hand over her protruding belly. "What is it like at home?"

"It's as you would imagine. There isn't a person on this land that hasn't been touched by her in some way, so everyone grieves."

He cautioned her about a hole in the ground before speaking again. "Although there'll be much sadness in the coming days, Unci will also be celebrated for the long, good life she led. I'm not sure you'll understand what you will experience, but I'll help you if you have any questions."

He looked to the sky as they walked but suddenly stopped. Anna followed his gaze until they stood together in awe. The entire big, blue winter Dakota sky was cloudless except for one large, lone cloud perched high above their home. It blocked the sunlight and shadowed the house as if the Creator understood what went on inside and shared in the pain.

People moved quietly and efficiently through the house. They still did what needed to be done daily, but often she heard the sounds of weeping and reverential tones as they spoke about Unci.

Anna set about learning a whole new set of traditions. Each meal a place was set for her as if she was still there with them. Every family member acted as if the old lady's wise eyes still saw all around the table.

This would take place for a year. They believed that was how long a spirit stayed around, and they welcomed the spirit. She was told this was called Spirit Keeping, and Anna was unsure whether to feel a bit creeped out or to welcome her spirit by their side.

Her wake, inside a large teepee set near the burial grounds, had been for three days. It had been tiring for Anna in the final days of her pregnancy, but cathartic for her family. Someone was always by Unci's side. She was never left alone.

Many came to visit and to share stories of their life with her. Anna was surprised to see laughter as well as crying when they shared their experiences. The grand old woman's life was celebrated, and stories in the Lakota tradition of her generosity, wisdom, fortitude, and family kinship were cherished.

Unci was buried on their own sacred grounds. Dakota had set aside an area years before when he took over the farm, once more reaffirming Anna's belief that this entire farm had been set up as an individual self-sufficient nation. That these people took care of their own was vividly apparent, and Anna warmly welcomed their strong love and harmony within her heart.

After the burial Dakota took on the huge task of feeding everyone on his farm, plus those who had traveled from far away to mourn and celebrate. The atmosphere was somber, at times happy, but always respectful. People were kind and considerate to each other, no matter how they chose to mourn.

She was surprised that someone had prepared a video they showed after the meal. Every picture of his grandmother that could be found was displayed on the large screen, plus those few of her husband and her family. A picture of every child Unci had ever birthed followed, ending with the birth of Anna's triplets. As she watched the video, she laid a hand across her active stomach, crying quietly in heartbreak that grandmother would never see her fourth child.

Some of grandmother's great lace-making sat in display around her coffin. The tribute was a shining example of what those twisted and distorted fingers had still been able to do up until the day before her death. The final article of clothing was Anna's wedding dress, and Anna touched the lace reverently, knowing grandmother had known all along that she and Dakota would join together.

Anna grew tired, needing to rest after the long, emotional day, and she exited the large canopied tent to make her way to her bedroom. Her children were down for a nap, and she planned to use the time to do the same.

Dakota caught up to her as she mounted the steps to the large patio and pulled her into his arms. "Where're you going?"

"To nap while the children sleep. I'm tired."

"Can I join you?"

She might be tired, but she was not a fool. This could be the last chance she'd be able to be with him for a while. She blinded him with a seductive smile and grasped his hand, tugging him up the final steps.

So much had changed in the past two years of her life, but none more welcoming than the man she clung to. She'd been a broken shell without even realizing it. She'd gone about her life believing she was living it to the fullest, but she'd been wrong. Little by little and piece by piece, this man had opened her eyes, and once they opened, she found life could really be more than what she imagined.

He'd walked into her life on a hot fall day and changed her. Leaning into his strength, she stopped outside their patio door and wrapped an arm around his neck, pulling him close. She didn't care that others stopped what they were doing and watched. She poured out her love in a kiss that was heartbreakingly soft and gentle.

"I love you, Dakota."

Far above them a regal bird called out to his mate. Joining together, they circled the sky in gentle arcs until as one they soared away.

EPILOGUE

She awoke by his side and felt the first of her contractions begin. By the end of this day, they'd have their fourth child.

She'd welcome this child as she had the others, with love and hope for their future. She snuggled back against the warm strength of her husband, knowing that hours of pain would come soon. She would enjoy him while she could.

Her eyes filled with sorrow as she thought about Unci and that she wouldn't be here to birth this baby. She'd wanted to name the baby after her, but Lakota tradition wouldn't allow it. She thought it would be a kind tribute but had to reluctantly acquiesce to their wishes. This birth would be overshadowed by the loss of the greatest woman she'd ever known, but it would still be celebrated. It was going to be another strange time in her life.

A small giggle rose within her as she felt her husband's thick morning erection against her backside. It was the reason for the tightening around her abdomen even as she giggled. She didn't fear this labor, even without his grandmother to guide her way. She knew what to expect and to do, and Mina would be by her side. The woman would take over the role Unci had vacated.

Seven months she and Dakota had been married. The triplets were now taking tentative steps around the house and exploring the fields beyond. Elan was bold and pushed aside every obstacle in his path. Mika took her time and thoughtfully studied each obstacle, as if she would create a new way to clear it. Dyami, her precious, tiny, third born, walked around each obstacle in his path, seeking the surest and kindest route. Out of all her children, he was the most like his father, peaceful and caring. They were three distinct personalities, and she cherished each moment as she watched them grow.

Chumani and her husband had been asked to take over the duties at her farm in Kansas, and they were only too happy to do so. It'd been too hard on Chumani to see the happiness she and Dakota shared and hard on Anna to see her pain. It was the kindest solution.

She and Dakota visited her farm often. They especially loved visiting the gazebo. Dakota had built an addition to his farm, a wheat mill. The wheat that grew in Kansas was trucked to South Dakota and transformed into breads that were shared with the clan. Any they didn't use was sold. No longer did he have to buy the wheat from outside vendors. Her farm was helping to make their family even stronger and more financially independent, and it warmed her heart.

Pride surged through her that she'd held onto her children's heritage, despite all that threatened to tear it away. Her children would never have to know what it was like to go hungry or to struggle to pay a bill. For that she was grateful. She knew when the day came that she passed from this life, she would do it with the knowledge she'd done all she could for them.

Another contraction ripped across her stomach, and she glanced at the clock on the wall. The contractions were very close. This birth would be so much quicker.

She eased her tightened stomach around to face her husband, and an overpowering rush of love for the man surged through her. She stared at him, at the thick black lashes that hid the eyes that spoke only of his love for her and at the lips that always touched her so reverently.

A lump formed in her throat. She'd been sleepwalking through life, never really seeing or feeling until he woke her. She had never even realized that the man who picked her up from her driveway so long ago would hold all the answers she sought. She woke him with a kiss.

"Dakota?"

His lips were warm and inviting, and as usual, she didn't want to let them go. With a whisper against the lips that she would love forever, she spoke to him softly.

"Dakota?"

He smiled a sleepy smile.

"Dakota, your child wants to be born."

Instantly awake, he lowered his startled wide brown eyes to look at her stomach, and a loving hand reached to lie on the tight protrusion.

"I'll get Mother." He flew from the bed, jumping into a pair of black jeans on his way out the door.

As she lay there waiting for the outcome of the day, she thought of the man who'd become her life. She'd become bound to him and him to her. She had loved Charles, but nothing had prepared her for the all-consuming power of the love she felt for Dakota.

Another contraction ripped along her abdomen, and she made a vow. As long as the seas continued to wash towards the shore, as long as the sun shone in the sky, and as long as the wind whipped across the land, she would love him. Even far past this earthly life, she prayed she would remain bound to him and him to her as they took their place among the stars.

The End

ABOUT THE AUTHOR

Born and raised in Baltimore, Maryland, Karen Louise dreamt of a time she could write. Though it was always a calling, work in the medical field, a home, and motherhood interrupted those dreams, and grand-motherhood followed soon after. At long last, there was time for writing. With three fledgling attempts at books behind her, she sat down with an idea for this book, and the words flowed.

www.ingramcontent.com/pod-product-compliance
Lightning Source LLC
Chambersburg PA
CBHW062011170626
46813CB00001B/116